GLADDEN THE HEART

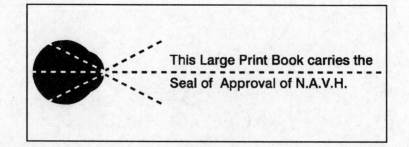

This Large Print Book carries the
Seal of Approval of N.A.V.H.

AMISH TURNS OF TIME

GLADDEN THE HEART

OLIVIA NEWPORT

THORNDIKE PRESS
A part of Gale, a Cengage Company

GALE
A Cengage Company

Farmington Hills, Mich • San Francisco • New York • Waterville, Maine
Meriden, Conn • Mason, Ohio • Chicago

LIBRARY OF CONGRESS CATALOGING-IN-PUBLICATION DATA

Names: Newport, Olivia, author.
Title: Gladden the heart / by Olivia Newport.
Description: Large print edition. | Waterville, Maine : Thorndike Press, 2017. | Series: Amish turns of time ; #5 | Series: Thorndike Press large print christian romance
Identifiers: LCCN 2017023035| ISBN 9781432842017 (hardcover) | ISBN 1432842013 (hardcover)
Subjects: LCSH: Amish—Fiction. | Large type books. | GSAFD: Love stories. | Christian fiction.
Classification: LCC PS3614.E686 G57 2017 | DDC 813/.6—dc23
LC record available at https://lccn.loc.gov/2017023035

Published in 2017 by arrangement with Barbour Publishing, Inc.

Printed in the United States of America
1 2 3 4 5 6 7 21 20 19 18 17

GLADDEN THE HEART

CHAPTER 1

Kishacoquillas Valley, Pennsylvania, 1847

A tent in July seemed overdone, but the *English* had their ways. At least the white canvas intercepted the sun, and sagging gaps in the tent walls just below the ceiling permitted an exchange of air. One more step could not hurt. On the day the tent went up, in anticipation of the Reverend Baxton's revival meeting, Susanna Hooley passed through the grassy clearing three times. The usual course of her day would have given her the opportunity, and collecting roots and wildflowers from the edge of the forest allowed her to watch the progress. She could not help but calculate how many people the benches within the tent could accommodate.

Most people traversed the narrows alongside the river at least once a month — far more often if they had produce or wares to sell in the town square in Lewistown. The narrows made Susanna feel as if her head was being squished, but it was not as if there were another way through the gap. Susanna was inclined to live as much of her life as possible east of the river and south of Jacks Mountain, content with where her parents had located their farm before she was born. Yeagertown, Milroy, Reedsville — they had opportunities. The Amish congregation was well settled in the valley by the time Elias and Veronica married. But they chose a wide, welcoming farm east of Lewiston, where Jacks Mountain was always part of the view, and if Susanna had any distance to drive, she had the Old Arch Bridge to look forward to.

Susanna slid a scuffed, square-toed brown shoe forward, nearer the tent. Her fingers found a gap between the panels hanging from a scaffold of metal rods, and she moved one panel to the right about three inches. Curiosity got the best of Susanna, her mother always said. Susanna tilted her head so one eye could get a clear view of inside the tent. The booming preacher's voice had deterred Susanna's determination to walk an aloof swath around the tent on her way home. She did not have to see him to be certain the voice did not belong to the only *English* minister she knew, Reverend

Baxton — who was an open-air preacher, a Methodist circuit rider, and her friend Patsy's father. The tent, and the afternoon revival meeting rather than an early-morning sermon, distinguished the guest preacher Reverend Baxton had invited to come all the way from New York to the central Kishacoquillas Valley. Under the circumstances, curiosity seemed reasonable.

She would not go inside, of course. Even curiosity had limits. Susanna was a grown woman of twenty-one, but she knew well the scowl lines of her mother's face, and she had no interest in explaining that she had gone inside a Methodist revival tent. Besides, she could hear quite well from outside the tent. Did the preacher always speak this way, or did he have a particular voice for sermons, as some of the Amish ministers did?

"Do you know that God desires the repentance of your heart?" The man's words smashed through the air. "Do you know that offering God your repentance will open new lands of mercy and grace to you? Let this be the day that you surrender to Jesus, so that on Judgment Day, when you stand face-to-face with God, you will know that Jesus has already stood there in your place."

In the far corner of the tent, a low voice

began to sing. Soon others joined. Hymns started this way in the Amish church services as well, a lone male voice singing the first line or two before the congregation joined. The only hymns Susanna knew were in German, and her brain stumbled for a few seconds trying to make sense of English words in church singing.

"Rock of Ages, cleft for me," the congregation sang. "Let me hide myself in Thee. Let the water and the blood, from Thy wounded side which flowed, be of sin the double cure; save from wrath and make me pure."

With rocky ridges as the backdrop to the tent's site, the choice of hymn was apt. Swelling voices were no hindrance for the preacher, whose own intonations ascended above the harmonies with a plea for the sinner to hide in the safety of Jesus, the Rock.

Susanna's feet had no urge to "go forward," as her friend Patsy called it, but she could not dispute the conviction and persuasion that filled the tent. If she kept watching, perhaps she would discover whether it was true that people rolled and twitched during these meetings.

Patsy Baxton resisted the urge to fan herself with the Bible in her lap. If she had been

10

anyone else's daughter, she might have, but her father was the Reverend Charles Baxton, and waving a Bible in desperate hope of a feeble air current was not what he meant by allowing the Holy Ghost to move through a revival. She tried to catch her father's eye and give him a signal that the temperature in the tent might mean that anyone who passed out was not slain by the Holy Ghost but simply overly warm. Surely the Holy Ghost could have blown a breeze through an open-air meeting even in the presence of a revival preacher who had learned how to give a sermon from Charles Finney himself, even if Finney was a Presbyterian and this preacher a committed Methodist.

Patsy had no intention of being the focus of such scrutiny. She needed air that moved against her face, not above her head. An onlooker might think that the hymn and plea for repentance meant the end of the meeting was near, but Patsy knew better. Another hour — or two — easily lay ahead. People came and went as they were able, and the preacher kept preaching in order that no soul would miss the call to salvation simply because of a tardy arrival. Household and business demands were bona fide. Not everyone could attend a meeting at a precise

11

time. Once, an entire congregation turned over one soul at a time, some arriving as others left. When the preacher began again speaking his original sermon, Patsy seemed to be the only person who noticed.

Her lips moved with the words of the hymn. "Not the labors of my hands can fulfill Thy law's demands: could my zeal no respite know, could my tears forever flow, all for sin could not atone; Thou must save, and Thou alone." But as she sang, Patsy tallied the steps required to reach outside air. She would have to excuse herself as she squeezed past six people in her row to reach the center aisle, but going toward the back of the tent in the main aisle would not do when others were pressing their way forward to meet the Lord. Her father's eyebrows would remain raised all through supper if she did that. Instead, she must gather her skirts and excuse herself to ten people to reach a side aisle. When the congregation rose to sing with more fervor, many swaying with the gentle rhythm of the song, Patsy made her way toward relief.

"Nothing in my hand I bring, simply to the cross I cling; naked, come to Thee for dress; helpless, look to Thee for grace; foul, I to the fountain fly; wash me, Savior, or I die."

The bonnet is what gave Susanna away. Its black quilted fabric crept farther into the tent with each tilt of her head. Patsy smiled. She had said all along that Susanna could not stay away.

The load of fresh-milled white oak was too heavy to expect the team pulling the wagon to gather much speed on an incline. Adam Yotter had resigned himself to this truth more than an hour ago. The Amish mill was on the outskirts of the sprawling district, nearest the forest. Driving out to the mill, checking the order, helping to load the lumber — for furniture and trim, not the walls of a log cabin house — and driving back at a decreased speed had consumed the entire day. By the time Adam got back to the farm of his *onkel,* his *aunti* would be pressing to get supper on the table. Adam knew little of lumber and would have preferred his uncle Niklaus send his son, Adam's cousin Jonas, to fetch the order. After all, it was because of Jonas's impending marriage — not yet announced but widely suspected — that Niklaus was adding on to the family home. The youngest of Niklaus's children and the only son, Jonas would inherit the farm one day.

Adam's two years in the Kish Valley

seemed like a moment, time flitting as nothing in the eyes of God. Niklaus would let him stay as long as he liked. His future would be less certain once Jonas took over the farm, but by then Adam would have a plan of his own. He hoped he would. His plan should have been firmer by now. Instead, he told any who inquired that he continued to wait on *Gottes wille.*

He had no wish to disturb whatever was happening under the tent. It was not his business. That was for the *English,* born out of a religion that marched right into the world rather than living apart as the Bible commanded. They would be responsible to God for their actions, not to a young Amish man who ought to have been married and settled by now. If he had been, his father might not have sent him off to his uncle's district.

But if he had been, he would not have met Susanna. None of the young women in his home district sparked in him what Susanna did. His father wanted Adam to marry sensibly, but if he met Susanna, surely he would see that sensibility and affection did not exclude each other.

On the slight incline approaching the tent, the horses slowed, and Adam urged them forward lest they lose the momentum required for the forward journey. As the land flattened again, details of the tent meeting came into focus. Horses and wagons were parked outside. Strains of the harmonic hymn thickened with every yard closer to their source.

Adam knew some of those horses and wagons. They belonged to the Amish. Confusion twisted through his gut. Perhaps it was simple curiosity, as Susanna said. She just wondered. Was there anything wrong with wondering? Adam could not rightly tell her there was, yet the heat in his stomach at the thought of Susanna inside the *English* tent betrayed that he did believe something was wrong with going where wondering might beckon into deep waters.

He scanned the array of horses, looking for an animal from the Hooley farm. Sometimes Susanna drove a cart with a sagging mare. More often she walked, if she could spare the time, because it was easier to spot wild berries or plants that she might use to create her dyes. He looked now for the basket she always carried over her arm, ever ready to collect something she might use.

There she was. She was not in the tent, but her face was.

Susanna lost the thread of the hymn. People

still sang, but now a second hymn had begun on the opposite side of the tent, and the notes and words melded, indiscernible. *Jesus. Faith. Calvary. Heart.* The words could have belonged to either song — or both, springing up in poetic renditions. In the beginning, the unfamiliar hymn had intrigued her enough to try to listen more carefully, but the cacophony of two songs at one time in the same tent, not to mention at least three people praying loudly from their far corners with hands raised taxed inquisitiveness. Over it all, the preacher continued, with rising urgency, the call to repentance.

Did not Genesis say that God walked in the garden in the cool of the day? Did not Elijah hear God's still, small voice? Did the Methodists think God was deaf and would hear only if the commotion were loud?

She ought to pull her head out from the opening in the tent flaps. She ought to step back and shake what she had seen and heard out of her mind. She ought to be on her way if she was going to be home to help her *mamm* with supper.

But Susanna did none of that. She stood still and watched. From time to time, a tearful woman or reluctant child prodded by a firm father stepped into the center aisle and

16

went toward the front of the gathering and knelt. While the guest preacher continued, Reverend Baxton towered over each penitent sinner and placed a massive hand on a bent head. What happened then? Was this the moment the person repented? Was this when forgiveness came? Was this the way the Holy Ghost arrived? How did any recognize the moment that one was converted if it looked so little different than the usual hours of the day? None of this happened in Amish church services — and maybe not in ordinary Methodist services. Susanna would ask Patsy to explain it all.

Susanna could easily slip through the open flaps. If she watched enough, she might sort out for herself what was meant to be happening. If God was a God of order, what did He think of all this?

Just as the singing and prayers had swelled, rising from small beginnings, now the wave receded. The preacher, keenly in tune, matched his descending tones to the space opening up. His urging for repentance continued, but in timbres cushioned with assurance. If you repent, God will forgive. If you but ask for salvation, God will give it. If you but acknowledge your need, God will meet it.

Susanna jumped at the poke in her ribs.

CHAPTER 2

Patsy laughed. "My apologies."

Susanna scowled. "You are not sorry at all. Have you heard even one word of the sermon on repentance?"

"Ah!" Patsy jabbed Susanna's rib again. "So you have been listening."

"You have been getting me into these situations since we were little girls."

"That's what happens when a lonely only child like me lives on a farm neighboring a big and busy family like yours."

"We might never have met over the back fence," Susanna said, "if you had not been out there chasing a cow so that you would not have to tell your father you let it out when you were not supposed to."

"I remember the day." Patsy pulled open the tent flap Susanna had been peering through. "Papa is gone so much. It was the hired hand's idea that I had to learn to manage the cows."

"You were five."

"Your mother expected no less from you when you were five."

"I will not argue with you on that point." Susanna laughed.

"What do you think of our revival meeting?" Patsy asked.

"Are all Methodist church services like this?"

Patsy shrugged. "I have not been to many church services. Papa is always on the circuit. But when he is home and we gather a few families, it's not as dramatic as this. We sing and pray and Papa gives a sermon."

"Is the preacher staying with your family?"

Patsy nodded and then looked around. "Many of your people are here."

Susanna glanced toward the rank of horses and wagons. "I recognize the rigs, but I was not sure how many of them actually went inside."

"More than you might think."

"They are hungry for the Word of God," Susanna said.

Patsy tilted her head at the remark.

"I did not mean that we do not hear the Word of God in our own sermons," Susanna said in a rush. "But can one ever receive too much of the Bible?"

"You do not think it means anything more?"

"More? What else could it mean?"

Patsy looked away. She had no clear answer to the question, and no good would come from upsetting her friend with the possibilities that the church she had grown up in might not have taught her everything she needed to know for the assurance of salvation.

"What have you been up to — before listening in here?" Patsy said.

"I was just passing through," Susanna said.

"You are always just passing through somewhere."

"Bark, roots, berries, flowers." Susanna lifted her basket in evidence. "I can only grow some of what I need in my own garden. The rest I receive as a gift from God in the world He created."

"Sometimes I suspect you only began making dyes because it would give you an excuse to go out collecting supplies. You just like to be out and about at the edge of the forest."

"Shh," Susanna said. "As long as I make and sell dyes, my *mamm* cannot complain — too much."

Patsy laughed. "Deep down I truly like

your mother. I wish she didn't dislike me."
Patsy's words were sincere. Veronica Hooley
was a fascinating meld of gentle, patient
motherhood and fierce protector who would
not allow harm, whatever its form, to
threaten her children. Patsy had seen grown
men back down without Veronica ever raising her voice.

"My *mamm* does not dislike you," Susanna said.

Patsy narrowed her eyes.

"I mean it," Susanna said. "She does not
dislike you personally. It is simply that our
friendship reminds her that the world is
closer to our people than she wants to
admit."

Patsy's eyes went murky. Susanna reached
for her friend's hand.

"I am sorry," she said. "Did I hurt your
feelings with my hasty words?"

Patsy shook her head. "The world is
changing. It's not the same as it was a
hundred years ago when your people — or
mine — came to Pennsylvania."

"God does not change," Susanna said.
"His ways are higher than our ways."

"But He might change our understanding
of Him," Patsy said. "Perhaps we are the
ones who must change."

Susanna shifted her basket to the other arm and squinted between the tent flaps again. "Is that what the preacher is trying to say with all his talk of repentance?"

"Your church believes in repentance. I know you do."

"Of course. God calls us to Himself by repentance."

"Then what is so wrong with other churches that also preach repentance?"

Susanna shrugged. " 'Tis hard to explain."

"Maybe it shouldn't be."

Susanna did not seek a quarrel. After the day she first saw Patsy over the fence and the two had shyly grinned at each other, they never knew when they might see each other. As they grew older, they managed more frequent visits. Their parents knew each other by brief acquaintance but lived in separate worlds. Somehow the Methodist circuit preacher ended up living amid Amish farms — or rather, Patsy and her mother did. Charles Baxton was home only a few days at a time, long enough to check in with the hired hand who kept his farm running sufficiently to at least provide food for his wife and daughter. When Susanna, as a fourteen-year-old, began teaching herself to create dyes, collecting supplies and selling dyes and cloth gave her increasing freedom to leave the Hooley farm.

"Why don't you come inside?" Patsy said.

"Inside the tent?" Susanna's heart lurched.

"Yes, of course, inside the tent. We're standing right here. Other Amish people are here."

"I could not do this." Susanna took two steps back from the tent.

Another hymn had begun with a clear tenor somewhere inside. "Arise, my soul, arise; shake off thy guilty fears. The bleeding sacrifice in my behalf appears."

Susanna pulled against the tune tugging her toward the tent. This was not the first time Patsy's father had organized a revival meeting and not the first time Patsy had urged her to attend. But this was the first time Susanna had gotten close enough to see inside, even if only through a slit in the tent, or to try to make out the words of an English hymn.

"We could just stand in the back," Patsy said, "just inside the tent. Is that so different than standing just outside the tent?"

Susanna stepped back another two paces. Patsy was right. Like a line drawn in dry dust and scuffed over by many steps, this line would also disappear if Susanna were not careful.

"My *mamm*," Susanna said. Whatever choices the other Amish made were on their consciences. But if she went inside, they would see her, and word would reach Veronica before supper. Her mother loved her children and sacrificed every day for them. Susanna saw no reason to crack open her mother's heart for the sake of curiosity.

"Never mind," Patsy said. "It's enough that your mother finds me a dangerous influence. If you came to our meeting, I would be a true villain."

Susanna stifled a sigh. She loved Patsy. But Patsy was outside the church — the Amish church — and she would never understand what it was like to be inside, any more than Susanna could understand the Methodist hymns.

"Shouldn't you go back in?" Susanna asked.

Patsy waved off the immediacy. "I have been here nearly three hours already." But she turned her head and began to hum as voices within joined the song.

"Sing the words." Susanna had not meant the thought to find voice, but Patsy complied.

"The Father hears him pray, His dear anointed one; He cannot turn away the presence of His Son: His Spirit answers to the blood, and tells me I am born of God."

" 'Tis pretty." The tune moved and pitched toward joy, without the somber tempo of the hymns Susanna was used to singing in church. "Thank you."

"I will sing as many hymns for you as you like."

"This one will do for now," Susanna said. *His Spirit answers to the blood, and tells me I am born of God.*

"Do you think Adam would come to a meeting?" Patsy asked.

Susanna's gaze snapped up. "Adam? Is he in there?"

"No. I only meant to inquire if you thought he would ever consider it."

"No, I do not believe so."

Patsy nodded. "Another reason you will not come in."

"Adam does not tell me what to think."

"No one tells you what to think," Patsy said. "But you do not like to make people unhappy."

" 'Tis nothing wrong with a charitable spirit."

"Certainly not. But if you are to marry Adam . . ."

Susanna raised a hand to her warming face. "You must not let anyone hear us speak of this."

25

"Sometimes you do not have to speak to know something is true." Patsy's voice lilted, teasing.

"Adam and I have not known each other long enough."

"Two years!"

"He is from another district, and he will want to go back someday."

"With a bride. And you have known his uncle and aunt all your life. Is it not a fitting recommendation that they would take him into their home?"

Susanna seized at the opportunity to change the subject. "Niklaus Zug is one of our ministers, you know."

"I do know. My father knew him when they were young men."

"Of course. My point is that Mr. Zug is quite an accomplished preacher. You might enjoy coming to one of our church services to hear him."

Patsy laughed. "What deftness you have used to turn the conversation around."

" 'Tis only an invitation. Visitors are welcome."

"Do you and Adam stare at each other across the aisle?"

"Certainly not!" Susanna at least tried to focus her attention in church. "Hardly ever."

The dance in Patsy's eyes matched her

smile. "I have seen the two of you out looking for berries. He cannot keep his eyes off
you."

"Now you are being silly."

"Am I?"

Adam let the wagon come to rest. The clearing was a flat space, and if he could not get
the horses going again uphill, he would turn
them downhill to gather momentum anew
and keep them moving. For now a few
minutes reprieve for the horses would
benefit the remaining journey, and he could
do with a gulp from his jug of well-water
kept cool out of the sun under a blanket
beneath the wagon bench. He retrieved the
jug and swallowed a long draught.

To his relief, Susanna had stepped a
couple of yards away from the revival tent.
Yet she was talking with Patsy Baxton, so it
was premature to think she had dismissed
the possibility of going inside. Adam tilted
his head back and judged the sun in the
early phases of its descent. Perhaps the
meeting would be over soon, and the question of whether Susanna might attend an
English tent meeting could be put off. After
another day, the revival would conclude,
and the questions that it posed would dissipate. She was not curious about the

Lutherans or Presbyterians and their established churches. All of this would pass.

Methodist tent meetings might confuse Adam, but his feelings for Susanna did not. His affection for her was a certain and true north. Adam plugged the jug again, stowed it safely where it would not roll around, and dropped from the bench to the ground. The team could have a few more minutes. With a firm grip on the reins, he led them to a spot of shade and tied them to a tree. Then he pivoted toward the private huddle between Susanna and Patsy. Being so near to Susanna, if he did not make himself known, he would regret the missed opportunity in all the hours before he dropped off to sleep that night, and she would overflow his dreams more than ever. Patsy's presence was no impediment. She was always pleasant toward him — though scheming with Susanna over something unspoken.

Adam waved, and Susanna's black bonnet bobbed above an inviting smile. Patsy's smile was slyer. Even Adam, with his limited experience with women, knew that unmarried women confided to each other about men.

"I was driving by and saw you," he said, his eyes fixed on Susanna.

"You two are always happening by," Patsy

said. "I don't want to get in your way."

"You are not in the way," Susanna said.

But Patsy had already pivoted to slip through the flaps of the tent, and Adam had no urge to stop her. What Patsy said was true. If he and Susanna did not conspire in their malingering, they might never see one another. At least not alone.

" 'Tis a warm afternoon," Adam said.

"Yes. 'Tis."

"The wagon will save you the heat," he said. "Might I drive you home?"

" 'Tis out of your way," she said. "And you have a load."

"Lumber will not spoil. Surely your *mamm* would be glad to have you home in time for supper."

"And your *aunti*?" Susanna's dark eyes glimmered in that way that made Adam want to take her face in his hands. He had once, and he did not dare again.

"Ah," he said, "there is a difference between an *aunti* and a *mamm.*"

CHAPTER 3

Morning sun bore down with the pledge of summer heat the next afternoon. Niklaus Zug had never liked heat. Keeping cool was too absorbing a task when there was always much to do. But the fields needed the sun at this time of year. Jonas was already out in the fields looking for signs of blight or infestation, which they had not suffered for years. The corn had achieved sufficient height to reassure that the ground carried adequate water and nutrients, and the wheat would yield plenty to grind and keep his wife in bread through the winter. Deborah's vegetable garden overflowed with squash and beans. Adam stood in the farmyard throwing slop to the chickens. This had always been Deborah's task, but Adam was a helpful soul and picked up the bucket more mornings than not. Whatever irritation made Adam's father send him to Niklaus was of no consequence now.

Niklaus was glad to have him. Despite the heat, Niklaus whispered a prayer of thanks for a bountiful life. But Adam needed more than a warm welcome from his uncle. He needed to find his place with skills more challenging that feeding kitchen scraps to the chickens or in the fields doing only what he was told. Niklaus had just the project in mind.

"Adam!" Niklaus called from the open barn door. "Come help me with the hay."

Adam's head rose from his task and rotated toward Niklaus before he dumped the remains of the bucket and walked to the back porch to leave it for Deborah's convenience. Beyond Adam a horse neighed and snorted. Its rider urged a brief, dramatic gallop that churned the dirt in the yard and sent the chickens into a burst of unaccustomed flight.

"Charles Baxton." Niklaus leaned against the door frame and crossed his arms over his chest. "A man who spends as much time on a horse as you do ought to know better."

"What would you know?" Charles dropped off his horse. "You ride only of necessity and close your heart to the sheer joy of it."

Niklaus laughed. "Nice to see you, Charles."

"The friends of our youth are the most tightly bound." Charles tied his horse to a hook in the side of the barn.

"You are speaking proverbs now?" Niklaus said. "I should write that down."

Charles's words lacked no merit. Niklaus had met Charles a quarter of a century earlier, when he had briefly worked for an *English* lumber company to fund the purchase of the land he stood on now. Charles was foundering, wrestling with his call to ministry, when he had already given his heart to Mercy, though he was years from offering her a life. Charles showed no aptitude for cutting lumber, but Niklaus inspired him to stay at it long enough to put money down on a small plot of land in the Kish Valley. If he proposed to marry yet also become a Methodist circuit rider, he could at least offer his bride a place to call home. And Niklaus would live within easy riding range to keep an eye on things.

"Patsy tells me she saw your nephew driving a wagonload of lumber yesterday," Charles said.

Niklaus nodded.

"Getting ready to build something?"

"I thought I might plant it. With enough care, an oak plank will grow a tree, will it not?"

Charles lifted his black hat off his head and scratched his hairline. "Sometimes I wonder why I put up with you."

"Seems to me you are always galloping away." Niklaus curled his fingers to beckon. "Let me show you what I have in mind."

"Does this have something to do with Jonas?"

"Might be so." Jonas was not yet officially betrothed. There would be plenty of time to spread the news once he was.

They strode around to the back of the house.

Was he supposed to follow? Or should he work on the hay by himself? Adam was not sure. It could not hurt to work on throwing one bale down to the barn floor on his own.

Adam did not dislike Charles Baxton any more than he disliked his daughter. The Baxtons were genial and hospitable, but they made him nervous. He never had a friend outside his own church or a neighboring district. That his uncle and Susanna, both of whom Adam adored, had deep and abiding friendships with an *English* family befuddled him.

Adam had thrown down two bales of hay from the barn loft and was descending the ladder to the floor when a wagon rattled into the yard. Unsure whether the temperature was rising faster inside the barn or outside, Adam dragged an arm across his sweaty forehead, dampening his shirtsleeve, and looked out the barn door. Bishop Hertzberger was securing his wagon and glancing around.

"*Gut mariye,* Bishop Hertzberger," Adam said, moving into the farmyard. "My *onkel* is —"

Coming across the yard, Niklaus interrupted him. "Shem! Thank you for coming."

Uncle Niklaus got along with everyone. Adam had never seen him less than glad to welcome a guest, and no matter his schedule, he paused to offer a greeting in the middle of the road. Now Niklaus stood between Charles Baxton, Methodist minister, and Shem Hertzberger, Amish bishop. Niklaus himself was a minister in the Amish congregation. Adam thought he ought to withdraw and stepped a few feet away.

"Is my arrival ill-timed?" Shem asked Niklaus. "Did we not agree I would come today to look at the wood?"

"You are right on time," Niklaus said.

"It is I who has come without prior arrangement," Charles said. "Niklaus tells me you will be working on his project."

Shem nodded. "And young Adam will assist me."

"By God's grace," Niklaus said, "I am a competent farmer, but by His will, I am no builder. My wife would rather do without the extra room than live with the mess I would make of it."

"I'm sure that's not true," Charles said.

"Adam will learn far more about carpentry from Shem than he would from me," Niklaus said.

Adam watched three faces. Niklaus's bore the smile it always did. Charles's eyebrows were raised slightly as he looked at Shem. The bishop was not an unkind man, but at this moment his eyes narrowed slightly as he took stock of the Methodist minister.

Niklaus rubbed his hands together. "The wood is still in my wagon. We can have a look, and if it is not sufficient for the trim and shelves and bed board, I will send Adam back on Monday."

"I will leave you to it," Charles said. "Perhaps the next time I am home, I will come and inspect the progress."

Susanna had not expected a gathering in the Zug farmyard. Her open cart, pulled by the smallest and oldest mare in the Hooley stables, carried fifteen yards of cotton dyed

35

especially for Deborah Zug and neatly folded and protected by a clean flour sack. Some of the Amish women were delighted simply to have a small jar of Susanna's dye to use on their own. Others welcomed Susanna's service to dye their cloth and return it to them ready to be cut and stitched into garments. Deborah belonged to a third category, those who had particular preferences for colors and would gladly pay handsomely — though in barter — for someone who could match the hues of their imagination. Of course Susanna would make a polite visit out of the excursion to deliver finished cloth, but she had not anticipated any of the men would be in the yard in the middle of the day. Adam and Niklaus stood with feet braced and hands on their hips — Adam was more like his uncle all the time — and Reverend Baxton and Bishop Hertzberger leaned slightly away from one another.

Adam's head was the first to turn in the gesture that warmed Susanna now as much as it had two years ago. One side of her mouth twitched up before she caught herself. It would not do to appear overeager in front of the others.

"Susanna!" Adam's clarion voice sounded,

and the others looked in her direction now as well.

Susanna guided the cart to an easy stop. *"Gut mariye."*

"That means 'good morning,' doesn't it?" Reverend Baxton said.

Niklaus clapped his old friend on the back. "I may yet persuade you that our language is the language of heaven."

"If that is *Gottes wille,*" Reverend Baxton said. "Perhaps I should pray for a special gift of the Holy Ghost, for I fear languages are not my strength."

Susanna offered the smile that seemed appropriate when Patsy's father smiled at her. He had always been amiable, but he was only home a few days at a time between his circuits, and Susanna generally did not see him. When she did, he made her feel glad. The glint in his green eyes was irresistible, and it explained the shine Susanna often saw in Patsy's.

" 'Tis nice to see you, Reverend Baxton," she said.

"Likewise," he said, "but I must be on my way and let these men get about their work."

As soon as Reverend Baxton was on his horse, the bishop glanced across the yard to Niklaus's laden wagon. "Your friend is right. We must get to work."

Niklaus and the bishop matched forward strides toward the wagon. Adam only shifted his weight from one foot to the other.

"Do you not need to go with them?" Susanna said.

Adam shrugged. "Either the lumber is acceptable to the bishop or it is not. My presence will not determine the outcome."

"But perhaps your *onkel* needs you."

"Are you trying to shoo me off?"

Susanna smiled freely now, with Adam's the only eyes on her. "Just testing how easily you might go."

"Not easily at all," he said. "Have you much time?"

"This is my last stop for today. I only hope your *aunti* is pleased."

"Of course she will be."

Susanna glanced around. "Do you know where she is?"

"I will look with you."

Niklaus's voice burst between them. "Adam, come. If you are going to be a carpenter, the first lesson is learning to judge wood."

Adam's shoulders sagged an eighth of an inch.

"Go," Susanna said. "You must not let down your *onkel.*"

"Or the bishop," Adam said.

38

"Or the bishop."

Amused, she watched him turn his torso, and then his legs, leaving his gaze to last in a display of reluctance. Then she turned her own body toward the task at hand. The slumping mare was not a wanderer and lacked the energy even to be properly spooked, so Susanna did not bother to tether her. The package in the cart required both hands to carry with care as Susanna speculated where Deborah might be.

She found Deborah a few minutes later on the back porch, churning butter.

"Susanna!" Deborah abandoned her grip on the paddle. "Is it finished? If you have come to break my heart and tell me you could not dye the cloth after all, you can turn around and go straight home."

Susanna laughed. " 'Tis finished. I hope you will like it."

Deborah snatched the package from Susanna and laid it on the rough-hewn worktable.

"Did you spin the cloth yourself?" Susanna asked. " 'Tis some of the finest I have ever seen."

"My sister sent it to me. A spinner in her district is the best in the state." Deborah opened the package. "Oh my. Susanna, you have outdone yourself."

"Is it close to the color in your mind's eye?"

" 'Tis exactly right. Exactly."

Brown, Deborah had requested, to remain within the confines of plain and unadorned, but with an echo of red to liven things up. She had winked when she made her request. Susanna had taken her cue from a reddish mud she once came across.

Deborah methodically unfolded several feet of cloth, careful that it should not be soiled by its surroundings.

"You have a gift," Deborah said. "No one can dispute."

"Thank you," Susanna said. The next time she came across a length of fine cotton for herself, she might try to reproduce Deborah's color. She had kept careful notes about the bark and berries she used and how long the cloth sat in the dye bath.

"Pie!" Deborah said. "We shall have pie. I may not be able to color cloth as you do, but my piecrust never fails."

When Niklaus climbed the steps of the back porch, with Adam a few yards behind him, half the pie was gone and two plates were scraped clean.

"You have had pie without me," he said.

"When you can dye cloth to please me,"

Deborah said, "you shall have pie."

Niklaus laughed.

"Adam," Deborah said, "get two more plates."

Niklaus stepped out of the way to let his nephew pass, and Adam returned a moment later with plates and forks.

"Has Shem approved the wood?" Deborah asked while she served generous slices.

"He seems to think Adam did well in the choosing." Niklaus plunged his fork into the pie and moved a bite to his mouth. He closed his eyes and chewed slowly, letting the flavors linger on his tongue before swallowing. Blackberry rhubarb was his favorite. Nothing would persuade him that his wife had not made this pie with him in mind, if not to please him then to taunt him.

"How soon can he begin?" Deborah slapped away her husband's hand as he moved toward the pie tin. "The last slice is for Jonas. Leave it."

"Next week," Niklaus said. "I told Shem I will spare Adam as often as he needs him."

He glanced at Adam, who was chewing pie with his eyes fixed on Susanna. Their countenance changed when they were near each other. Did they know that? They could only see each other, not the whole that they made together. Adam should not drag his

41

feet about proposing. Niklaus would do whatever he could to help the young couple as if they were his own children. He could also add another room. Once Shem made a carpenter of him, Adam would know how to build the second room on his own. Niklaus ran his fork around the plate seeking every remaining morsel.

"You two should go for a walk," he said. "Susanna probably used up some of her best supplies earning this pie. There is yet time in the day to walk along the edge of the forest and replenish." One pie was not sufficient payment for dyed cloth. Niklaus suspected his kitchen held enough meat and fruit pies to feed the entire Hooley family for two days. He would help Deborah put them in Susanna's cart.

"I am sure Adam has much to do to help you here." Susanna blushed.

"Hay," Adam said. "I do not know if I threw down all you intended."

"How much did you throw?" Niklaus said.

"Two bales."

"That is sufficient. See? You have time for a walk after all." Building the room for Jonas and Anke would also build Adam's confidence. There was no telling what he could do once he believed in himself enough to try.

When Susanna and Adam had left, Deborah stacked plates.

"You are turning into a silly old man," she said.

"When it comes to those two, have you any objection?"

"None."

"Then I will be silly all the day long."

Chapter 4

If one of the ministers knew he was her favorite, it might lead to pride. Susanna would never thank Niklaus Zug for preaching with any more enthusiasm than she offered to the others. But he was her favorite. When Niklaus preached, she leaned a little farther forward, every part of her body ready to listen.

The church service had ended three hours ago. The meal the congregation shared after worshipping was nearly over. Some of the women were wrapping leftover food in flour sacks. Mr. Zimmerman, as always, was ready to begin loading tables and benches in the wagon that would carry them to the farm of the family who would host the congregation in two weeks — the Zooks, Susanna thought. Or was it the Planks, who might have traded with the Zugs? While she understood the practicalities of bringing to a close a long morning of worship and the fellowship of a meal, this was Susanna's favorite part of church Sundays. Friends lingering over a last bit of conversation before parting. Women sharing their recipes while jiggling *boppli* on their hips. Men remarking how much closer the harvest was than half a month earlier. Barefoot children chasing and squealing through the grass or perching on the fence along the pasture to admire the horses. Young men daring to greet the young women to whom they hoped to offer a ride home, as Adam often did for Susanna. Amid it all, sitting alone on a bench, Susanna found a stillness, a secret inner place to absorb the love that bound family to family.

This was church.

She might be curious about the Methodists and their ways, but she recognized where she belonged. Here.

Noah Kauffman was not far off. He was her family, her mother's cousin's son — and another of Susanna's favorite people ever since she was a small child. Noah was fifteen years older than Susanna, yet he never let on that she might be bothersome when she perched on a fence or hung over a stall wall in the barn just to watch him work. For the moment, he stood alone, and Susanna pressed her feet into her heels and stood up. A moment with Noah would bless her day. He was such a gentle soul. In a room full of men, his was not the voice Susanna would hear rise above the din, but in private conversation, he was the one who made Susanna feel he truly saw her. She approached him.

"Good morning, Cousin Noah."

"Hello, Susanna. I pray God met your heart today."

"He did. The sermons were indeed a blessing."

"If I could preach the way Niklaus does, perhaps the thought that I might be chosen to be a minister would not perplex me the way it does."

"If God chooses you, it will be for a reason, and I would not want to miss a word He gave you to speak."

Noah winked. "Speaking of choosing, I hear some of your friends are arranging an afternoon's recreation."

"What has that to do with choosing?"

Noah winked again, his cheeks reddening in pleasure. "Adam will choose to walk with you."

It was safe to smile in Noah's presence. Susanna would go on the outing even if Adam did not, but it would be so much nicer if he did. His voice would supply the missing tones in the forest, his step the patter to match her own. Others might pair off, but if another walked with her, it would only be until Adam threaded his way toward her.

"Cousin Noah?"

"Yes, Cousin Susanna?"

"People say you pray something fierce when you seek *Gottes wille.*"

"That is the way my *daed* taught me. Finding the will of the Lord is a serious matter."

Susanna looked down at the toes of her shoes peeking beyond the hem of her skirt while she composed her features. When she looked up again — only a few seconds later — the color had washed out of Noah's face.

"Cousin Noah?" Susanna touched his arm. "Are you all right?"

He gave no response. His eyes started to roll.

"Cousin Noah!"

Adam knew every move Susanna made on a church Sunday — whom she greeted, which dishes she carried out from the host's kitchen, which child she took into her lap. Once their friends went off together, it would be more fitting for him to be at her side. In the meantime, Adam was adept at turning his head so that wherever Susanna was, she was in his peripheral vision if not his direct view.

"Where are the benches going next?" It was Susanna's brother Timothy who asked. He had just turned sixteen, five years younger than Susanna.

"I am not sure," Adam said, his head tilting to bring Susanna into his gaze. "Zooks? Planks? Or it may be my *onkel*'s turn. Mr. Zimmerman should have the schedule."

Susanna's hand cupped her cousin's elbow now. Even in profile, and even with most of the farmyard between them, Adam saw the concern that skittered into Susanna's face. Then she dipped her bonnet at an angle that obscured her face from Adam's view. He shifted over one step.

"Are you going to help load the benches now?" Timothy asked. "I will come."

"Not quite yet," Adam muttered.

He took a slow step toward Susanna. Both her hands held Noah's wrists now. Susanna said often how fond she was of Noah, but Adam had never seen her touching him this way before.

"Excuse me, Timothy," Adam said. "I will meet you at the bench wagon in a few minutes."

"Where are you going?"

Adam let Timothy's voice fade without responding. His eyes were on Susanna and Noah. Perhaps Noah had gotten too warm in the full sun and Susanna wanted him to sit down. But there were no benches near them. Adam picked up his pace.

"Adam!"

If the call had come from Susanna, Adam would have launched a sprint. But it was his own cousin, Jonas, who sat with a group of young men.

"Come here and weigh in," Jonas said. "We are trying to choose where to walk today."

"Anywhere is fine," Adam said, still moving.

"But you know the best trails, as you like to remind us at every opportunity."

"I do know the best trails. I will come back." Adam persisted forward, weaving through huddles of conversation and nearly stumbling over a toddler who did not quite have his balance and fell on his bottom and wailed. Adam swooped him up and placed him safely in his mother's arms in a single fluid motion that did not detour from his path.

Susanna's face flushed in alarm as her weight shifted to support the now slumping Noah. Her gaze swept in a half-circle, find-

49

ing Adam's eyes.

He dashed the remaining yards between them.

Noah was a slight man, but even so Susanna could not hold him upright indefinitely. And he was in no condition to walk.

"Noah!" she said. "Can you speak?"

"Speak?" he echoed, dropping in her arms.

"Does something hurt?" She moved behind him and slipped her arms under his.

"Hurt?"

His collapsing weight took Susanna to her knees, but she kept him from a free fall. At least they were on soft ground at the edge of the yard and not the rocky lane.

"I have him." Adam's hands grasped Noah's shoulders.

Susanna surrendered Noah's weight and moved out of the way. Adam laid Noah flat.

"What happened?" Adam said.

"I do not know." She could not control the tremble in her voice while her fingers still remembered the tremble in Noah's arms. "We were simply talking, and suddenly he was unwell. But he told me nothing of how he felt."

"Noah," Adam said. "We will help you. Tell us what is happening."

Noah's response was a jumble of barely

50

audible words.

"Did you understand any of that?" Adam asked.

Susanna shook her head.

Noah's head fell to one side.

"He is unconscious!" Susanna's voice pitched sharply up. "We have to get help."

When she stood, she pressed against Adam's aunt Deborah. Niklaus was there, and Timothy, and Jonas and a half dozen others.

Niklaus knelt beside Noah and picked up an arm. When Niklaus released it, the limb fell limply back to the ground.

"Check for a pulse," Deborah said.

Adam's hand went to Noah's wrist. " 'Tis there, and strong."

"He is breathing," Niklaus announced. He took Noah's clammy, ashen face in his hands. "Noah! Noah! Wake up!"

"I have to find Phoebe," Susanna said. The crowd around Noah enlarged, but Phoebe was not in sight.

"Yes," Adam said. "Go quickly."

Susanna turned to navigate out of the growing throng. The entire church district seemed determined to occupy the same two square yards of dirt.

"Has the good Lord taken him from us?" someone asked.

"Gottes wille," someone else said.

"Hush," Deborah said. "Noah has not passed. He has simply fainted."

Susanna scrambled through the crowd.

"He is trembling mightily," someone said. "His limbs are not his own."

Susanna halted, pivoted, and peered through the onlookers to witness the truth of the statement. Something had seized Noah.

"A demon!" With hushed voice, a woman took steps back, away from Noah. "Like Legion in the Bible."

"No," Niklaus said. "He is simply ill."

"Ill unto death, I believe."

Susanna's heart clenched, and she lifted her skirt sufficiently to allow her feet to run.

The house, the outdoor kitchen, the stables, the barn. Susanna checked them all while a giant clock tick-tocked in her mind. If she did not find Phoebe soon, it might be too late.

Too late for what? *Ill unto death.* No. Susanna refused the thought.

Breathless, Susanna emerged from the back door of the barn. There, among the chicken coops and with a hen in her arms, Phoebe stood talking with Mrs. Satzler well beyond the commotion that had spurred Susanna's search.

"Phoebe," Susanna said. "Come."

"What is it?"

"Noah is ill."

Phoebe's grip on the chicken went lax, and the bird cackled and fluttered toward freedom. Susanna grasped Phoebe's hand, and together they ran back to Noah. When he came into view again, Susanna expelled breath. Noah was on his feet. All would be well.

"Repent!" Noah shouted.

Susanna twitched. The crowd around Noah gave a collective gasp.

"Do you not know," Noah said, "that what the Lord requires of you is a repentant heart? A contrite heart? Will you offer this to God, who offered to you His own dear Son?"

Not ten minutes ago, Noah had confessed his anxiety should he ever be called upon to preach. And now he was preaching — but not like Niklaus Zug. It was more like the Methodist revival preacher Susanna listened to outside the tent two days earlier.

Noah was not a preacher.

Noah had never preached.

He was limp and unconscious only moments ago.

Whose effort had successfully wakened Noah?

How did he have the strength to stand and preach in the same full sun that had weakened him?

This made no sense.

Adam stood with a hand gripping the back of Noah's shirt.

Do not let go. Stay where you are.

The assembly parted for Phoebe, and Susanna tailed her.

Noah raised his arms, devoid of weakness, and spread them wide. "If you but come to God, He will come near to you."

Susanna had known Noah all her life, and he hesitated even to pray aloud. Her mouth hung open. Voices around her echoed her confusion.

"What is he doing?"

"Why is he saying such a thing?"

"Did he get hit on the head?"

"Does he think we do not have enough ministers?"

Still threading toward Noah behind Phoebe, Susanna caught Adam's eye. His shrug was slight. He had no explanation.

Stay with him.

Their eye contact broke when the bishop shouldered his way in from the periphery and his wide frame stood between Phoebe and her husband.

"Noah Kauffman!" Shem Hertzberger

thundered. "What kind of disturbance have you called upon our peaceful Sabbath?"

Susanna's ears rattled. The bishop was one of those preachers with a distinct voice for sermons, and he could work up fervor for the Word of God. But never had Susanna heard him address one of the church members in such a tone. How could he be angry about what happened when no one was sure what, exactly, had transpired? Noah gave no sign of hearing anything. His cadence did not falter, nor his motions hesitate, as he looked right through the bishop.

"The Bible is a story of mercy and judgment," Noah said, his voice lower and fuller than Susanna had ever heard it. "This truth runs through the Holy Scriptures, and we must choose which side we are on. Will we know our own sin and therefore God's mercy, or will we deny our sin and know only His judgment?"

The listeners sobered.

Susanna leaned forward and whispered in Phoebe's hear. "God has anointed Noah. Perfect love casts out fear. He will have no need to fear preaching after such a wonderful beginning."

"Noah," Shem said, "I demand you speak to me."

Air rushed out of Phoebe and her face clouded.

CHAPTER 5

Even the children stilled at the sight of Cousin Noah preaching. He was the man who offered sweet treats, spoke kindly, and sewed leather around balls of string for them to play with. He wasn't wearing a frock coat, such as the ones the ministers wore when they preached, so the sermonic words coming from Noah's mouth made the children tilt their heads and examine him curiously.

"We see God's mercy and judgment right at the beginning of the Bible, in the book of Genesis, and we trace it through Holy Writ until the great white throne of Revelation," Noah said. "It is not God's desire that we should fall into the lake of fire. It is God's desire that we hear His voice and answer Him when He calls us each by name. Do you hear Him calling you by name?"

"Noah, what are you doing?" Mr. Zimmerman said. "We have benches to load. You always want to help."

Noah preached on.

"Noah, the bishop pronounced the benediction hours ago."

Noah preached on.

"Brother Noah, let us worship in reasonable order."

Noah preached on.

Susanna turned toward the tug on her elbow. Timothy had edged his way in.

"What is he doing?" Timothy asked.

"I do not know any more than you do," Susanna said.

"You were with him when it started."

"When I left him, he was ill," Susanna said. "He said nothing to me about this. In fact, he spoke only of admiration of the way others have the gift to preach while he does not."

"His eyes do not look right."

Susanna concurred. Noah's eyes moved from person to person but with a glaze that resisted focus. When he looked at her, she did not feel seen.

Noah preached.

Babies cried, mothers soothed them, fathers readied the wagons, and Noah preached.

Women gathered their things, and Noah preached.

Younger adults, some married and some hoping to be, debated their walk in the woods, and Noah preached.

Phoebe took her place beside him, trying to still his gesturing hands, and Noah preached.

Susanna and Adam exchanged glances every half minute, and Noah preached.

The bishop demanded that he stop, and Noah preached.

One hour. Another half hour. Two hours.

Phoebe's face wrenched in distress, and Susanna believed that if Phoebe could have made Noah stop, she would have. But he responded to no touch, no word, no expression, no urging.

Susanna inched closer as others inched away and the afternoon wore on.

"What should we do?" Adam said at the two-hour mark.

"There is nothing to be done," Phoebe said.

They spoke from either side of Noah, but he did not hear them.

Families with long drives ahead of them rolled their wagons off the Satzler farm. Young men gave up on snatching a few minutes with one of the young women.

"We are going now." Susanna's mother was suddenly at her side. "The children are tired, and the animals will need tending. And Philip is starting to look sickly."

"I cannot go now!" Susanna said. It flabbergasted her that her mother would suggest departure for any of the Hooleys.

"You must," her mother said. "Walking home from one of the nearer farms is reasonable, but this is too far for you to walk, and I do not think your friends will go on an outing after such excitement."

Adam, still at Noah's side, spoke. "With your permission, Mrs. Hooley, I will see that Susanna gets home."

Susanna stifled the urge to clasp him around the neck. "Please, *Mamm*? Noah is your cousin, too. Let me help care for him."

Her mother looked from Adam to Susanna and back again before finally nodding. "I will tell your *daed,* but please try not to be late. The sooner we all get back to a normal routine, the better."

"Not a minute later than necessary," Susanna said. "I promise. *Danki.*"

Niklaus, Bishop Hertzberger, and Yohan Maist, the three ministers of the district, conferred. But when they lined themselves up before Noah like a wall, he merely stepped to one side and shifted to prayer.

"Catch him," Phoebe said suddenly, perspiration dripping from her face after so long in the sun at her husband's side amid the debate about his well-being.

"What do you mean?" Adam said.

Susanna stepped closer, listening to Noah speak the Lord's Prayer. *Lead us not into temptation.*

"Catch him," Phoebe said. "Now."

And Noah slumped against Adam.

"Cousin Noah!" Susanna pressed in.

"Adam, will you help me with my wagon?" Phoebe said.

"Of course."

"We can make him comfortable in the bed of hay."

"But he is unconscious again," Susanna said. "He is most certainly unwell." If they had waited so long to take him home, should they not allow a few more moments for his recovery?

"I want to get him home," Phoebe said. "Now that he stopped preaching, the ministers will be full of questions I do not wish to answer. I do not want Noah to wake with their faces staring down at him. He will be mortified, and I will not put him through that."

"We only want to help," Susanna said. Though the bishop had spoken roughly, trying to startle Noah, even the ministers only wanted to help.

61

"Then please bring my wagon and help me lift him."

"I will go now for your team," Adam said.

Susanna knelt and received Noah's lolling head into her lap. "Your *onkel* is coming," she said to Adam.

"Good," Adam said. "I will ask him to keep the others away. You and I can follow Phoebe and make sure Noah is all right before I take you home."

She wanted to throw her arms around him and kiss him. At the soonest opportunity, she would.

Susanna pulled her cart onto the Kauffman farm at midafternoon on Monday. All day she had ached to know how Cousin Noah was. Phoebe put him straight to bed the day before and shooed off Adam and Susanna with assurances that Noah would be fine with a good night's sleep.

What could they do to help care for Noah?

Was Phoebe sure he would be all right when he had not yet come to consciousness?

What about something to drink? Should they not try to get Noah to swallow some liquid?

And supper? Susanna could put something in the oven.

These questions and more bubbled out of Susanna, but Phoebe's only response had been patiently making sure of her husband's comfort as he slumbered, until Susanna could no longer resist Phoebe's encouragement that she and Adam should go on home to their waiting families.

Susanna barely slept. During the early morning hours, something had come to her: Phoebe had been distressed but not surprised at Noah's behavior. What could that mean?

Susanna was up before first light to dispatch her chores with the animals, mix up three batches of dye, and color two dress-lengths in a dye bath and hang the fabric from the line to dry. Only then, and with a promise to her mother to be home for supper and evening devotions with the family, was she free to drive her cart over to the Kauffmans'. It was too late to walk and still keep her promise.

The fragrance of bread wafted from Phoebe's summer kitchen, and the ring of a hammer from behind the barn witnessed to Noah's labors. The cows were in the pasture and the chickens pecked the ground as they always did. Smoke swirled from the outdoor oven.

All the usual activities of farm life, Amish or not.

Perfectly normal.

Susanna exhaled relief. Phoebe had been right. Noah was fine after a night's rest. Leaving the cart in front of the house, Susanna circled to the back on foot.

Phoebe gently removed a loaf of bread from its pan and lined it up beside five others cooling on the covered wooden table. She looked up.

"Susanna."

"I came to see how Noah is — and you," Susanna said.

"As you can see, we are quite well." Phoebe smiled. "I have a loaf cool enough to slice. Can I tempt you? Butter and honey, perhaps?"

Susanna's mouth salivated in immediate response. "No need to trouble yourself."

" 'Tis no trouble." Phoebe picked up a knife and deftly sliced into the loaf. "I suppose you will want to see for yourself that Noah is well."

"If you say he is well, that is enough," Susanna said.

Dubious, Phoebe shook her head. "You are too fond of him to settle for that."

"Well, he is my favorite cousin. He always has been. He was nearly a man and I was not yet old enough for school, but Noah looked out for me."

Phoebe nudged a bowl of butter toward Susanna and handed her a table knife. "I will fetch him."

While she waited, Susanna bit into the bread. Every Amish girl in the district learned to bake bread competently before her twelfth birthday. Susanna herself made the Hooley household bread many times when her mother was busy with the younger children or looking after a cow threatening to go dry, and no one in the family detected the difference between the loaves Susanna and her mother baked. But the sensation on her tongue now was a rare indulgence. There was no point in asking Phoebe what made her bread taste like it was sent from heaven. She would only shrug and say it was just bread.

Phoebe returned with Noah, handed him a slice, and said, "Shall we go sit in the house? I have a jug of milk calling for someone to drink it."

Susanna helped Phoebe gather the loaves and take them into the house to finish cooling.

"As you can see," Noah said once they were comfortable in the Kauffman front room, "I have fully recovered from my malady."

"I am so glad. You gave everyone such a fright."

"Did I? I do not recall."

"I suppose not. You were quite unwell."

"I am sure it was not as bad as that."

Susanna's stomach lurched. "It was, indeed." People often did not remember details of an illness, but surely Phoebe would have told Noah how ill he had been only the day before if for no other reason than to encourage him to rest today as well.

Noah glanced at Phoebe. "Then I shall take care not to frighten you again," he said.

"I am not concerned for myself but only for you," Susanna said.

Noah spread his hands wide. "I am quite well."

"I did not know you could preach."

"I do not preach." He glanced again at his wife.

"But you did — and very well," Susanna said. "I would sit through an all-day service if it meant hearing you give the sermon."

Noah readjusted himself in the chair. "If I muttered something that would pass in your mind for spiritual wisdom, you flatter me. Be careful, lest you tempt me to pride."

"But Cousin Noah —"

Phoebe stood up. "I hope you will greet your mother for us. We are always glad to see any of the Hooleys. A morning visit would be nice."

Phoebe's abruptness, however kind, flustered Susanna.

"Of course," she said, standing as well.

"I may have had too much sun again today," Noah said. "I feel in need of a rest after all."

"Then you shall have one," Susanna said.

Noah leaned back in the high-back overstuffed chair and closed his eyes. Within seconds he was asleep.

"I will go," Susanna said softly, never imagining that Noah could drop off so quickly. When he slumped to the left, his head weighting forward, she startled. He began to tremble.

"Phoebe, what is wrong with Noah?"

"Noah is fine."

"I do not agree."

Noah bolted out of his chair. "The mercy of God is wide and deep, and He invites us to step into the river of His love and be washed clean."

"Phoebe," Susanna said.

"He is fine."

Noah stared out the window, shutters flung open, as if preaching to the chickens and cows. "If you have any doubt of the love of God, this is the day to set your heart at ease. For God is love. We love one another because God first loved us. His way is the way of love."

"He is preaching," Susanna said. "No one else is even here."

Phoebe said nothing.

"This is what happened yesterday," Susanna said, "and you knew exactly what to do for him."

Distressed but not surprised.

Noah reached to pick up his German Bible from the table beside his chair and turned again toward the window.

"There is no greater message in the Holy Scriptures, which God Himself has written for us, than that we are His beloved. Let your heart hear the beating of God's heart for you."

Phoebe shuffled toward her husband. "I see his true heart, a heart after God, when these times come."

"This has happened before," Susanna said. "How often?"

Phoebe hesitated. "At first only once a year or so. He would wake in the night, come out here to the window, and begin. I would only wake when I heard his voice or got cold from the draft in the middle of winter."

"And then?" Susanna spoke over Noah, her attention pulled to his words even as she asked the question.

"Then it was more often. Now it is quite often."

"Why would he not want the ministers to know he has such a gift? Or the congregation? Surely they would vote to make him a minister as well."

Phoebe shook her head. "He only knows that he preaches because I have told him so."

"I do not understand."

"He has no memory of yesterday," Phoebe said. "And tomorrow he will have no memory of today."

"You might be well familiar with John 3:16," Noah said. "Are you also familiar with the other many, many, many verses that lead you into the deep well of God's love?"

"How has no one discovered this before?" Susanna asked.

"It used to happen during the night," Phoebe said, "and then in the evenings after supper."

"And all our people are scattered on their own farms and stay in their own homes in the evenings." The Zugs were the Kauffmans' nearest neighbors, but they were still a couple of miles away.

Phoebe nodded. "Now it has begun happening in the afternoons but never as early as yesterday. If I had thought there was any risk, we would have come straight home after the service finished."

"How long will he preach?" Susanna said. "As long as yesterday?"

"Most likely. Once it begins, there is no interrupting. You saw for yourself. You can trust me when I say that I have tried many times to no avail."

"Yesterday you knew when he was nearly finished."

"He always concludes with the Lord's Prayer." Phoebe moved a loose rug away from the path Noah had begun to pace as he preached.

Susanna sighed. "Bishop Hertzberger was unhappy."

"Shem has been a faithful minister for us, but he does have particular views." Phoebe pulled a small table closer to the wall. "I try to keep him away from anything he might trip over. He does not even see the furniture. I suppose if he is going to do this every day, I will have to find a way to arrange the furniture more permanently. I was hoping not to have to explain to him why I am moving things around after so many years with an arrangement that has suited us well."

"The whole congregation saw it happen yesterday," Susanna said. "There will be questions."

Phoebe picked up the glasses the three of them had drunk milk from only a few minutes earlier. "It would not be an untruth to say he is unwell and needs rest. We did go to an *English* doctor once, when we visited Noah's brother in Somerset County, and that was the only advice he had for us. Rest and close observation to be sure he does not choke during a seizure."

The medical opinion did not strike Susanna as particularly helpful.

"I thought about it a great deal last night," Phoebe said. "We will stay home from church for the next couple of services. That will give us six weeks to see what might change. It might all subside, or at least rotate back to the evenings."

"I want to help," Susanna said.

"You must not tell anyone what I have confided." Phoebe's tone sharpened. "You must promise me. Even my own sister does not know. If the preaching ceases, there is no reason to concern anyone — or to make Noah feel more badly than he does that he cannot recall any of this."

Susanna watched Noah, still preaching out the open window. She would do nothing to intentionally bring harm to him.

"If no one else sees it and has reason to mention it to Noah, he does not even have to know it happens. Let us allow him that happiness."

Susanna nodded.

"Not even Adam," Phoebe said. "No one."

Susanna nodded.

"Your *mamm* will want you home for supper."

"I cannot leave now."

"You must. If you want to help Noah, do not raise questions for anyone."

Susanna swallowed and nodded one last time.

If he had not noticed the loose fence railing when he did, Adam would not have been up along the road when Susanna drove by. It did not seem like she was driving, though, but rather trusting the mare to find the way from the Kauffman farm — the only point beyond his uncle's farm that she could have taken the cart — past the Zug land, through the Baxton property, and home to the Hooleys'.

But he had noticed the fence, and he was up at the road to fix it just as Susanna happened by. He hoisted himself over the top railing and waved at her in the road. They did not get to wander with their friends the day before, so he proposed to invite her to explore a new trail into the forest. Uncle Niklaus seemed to turn his head when Adam slipped away with Susanna, no matter how much work there was to do, a tendency Adam could not resist exploiting. Her cart was moving slowly enough that he could easily trot beside it.

"Oh," she said. "Adam. Hello."

"Is that the best I get?"

She turned her face to him. "I am sorry."

"Are you all right? Is your cousin all right?"

"Noah is fine. He is fine."

"So you have been to see him?"

"Yes. Where else could I go down this lane?"

Adam furrowed his forehead. "Susanna, what is wrong?"

"Nothing." She picked up her reins. "Nothing."

"It does not sound like nothing."

"Well, it is."

He trotted beside her, thinking what else to say.

"I found a new trail," he said. "I do not know who tramped it down, but it is easy to follow. We would not get lost. We could look for roots."

"I have no need of more roots right now."

That had never mattered before. Susanna had been as complicit as Adam in finding times and reasons to explore God's creation together. Adam reached a long arm over and tugged on the reins. The old mare required little convincing to stop.

"What are you doing?" Susanna asked.

"I am trying to talk to you."

"My *mamm* does not want me to be late for supper and devotions."

"You have time," Adam said. "What report will you give her on your cousin?"

"I told you. Noah is fine."

Why did he not believe her? "Susanna."

"Adam, we will talk another day. I must get home." She took the reins again and urged the horse forward.

Adam stood in the road and watched her until she rounded the bend and went out of sight. She had never done that before.

CHAPTER 6

The sight of her father cooking an egg mesmerized Patsy Baxton, not because she had supposed that he was incapable but because it so rarely happened. He had been home for a week now, and that in itself was unusual.

"Papa, let me make you some toast to go with your egg." Standing beside her father at the stove, she opened a burner and used tongs to hold a thick slice of bread flat over the lapping flames.

"Egg and toast," Charles said, "and strong black coffee. What better breakfast to send me off on my horse."

Patsy inhaled her father's scent — the fragrance of the soap he'd used on his bushy gray-streaked hair mixing with the smells of his freshly laundered shirt and his well-traveled light wool frock coat. This is what her fathered smelled of — readiness for the journey.

"You could stay home another day." Patsy slowly rotated the bread to brown both sides evenly.

Charles shook his head. " 'Tis Thursday already, and I am promised to a revival meeting on Saturday that is two days' journey."

"The toast is ready," Patsy said.

"And the egg." He reached for a plate and carried his breakfast to the table. "What will you eat?"

"I've had my porridge."

"Ah. I will have my fill of porridge during my circuit. A favorite of hosting families."

Patsy arranged herself in a chair across from her father, filling her mind with this ordinary image of him. A man eating his breakfast. That is what he was just then. An hour later he would be the minister on his horse.

"How did you feel about the revival meeting here?" Patsy planted her elbows on the table and cupped her chin in her hands.

Her father swallowed a bite of egg. "We reached many souls, and I believe many have genuinely turned their hearts toward God."

"I saw the one woman who was so happy to be converted that she was crying."

"She knew in that instant that she was

76

saved. The knowledge took great weight off her shoulders."

"Some of the Amish were there," Patsy said.

"On one night, yes. I do not expect the Amish will easily convert. Their teaching, as I understand it, leaves little room for true knowledge of salvation."

"But Niklaus Zug is your friend, and you think he believes. I'm sure Susanna does."

"But do they have a testimony? The fruit of faith?"

"Did any of them go forward?"

He shook his head. "Nary a one. But I continue to pray that God will work renewal among our friends."

Patsy sat back in her chair. "Will you ever leave the circuit?"

Most Methodist circuit riders were young men. Her father was forty-one, an age when most riders had settled down. Over the years, Patsy heard stories of men her father knew who had given up the work in a state of ill health — or even been found dead on the circuit. She did not want his next journey home to be so riddled with illness that the end of life was in sight.

Her father reached over and grazed her cheek with his fingers. "I do as the Lord bids me. My heart aches for you whenever I am away. But your mother's inheritance — which we never expected — allows us to have this farm and helps to run it. Is this not God's provision for the ministry?"

Patsy wrapped her fingers around her father's hand against her face. "I love you, Papa."

"Do you believe this is absolutely necessary?"

Susanna sucked in her lips before turning to meet her mother's examination.

"This is the third time this week you have run off to the Kauffmans'," her mother said.

Veronica scrubbed a man's work shirt against the washboard. Susanna presumed it was her father's, but Timothy was of stature to fill a man's garment as well.

"I only want to be helpful," Susanna said, wringing out a frayed apron before pinning it to the clothesline.

"But you said yourself that Cousin Noah is better." Her mother scrubbed again.

Susanna chose her words carefully, as she had done all week. "I did say he is stable. But I have seen in my visits that his condition may take longer to resolve than Phoebe had hoped, and if she does not take care, she will need tending as well."

Stable not *well.*

Condition not *illness.*
Resolve not *cure.*

"Phoebe is a dear wife," her mother said, "and with no children, she certainly provides all the attention of a dedicated nurse."

"Caring for someone who has not recovered in a few days is tiring," Susanna said. "There is a farm to run. A helping hand goes a long way."

"There is much to do right here at home. The truth is, your four younger brothers are more help to your *daed* than to me."

Susanna swallowed. Timothy was sixteen, and Daniel twelve, both old enough to work in the fields or in the barn. At nine and seven, Philip and Stephen were still doing lessons, and Susanna gladly had taken on their instruction. They would start up again right after the harvest. She milked the cows more than any of her brothers, and she kept the family of seven in cloth. She planned to stay right beside her mother until the family's weekly laundry was hung that day. Vegetables for the Hooley supper were laid out in the kitchen. What more could her mother ask of her?

"You are always very generous with the candles you make," Susanna said. "Phoebe could use some new tapers. I said I would bring some — if you can spare them."

"I can spare them," her mother said. " 'Tis you I cannot spare."

"I will not walk nor stop to collect any colors," Susanna said. "I will go directly in the cart and come home directly as well."

"Perhaps another day." Veronica dropped the scrubbed shirt into the pail for Susanna to wring.

"Tomorrow, then."

"We will see."

Susanna angled herself away from her mother to wrest moisture from the garment. Controlling her daughter's comings and goings was not like Veronica. If she knew the truth — that Phoebe needed help keeping Noah safe while he preached — would that make a difference?

"Like this?" Adam held the corner together as Bishop Herztberger instructed, two logs meeting.

"Is it perfectly square?" the bishop asked.

Adam looked at the array of tools on the floor and settled his eyes on a right angle piece of metal.

"That is right," the bishop said, following Adam's gaze.

"I cannot let go to pick it up," Adam said.

The bishop laughed. "This is why a good carpenter always benefits from an assistant."

He picked up the angle and demonstrated how to use it, checking both the bottom and the top of the joint Adam had begun to create.

"I have never done this before," Adam said. "I want it to be right for my *onkel* — and my cousin Jonas."

The bishop nodded. "You have learned much this week already. Lock the notches in place, and we will check the angles once more. We already have the basic shape of the pen, but we must be careful that the angles do not migrate wider or smaller, or Jonas's wife will never be happy with the way the furniture fits!"

Adam chuckled. His own mother had complained for years about a drafty corner that left a gap. She was compelled to keep a substantial chest of drawers there whether it suited her or not.

"Do not fret," the bishop said, "we have plenty of time before any harvest weddings, and the newlyweds will visit around to their relatives before settling in here."

They set notched logs that Niklaus had selected and felled with Jonas. Adam grew up in a house his grandfather had built, and his limited experience with barn raising taught him little about home construction. At least he recognized the shape of an emerging rectangle.

"You are doing well, Adam," the bishop said as they began the process of setting the next set of logs to shape the room.

"Danki."

Adam was unsure with every cut or notch, yet the bishop commended him. The patience Adam witnessed in this carpenter in common work clothes did not form a clean corner in his mind with the stern minister of Sunday who chastised Noah Kauffman for speaking truth from God's Word. How could donning a black frock coat to lead a worship service, as all the ministers did, change the demeanor of a man? Perhaps if Adam began an extemporaneous sermon, the bishop would chastise him as well.

Bending to blow sawdust out of the latest notch before setting the crosspiece, Adam shook off the thought. He could not explain what happened to Noah, but it was not his place to judge the bishop's response. When he was baptized, he vowed submission to the church. Certainly the vow held when he moved to a new district.

"Very nice work," the bishop said. "Now do you think you can manage cutting some notches on your own?"

"Surely I am not ready!"

The bishop ignored Adam's hesitation.

"We will begin with three logs. I will try to come again tomorrow or the next day, and we will see how you have done."

"You are leaving?"

" 'Tis nearly suppertime, Adam. You have worked well and hard today. Try the notches. A dovetail takes the most time to cut, but it also gives the tightest hold."

"I am not ready. I will make a mistake."

The bishop gestured to a pile of mismatched ends of logs cut from the pieces that formed the walls so far.

"Practice on some scraps. Remember to keep a steady hand. If you are uncertain, your *onkel* can help. He does not make a very square corner, but he is not bad with an ax if he tries, and he will try for the sake of Jonas."

The bishop picked up his tools and mounted his horse. His farewell was a simple tip of his hat, and Adam was left standing alongside a framed pen four logs high. If the day's heat had not already drenched Adam's shirt, the thought of taking any step in the construction on his own would have. It was Niklaus's idea for Adam to learn carpentry, but Adam had only imagined himself as the assistant to an experienced laborer. As he puffed his cheeks and blew out his breath, he picked up a piece of scrap wood and an ax. Disappointing either his uncle or the bishop was not an acceptable alternative.

CHAPTER 7

The brush snagged on a burr in the stallion's mane, and Adam tugged harder. Belgians were beautiful animals and never disappointed in the fields, pulling plow or the work wagon full of harvest. The pair that Adam and Jonas were brushing now had been Jonas's choice, his first independent purchase of farm animals that he hoped to have for a long time.

"He is your favorite, *ja?*" Jonas said from the side of a young mare.

"*Ja.*" Denying it would be insincere. The horse Adam rode came from his father's stables, and while his relationship with the stallion was amicable, he was a serviceable riding horse with little to remark on. His color could be named neither white nor gray, and the brown streak down his nose was crooked. But Jonas's stallion was a creature of beauty. Along with a silky chestnut coat and flaxen mane, he had the ability to haul tremendous weight.

"Mine too," Jonas said, glancing around to surrounding stalls. "He is stalwart and loyal and handsome, and I pray he will breed well for many years."

"Surely it will be so."

"You were up very early this morning." Jonas exchanged a curry comb for a dandy brush.

"The bishop gave me an assignment. I did not want to disappoint." Adam slowed his brush. "Will you be helping to build as well?"

Jonas met Adam's eyes. "You are wondering why my *daed* offered your services to the bishop rather than mine."

"I am happy to do as your *daed* asks," Adam said, "but 'tis a curious question."

"Truly. Perhaps you will be the one to teach me to build."

"I have just begun to learn," Adam said. Jonas was barely nineteen, several years younger than Adam, and already on the verge of betrothal.

"I do not always understand my *daed*'s decisions, but I have learned to trust what I do not understand." Jonas glanced out the small window in the stable wall. "Here comes the bishop now."

Adam returned his brush to its hook on

the wall, inhaled and exhaled a deep breath, and stepped out into the yard just as the bishop tied up his horse.

"*Gut mariye,* Adam," the bishop said. "I trust one day has been enough time for you to try your hand at notching."

"I have done my best," Adam said.

"Was Niklaus able to advise you?"

"I did not ask him."

The bishop raised an eyebrow. "Then let us see the work of your hands."

Adam led the bishop around to the far side of the house, where Jonas's room would rise one log at a time. Three logs, each one notched at both ends, lay in equally spaced parallel lines.

Bishop Hertzberger squatted and lifted one end for closer inspection. "Well done."

And the next, and the next.

"You have done extremely well," the bishop said. "You must have practiced first."

"I did."

"May I see the scraps?"

Adam pointed to a row of twelve log ends, all with dovetail notches.

"But these are perfect as well," the bishop said, picking up one and running his eyes down the row. "Where are the mistakes? We learn from our mistakes."

"This is all of them," Adam said.

"When you are learning, mistakes are nothing to be ashamed of. You need not hide them from me."

"I am hiding nothing," Adam said. He would not lie to the bishop, of all people.

"Perhaps one or two that you threw on the fire last night?"

Adam shook his head.

The bishop dropped the scrap in its place beside the others. "If you take such care with simple notching, God will be pleased with the beauty of what you create."

"I hope so."

The bishop shook a finger. "But do not become proud."

"No, sir."

"Then let us begin."

"Yes, sir."

Niklaus rounded the corner. "Shem! Jonas said you had come again."

"Your nephew is a talented young man," Shem said to Niklaus.

"All I did was notch a few logs," Adam said.

Shem clasped his hands together. "It is the spirit of your work that you offer to God, and you have offered Him your best."

"I try to," Adam said.

Niklaus clapped his nephew's back. "You

are careful with the details in all that you do."

"And such care is what will make you a carpenter," Shem said. "Someday a young woman will be blessed to have a husband who can bring God's beauty right into the home."

Niklaus contained his smile. Susanna was the young woman who should be so blessed.

"Adam has a good head on his shoulders," Niklaus said, "and a good heart. Deborah and I are delighted to have him in our home."

Adam had arrived two years earlier, tentative, reluctant, hesitant at every turn. His father had decided it was best that Adam leave, and his mother — Niklaus's sister — did not object. She must have seen for herself that Adam would not thrive under the direction of a man who imposed an hourly schedule on his children, even after they were grown. Niklaus was happy to have his sister's boy. If you are a child's favorite *onkel* when he is small, it is only right to take him in when he is in need. Adam should have married sooner, in his father's opinion. But someday — soon, Niklaus hoped — Adam's parents would meet Susanna and understand that God's hand had not left their son. In the meantime, if the bishop recognized and commended Adam's abilities, great blessing would fall on Adam and spill over to Susanna.

"I will get my tools," Shem said, "and we will begin. Niklaus, are you helping us today?"

"Perhaps I will," Niklaus said. "The chores are in hand, and the corn and wheat will grow no faster if I sit in the field and watch it."

"Then you may stay," Shem said, "but you will do as you are told."

Niklaus bowed his head slightly. "You are the master. I am but a lowly servant."

"Do not mock me," Shem said, but his eyes twinkled. "I will be right back."

"How do you dare make fun of the bishop?" Adam asked once Shem was out of earshot.

"Shem and I were boys together, and we are ministers together."

"But he is the bishop."

"And I respect him. But he is not God."

"I try to understand him," Adam said. "He has overflowed with patience toward me as I learn, but sometimes he also spills over with authority."

"You are talking about Noah on Sunday."

"Yes, partly."

"That is difficult to understand," Niklaus

said. "The circumstances are unusual. Knowing how to respond is also difficult."

"What will the bishop do now?" Adam asked.

"Phoebe made it clear she did not want a visit from one of the ministers. I have recommended that we respect that. But in all things we must make room for God."

Patsy eased off the reins and pressed her knees into the horse's sides.

"Hup!"

Tired of waiting for her father — who spent most of his time on a horse — to teach her to ride, years ago she begged the farm's hand to put her astride. There was never any question of learning to ride sidesaddle. Patsy's mother always took a buggy and Harvey, the farmhand, was unskilled in the genteel ways of ladies' recreational riding. He simply lifted the little girl into a saddle and began the lesson.

Patsy never looked back. If she went fast enough — and she did — she heard nothing but the wind whirling through her ears. The rhythmic vibration of the hooves shivered through her body with an abandonment she found nowhere else than giving her horse his head.

Galahad, the golden stallion, galloped with

minimal encouragement. Rider and horse were a matched set. The smooth gait of a gallop, which needlessly terrified so many children, was more comfortable to Patsy than the more common trot or canter. She lifted off the saddle, her right hand tangled in the mane, leaning forward to hang on to her center of gravity as the horse's weight shifted from rear to front. Nearly out of her stirrups, and exhilarated, Patsy adjusted the angle of her hips again as the horse went from front legs to rear and back again. Over and over, this automatic motion united them in shared triumph. The speed. The energy. The freedom. Tears from the wind — or joy, Patsy was never sure which — formed rivulets on her cheeks.

They charged at the base of Jacks Mountain, which had never frightened either of them. Though she wanted to, she did not take the horse all the way up to the ridge. Instead, Patsy reined in the stallion and followed an inclined forest to her favorite overlook above the Kish Valley. She had never lived anywhere else, but the rolling farms of the valley between Jacks Mountain and Stone Mountain made her hesitate to believe she could be happier anywhere else on God's earth. Below her lay own family's land, the Hooleys', the Zugs', the Kauffmans', the Hertzbergers', other Amish farms in one direction, and farms and shops of the people of other faiths in the other. Milroy, Lewistown, Reedsville — all towns of hope for the future. The valley cradled them all, twin shoulders of the mountains rising in grandiose reminder of the blessing of the land. The stallion nuzzled the ground while Patsy gazed at fields of green corn and white, willowy wheat, colorful vegetable gardens that would see the valley residents through the winter, cows grazing. With little effort she could pick out the new courthouse on the town square in Lewiston, the train tracks that ran through the valley, the narrows, the market house with its meat and vegetable stalls.

Nowhere. She would live nowhere else, ever, even if that meant becoming an old maid.

Finally, Patsy descended, more slowly than she had charged up but satiated with gratitude. She kept a hand on the reins, lest the horse break into a gallop again.

She needed no watch to tell her the time. The farmhand — still Harvey after all these years — would be sure any other horses he had used would be cooled and brushed, but it was Patsy's job to be sure the single Baxton cow was milked and the chickens were rounded up before nightfall. She had plenty of time — hours. The slow, scenic route home would hold her in her refreshed mood.

Her gaze lifted to the horizon so steadily that she nearly did not see the figure waving in the road. She tugged on the reins while she rummaged for the Amish woman's name.

"Mrs. Zimmerman."

"You are a friend of Susanna Hooley, *ja*?"

"Yes, that's right."

"I have just come from the Kauffmans'."

A lump took shape in Patsy's throat. "Is everything all right?"

" 'Tis hard to tell, to be honest. I only stopped in for a friendly visit, but Phoebe seemed most eager for me to depart."

"What do you mean?"

"She did not even offer me a slice of pie — and only one cup of *kaffi.*"

"She must be busy."

"Too busy to visit? That is not our way."

"Or perhaps she was tired." Had Mrs. Zimmerman flagged her down to report on Phoebe Kauffman's unacceptable etiquette? "Did you need something, Mrs. Zimmerman?"

"Susanna."

"What about Susanna?"

"That is what Phoebe wants. She wants Susanna. Why she should send me out when I was right there and then turn around and ask for someone who is miles away befuddles me."

"Susanna is family," Patsy said. "Perhaps it is a family matter?"

"I simply thought that after what happened on Sunday she would be grateful for whatever hand of help came her way."

Patsy scrunched her face. "What happened Sunday?"

"Why, Noah, of course."

"What's wrong with Noah?"

"He was taken quite ill. After church. I thought you would have heard."

Patsy had ridden by the Hooley farm twice earlier in the week, but both times Susanna's cart was missing from its usual spot alongside her shed, and Patsy had passed on by. That she did not see Susanna for five days was not unusual, but if Susanna's favorite relative was ill, she would be distressed. And that Patsy could not bear.

"If Phoebe wants Susanna," Patsy said, "I will make sure she gets the message."

Susanna wrapped the bark in an old cloth and carefully pinned a label to it. *Oak.* Another label on another package said *White*

Oak. She did not want to confuse them because it would change the color of the dye. Placing both bundles on the same shelf, she evaluated her bark supply. Adam would be glad to know that soon she would need to collect more, and she would be foolish not to pick wild berries while they were plentiful. The blues and reds would be in demand for the purple cloth that some of her Amish neighbors increasingly favored. She first had to be confident she would not speak to Adam of Noah's condition.

The door to the windowless shed where she worked was propped open for light. Susanna looked up when a shadow moved through the shaft of illumination she depended on.

"Hello, Patsy."

"Susanna, why have you not told me Noah is ill?"

Susanna stiffened. "Who told you that?"

"Mrs. Zimmerman."

"She told you what happened?"

"Not precisely. Only that Noah took ill on Sunday — and that Phoebe is asking for you. She asked Mrs. Zimmerman to get a message to you."

Susanna gasped. Phoebe would not have asked anything of Mrs. Zimmerman if the situation were not urgent. Susanna pulled the pins out of the top of her work apron and tossed it on her workbench.

"I want to help," Patsy said. "Tell me what to do."

"Help me put out the fire." Susanna pushed past Patsy and out of the shed. The water was nowhere near hot enough to begin the dye bath. The lot would have to wait another day. "I must hurry."

"Hurry where?"

Susanna spun toward her mother's voice.

CHAPTER 8

"Where are you off to?" Susanna's mother moved toward her, trailed by Timothy and the younger boys.

"Good morning, Mrs. Hooley," Patsy said.

"Hello." Veronica turned a hospitable, if not welcoming, gaze upon Patsy. "I pray the day finds you well."

"Yes, and you?"

"Very well," Veronica said. "Thank you for asking."

"I ran into one of your friends in the road," Patsy said, "and she asked me to deliver the message that Phoebe Kauffman would like Susanna to visit today."

Susanna softly cleared her throat. Patsy meant well. She always meant well.

"I understand Noah has been unwell." Patsy was undeterred.

"I should take Phoebe those tapers I promised. I have them right here." Susanna reached for a half dozen candles, their wicks hanging long. "I thought it would be all right if I just took the odds and ends."

"Phoebe is welcome to my best candles," Veronica said. "Perhaps I will take them myself and see what she needs."

"No." Susanna lurched. "There is no need for you to disturb yourself. I am sure you have a busy afternoon planned."

Her mother turned toward the fire Susanna had laid under a pot. "You were getting ready to dye a cloth."

"The water is still cold," Susanna said, "and I have not promised the cloth for this week. No harm will come if I run over and see what Phoebe needs."

"No!"

Susanna held her breath, and her little brothers startled at the uncharacteristic volume of their mother's voice. She had not thought it possible for Veronica to magnify her objection in such a manner.

Even Patsy stepped back, slipping her hand in her stallion's bridle and leading it away and out of sight into the grove of apple trees. Susanna eyed her path. Patsy had done what Mrs. Zimmerman asked and delivered the message. There was no need for her to be caught up in the whirlwind of the objections Susanna's mother would spin.

Timothy's shoulders were broad beyond his years, and he stepped onto the space Patsy left vacant. "You were going to ask Susanna to help you with the rugs," he said, "but I will do it. Let Susanna go see Cousin Noah."

Timothy was nosy, but he was sweet.

Even before her mother spoke again, Susanna surrendered to befuddlement. Every child grows up knowing the tone in a parent's voice that means business, but her mother's obstreperous umbrage to Susanna visiting Noah and Phoebe bewildered her. They were relatives and fellow church members, and they had a need. Susanna had learned from her mother the call of God for compassionate response.

"*Mamm,* Phoebe would not ask if it were not important," Susanna said, fortified by Timothy's support. She dropped the candles into a patched flour sack and picked up the poker to push the flickering logs apart.

"What do you think you are doing?" Veronica gripped Susanna's arm.

"I must go." Susanna was not a child of defiance and never had been. She had not learned submission through repeated punishments for displeasing her parents but rather from the pleasure of pleasing them. Why could her mother not see what was so

100

clear to Susanna?

"We allow you great freedom, Susanna, and for the most part you are a sensible girl. But I am still your *mamm.*"

Susanna used her boot toe to kick dirt onto the only piece of wood that had not stopped flaming as soon as it was separated from the others. With a tin cup, she splashed water on the logs.

"Susanna," her mother said, "are you listening to me?"

"Yes, *Mamm.*"

"Then you will heat your water and dye your cloth. I will go see Phoebe."

"Mamm," Timothy said, "I finished my chores. You have been saying for days that the rugs need beating. We can do them now."

"Timothy, take the boys and go find your *daed.* I know he has work for all of you."

Timothy tapped the shoulders of the younger boys, and they scrambled past the orchard toward the house, relieved to be dismissed from their mother's rare wrath. Patsy was gone. Timothy was gone. Susanna was on her own.

"Noah must still be unwell," Susanna said. "Phoebe does not have a house full of children to help her. I want to help."

"They have neighbors who live much

closer." Veronica fingered the hem of her apron. "The Zugs are on the next farm over. Surely they will have inquired."

Susanna eyed the sun. If Deborah or Niklaus Zug had stopped by in the morning, they would have found everything well. If Noah's new pattern had persisted through the week, Phoebe would not be eager for visitors in the afternoon. Yet she was desperate enough to send a message through Martha Zimmerman.

"Noah has been up and down," Susanna said. It was the truth. "He tries to keep up with the chores but wears out in the afternoon. He needs rest."

"But it will be difficult to keep him down," her mother said.

"That is my concern. You can imagine it is wearing on Phoebe as well if he tries to do too much."

"He has a peculiar illness. It unsettles me that you should be exposed to it."

"It is not catching, *Mamm.*" Susanna's heart started to slow. Finally, her mother's anxiety became clear.

"He must have been delirious on Sunday," her mother said. "That is the only explanation I can think of. Delirious from the heat. Acting like one of those *English* revival preachers."

Susanna said nothing. Perhaps her mother would find her own way back to compassion. Susanna glanced at the logs, satisfied they would pose no danger if she left. Slowly she put the lid on the pot to keep the water clean for later.

"I must think of what is best for you," her mother said.

"This is Cousin Noah," Susanna said. "Surely we must think of what is best for him."

Her mother pressed her lips together. "He is my favorite cousin."

"Mine too!" Susanna could have her cart hitched up within minutes and be on her way. When footsteps crunched, she turned her head.

"Not now, Timothy," Veronica said.

"But *Mamm*."

"Not now."

Timothy caught Susanna's eye and shrugged. Then he pointed with a thumb over his shoulder.

Daed! Timothy, *Mamm*, Daed. A simple visit to dear relatives was becoming a family decision. Never had she argued with a decision of Daed's, nor would she. He was the head of the household.

Elias tramped along the edge of the apple orchard. "Veronica?"

"There was no need for you to come down here." *Mamm* glared at Timothy, who fell into step with his father.

Susanna dragged a shoe through the dirt. Just when *Mamm* was on the brink of relenting, Timothy had to stick his nose in. Could he not, for once in his life, do as he was told? He thought sixteen was far older than it was.

"Timothy tells me Phoebe is asking for Susanna." Elias addressed his wife. "Noah is still unwell."

"*Ja,*" Veronica said, "but perhaps someone should ride into Lewistown to see if the *English* doctor can pay a call instead."

"Phoebe will know when it is time for a doctor," Daed said. "In the meantime, what harm can come if Susanna visits?"

Her mother met her husband's eyes, some secret language passing between them. Susanna had witnessed the language before but was not a fluent interpreter. One day she might understand a secret marital language. Adam's face filled her mind.

"It will be all right, Veronica," Elias said softly. "Susanna has a level head on her shoulders. She wants to help. Is this not how we have raised all our children? She may go as freely as she thinks prudent while Noah is ill."

"Thank you, Daed," Susanna said. *And thank you, Timothy.* She had her father's blessing — not just for today but for as long as Noah was unwell. Susanna pulled the door to her shed closed and made sure it stayed. If the boys had let the horses into the pasture, it might take her longer than she wished to summon her mare and lead it to the cart parked alongside her work shed.

"The younger children are not present," Veronica said. "Perhaps this is the time to tell the older ones what we have been discussing."

Susanna's gaze snapped up again.

"It may be too soon," her father said.

"What?" Timothy said. "What have you been discussing?"

"I would not call it a discussion," Daed said. "An idea. A passing thought. That is all."

"Then what is the idea?"

Susanna's toe twitched inside her boot. Timothy had just done a sweet thing for her, it turned out. Did he now have to undo his kindness by prolonging a conversation that would keep her from Noah?

"We have been talking about moving," Veronica said. "Farther west."

"Why would you feel we should move?"

Timothy asked. "The farm is doing well, is it not?"

"Very well," Elias said.

"Our physical livelihood is not the only matter of importance," Veronica said. "We must also be mindful of our spiritual well-being."

Timothy bunched his features, a man becoming a confused small boy once again.

"Certain influences are taking hold," Veronica said.

Influences? Susanna tied closed the sack of candles. Could they not speak of influences later?

"Phoebe will be waiting," Susanna said.

"A few more minutes will not matter," her mother said.

They might. What if something had already happened and that was why Phoebe had sent for Susanna?

"Your *mamm* is concerned that the *English* revivals might have a harmful effect on our congregation."

"You must admit, they have some peculiar ways," Veronica said. "And they seem quite eager to convert our people to their ways."

Patsy's father. That was what this was about. The Methodist preacher held a revival meeting, and some of the Amish church members went to hear the preach-

106

ing. Susanna was being restrained because of the choice of others.

"Three families have already moved west, including my own dear friend Marianne," Veronica said. "Others are thinking of it. It may be the best thing for our young people not to be exposed to *English* influences."

English influences? Is that what her mother thought of Patsy's family?

"Is this a serious idea?" Timothy said.

"An idea," Daed said simply. "One that will require great thought and will not be decided standing here. Your *mamm* and I will pray and wait on the Lord for guidance."

"I have had letters from Marianne in Indiana. They are quite happy there."

"We must not hold up Susanna any longer," Elias said.

Susanna inspected her work area again. The fire was out. The lid was on the pot. The shed door was closed tight. The poker was the only tool left outside, and it would come to no harm.

"Go, Susanna," her father said. "Assure Phoebe and Noah of our affection and bring us a good report."

Patsy's horse snorted. The sound flickered and died with one second, but Patsy knew well that the air passing through a horse's nostrils could be heard from yards away. But only Susanna's eyes rose toward the orchard. The horse had already relaxed. Whatever scent of danger made him raise his head had passed, and he nosed around on the ground.

Susanna hurried toward Patsy as if beckoned by the horse.

"You stayed!" Susanna said.

"Of course I stayed." Patsy stroked her horse's long nose. "I am not one to deliver an urgent message and then wash my hands of the matter."

Please don't ask me how much I heard. Enough of the Hooley family conversation had wafted toward Patsy to know that her father's actions were under scrutiny. But every family had its ways. Her own parents could have a protracted disagreement — usually about her father's absence — without ever speaking a word. Patsy saw no point in embarrassing her friend by probing into private family matters.

"I must hurry," Susanna said. "I think my mare may be in the pasture, and she is a slowpoke at the best of times. At least the cart is handy."

"Taking the cart is a waste of time," Patsy said.

" 'Tis faster than walking."

"But not nearly as fast as my horse."

Susanna's eyes widened.

"If I scoot forward in the saddle, there is room for two," Patsy said.

Patsy lifted the hem of her skirt, gripped the saddle horn, put one foot in a stirrup, and hoisted herself up. Then she cleared the stirrup and offered a hand to Susanna.

"You do not have to get involved in this," Susanna said.

"I choose to. Just because I'm not Amish does not mean that I can't be a good neighbor."

"I did not mean to imply that it did."

"We are friends, no matter what." Patsy wiggled her fingers and once again held her hand out to Susanna. "Just get on."

This time Susanna took it and squirmed into place behind Patsy.

"Hang on tight," Patsy said, "and get ready to ride like the wind."

CHAPTER 9

They had last ridden like the wind together when they were young enough to be excused for a childish choice, though they should have known better. The saddle was roomier then. Though the gelding then was no Galahad, they galloped through the valley for the sheer joy of it, both of them leaving their chores behind. In the years since, Susanna had not dared wish for another afternoon like that one, and Patsy must have known better than to offer, because she never had.

Until today.

Until this moment of need.

Until this purposeful choice in young womanhood, not the folly of children.

"Thank you!" Susanna shouted.

"What did you say?" The wind pushed Patsy's syllables toward Susanna's ears, only inches away, but they arrived fragmented.

Susanna hunched forward. "Thank you!"

Still they galloped. This was Susanna's

first time on Galahad's back, but she would be as disappointed as Patsy when one day the stallion could no longer offer this exuberance. Only after they rounded the last curve beyond the Zug farm did Patsy slow the horse to a canter.

"I should explain," Susanna said, now that they could hear one another.

"You don't have to explain anything to me."

"Please allow me. If you come inside with me, you may be shocked."

Susanna explained Sunday's fit or seizure or whatever medical term might be appropriate but which she had no grasp of. The collapse. The unconsciousness. And the sermon. And the sermons in the days since.

"You cannot tell anyone," Phoebe had said. *"Not even Adam."*

But Patsy had delivered Phoebe's message and now was delivering Susanna. It was hardly fair to ask her to wait outside without an explanation. Susanna would make it right with Phoebe.

So Susanna explained. Patsy's eyes turned to bottomless bowls of curiosity.

"When I promised to help," Susanna said, "I did not know my *mamm* would object."

"But your father has given his blessing," Patsy said.

111

"If Noah continues to preach in the middle of the day, Phoebe will need more help." Patsy's father was gone a great deal, and her mother was the most easygoing person Susanna knew. "What if this 'illness' continues? My *mamm* will put her foot down again. Maybe you and I might split the days."

The horse came to a stop beside the front stoop of the Kauffman house. Susanna slid off, with Patsy hitting the ground next to her.

"Are you sure I should go inside?" Patsy asked. "What if Phoebe is upset that I've come?"

"I will explain my proposal." Susanna would not repeat to Phoebe — or Noah, if he was conscious — everything her mother had said. But Phoebe would understand the simple practicality that it might be hard to get off the farm every day. "If she knows that telling you means she will have help every day, I am hopeful we will ease her distress."

And every day was what Phoebe needed. Susanna was sure of it.

Patsy tied up the stallion. "You choose your days. Our farmhand will make sure I can get away on my days."

"You cannot tell him why!"

Patsy smiled with one side of her mouth. "I won't have to tell him why. But what are you going to do about Adam?"

Susanna ignored Patsy's question and knocked on the front door without waiting for a response before swinging the door open. Patsy followed her inside. The farmhouse was smaller than most in the valley, perhaps because the Kauffmans had no children and no need to add on. Patsy had been inside the Hooley house from time to time, but this was the only other Amish home she had seen up close. The furnishings were sparse but functional. Chairs. Tables. Dishes. Shelves. A main room with doorways leading in two directions. One must be the way to the kitchen, and the other to the bedrooms. There could not be more than two. There was no second story, and Patsy doubted there was a cellar beneath them. More likely there were steps behind the house descending into an outbuilding halfway beneath the ground.

What surprised Patsy most was Phoebe. They had only met a few times in passing, usually when Susanna was present, but the bags beneath Phoebe's eyes and the slump in her shoulders were new.

Phoebe's startled eyes darted from Patsy

113

to Susanna.

" 'Tis all right, Cousin Phoebe," Susanna said. "Patsy brought me your message from Mrs. Zimmerman and carried me here. I trust her, and I know you can as well."

Phoebe moved her wordless glance to Noah, who stood before the open window, his wrists crossed behind his back and his shoulders squared.

"I want to come whenever I can," Susanna said. "But Patsy can help, too. You will not have to be on your own so much."

Phoebe exhaled and nodded. Patsy did not mistake the gesture for approval so much as surrender.

"He is not speaking," Susanna said.

" 'Tis but a brief interlude," Phoebe said. "He collapsed hours ago. He stops and starts, but he will not agree to sit down. He does not hear my pleas. I do not dare let him out of my sight."

"But Mrs. Zimmerman," Patsy said.

Phoebe raised both hands to her cheeks. "I managed to entertain her briefly in the shade outside."

"She was quite put out at the lack of pie," Patsy said.

Phoebe rolled her eyes. "I had to give her something to do. I thought it might as well be useful, so I asked her to get a message to

Susanna."

"She will tell half the district," Susanna said.

"She did not see anything to tell them," Phoebe said. "Noah was still awake, but I knew he would start preaching soon."

"And have you opened your hearts to the Lord?"

Patsy gasped at the force of Noah's voice.

"Do you hear His voice? For the Scriptures assure us that He knows our names and the number of hairs on our heads. We are worth more to Him than all the sparrows in all the fields of all the world."

Patsy gulped. "I thought he would be . . . mumbling . . . or whispering. He is preaching with enough force to fill one of my father's tents."

"Susanna," Phoebe said, "I have decided I must remove the rag rug for good."

"But it makes the room so cozy," Patsy said. It must have taken Phoebe years to collect the remnants to make such a large rug. Blues and browns and reds and whites were braided tightly and wound into a perfect oval before the fireplace.

" 'Tis dangerous," Phoebe said. "Sometimes Noah paces. He does not know where he is."

"If he were to trip . . . ," Susanna started.

Patsy nodded. Now she understood. "I'll help you roll it up. Susanna and I can carry it out. Would you like it in the barn?"

Phoebe looked distracted in addition to exhausted.

"Of course we will take the rug out," Susanna said. She lifted a small table off the rug and placed it safely against the wall. Phoebe was already tugging the davenport clear of the rug.

"I hope your mother will understand if you are not home to help with supper," Phoebe said. "I need more than help with the rug."

"What is it?" Susanna said. "Anything."

"You know my sister."

"Of course."

"Her back is out again."

"I am sorry to hear that."

"I have to drive over there and see to her, but I cannot leave Noah alone."

"We are here now," Susanna said. They had come together on Patsy's horse, and they would leave together only when Noah was safe.

"What if he . . . wakes up?" Patsy said. "Is that the right word?"

" 'Twill do."

"What if he wakes up while you are gone?"

"Susanna knows what to do. He will come

116

to himself and then be asleep very quickly."

Susanna nodded. "I will make sure he lies down."

"The davenport will do," Phoebe said. "He likes a quilt if it is not too warm."

"God yearns for you? Do you know that?" Noah stabbed the air with a forefinger. "Why else would He send His only begotten Son to die on a cross for your salvation? He yearns for you to come to Him, to find your refuge in Him, to trust your future to His loving-kindness."

Patsy's jaw hung open, and Susanna nudged her friend back into action to roll up the rug.

"I'm sorry," Patsy said. "I've never seen anything like this — not when someone is asleep."

"Call it what you will," Phoebe said, "but he is not himself. He will know nothing of this later."

Susanna began rolling the rug and tugged on Patsy's skirt. If Patsy was going to stand there and gawk, she would be no help at all.

Patsy knelt beside Susanna, and together they rolled the rug evenly. "What a true gift from God!" Patsy said.

"He could get hurt." Phoebe's tone was stern. "If you want to help, you must keep

117

your mind on his safety and not on his words."

"She understands," Susanna said. " 'Tis new for her, but she understands."

"You cannot guide him," Phoebe said. "He will pace at will. You must only try to keep yourself between him and danger. The fireplace, the stove, the furniture, the lamps, anything glass, the steps if he goes outside."

"It will be as if he does not see it," Susanna said.

"He truly does not know it is there," Phoebe said.

Patsy nodded.

"And when you yield your heart to Him," Noah said, "you will find His heart ever ready to receive you. As the Word of God assures us, when we confess our sin, God is faithful to forgive us."

Patsy had stilled her motions again.

"Patsy," Susanna said.

"I'm sorry. Truly," Patsy said. "What a wondrous thing."

Phoebe caught Susanna's eye. "Are you certain this will work?"

"Yes. Surely. Go to your sister. We will be here when you return."

"And one of us will come every afternoon," Patsy said.

Phoebe fixed her eyes on Patsy. "You must

not tell anyone. I pray that these daytime occurrences will fade and it will not be necessary to cause any stir."

"I understand," Patsy said. She picked up one end of the rug. "You can depend on me."

After Phoebe left, Patsy leaned against the wall in the main room, beside the window, watching the glow in Noah's face. His eyes were fixed on something — or perhaps nothing at all — outside, well beyond the house.

"He is standing up and talking," Patsy said. "How can he be asleep or unconscious?"

On the other side of the window, Susanna shrugged one shoulder. "Does it matter whether we can explain it? 'Tis happening. We see with our eyes and know with our hearts it is true."

"Won't he miss the rug when he wakes?"

Susanna nodded. "Phoebe will have to decide what to tell him."

"He truly doesn't remember?"

"No, but he knows he has spells. Phoebe has never kept the truth from him."

"He recovers quickly?"

"With some sleep."

"How many times have you seen this?"

Patsy leaned in for a closer look at Noah's face. He showed no awareness but only kept speaking, quoting a long section from the Good Shepherd passage in the book of John. Patsy knew it well. It was one of her father's favorites.

Her father.

Perhaps by the time he next returned from his circuit, Noah would be himself all the time. Patsy was not sure whether she hoped he would be or would not be. But it would be hard not to tell her father about something that would delight him so deeply.

CHAPTER 10

Susanna mixed dyes and stirred cloth in the bath all afternoon the next day. Even knowing that Patsy planned to go to the Kauffmans' to see if Phoebe needed help did not keep her mind off Noah. After speaking the Lord's Prayer, just as Phoebe said he always did, he had collapsed at the end of his trance straight onto the davenport and slept heavily. Though Susanna and Patsy watched him for several hours, he did not awaken. He would never even know they had been there or that Phoebe needed to leave, but would wake to see his wife knitting by firelight.

Sunday was Susanna's turn, and since it was a visiting Sabbath rather than a church Sabbath, little explanation was required. Her parents had taken the younger boys and driven halfway across the district for their own visit to the Maists. Susanna slowed her cart as she went past the Zug farm, wondering if Adam was home, but she resisted the temptation to put herself in his path. She would not have time for a walk to gather roots or bark, and he would want to know where she had to hurry off to and why they had not happened to see each other all week when they had become so adept at it, especially in the last few months.

Noah had not preached on Sunday. Instead, Susanna had a true Sabbath visit with her favorite cousin — and gave her parents a forthright account. Veronica asked several questions that Susanna had answered with sufficient detail to satisfy her mother.

On Monday Susanna prayed under her breath all afternoon — for Noah, for Phoebe, for Patsy who had promised to be at the Kauffmans'. Had he preached to an invisible congregation outside the window on Monday? Susanna did not see Patsy to inquire, and on Tuesday when Susanna arrived, Noah already stood at the window.

"You are sure?" Phoebe said, the two of them standing behind Noah.

"Yes, I'm certain. Go clean the chicken coop," Susanna said. "Or I can clean the coop if you would rather stay with Noah."

Phoebe hesitated. "I could use the distraction of the task. And you have enough chickens to clean up after on your own family's farm."

"Do whatever you wish," Susanna said. "I am here to help in the way you deem best."

Phoebe glanced out the window. "I might need to walk out to the other side of the pasture and check on the fence. I think Noah may have forgotten he said he needed to fix it, and I am not sure how bad the disrepair is."

"Take your time. I will be here." Susanna's impulse was to volunteer Adam to repair the fence, but first she would have to persuade Phoebe to allow her to confide in him.

Susanna pulled a straight-backed chair up closer to the window, allowing plenty of room for Noah to gesture and pace while still keeping him within view. She was a congregation of one, and the Holy Ghost blew through her cousin's words.

" 'Charity suffereth long,' " he said, quoting the thirteenth chapter of 1 Corinthians, " 'and is kind; charity envieth not; charity vaunteth not itself, is not puffed up, doth not behave itself unseemly, seeketh not her own, is not easily provoked, thinketh no evil.' "

Susanna had no trouble suffering long for Noah. It was her mother who challenged her. But what challenged her mother? The last few days were as if someone had dropped a burlap bag over *Mamm* and carried her away, leaving a fearful soul in her place. Trying to forbid Susanna from visiting Noah. Talking of moving farther west, to a new district in a new state when their ancestors had been among the first Amish to come to Kish Valley. Raising her voice to the boys. Murmuring in that urgent tone she had taken on of late. Her *mamm* had lost the peace of Christ, and Susanna wanted her to find it again — soon. Veronica was ill-suited to a disposition of anxiety, unpracticed at managing her daily affairs in the unfamiliar surroundings of fear.

" 'Charity beareth all things, believeth all things, hopeth all things, endureth all things,' " Noah continued. " 'Charity never faileth.' God's charity toward us is eternal. Surely our charity toward one another can endure the length of our days."

Susanna nodded, as she might have if she were sitting in church. Whatever was churning up her mother's spirit would surely pass, and with God's help, Susanna would wait patiently and with charity until it did. Noah even turned his head as if he were speaking directly to her with his admonishment, but his gaze found no focus. When he began to pace, continuing to quote Paul's letter to the Corinthians, Susanna snapped her attention back from her own uncharitable failings. She was not here to examine her heart. Her task was to make sure Noah remained safe.

Outside the window, a flash of blue fabric caught Susanna's eye, and she pivoted to absorb the sight of Mrs. Zimmerman coming down the lane.

With determination.

And without distraction.

Susanna scanned for Phoebe. Had she gone around back to the chicken coop, or had she availed herself of the opportunity to walk along the fence?

On the one hand, Susanna was surprised Mrs. Zimmerman had not been back before this — or perhaps she had, at a time when Noah was himself and Phoebe had invited her in for a proper visit. On the other hand, it was imperative that Mrs. Zimmerman not enter the Kauffman home this afternoon under any circumstances.

Noah paced and preached, with no sign that the Lord's Prayer would pass his lips anytime soon.

Susanna shoved the davenport from its usual angle to a position where it would block Noah if he tried to walk toward the fireplace. At least he would not fall into the stone. Moving the lamp off the side table and to the mantle would keep him from swinging his arm into glass. Leaving Noah was undesirable, but under the circumstances she had no choice. Susanna scampered across the room to pull closed the door to the kitchen and then to seal off the bedrooms. Last, she closed the shutters in the front window before hurtling outside and into the yard. Her last task might not have been worth the effort. The slats were widely spaced and three were missing altogether. Detecting the presence of someone inside the house would not be difficult.

"Good afternoon, Mrs. Zimmerman."

The older woman stopped about forty feet from the house. Susanna circled around her to draw her eyes away from the house.

"I did not expect to find you here," Mrs. Zimmerman said.

Susanna forced a light laugh. "My secret is out. Noah is my favorite cousin."

"The book of James cautions us against favoritism, Susanna."

"You are right, of course, but love binds us together. 'Tis the greatest gift, is it not?"

Mrs. Zimmerman's eyes narrowed. "Should you not be at home helping your *mamm*?"

Susanna heard a gentle rise and fall of Noah's voice, even at this distance. But it was common knowledge that Mrs. Zimmerman had begun to be hard of hearing.

"I am afraid Phoebe is not in the house," Susanna said.

"Where is she?"

"On the farm somewhere," Susanna said. "With just the two of them, there is always work to do."

"Why are the shutters closed in the middle of the day?"

"To keep out the heat," Susanna said.

Mrs. Zimmerman wrinkled her face. "If Phoebe is out, then what are you doing here?"

"I offered assistance with a few things in the house," Susanna said quickly. She looked over Mrs. Zimmerman's shoulder and through the shutters saw Noah pace past the window. "I will be sure to tell Phoebe you were here."

The fence and then the shutters. As soon as she was allowed to speak to Adam, Susanna would corral his help.

"Mmm. Perhaps I will have a look around before I give up entirely. Phoebe and Noah might be quite nearby."

"Yes! Of course you are right." Susanna was happy to have Mrs. Zimmerman look for Phoebe anywhere on the farm, as long as she did not come nearer the house. Noah reversed directions and passed the window again.

"If I fail to find them," Mrs. Zimmerman said, "perhaps you will be kind enough to let them know I stopped by to inquire."

"Of course."

Mrs. Zimmerman's gaze went toward the pasture.

"Phoebe did mention checking the fence," Susanna said. "On the far side of the pasture."

" 'Tis always the far side." Mrs. Zimmerman sighed. "She could be anywhere on the farm."

"I am afraid so."

As Mrs. Zimmerman strode back up the lane, Susanna ran back to the house, through the front door, and into the main room to find Noah now quoting from the book of 1 John.

" 'Hereby perceive we the love of God, because he laid down his life for us: and we ought to lay down our lives for the brethren. But whoso hath this world's good, and seeth his brother have need, and shutteth up his bowels of compassion from him, how dwelleth the love of God in him? My little children, let us not love in word, neither in tongue; but in deed and in truth.' "

Susanna's heart rate slowed. Noah had

wandered no farther than back and forth across the front room, still preaching a convicting sermon about the necessity of love. She took her seat in the chair beside the window once again as Noah planted his feet in his habitual way. It disturbed him not at all that the shutters were closed. Fixing them might be one of the most helpful things Susanna could arrange. She peered out and welcomed the sight of an empty farmyard. Mrs. Zimmerman had wasted no time in her search for Phoebe.

Then the clatter came from the kitchen. Susanna sprang from the chair, quickly assessed Noah's stability, and crossed the room. Her fingers were on the knob when it turned and the door opened.

"Mrs. Zimmerman!" Susanna's stomach thudded like a dropped pail.

"It occurred to me that you were unclear about Noah's whereabouts," Mrs. Zimmerman said.

"Shall we chat in the kitchen?" Susanna gripped Mrs. Zimmerman's elbow to try to turn her around. For the moment, Noah was silent. From this angle, it appeared he was simply surveying his land — if only the shutters were not closed.

"What is going on?" Mrs. Zimmerman pushed past Susanna. "Noah, I am delighted to see you are on your feet again."

Noah spread his hands wide. "There is no greater gift in the world than love, but it must never be selfish love but rather selfless. Think of what your neighbor needs rather than what you might wish for yourself."

"Ja," Mrs. Zimmerman said. "That is exactly why I have come. I am here to help."

Susanna's stomach burned. Noah did not turn around.

"Have you known any need that love did not meet? I call upon you to speak of it, though I do not believe you will able to do so. Charity never faileth."

"Who is he talking to?" Mrs. Zimmerman said.

Susanna said nothing.

"Is this another sermon like the one he gave on our last church Sunday?" Mrs. Zimmerman crossed to the window and threw open the shutters. Another slat dropped out of place.

Susanna swallowed her silence. She and Phoebe had not talked about what to do if this happened — though of course Mrs. Zimmerman should not have barged into the house.

"Susanna Hooley, I believe an explanation is due."

Susanna shrugged. "You can see for yourself."

"The bishop will not approve. Noah, you must stop right this minute."

Noah moved on to talking about the brotherly love between David and Jonathan.

"If he will not listen to me," Mrs. Zimmerman said, "then you must intervene."

"He is asleep," Susanna said softly.

"Then wake him up." Mrs. Zimmerman reached for Noah.

"Please do not touch him," Susanna cautioned.

The front door opened, and Phoebe came in.

"I am sorry," Susanna said immediately. "She came in through the back. I did not realize."

Phoebe wiped her hands on her apron. "Susanna, is Noah all right?"

Susanna nodded. "He has come to no harm."

Mrs. Zimmerman snapped her fingers in front of Noah's eyes. "This is what you did not want me to see the other day."

"Martha," Phoebe said. "Please do not interfere."

Mrs. Zimmerman planted a fist on one hip. "What am I interfering with? Do we not all want what is best for your husband?

131

He must not persist in disobedience to the bishop."

"He cannot help it," Phoebe said.

"I suppose if you had children, you would excuse them as well." Mrs. Zimmerman sobered her features. "If he cannot help himself, someone will have to help him."

"We are helping him the best way we know how," Phoebe said, "by keeping him safe during his spells."

"Then perhaps you need some help as well."

"I am helping," Susanna said, indignation welling.

"I have in mind another kind of help," Mrs. Zimmerman said. "What affects one household in the congregation affects us all. We must think of the good of all."

"Martha, perhaps we can sit down and talk about this," Phoebe said. "I will make *kaffi* and answer your questions."

But Mrs. Zimmerman waved her off. "I have seen enough. It's quite clear what is going on."

She stomped out of the house, leaving Phoebe and Susanna staring at each other while Noah continued to preach.

"The news will be everywhere by the morning," Phoebe said softly. "Everyone will know that what they saw at church that day was not merely an illness that overtook Noah of an afternoon."

"What do you think will happen?" Susanna said, sitting on the arm of Noah's stuffed chair.

Phoebe drew a long breath.

CHAPTER 11

Niklaus ran his hand down the cow's back. "Noah will have a suggestion," he said. "Perhaps an elixir to give the cow."

Adam nodded. "I will ride over and ask."

"We can both go. It will not take long to ask a question."

"He might be free to come back with us and look for himself," Adam said.

If Noah offered, Niklaus would not object. No one else in the district could assess an animal's health as swiftly and accurately as Noah. Adam could have carried the question on his own and brought back a reliable answer, but Niklaus had not seen Noah since his attack of delirium ten days earlier. Having his own eyes on his friend and neighbor would be reassuring.

They took a pair of stallions for the two-mile ride.

"What in the world?" Niklaus said when the Kauffman house was in sight. Noah and

Phoebe were quiet people living a quiet life. When it was their turn to host the congregation for worship, they happily did so. Otherwise, it was rare for a gathering to take form on their land — especially on a Wednesday afternoon.

"Did I doze off during an announcement at church?" Adam asked.

"Shall I consider that your confession?" Niklaus nudged his horse closer to the commotion. Deborah usually made sure Niklaus did not forget a church activity. She said nothing about this gathering, though most of the dozen or so people milling in the Kauffmans' yard were women. Martha Zimmerman seemed to be in the middle of things. She spotted Niklaus and pushed out of the tight circle.

"So you have heard," Martha said.

"I came only to speak to Noah about a cow," Niklaus said.

"You are his nearest neighbor — and a minister. I am surprised that you have not come to see for yourself before this."

Niklaus slid off his mount and glanced toward the barn, wondering if Noah might be there.

"If you have organized something with the women," Niklaus said, "I have no wish to disturb you."

"Niklaus Zug, you must know what has drawn us here."

"No, Martha, I do not. As I said, I only want to speak to Noah about my cow who is feeling poorly. Do you happen to know where he is?"

"Inside resting. At least, that is what Phoebe said."

"Then I have no doubt he is inside resting," Niklaus said.

The front door opened. Susanna and her friend Patsy stepped out onto the stoop.

"Phoebe asks that you all please be on your way," Susanna said.

"I told them what I saw with my own eyes," Martha said.

"Yes, I supposed you had," Susanna said. "But let us all be respectful and not turn the Kauffmans' home into some sort of *English* curiosity."

"We have a minister here, now," Martha said. "He can judge for himself."

"I am not here to judge anything," Niklaus said, "other than the health of a cow threatening to be unfit to breed."

"Noah is not available to speak or go anywhere," Patsy said. "He is resting."

"Susanna," Martha said, "what has your *English* friend to do with any of this?"

"Martha," Niklaus said, intending the

136

warning his tone carried.

Adam walked slowly toward the stoop and caught Susanna's eye. She flushed.

"If he begins preaching," Mrs. Zimmerman said, "why should our people not see what is happening among us? Then they can judge for themselves."

Preaching?

Adam tilted his head, pointing with his brow toward the side of the house. Susanna might not come, but Adam strode away from the gaggle.

"He stood right there," Mrs. Zimmerman said, "right in front of the window, plain as day."

Adam leaned against the house and peered around the corner where he had taken refuge. Susanna was off the porch now.

"Please go about your days," Susanna said. "We will make sure Phoebe knows you were here, and when there is news of Noah's recovery, we will make sure everyone knows. In the meantime, we covet your prayers."

"We are not hurting anyone by standing out here," Mrs. Satzler said. "We just want to see if it is true."

Mrs. Zimmerman huffed. "Is my word insufficient for you? I saw him preaching — about love — just the way you all saw him

137

preach after church."

Susanna came toward Adam and leaned beside him against the house and sighed.

"Is it true?" he asked.

Susanna swallowed, her slender neck rippling in movement. "Noah continues to be . . . unwell."

"He preaches?" Adam said.

"There is no one to listen," Susanna said. "He just stands and looks out the window. Until today."

Adam studied her features. Keeping them unperturbed required more effort than usual.

"And . . . why are you here?"

"Phoebe needs help."

"The kind of help we gave her after church?"

"You are asking many questions, Adam," Susanna said.

"I want to understand."

"Noah's condition or my choices?" Now Susanna became the questioner. Had his queries stung as much as hers?

"I must be honest," he said, "a bit of both."

"You did not hesitate to help at church," Susanna said. " 'Tis no different if I come to help at their home."

"Surely he has not been ill all this time,"

Adam said.

"Most of the time he is himself."

"But the preaching? Every day?"

"No. Not every day. But often enough that Phoebe needs help. When it happens, Noah does not keep up with the chores. And Phoebe's sister's back is out again, so she goes back and forth."

"If she needs help, she should call on the congregation. Others would want to help."

"Would they, Adam?" Susanna pushed off the wall and turned to face him squarely. "Mrs. Zimmerman only found out yesterday, and look what has happened. Not one person has offered to do the milking or weed the garden. They only want to know if there will be a show. That is no help to Phoebe or Noah."

Susanna was right.

"They should all go home," Adam said.

"Yes, they should."

"So let's make them leave."

"I have asked with increasing insistence to no avail."

Adam pivoted around the corner. Niklaus huddled with Mrs. Zimmerman off to one side, both of them gesturing. Patsy barred the door with her body. Phoebe was out of sight. The crowd straggled farther from the house, but no one had left. The window was empty, which was for the best. With nothing to see, this would come to nothing. A year from now no one would remember it had happened at all.

Adam began speaking to individuals, moving from one to another with the same message.

"This is a matter for the ministers."

"What Noah needs is peace and quiet."

"Our prayers would be our greatest gift to Phoebe."

Niklaus and Mrs. Zimmerman parted, and Niklaus stood on the stoop. "Let us peacefully disperse," he said. "I will see how we might minister to our brother and sister in this time of illness and call upon you in due course."

Several women began walking up the lane. Another pair climbed into a shared wagon. Mrs. Zimmerman glared at Patsy — no doubt seeing her as an intruder — but surrendered her goal and shuffled away from the house.

"*Danki,*" Susanna said to Adam. "They started coming and would not listen to me."

Adam studied her face. The lines in her forehead meant she felt anxious. Loose tendrils of hair springing from her bonnet meant she was too distracted to notice. The set of her mouth. A slight tearful glaze in her eyes. He needed no interpretation because he knew Susanna. What was on her face was also in her heart.

Yet she had kept this from him. She had stayed away for days.

Now he saw a crack between them.

When Patsy arrived at the Kauffmans' three days later, Susanna was already there. Their schedule of alternating days meant little after Tuesday's spectacle in the yard. Phoebe would need them both.

Riding her stallion, Patsy circled around the edge of the clearing between fields that held the Kauffman home, barn, chicken coop, and stable. Patsy didn't trust the stable's structure, though. Its ramshackle slight lean in one direction deterred her from putting Galahad inside, though the Kauffman horses were there. Instead, she had taken to tying a long lead to an oak tree that bathed a portion of the rear part of the property in shadow. Susanna had unhitched her cart and left her drooping but trustworthy mare to graze.

Noah had preached only once in the last few days, on Thursday afternoon, but enough people had arranged excuses to be on the Kauffman farm at the time that Noah had an audience outside the window whether or not he preached. Two more slats had fallen out of the shutters, so there seemed no point in trying to keep them closed. Patsy and Susanna politely encouraged people to leave. Some did — or it had seemed that they did. They were back soon enough, having only withdrawn from sight while remaining on the property. As Noah's preaching rose in fervor, they inched their way back toward the house, and nothing Susanna or Patsy said persuaded them to leave. Phoebe stayed out of debates. She had a farm to run and a husband to look after, so it was up to Patsy and Susanna to keep onlookers from pressing into the house.

After Thursday's sermon, the motley congregation returned on Friday and waited more than two hours only to be disappointed that the single matter Noah was attending to was his notations of the progress of his crops.

Now Saturday had come, and so had a larger crowd. For the first time, some in the Kauffman yard were not Amish. Anticipation quickened through Patsy's nerves. Inside the house, Patsy leaned against the wall in the main room. Susanna came to stand beside her. The furniture was already pushed back from the space Noah was most likely to wander into if he left the window.

"He just started," Susanna said. "The story of Elijah and the still small voice."

"One of my favorites."

"He used to tell it to me when I was small."

Noah flipped pages in the heavy black Bible supported by the span of his long fingers in one hand.

"He speaks in English," Patsy said, "except when he is reading from his German Bible. I'm sure my father would be happy to give him an English Bible."

Susanna's gasp surprised Patsy.

"Would it be so wrong for him to have an English Bible?" Patsy asked.

"His condition is a great strain," Susanna said. "And our people do not have English Bibles."

"But he speaks the word of the Lord," Patsy said. "The word of the Lord is for everyone. What if Noah's preaching is not a condition but a true gift from God?"

"Does God give gifts to people and not allow them even to know that they are serving?"

Patsy shrugged. "Maybe. Papa says he has seen the gift of tongues as surely as on the day of Pentecost in the book of Acts — and prophecy as well. Is it so difficult to imagine that God might work in this mysterious way?"

"Phoebe and Noah do not deserve for their life to be a spectacle," Susanna said. "If you will watch Noah, I will go clean the coop. Phoebe is in the barn mixing another elixir for the Zugs' cow according to Noah's notes."

Patsy nodded and Susanna slipped out the back door. A chicken coop could be cleaned or a cow tended anytime. Watching Noah, and hearing him speak, was the shining moment unfolding before her. She made herself stand away from the wall and away from the temptation of a chair, convinced it was possible to keep her eyes on Noah's physical safety while her heart opened to the message he spoke.

The rattle of the wagon a few minutes later disturbed both her intentions. Two men rode on the seat, their load of benches creaking with the wagon's sway.

Niklaus followed the wagon onto the Kauffman land with a clear view of the load. Those benches belonged to the congregation. They were meant to move from farm to farm as church services were held and should have been safely parked on the Zook farm for tomorrow's service. Then they would be moved to his farm. The Kauff-mans were not on the schedule for the near future. Most of the benches had been removed from the wagon, leaving only four.

Zaccheus Swigert and his young married son, Nathaniel, were the men in the wagon. Niklaus was off his horse before they had set the brake.

"Has Phoebe or Noah asked you to do this?" Niklaus said. He had to be certain he was not misinterpreting what he saw.

"We took it upon ourselves," Zaccheus said. "We never use all the benches in the wagon for church. They can serve a purpose here."

"This is Noah's home," Niklaus said. "I think it is best if you take the benches back where they belong."

Zaccheus gestured toward the curtainless window with the decrepit shutters. In the waning days of July, the hinged glass was swung open, no doubt seeking a cross breeze through the house. Niklaus could advise Phoebe to keep her windows closed, or he could insist that the spectators vacate.

"We sit for the sermons in church," Zaccheus said. "Someone might faint in the heat out here if there are no benches."

"Please do not mistake this gathering for church," Niklaus said.

Phoebe emerged from the barn. "What now?"

"I am asking our brothers to take the benches and go," Niklaus said.

"Thank you," Phoebe said. "I have your mixture for the cow. Noah will come in the morning and have another look at her."

Zaccheus jumped into the bed of the wagon and began to shove a bench into the waiting hands of his son.

Niklaus slapped the side of the wagon. "You know Phoebe would like you to leave. So please leave."

Zaccheus abandoned his effort — for now — and sat on the edge of the wagon, turning his attention to Noah's words.

Irritation roiled in Niklaus. Members of his own church were willing to turn the Word of the Lord — if that was indeed what he was witnessing — into an excursion for their own amusement.

"I am sorry I cannot stay," Niklaus said.

"Your cow," Phoebe said. "I am sorry she is not better by now."

Niklaus gripped the small vial she had handed him. No doubt Zaccheus and his son would unload the benches the moment he was out of sight. It was not that Noah preached or that people wanted to listen that disturbed Niklaus. Rather, it was the disregard for Phoebe's wishes, the grasping at their own desires above hers. The district was headed for a spiritual crisis.

CHAPTER 12

Sizzling bacon could wake Patsy from the deepest sleep. She inhaled before turning over in bed to see that the day had not yet begun. She had not slept late. Rather, breakfast was early. Her senses awoke more fully, and she discerned coffee in the melding aromas. At the end of the bed was a light yellow cotton robe, tattered and thin but still her favorite. It would do. Early morning bacon meant one thing.

Her father was home.

With feet bare and her robe hanging loose, Patsy padded down the not-quite-even steps to the kitchen, stopping twice to breathe deeply the scents of her father at home. Most mornings she attended to a few chores before sitting down to eat. Today she was famished by the moment she reached the final step.

"Papa."

He turned his head and gave her the

broad grin that made her heart sing through her childhood. When he spread his arms, Patsy moved into them to press her head against his chest and feel his strength around her.

"I thought you would be out one more day," she said. "When did you get here?"

"Four hours ago. I'm grateful for a horse surefooted enough for the dark."

"How was the circuit?"

"One wedding. One young widow finally giving her grief to the Lord."

"And the Tabor boy?"

"Still quite ill. He will live, I believe, but he won't walk."

"That is sad news." Patsy anchored an elbow on the table and set her chin in her hand.

Her father slid a fork under four slices of bacon, one at a time, and set them on a plate in front of her. "Bless your food so you can eat while it is hot."

Patsy closed her eyes and gave thanks, saying *Amen* at the same moment her fingers moved to the bacon.

"Scrambled eggs," her father said, sliding a generous portion onto Patsy's plate. "What is the news around here?"

Patsy swallowed her food. "Noah Kauffman has become a preacher."

He looked at her, eyebrows arched. "The Amish man?"

"You've met him."

"Several times. I almost bought a horse from him once. He has never struck me as a preacher."

"It's a new gift." Patsy scooped up a bite of eggs. "He is quite good."

"You've heard him?"

Patsy explained. The trances. The safety concerns. The onlookers who grew in number each day. The weight on Phoebe's shoulders.

"I would like to hear him," her father said. "This afternoon. One more curious man in the congregation won't hurt."

"It's not precisely a congregation," Patsy said. Susanna would not use the term, nor Phoebe.

"Is he ministering to them?" her father said. "He is preaching and they are listening, yes?"

"Yes."

"I must see this."

"It doesn't happen every day," Patsy said.

"But when it does, it is at about the same hour each time?"

She nodded.

He turned over a half dozen slices of bacon on the griddle. "I will wake your mother for her bacon. Then you and I will make our plan."

Eight hours passed before it was time to leave, hours full of barn chores, inspecting the progress of the crops, consultations with the farmhand, a midday meal with both of Patsy's parents seated at the table with her, chatter about the Kish Valley and the circuit Charles Baxton rode even as more and more towns had their own Methodist churches. When midafternoon came, Patsy and her father mounted their horses, both stallions, one golden and one deep brown, to ride to the Kauffman farm.

They went early — or so Patsy thought. Her intention was to arrive before the time a crowd would be gathering, but already eight people milled in the Kauffman yard, glancing periodically at the front room window.

"Benches," Charles said.

"They were not Phoebe's idea," Patsy said, "and they are confusing to Noah when he is in his right mind."

"Do you suggest that when he preaches he is not in his right mind?"

"It's hard to explain," Patsy said. "He's different. He hardly seems like the same man. When he is himself, he would not think of trying to preach, and when he is preaching, he knows nothing else."

"We will let God be the judge of a man's right mind and right heart," Charles said.

Patsy nodded. "I must go inside. If he preaches today, you will see from here."

Her father nodded, squared his feet before the window, and raised his face in expectation.

Patsy paced around the house and knocked gently on the back door. Susanna answered.

"How is he?" Patsy asked.

"So far he is well," Susanna said. "Phoebe does not wish for him to be out on his own at this time of day, and it distresses him to look outside."

"Perhaps we should at least close the windows," Patsy said, watching Noah squirming in the stuffed chair meant to keep him comfortable.

"She tried that. Noah opens them."

"Uh-oh." Patsy lurched toward the front room with Susanna right behind her.

Noah slumped in the chair, and it took both of them to keep him from sliding to the floor unconscious. Patsy had only twice been present at the onset of one of Noah's . . . she was not sure what word to use. *Episodes? Incidents? Spells?* But she knew what would come next. Beneath her touch,

Noah's form found its shape again. Muscles tightened, his eyes fluttered open, and he pushed up out of the chair. Patsy and Susanna held his elbows until his balance was firm and he picked up his Bible, and then they followed him toward the window. Afternoon light spilled through at an angle that illumined Noah's face like the religious paintings Patsy's parents had once taken her to see in a Philadelphia museum. His face transformed, shimmering in grateful anticipation of what he was about to do. Even if he never remembered a single syllable he uttered during one of his anointings — Patsy settled on the term for now — it was as if his face shone with the rays of Christ. How could this be anything but the blessing of God?

At the window, Patsy was careful to stay out of sight as much as possible, but she couldn't help but catch a glimpse of her father's transforming face as Noah began to speak.

Focus on Noah. Periodically she reminded herself what she had promised to do for Phoebe — keep Noah safe. Exchanging a glance with Susanna, Patsy constrained her attention to notice any shift in Noah's physical demeanor. His eloquent words must not distract her from her call to this unique service.

Twenty minutes passed. A sound in the kitchen pulled Patsy's glance at the same time that Susanna lurched toward it.

"I'll go," Patsy said softly.

It wasn't the first time an onlooker from the outside had decided to attempt a closer look. She must have forgotten to latch the door when she came in. Pushing open the door to the kitchen, she prepared to chastise kindly but firmly. No one would be allowed in the front room under any circumstances.

"Papa," she said, startled. "What are you doing?"

"Please don't think I was doubting you," Charles said. "If anything, you were restrained in your description. What a marvel this is!"

"Papa, no one is allowed inside the house."

"I won't disturb Noah," Charles said. "Not when he is boldly and rightly declaring the word of truth."

"Phoebe would be upset to find you here," Patsy said. After Mrs. Zimmerman's intrusion, they had taken such care to keep people out of the house. Patsy could not make an exception even for her own father.

"Where is Phoebe?"

"In the bedroom working on the mending

pile. When Susanna or I are here, we want Phoebe to be free to do what she feels is needful or restful.

"Of course, of course." Charles looked past Patsy into the room beyond. "What an opportunity! You see for yourself how eagerly the crowd gathers to listen. With a gift like Noah's, my heart beats to know what God might do at a revival meeting."

"Noah? At a revival meeting?"

"Yes, yes. Surely you can see the possibilities. I know that families on my circuit would be glad to have a visiting preacher for a few nights of revival with a speaker such as this." Charles's features lit. "Oh, Susanna. It's always good to see you."

Patsy whirled. "Shouldn't one of us be with Noah?"

"Phoebe came out of the bedroom for a few minutes." Susanna's face clouded. "Surely you do not mean to make a visiting preacher of Noah."

Patsy hadn't made up her mind what to think of her father's suggestion, but in this instant the picture came clear.

"It would be a wonderful opportunity for the gospel," Patsy said. "We might convert many souls to the kingdom of heaven."

"Patsy Baxton! What are you saying? You know this cannot be." Susanna's face flushed crimson.

"Perhaps it can be after all."

"It is not for Noah's sake that you suggest this." Susanna's jaw set as solidly as Patsy had ever seen it.

"My own father is a minister of the gospel," Patsy said. "Can he not verify that Noah has a true gift from God? If this is the case, why would we want to hold Noah back from exercising the gift?"

Charles stepped toward Susanna, his head tilted in kindness. "Did not the apostle Paul write to the Ephesians that some are appointed to preaching? Can there be any doubt that Noah has been so appointed?"

"Phoebe would never consider such a proposal," Susanna said.

"Perhaps not," Charles said, "but we might at least introduce a conversation."

Patsy's enthusiasm quickened. "What can it hurt to ask? Although Noah does not remember the preaching, he knows it happens. And when he has not . . . fallen ill . . . or come under anointing, he is more than able to make his own decision."

"No one would force him," Charles said. "Of course we would not compel him if the Holy Ghost does not do so. But who are we to make a decision that is only Noah's to make?"

Susanna wavered. Patsy saw it in the quivering corner of her lips.

"Not today," Susanna said. "You cannot think to raise the matter today."

"Susanna is right," Patsy said. "Noah will sleep for hours after the preaching. We would have to speak to him early in the day, when he is himself."

"Then tomorrow it shall be," Charles said. "I dare not quench the Holy Ghost by failing to act on His urging."

The firmer her father's determination became, the more Patsy imagined that his idea could come true. They discussed it over supper in the dining room, in the evening while they sat in the parlor, and then over breakfast in the kitchen the next morning.

"Shall we go?" her father said when the breakfast dishes had been cleared.

Patsy nodded.

"Will Susanna be there?"

"I'm not sure," Patsy said. It was early in the day. Susanna might be fully occupied with her dyes.

But Susanna's rickety cart was unhitched and idle in the Kauffman yard and her mare grazed in the pasture. And it was Susanna who appeared on the Kauffman front stoop and took a half dozen steps into the yard to greet them.

"Good morning," Charles said.

"Good morning," Susanna echoed.

"How are your parents? Well, I hope."

Patsy flinched at her father's inquiry. For the last few days, Susanna had said little about the price her visits to Noah might have cost her at home with her mother.

"We are praying for a good harvest," Susanna said. She gestured toward the house. "I assume you have not changed your mind."

Charles shook his head. "I sense great confirmation from the Lord that we should take this step."

"Then please come in," Susanna said. "I will let Noah and Phoebe know you are here."

Susanna rounded up Noah from the stable and Phoebe from the chicken coop, and lit the stove to make fresh coffee as they sat.

"Patsy has been so helpful," Phoebe said, pouring coffee in the front room a few minutes later. "Thank you for allowing her the freedom to minister to us as she has."

"Of course. I am pleased in her choice to do so." Charles put his hands on his knees and leaned forward. "Noah, your own ministry has been on my mind. I have thought of little else since yesterday."

"My ministry?" Noah said.

Patsy glanced at Susanna, who calmly sliced into a raspberry coffee cake, laid a piece on a plate, and handed it to Patsy. In the swift moment of transition when both their fingers grasped the plate, Patsy tried to hold her friend's eyes, but Susanna would not offer them.

"My daughter has explained the matter to me," Charles said. "I have some understanding of the complexity. I realize that your preaching only occurs under peculiar conditions that cause others to be concerned for your welfare. But as a man seemeth in the heart, the Scriptures tell us, so is he. I believe you have a gift, and I believe God would be pleased to see you use it for His glory."

With considerable deliberation, Phoebe handed Charles his slice of cake. "Things have gotten out of hand with those people turning up to watch as if Noah is a theater show. 'Tis been no gift to us."

"I understand," Charles said. "I will state my proposal, and you may consider it or dispose of the matter as you see fit."

Phoebe nodded.

"Noah," Charles said, "I propose to take you on a short preaching tour — just three or four days. And if the Holy Ghost moves, we will preach together."

"I cannot preach." Noah's protest was immediate.

Now Susanna caught Patsy's eye, as if to say, *I told you.*

"But you do preach." Charles pressed on. "I saw it myself yesterday."

"I am not myself during these episodes." Noah set his coffee aside.

"Perhaps not," Charles said. "That does not mean you cannot be a vessel for the Lord. You could be a vessel not only in your own home but on my circuit, for people who need to hear the message you bring."

"Mr. Baxton." Phoebe's tone rang sharp. "What you suggest is impossible."

With God nothing is impossible. Patsy held her tongue, sure her father would offer the same thought.

"With God nothing is impossible."

The voice who spoke the words was Noah's, not her father's.

"Noah, this is not wise," Phoebe said.

"Might we at least pray on the matter?" Noah said. "Have you and I not taken all our decisions to the Lord? Why should this be different?"

Excitement gurgled up in Patsy even as Phoebe nodded once, slowly, and alarm shaped Susanna's face.

"Two days," Noah said. "I will wait on the

Lord for two days, and then we will settle
the matter."

CHAPTER 13

Two days. As Susanna went about her work with the dyes, tended the gardens yielding both her mother's abundant vegetables and plants Susanna selected for the colors they would offer, she was grateful Noah had not rushed into an answer. He might still conclude that doing what Reverend Baxton proposed was ill-advised. She also wondered if two days were enough. He could have said he would take a week. That would have allowed time to consult with Shem Hertzberger or Niklaus Zug or Yohan Maist — ministers from among his own people.

The bishop, of course, would forbid it on all counts. Susanna was surprised Shem had not yet turned up on the Kauffman farm to forbid Noah's sermons on his own land — which would not have stopped the preaching. Yohan Maist would take his lead from the bishop. At some point, Shem would have to understand that Noah was not choosing what happened. Niklaus might see no harm but also no edification for the Amish congregation. And he would point out that while Noah might not be choosing to collapse and preach, going on the circuit was a choice.

But was it the right choice?

Susanna swayed in her cart with the final turn onto the Kauffman farm, two days to the hour since Noah agreed to think about preaching where Charles usually preached. The Baxton horses were already tethered to hooks on the side of the barn. Susanna discarded her hope for a private moment with Noah where she might have judged which way he leaned. She would hear the news with everyone else.

Inside she extended greetings, declined Phoebe's offer of coffee — she drank three cups at home that morning — and settled on the davenport between Patsy and her father.

"I have made a decision," Noah said. "It has been prayerful, with my Bible in my lap many hours. In silence I have waited on the Lord."

Susanna moistened her lips. Beside her, Patsy leaned forward slightly.

"Reverend Baxton," Noah said, "I am humbled that you would think me worthy of preaching the gospel alongside you."

Charles nodded. "It is I who would be humbled to share a pulpit with you."

A bead of perspiration crawled down Susanna's spine. Noah was taking his time, and Phoebe's face betrayed nothing. If she knew her husband's decision, she hid it well.

"Noah," Patsy said. "Please tell us what you have decided."

Noah met their eyes, one pair at a time. "I have decided to go."

Patsy clapped her hands. Charles stood up and offered Noah a hearty handshake. Susanna's startled gaze returned to Phoebe.

"I will begin making arrangements," Charles said. "I have no doubt that all who hear you will be blessed."

Phoebe stood up. Susanna examined her face once again. Phoebe was not surprised, but neither was she pleased.

"Reverend Baxton," Phoebe said, "I am sure your daughter has made clear to you that my husband has particular needs. Someone who knows him well must accompany him."

"Of course we would be delighted to have you travel with us," Charles said.

Phoebe shook her head. "I am afraid I cannot undertake the journey."

"Only three or four days," Charles said.

Phoebe shook her head again.

"You have the farm and the animals," Charles said. "I understand. I will arrange for someone to look after things while we're away."

"I have my sister to think of," Phoebe said. "Her back continues to trouble her, and she cannot keep up with the cooking and washing on her own."

Fatigue hung from Phoebe's face. Susanna should have seen it sooner. Even if her sister did not need attention, Phoebe was too weary to journey.

Susanna had hoped Noah's decision would be different. But his face radiated with contentment and anticipation. No hesitation remained in his frame.

"Of course you cannot travel," Susanna said. "But you might have a break. I could send my brother Timothy over to look after your animals. You could go spend a few days with your sister without having to run back and forth."

Phoebe blinked twice, the idea settling in. "My sister would be grateful. But someone still must go with Noah."

"Susanna will come." Noah's statement was definitive. "You have assured me she knows my habits when I do not."

"Yes, she does," Phoebe said. "Unquestionably."

Susanna's pulse pounded in her ears. "Me?"

"You are a logical choice," Noah said. "When I am in my right mind, I can see that. And I would love to have the companionship of my favorite cousin."

"My *mamm* will not agree." Susanna raised her shoulders and let them drop. The conversation at home would be impossible.

"I will have a word with your parents," Charles said.

Her eyes widened. A request from Charles Baxton, however well-reasoned, would not have the effect he supposed.

"Maybe I can sort it out," Susanna mumbled. If she could manage a private moment with her father, he might hear her out. If he approved, her mother would not forbid Susanna to go — at least, not with words.

"Niklaus might go with us as well," Charles said. "Susanna understands the way the Holy Ghost moves through Noah, but it might also be wise to have one of the men from your church as well."

Noah nodded. "Niklaus is a good choice. One of the ministers and a good neighbor."

"We are old friends," Charles said. "I am certain to persuade him."

Charles Baxton seemed to get his way. He might well convince Niklaus, but Susanna's

166

mother would not be easily felled.

"Mrs. Kauffman, have we addressed your concerns satisfactorily?" Charles said. "I do want you to feel at ease with the arrangements."

"If Timothy agrees to look after things here and Susanna accompanies Noah," Phoebe said, "then I know things will be well in hand. There is just one problem."

"What is that?" Charles said. "We will solve it."

"Veronica," Phoebe said. "She will not agree to the scheme. Certainly she will object to Susanna's participation, and she will not be easily persuaded that Timothy should be involved if she knows what Noah is up to. It will look like she supports Noah's endeavor."

Susanna sighed. Phoebe was right. Her mother's personal convictions aside, she would not agree to give the appearance of approval to something she disapproved of. "We will have to think of something else."

"I could go," Patsy said. "I also know how to watch out for Noah's welfare."

Envy flashed through Susanna, and instantly she wanted to take the journey.

"That will not be required," Charles said. "I will have the necessary conversations.

Niklaus can go with me to talk to the Hooleys."

Susanna thought that might work.

Charles turned to Susanna. "Your parents are fond of Niklaus, are they not?"

She nodded.

Noah was the one to object. "Veronica does not need ministers ganging up on her. Despite what you think at the moment, she is not an unreasonable person. And she is my cousin, so it is fitting that I be the one to ask her permission to take her daughter on this excursion."

Patsy ignored her father's outstretched hand of assistance and hoisted herself into the saddle. How did he think she got on a horse when he was gone? She had long ago abandoned ladylike decorum when it came to her stallion. If she needed to go somewhere, she got on the horse and went, letting her skirts fall where they may. Now she pressed her knees into the animal's side and put him immediately into a trot before her father had managed to get astride his own mount.

Once out of the farm lane, she urged more speed. Behind her the feet of her father's horse pounded faster.

"Patricia," Charles called. "Slow down."

Her first impulse was to push harder,

maybe even take her horse toward Jacks Mountain. They could go all the way to the high ridge. Instead, she blew out her breath and slowed the horse. Her father rarely called her by the name written in the family Bible.

Charles came alongside her. "What has gotten into you?"

"Never mind." She paced her horse to his. She could charge up Jacks Mountain later and work off the discontent of this moment.

"Well, this is exciting," Charles said. "Now that Noah has decided to go, there is much to do. I wonder if he will be all right on horseback. I must think of his safety rather than my own habits when I ride alone."

"Of course you must."

"Has he ever fallen under the Holy Ghost in the morning?"

"Not that I know of. Midafternoons."

"Then we shall plan to travel in the morning. After a midday meal, we will be sure he has a place to rest."

"That would be wise."

"Perhaps we will only go as far as we can in a half day's journey. I know a place where we can easily gather a congregation."

Patsy urged the stallion forward, one length ahead of her father and then two and then three.

"Patricia."

Twice in one day. Patsy slowed again.

"You must explain yourself," Charles said.

" 'That will not be required'?" Patsy threw his words back at him. "Really, Papa."

He was silent for a few yards.

"Are you suggesting that you want to go on the preaching trip?"

"I offered, didn't I?"

"Yes, you did. I'm sorry I brushed you off."

"Even if Susanna's parents are persuaded she should go," Patsy said, "do you expect it will be wise for her to journey with three men and no female companion? Would you allow me to take such a trip?"

"No, I would not. I see your point."

"Then I can go?"

"We will be a group of five," he said. "We will take a proper wagon and everything we need for you and Susanna to be comfortable. And a wagon will give me an opportunity to distribute Bibles and hymnals as well."

"Thank you, Papa."

"It's resolved. We have no hard feelings between us. Now you may give your horse his head."

"You should come with us." Niklaus set his

eyes, expectant, on his nephew.

"With Noah and Reverend Baxton?" Adam looked through the door frame he had cut yesterday to give Jonas and his bride access to the outdoors without having to walk through the house.

"And Susanna," Niklaus said. "Have I mentioned they want Susanna to go?"

"Several times, Onkel."

"Jonas is here for the animals, and the crops need nothing but time to grow," Niklaus said. "You and Shem are ahead of schedule out here. And have I mentioned that Shem believes you can have a life ahead of you as a carpenter if you would like?"

"Several times, Onkel."

Privately Shem had told Niklaus he planned to take Adam on as an assistant and continue teaching him. If he learned to make cupboards and cabinets, as well as build rooms, he would earn enough to think of marriage. Niklaus was ready with an enthusiastic *ja* for the moment when Adam and Susanna asked him to officiate at their wedding.

"Come with us," Niklaus said. "A break would do you good."

"Are you certain Shem would want you to go?"

"I am certain Noah wants me to go and

that I want to go," Niklaus said. "Noah is one of my sheep."

"But the congregation."

"Does not a good shepherd leave the ninety and nine to find the one?"

"Do you think Noah is a lost sheep?" Adam said.

Niklaus turned up his palms. "If he begins to lose his way, should I not be there?"

Adam twisted his lips. He had done that ever since he was a little boy whenever he got an answer from an adult that he did not like but would not challenge with his own words.

"We leave Monday morning. You can change your mind up to the last minute," Niklaus said. "There will be room in the wagon, and we have plenty of provisions."

On Monday morning, before Deborah had the breakfast dishes washed up, Niklaus climbed to the bench of the wagon Charles drove onto his farm. Adam stood beside the barn.

"We could wait a few minutes if you want to gather your things," Niklaus said.

Adam glanced at Susanna, seated with Noah and Patsy in the wagon bed, but shook his head.

CHAPTER 14

Limestone was plentiful in the Kish Valley, and Jonas's betrothed had simple tastes, so Shem had left Adam to craft a small fireplace. Once, when he was a boy and his father was not yet disappointed in him, Adam had helped to build a new fireplace. That one had been large enough to cook in and warm the main floor of the house. This one would only be called on to supply heat to a single room during winter nights. Adam was surprised how easily he recalled the necessary steps. He and Jonas together had selected and dug up the stones, but Jonas left to Adam the work of arranging them and filling the cracks between them. Jonas had not yet made up his mind whether the final product should be whitewashed. Adam was fairly sure Jonas was waiting for Anke, his future wife, to make her wishes known. If it were his fireplace, Adam would leave it be. Stone that God created was sufficient beauty, but the stones must be arranged in a way that sealed the chimney as tightly as possible.

Adam turned to the footsteps behind him. *"Gut mariye."*

Shem was already nodding as he looked around the room. "You have done well."

"Danki."

"But do not let it go to your head."

Every compliment from Shem came with the same caution, but the twinkle in his eye as he spoke the words or wagged his finger set Adam at ease.

Shem poked his finger upward toward large canvas tarps stitched roughly together and arranged as a makeshift ceiling over the opening the finished walls formed. Adam imagined what it would be like to lie in this room and look up at the stars, and he might even have brought a quilt downstairs to do so for one night if Shem's practicality did not demand protecting incomplete work from the possibility of rain.

"One inside door and one outside door," Shem said. "Two windows. Now all we need is a roof."

"Onkel Niklaus ordered the shingles. He expects word any day that we can pick them up."

With Niklaus gone, Adam would receive

the message and dispatch himself to pick up the shingles from the small store in Lewistown that would receive them from Philadelphia on the train.

"We have the wide boards, so we can ready them for the shingles. I suspect we will need Jonas and Niklaus to help set the frame. A steep pitch will shed rain and snow better than a slight pitch, but it is difficult to work on."

Adam nodded. He knew nothing of building a roof other than watching the occasional barn raising from the safe distance of children told to stay out of the way. Even when he was older, his assigned task was unloading shingles from the wagon. He was never part of the team that climbed the scaffolds and swung the hammers.

"Perhaps tonight you can ask them to help," Shem said. "We could start tomorrow."

"Tomorrow?"

"Yes, that's right. Ask your *onkel.*"

Adam shuffled his feet. "My *onkel* is away for a few days."

"Oh? Where has he gone?"

"Not far," Adam said. "He will be there by midday today."

"Where would he go and not mention to his old friend the bishop?"

Adam bent to pick up a hammer, though he had nothing to strike just then.

"Adam," Shem said.

"He and Noah Kauffman are together," Adam said.

"I thought Noah was still poorly. He missed church last week."

"I suppose he is." After all, he still had spells. "Yet Noah was determined to go, so Niklaus thought he should go as well."

Truth. Just not all of it.

Shem waited.

Adam moved the hammer to the other hand, still not finding anything requiring to be tapped or banged.

"Adam," Shem said. "You are a thoughtful young man, and I feel I have come to know you better in these weeks of working together."

"Yes, sir."

"You must feel free to be candid with me."

Adam studied the toe of his boot. "Charles Baxton invited Noah to preach with him at a revival meeting."

The rush of words brought instant relief, though Adam would have preferred that his uncle speak them.

The bishop paced across the room. "Did he encourage you to go?"

"He invited me," Adam said. The two

176

words did not mean the same thing.

"But you declined."

"I did not feel right about it."

Shem nodded. "You have chosen wisely."

Adam was less sure than the bishop's words sounded.

"We have lost enough of our people to the Methodists and Baptists already," Shem said. "When I meet with the ministers of neighboring districts, they say the same thing. It consumes considerable portions of our conversations. Your *onkel* should not be encouraging this."

"His concern was for Noah," Adam said. While he wished the entire trip had not come to pass, he could not fault his uncle — or Susanna — for caring for Noah.

"You must speak up when you are with the young people," Shem said. "I can preach in church, but I am not so foolish to think that they listen to every word. You are one of them. They would listen to you."

"Yes, sir." Adam could think of nothing else to say, and he doubted he had any significant influence among his peers.

"This revival business is going to split the church," Shem said, "if we cannot find a way to be of one mind in honoring our own traditions."

Shem reached for a large, flat limestone

and heaved it up to set at an awkward angle on top of the arrangement Adam had crafted so carefully.

Adam winced when Shem did not pull his fingers out quickly enough. In all the hours they had worked side by side, Adam never before saw Shem make such a rudimentary mistake — or any mistake at all in craftsmanship.

Susanna raised her face to the sun. Charles had kept his word and brought the group to a stop by two o'clock. If Noah were to "fall under the Holy Ghost," as Charles called it, he should not be in a situation where he might try to stand up, pace, and preach from a moving wagon. They would camp here for a few nights, Susanna and Patsy sleeping on hay in the wagon and the men on the ground nearby. Along with the team pulling the wagon, Charles had brought along a saddle horse, and he was off on the stallion now to let the closest families know that tomorrow afternoon and the day after that, open-air revival meetings would be held in the clearing. Niklaus and Noah had arranged the camp and now leaned against the wide trunk of a white oak tree.

"He seems fine." Patsy joined Susanna sitting on the open end of the wagon and dangling her legs.

"He does," Susanna said, "but that does not mean it will not happen." It could happen anytime after three and before supper with only a few seconds of Noah sensing that he did not feel well. Even if he felt a warning, he might not have time to mention it to anyone. He often fell under within seconds.

"If it does, he will be safe," Patsy said. "That's why we are here."

"I know."

"Do you hope nothing will happen?" Patsy said.

Susanna tilted her head. "I do not know what to think."

Noah was eager to cook beans over the fire to feed the group their supper, claiming to have stowed among his personal belongings the seasoning that would bring perfection to their taste. Onions, they guessed. Brown sugar? Molasses? Noah answered their speculations only with a wry smile. And falling under — maybe she would call it simply that — exhausted Noah. Would it not be better if he enjoyed his day, ate a hearty meal that gave him pleasure, and rested well tonight? Tomorrow would be the day that mattered. Even then, though, Susanna was unsure what to hope for. If Noah did not preach, Charles might let go of his notion and take Noah home. If Noah did preach, what would happen next?

"Whatever happens," Patsy said, "it will be God's will. Isn't that what you always say?"

Gottes wille. It was not Susanna who said it but the Scriptures. Even Bishop Hertzberger would concede that if an event happened, it must be God's will. Clinging to the teaching of Amish preachers for more than a century and a half was all that comforted Susanna's nerves now. Perhaps this truly was God's will. But sin that transgressed the teaching of the church was not God's will, and everyone from her own mother to the bishop had opinions about whether Noah's actions were willful.

Noah's voice rippled with laughter from the tree, a sweetness more delectable than every kind of pie that might enter the imagination.

"Noah is thoughtful and kind and generous and faithful," Susanna said. "Is that not enough for a life that pleases God?"

The women were silent for a few minutes, listening again as Niklaus's deeper laughter harmonized with Noah's. The joke, whatever it was, surely began with Noah. This was the Noah Susanna wanted people to know.

■ ■ ■ ■

"Do you hope he will preach?" Susanna asked Niklaus the next morning.

The question surprised him. They were side by side on the wagon's bench perusing a crude map Charles had drawn to identify pockets of farms or trading posts or small towns where the congregation he hoped to assemble later that day might draw from. Neither he nor Susanna had wanted to leave Noah, but Charles pressed the matter. He wanted time to help Noah understand how the meetings would be run, where the congregation would gather, where Noah could stand while awaiting the moment when he might fall under the Holy Ghost, how Charles would proceed if Noah did not. And, Charles said, if Noah did preach and there were no people, they would have brought Noah all this way for nothing. In the end, Susanna conceded that nothing was likely to happen to Noah in the morning hours, and Niklaus said that if he were to take the wagon out, he would appreciate her company.

"He did not preach yesterday," Niklaus said. "I am sure you know what to expect more than I."

"There is no pattern." Susanna squinted at the map. "Have we not spoken to enough people already? They will come or they will not come."

"Gottes wille." To himself, Niklaus admitted some curiosity about the ministerial life of his old friend. Otherwise he would not have consented to be the messenger for a revival meeting for which he had little personal leanings.

Susanna sighed and pointed to the left. "There. But after this stop, I want to go back to Noah."

"I agree." Niklaus glanced at Susanna sideways. "And perhaps we can find another topic of conversation to pass the time."

"Anything," Susanna said.

"Adam," Niklaus said. He turned his head in time to see her blush. "Harvest will be here before you know it. I have you to myself. The others will not hear anything you say in confidence."

Susanna turned her head away. "Perhaps not this topic of conversation."

"Then we will return to *Gottes wille,*" Niklaus said. "I find myself wondering if the reason Adam came to Kish Valley was not to learn to be a farmer or a carpenter but because it was *Gottes wille* for him to become a husband. Yours."

Susanna's blush now rounded to the back of her neck. Niklaus smiled.

CHAPTER 15

Susanna had never heard Charles preach before. The crowd that gathered on short notice impressed her. Though not large, it was far from paltry. Patsy had told her that when Charles preached on his circuit during the summer, he usually preached early in the morning before the farmers began their labors and the relentless sun began its path. All that was rearranged for Noah. If he was to preach at all, it must be in the afternoon. The Baxton family had handwritten a stack of announcements that now peppered the countryside, beckoning listeners to a brand-new messenger of God. And people had come, exchanging their plows and the baking and the wash on the line for wagons and benches to hear both the Reverend Charles Baxton, Methodist minister, and Noah Kauffman, Amish farmer.

The hymns were unknown to Susanna, their liveliness reminding her of what she had heard during the revival tent meeting with the New York preacher. A man with a lovely tenor voice offered another hymn as a solo. Charles prayed — for a long time — and finally began to preach. His theme, he said, was living the full Christian life.

Susanna turned her head to smile at Noah, who sat in the only plain wooden chair Charles had packed in the wagon. On the other side of Noah, Patsy stood sentry. They knew their duties, amended for this unusual circumstance. They stood off to the side, in the shade, where Charles could see them easily and where there would be little impediment to guiding Noah to the makeshift pulpit swiftly. Charles would be watching as he preached. If Noah began to fall under, Patsy would raise her hand and signal, and the two friends would wait for Noah to sink into unconsciousness, stiffen, and rise with the words of God in his mouth.

"God reaches out to the repentant sinner," Charles proclaimed. "We are wretches, but He is grace. This we know to be true because it is written in God's Word and we experience it every day. Is not the sun and rain that bring the harvest a sign of the grace of God? Is not the sweet fellowship we know with each other the grace of God?

The justifying grace and the pardoning love of God speak afresh to our hearts that God's mercies are new every morning."

"Has your father prepared an entire sermon?" Susanna whispered to Patsy.

"He speaks what God lays on his heart," Patsy said.

Between them Noah nodded, still sitting erect and showing no sign of feeling ill.

Charles preached on. "If you have not experienced the new birth that brings you to God's pardoning love, let this be the day."

He glanced at Patsy, who shrugged.

"After we are born again — a wondrous gift that comes to us in a splendid moment like no other we will ever recall — God's grace draws us into the fullness of the Christian life. Jesus came that we might have life and have it abundantly. This is God's love for you, made possible by Christ's sacrifice."

Charles glanced again toward Noah, who now leaned forward in his chair. But it was only genuine interest in Charles's words, Susanna knew, rather than a sign of falling under.

"John Wesley, the esteemed founder of my own Methodist tradition, described the Christian life as a heart habitually filled with the love of God and the love of neighbor, as

Jesus himself said that the greatest commandment is to love the Lord your God with all your heart, with all your soul, and with all your mind."

Another glance. Another shrug.

"Let the mind of Christ dwell in you. Then you will know this fullness of the Christian life to which He calls you and for which He gave his life. New life makes all this possible. If you do not yet know what it is to be born again, let this be the day."

Charles was beginning to repeat himself. Perhaps he always did so when he preached. Susanna could not be sure. But she could be certain that he was looking toward Noah more frequently and using the gesture to create pauses in which he gathered his thoughts.

He would just have to finish his sermon and give a benediction. He should never have even hinted at a guest preacher.

"Don't stop, Papa," Patsy murmured.

He'd only been preaching a few minutes. Yesterday he had seen for himself that Noah might be well and whole for an entire day with no sign of falling under. The people had come to hear a sermon, and her father would give them one, but Patsy suspected he would soon shift to a melding of sermons he had given before. Calling people to new birth was a favorite topic. Nothing gave him more pleasure than witnessing the moment of conversion, the moment a new soul entered the kingdom of heaven.

"Through the power of the Holy Ghost, we increase in our knowledge of God and in our love for God and neighbor," Charles said. "The joy of the gospel fills us to overflowing. Do you not want this great joy? It is God's gift offered to you. You must but accept it with a repentant heart and it shall be yours."

Another glance. Patsy shifted her gaze to Noah, whose eyes remained fixed on her father. Open and fixed, not glazed or closing. If Noah did not preach, at least he would be edified by the sermon her father preached. Patsy returned her own gaze to her father.

It was Susanna's movement, not Noah's, that caught in her peripheral vision a few seconds later. Susanna's hand moved to Noah's shoulder.

"Is this it?" Patsy said, her hand moving to Noah's elbow. "Noah?"

"I am still here," he said.

He twitched, but it could have been nerves. The stress of seeing the audience gathered and primed yet wondering what would happen next was enough to make them all twitch.

"Susanna?" Patsy said softly.

"I am not certain," Susanna said. "But I think so."

Noah leaned back slightly in the chair — or perhaps Patsy only imagined he had. The angle of his head shifted. She was certain of that. In an instant, color fled his face, leaving only a white clamminess.

Susanna nodded.

Patsy raised her hand to signal her father.

Noah slumped in their arms.

Charles made a smooth transition. "I have great delight in the Lord that today a man who lives the fullness of the Christian life has accompanied me on this journey to meet with you. Though I am a Methodist and he is Amish, we find ourselves of one heart in the joy of the Lord."

Charles swung one arm open wide, directing the gaze of his open-air congregation to Noah.

"Are we sure he's ready?" Patsy whispered.

"Do not let go yet," Susanna said.

With the dozens of gazes on them, Patsy kept one hand under Noah's elbow and the other behind his shoulder, her fingers hungering for the stiffening that would return his form and open his eyes.

"Mr. Noah Kauffman is here to share the Word of God with you," Charles said. "I know you will find great blessing as he brings to you a message from the heart of God."

Noah's knees bent at right angles as his weight shifted into his heels and he unfolded himself from the chair.

Niklaus bolted toward them from the edge of the crowd.

"Is he all right?" he said.

"He will be," Susanna said.

Noah claimed his full height now.

"Where is his Bible?" Susanna said. "He will want it."

Patsy scooped up the black-bound volume from the ground at Noah's feet. Susanna took it and placed it in Noah's hands.

"What happens now?" Niklaus asked.

"Now Noah will preach," Susanna said. "I will go stand with him."

"I'll go, if you like," Patsy said.

Susanna shook her head. "I will go first. But stay close."

"How many times have you witnessed this?" Niklaus asked Patsy as Susanna gently guided Noah.

"Quite a few," she said. "But you have seen it as well, haven't you?"

"I only saw him preaching after church on the day this all began," Niklaus said. "I would not have known the signs."

Susanna kept a hand on Noah's elbow, but Noah chose his own path.

"Where is he going?" Niklaus asked.

"He might be looking for the window at home." Patsy could only speculate. "Or he might be starting to pace. He sometimes walks around as he preaches."

Niklaus glanced around the clearing. While the trunks had been felled and removed long ago, enough stumps remained, spreading old roots like giant spider legs, to prove a hazard to a careless step.

"Susanna will stay right with him," Patsy said. "And when she tires, I will take a turn."

"Might I also?" Niklaus said.

Patsy inspected his face.

"He is my friend, after all," Niklaus said.

Patsy nodded. "He will likely preach longer than the congregation can stay."

"Will he not know to stop?"

She shook her head.

"Then I shall be ready to assist."

Noah held his Bible open in front of him, Susanna still at his elbow, and began to speak.

He spoke of God's love, of human failings, of faithfulness, of repentance, of redemption, of new life, of serving Christ with love toward one another, of unceasing prayer, of God's gracious gift of salvation.

"I don't see much difference," Patsy said.

"Between what?" Niklaus said.

"Between the way my father preaches and the way Noah preaches."

Niklaus could not disagree. What the daughter of a Methodist minister could not know was that Noah's sermons were not what she would encounter if she visited an Amish church service. His bright tone. His lively eyes. His plain speaking from the heart. His words of joyful Christian living. His appeal for repentance because of the gracious welcome awaiting the sinner in the arms of God. His assurance of the reward of repentance and faith.

It was indeed in the manner of Charles Baxton but not at all in the manner of Shem Hertzberger or Niklaus himself.

Noah pivoted, fixed his gaze on Niklaus, and grinned. Niklaus waved.

"He will not remember," Patsy said quickly. "He looks at you and makes you feel that if you were the only sinner on earth, Christ would have died for you anyway. But he does not see, and he does not remember."

Niklaus crossed his arms over his chest.

Noah's words resumed, with a lengthy quotation from the book of Romans without referring to the Bible in his hands. Niklaus found no fault in Noah's words. But the mystery of falling under the Holy Ghost and knowing nothing of what happened but what others told him — Niklaus found no sense in that.

CHAPTER 16

Uncle Niklaus had been home for two days. That meant Susanna was as well. Tomorrow was a church Sunday, but Adam did not want to wait that long to see Susanna and perhaps not have a moment to pull her away on their own. The Kauffman farm was just the next farm over. She could have been anywhere for the early part of the day — chores on the Hooley farm, walking and collecting items for dyes, delivering dyes or cloth. But now, in midafternoon, he was most likely to find her at the Kauffmans'. Noah's condition, willful or not, was changing his bond with Susanna. The pleasure in happening upon each other was lost in her efforts to be where Noah needed her. Her mind was in a place that had not existed a few weeks ago. Bracing himself for what he would encounter at the Kauffmans', Adam chose to walk rather than take a horse.

Since arriving home, Niklaus had said

little about the preaching excursion. Noah had fallen under during both open-air meetings and had traveled well otherwise. Niklaus's silence suited Adam. The less he knew, the less anyone could expect him to answer questions. The Hooleys knew of the trip. Adam's aunt Deborah and cousin Jonas knew. And, thanks to Adam, the bishop knew. It was no secret, yet the details made Adam uneasy. He would have been happier to hear that Noah had not preached, but he could not change what happened. *Gottes wille.*

If he could turn back time, Adam would go back to the Sunday when Noah became ill and find a way to keep it from happening. *Gottes wille* sometimes puzzled Adam.

And Susanna. If he were ever to take a wife, he would want only Susanna. Yet they had not even spoken in two weeks. The words he would speak to her now had not yet come together in his mind, but the impulse to see her persisted.

The scenario at the Kauffmans' was better than what Adam had imagined. A four-day absence of both Noah and Phoebe from the farm had thinned out the onlookers. Adam breathed a prayer of thanks. Perhaps *Gottes wille* for the preaching trip had been to deter their own people from gathering to

195

listen. Yet a handful were there, chatting in the yard and arranging themselves on the benches. Adam chided himself. He could have come and gotten those benches while Noah was gone and done his part to make this stop. He could still return later in the day with a wagon and Jonas to help load the benches.

What mattered now was that Susanna's cart sat idle alongside the barn.

Adam kept his head down as he strode down the edge of the yard. Eye contact with any of the gathered — all Amish — could be misleading. If Noah began preaching, Adam would take care not to be seen. He offered neither approval nor simple curiosity. But once Noah started preaching, Susanna would not answer the door, which she had taken to latching since the day Mrs. Zimmerman invited herself in.

He knocked on the back door of the Kauffman house.

"Adam." Susanna answered the knock, as he had hoped she would.

" 'Tis good to see you, Susanna."

"And you."

He feasted on her countenance. Strained. Befuddled. Yearning. All that he felt was in her eyes also. Yet she did not move toward him.

"Can you come out for some air?" he said.

The day was a stifling blend of heat and humidity that had sent a rivulet of perspiration down the center of Adam's back. Only the wide brim of his hat kept his face from puddling. Yet he wanted to speak to Susanna, and outside, away from Noah and Phoebe and Patsy, would give the most privacy.

She closed the door behind her, and they paced away from the house.

"How are you?" Adam asked.

"Well," she said. "And you?"

"Also well." Adam's heart beat a little harder. They were losing precious moments acting as if they were near strangers. "I miss you."

"Adam." Her breath caught slightly. "Everything is so confusing."

"We can go back and untangle it." He reached for her hand.

Her wide eyes met his. "I would not change anything."

"Even if what you are doing makes your parents decide to move west?"

Her gasp this time was full and deep as she took back her hand. "Where did you hear that?"

"Is it true?" Adam said.

"My *mamm* mentioned it. That is all."

"I heard it from my *aunti*. Your *mamm* was talking about it at a quilting bee a few days ago. At least a dozen women heard what she said."

Susanna dropped her forehead into one open hand. "I thought she was just annoyed with me. She would not really uproot our family, would she?"

Adam shrugged. How could he know what someone else might do?

"I do not know how to talk to my *mamm* these days," Susanna said. "My *daed*. I will speak to my *daed*."

"He will tell you the truth."

"I think he will." Susanna glanced back at the house, her face paler than it had been just five minutes ago. "I have to go back inside. 'Tis nearly time."

Her voice cracked with the tear that slid from one eye. She sniffled and wiped the back of her hand across her face.

"I did not mean to upset you."

"I have to go, Adam."

Susanna had heard so many of Noah's sermons in the last few weeks — and two from Charles Baxton — that she was not sure her mind could absorb three hours of words that Sunday's church service would bring. They were in the Plank barn this time, singing a long, slow hymn so unlike the ones Charles led. Her lips moved with the words.

"Oh God Father, on heaven's throne, you have prepared for us a crown if we stay in your Son, if we suffer with him the cross and the pain, if we surrender ourselves to him in this life and if we struggle continually to enter into his community. You tell us what we need to know, through your Son, if we have community with him."

Susanna's voice stilled. Why should there be so much struggling to enter God's kingdom? Reverend Baxton would say conversion brings assurance, not struggle. Plainly it should bring gladness.

Her mother nudged her, and Susanna joined the singing again. Surely her mother had not discerned the question in her mind.

"You gave your beloved Son to us to be our head. He has marked out for us the road we should take, so that we would not lose our way and find ourselves outside of his community."

Susanna preferred sitting on the rear of the church gathering because she could see nearly everyone present from that vantage point. Her mother rarely argued the logic. Raising a trail of spirited boys, Veronica had seen the practicality of being in the back.

Now that they were all old enough to sit on the men's side, she still liked to be able to keep an eye on them.

The hymn was coming to a close. One of the ministers, probably the bishop, would offer a lengthy prayer. Then the sermons would begin. Susanna bowed her head for the bishop's prayer, fairly certain that some church members used the occasion for a quick nap behind devoutly closed eyes.

At the *Amen,* Susanna's eyes opened and drifted to Adam. She could not see much but the back of his head or a glimpse of his profile if he should happen to turn his head. She should not have fallen apart yesterday and rushed away from him. She should have thanked him politely for his concern and inquired more fully about his own welfare. He was confused by recent events, she realized, just as she was. At some point, they would have to talk with genuine hearts, as they always had until recently.

And then there was Niklaus, who seemed unusually fixed on Bishop Hertzberger today. During the preaching trip, Niklaus took great care not to say he approved or disapproved of Noah's participation. He was a helpful friend to everyone in the group, tending the horses, making coffee in the morning over the campfire, making sure

Noah ate well. His deeds spoke the intent of his heart even without the agreement of his mind. Usually in church, as Niklaus sat on the preaching bench at the front of the church, he had his Bible open in his lap to read and follow closely as one of the other ministers preached. If it was his turn, he spoke words of edification in calm, reasoned tones. What he thought of Noah's preaching he kept to himself. But now he watched the bishop with great interest, each gesture of his hands, each lean of the head toward the congregation, each squaring of the shoulders, as if he were saying, *Listen!*

Susanna's gaze drifted to the bishop. His farm was not near the Hooleys', and she had little reason to ride that far out unless Mrs. Hertzberger insisted she would not wait until the next church Sunday for Susanna to bring her a jar of dye or a length of cloth. And given recent events, Susanna was not eager to encounter Shem Hertzberger on her own.

She missed Noah. Even though she saw Noah and Phoebe every day, over her mother's silent objections, she still missed them on a church Sunday. Phoebe should not have to feel unsafe coming to worship in her own congregation.

■ ■ ■ ■

Was the edge in Shem's voice new, or did Niklaus hear it differently now?

In their meeting just before the service began, the three ministers prayerfully discerned that Shem would preach first and Niklaus would follow. Yohan Maist would do his part by praying unceasingly for both of them to respond to the Holy Ghost. Shem had chosen to preach on the topic of submission. It was not an uncommon topic in an Amish church service. Every adult made baptismal vows to submit to the authority of the church. Children submitted to their parents. Wives submitted to their husbands. Husbands submitted to the headship of Christ. Niklaus could have called on any member of the congregation to recite the Bible verses that they all took seriously. Still, from time to time a sermon seemed prudent to remind everyone that the entire congregation would suffer should they become lax on this belief.

However, on this particular morning, Niklaus suspected that Noah Kauffman's preaching had more influence on Shem's choice of sermon text than did the whisper of the Holy Ghost. The first sermon was supposed to be shorter than the second, main, sermon, but Niklaus had never known Shem to make a distinction. Whether he preached first or second did not change the constraints of the sermon he delivered.

Niklaus inhaled through his nose, slowly filling his lungs and feeling his belly rise. He judged he had another forty minutes before Shem would end his sermon with a prayer and step aside for Niklaus to stand. Niklaus did not fault the words of his fellow minister, but he was unsettled. Shem's stern, authoritative pitch was not unusual, but today it bit into Niklaus.

Or something did.

Perhaps it was not Shem. Perhaps it was the Holy Ghost, on whom Niklaus would depend to guide his own sermon to follow. He imagined himself speaking the words Shem spoke. Would he change anything? Should there be more grace? Less judgment? More assurance? Less fear?

More than all else, should not a sermon be livelier? More lyrical? More a song of the heart than a reading of the law?

More like Charles Baxton.

More like Noah Kauffman.

Twenty minutes passed. As Niklaus breathed in and out, he questioned whether the Holy Ghost might breathe through his words today. If he relied on God to give him words, did it not also make sense to rely on God in the manner of speaking those words?

Another ten minutes passed.

Noah's words from the preaching trip rehearsed themselves in Niklaus's mind.

The love of God.

The wooing of God.

The welcoming of God.

The celebration of God and His angels when one sinner repents and enters the kingdom of heaven.

Niklaus had watched Shem preach for enough years to recognize when he was winding down. He was beginning to repeat the list of points he had made and the passages he had read aloud to the congregation. In another five or six minutes, he would begin his prayer, and then he would humbly nod toward his fellow minister for the main sermon. Niklaus inhaled and exhaled with thoughtful deliberation, seeking God's clarity.

It was not Noah's words Niklaus wanted — or Charles's. But he could not help wonder what his own words might sound like if preached in the lively style of the revivalists.

Shem began to pray. Niklaus shuffled his feet beneath the bench.

Shem pronounced the *Amen* and nodded at Niklaus.

Niklaus gripped his Bible and stood. The easiest choice was to preach in the style he was accustomed to and which the congregation — and the bishop — expected of him. Another two weeks before the next church service would allow him time to wait on the Lord on the matter.

On the other hand, the apostle Paul admonished believers not to quench the Spirit of God.

Shem sat down and turned his vigilant eyes to Niklaus.

Niklaus moistened his lips, opened his Bible, and began to speak. With every sentence, he was more certain he had made the right decision.

CHAPTER 17

Rocky anxiety tumbled through Adam's gut, and his head ached. His uncle's sermons were always easy to listen to, and the congregation committed fewer infractions of restlessness than when other preachers were speaking. But this morning it was as if the bishop had invited a guest preacher whom he had not previously heard speak. The voice falling on Adam's ears was the one he heard around the Zug home when his uncle was especially pleased or in the mood for winking and teasing. It was not his preaching voice.

But Adam had heard someone preach in this manner. Noah. Adam hesitated to call them *preaching* or *sermons,* because Noah was not a minister and the episodes happened outside of church. Matters would be far less complicated if Uncle Niklaus had not gone on that expedition with Charles Baxton.

At the front of the gathering in the barn, Bishop Hertzberger flipped the pages of his Bible while glancing up at Niklaus every few seconds. Shem Hertzberger was a man who knew what he thought. His words were as meticulously planned as the notches and corners of his carpentry work. Self-restraint permeated his personality and interactions — except when it came to Noah. The change began with Noah's spell in the Satzler yard, but just the other day, Shem had smashed his fingers under a rock in a careless moment. Now he used those fingers to fidget with his Bible. Adam's observation of the bishop caused his mind to lose the thread of his uncle's sermon. He swallowed hard and shifted his eyes back to Niklaus.

Niklaus glowed. Adam could think of no other word to describe his uncle's countenance. It was not the angelic brightness that Adam had once seen in an *English* painting — one his parents never knew he saw. Yet Niklaus glowed with pleasure and confidence and satisfaction — the expression that Adam was accustomed to seeing on Niklaus's face when all his children and grandchildren were gathered at the table and a meal of abundance was laid out before them. They bowed their heads in silent prayer, and when Niklaus spoke the

Aemen that broke the hushed mood, his voice caught on love.

Love in his voice. That is what Adam heard now.

Adam's father would not have approved of the way he now reached to scratch the center of his back in the middle of a worship service, but if he left the itch untended, it would only magnify and he would hear no more of the sermon than he did now. The contortion had one other benefit. It allowed him a brief glance at Susanna, sitting on the women's side toward the back.

Her eyes were wide, and with her hands gripping the bench rather than resting in her lap, she leaned forward slightly.

But what did that mean?

Agreement? Consternation? Inspiration? Conviction? Alarm? Encouragement?

Adam thought he knew everything about Susanna's face. But he did not know this.

Words welled up in Niklaus, colliding on their way from his mind to his mouth. Thoughts coming faster than he could put them into proper form was not a familiar experience to Niklaus. If this is what Charles had meant all these years when he spoke of being caught up in the Spirit, Niklaus had new appreciation for his friend's ministry.

"Do you seek the Spirit of God?" Niklaus said. "Or do you quench the Spirit? Do you hear the gentle whisper of God, or do you hear the voices of the world? I implore you, my brothers and sisters, to know the Spirit of God prompting your spirit and speaking assurance of how precious you are to God — so precious that He would send His Son to redeem you. Perhaps this is the day that you will know this to be true in your heart and in your home."

Niklaus would not say that heads were bobbing in agreement. Such enthusiasm would disturb the accustomed restraint of the district's church services. But as he looked around the barn, heads nodded here and there. The faces, so familiar that he could call them all by name, were fixed on him. No eyes strayed — whether in astonishment or agreement, he did not know. But this was a moment like none other he had experienced. He would quench pride at the first sight of it in himself as he preached, but the freedom of the Spirit he would not bridle.

He paused, gazing at the upturned faces, forming the thoughts that would next carry words of the Holy Ghost to the waiting listeners.

"Thank you, Brother Niklaus." The bishop

popped up from his seat, trapping his thick Bible between his arm and chest.

Niklaus glanced at his own Bible, open and balanced in one hand. Shem could not have thought he was finished after only thirty-five minutes.

"Let us meditate on our faithfulness to God," Shem said, "as we sing our closing hymn."

Shem began to sing, rather than waiting for one of the men in the congregation to feel moved to lead in the first phrases.

"We are scattered like sheep without a shepherd. We have left our houses and lands and have become like owls of the night, like game birds. We sneak about in the forest. Men track us down with dogs, then lead us like lambs back to town. There they put us on display and say we are the cause of an uproar. We are counted like sheep for slaughter. They call us heretics and deceivers."

The *Ausbund* was full of hymns recounting suffering the church had endured, by the grace of God. But had Niklaus enjoyed the opportunity to choose a hymn to follow his sermon, he would have chosen, "Those of us who have been washed with the blood of Christ and made free from sin are tied together in our hearts. We now walk in the

Spirit who shows us the right way and who rules in us."

Instead, though, Shem pressed on with his choice, and the congregation joined with the words that were two hundred years old.

"Oh Lord, no tribulation is so great that it can draw us away from you. Glory, triumph, and honor are yours from now into eternity. Your righteousness is always blessed by the people who gather in your name. You will come again to judge the earth!"

As they sang, Niklaus moved to his place beside Yohan Maist. When the ponderous hymn concluded fifteen minutes later, Shem offered a prayer and pronounced the benediction. Conversation buzzed in the barn as men rearranged benches into tables and women dispersed to prepare the food. Niklaus savored the moment, the sounds of the congregation fading from his ears as his heart opened in a way it never had before. Many times he had felt he had rightly taught the truth of Scripture, but the experience of doing it with such freedom and assurance was new. Even if his words fell on deaf ears, he himself was changed.

"Niklaus." Shem's voice shattered the moment. "May I have a word?"

"Of course." Niklaus turned toward his friend.

"Perhaps outside," Shem said.

Tables were going up in the farmyard, but beyond the confines of the barn, it was easy to stroll away from hearing distance of congregation members, which was Shem's clear intent. Niklaus kept pace.

"As your bishop," Shem began, "I feel it is incumbent on me to speak to you about your sermon."

Niklaus waited.

" 'Twas quite unlike you," Shem said.

"We all speak as the Spirit leads us," Niklaus said.

Consternation colored Shem's face.

"Have I spoken amiss?" Niklaus was so close to God in the doing that he could not now see what disturbed his fellow minister.

Shem crossed his wrists behind him and continued to stride along a fence line. "I feel in my spirit that you have spoken in a manner unsubmissive to the authority of the church."

"Surely you do not believe that was my intent," Niklaus said. "I was called on to preach, and I preached. This is the promise I made when I was ordained."

"Intent and result do not always align," Shem said.

"And what result do you perceive?"

"I held my tongue when some of our

people attended the revival meeting a few weeks ago," Shem said. "I have held my tongue regarding Noah Kauffman because I believe in due time God will call him to repentance."

"Repentance?" Niklaus said.

"And when Noah repents, God will be faithful and just to forgive, and this illness of his spirit will be healed."

Niklaus swallowed and ran his tongue across his bottom lip. "The matter of Noah Kauffman is a complicated pastoral challenge."

"I commend him for staying away from the congregation while he awaits his healing," Shem said, "though I am given to understand that more and more of our people are visiting his home in the hope that he will expound."

Niklaus nodded. "It would seem so. When I had the opportunity, I discouraged such gathering."

"Then I commend you for your discernment," Shem said. "Yet I cannot help wondering what benefit you thought would come to the church by encouraging him to go on a preaching mission with Charles Baxton."

"Charles Baxton loves the Lord," Niklaus said.

"Perhaps in his own way," Shem said, "but not in our way. You are Noah's closest neighbor, and I have always deferred to you to minister to the households closest to you. But I believe the time has come that I must intervene."

"Our people were not present on the journey with Charles," Niklaus said. "No harm has come to the congregation, and I doubt Noah will want to do it again."

"No harm?" Shem stopped walking and turned to face Niklaus. "Susanna Hooley is an impressionable young woman. Noah tasted the pride and fame of the outside world. And your own preaching changed after one short trip with Charles Baxton. I cannot accept the truth of your statement that no harm has come to the congregation."

Niklaus had not expected Shem would gush about a livelier style of preaching, but neither had he expected chastisement.

"Shem," he said, "we have been friends for many years."

"And I hope we will be friends for many more years. But I am the bishop. I have a particular burden on my shoulders for the spiritual welfare of the church."

"We share the duties as ministers," Niklaus said. "Yohan also shares in our work."

"Yet I am bishop," Shem said. "What is to become of the influence of Charles Baxton and his Methodist revivalism on the church? We are to shepherd our flock, not lead them astray."

Niklaus held Shem's eyes for a long half minute, blinking only twice before shifting his gaze.

"Here comes Adam," he said.

Adam was uncertain what he was approaching, with the bishop standing in such a posture and Niklaus seeming to pull away from him. He faltered, thinking to turn away.

"What is it, Adam?" Niklaus said.

"The tables are ready," Adam said. "I have been sent to see if the bishop will lead the silent prayer or if I should ask Mr. Maist."

"I will come," Shem said.

Against his volition, Adam's eyebrows pinched toward each other. He had interrupted something more than a friendly stroll between two old friends.

His uncle put a hand on Adam's shoulder. "Someday perhaps Adam will be the minister called on to pray."

Adam gulped. When he married, he would also be promising to serve as minister if he was called upon, but he could think of no young man more unworthy of such a spiritual calling.

"I am certain Adam will honor his baptismal vows," the bishop said. "He understands the serious nature of the promises we all make to submit."

Adam's chest tightened. He had come only to find someone to lead a time of prayer but was caught in a debate about his intentions to keep his promises.

"Adam is a reasonable young man." Niklaus tapped Adam's back twice. "In his heart and in his way, he wants to follow the Lord."

"His way will be the way of our people for two hundred years," Shem said.

Adam inhaled deeply. "The prayer? One of you will come?"

"Of course I will come," Shem said. "I am the bishop."

CHAPTER 18

The walk along the edge of the forest at the base of Jacks Mountain with people his own age brought Adam respite from feeling stretched between his uncle and his bishop. Shem had strode back to the farmyard to lead the beginning of the meal, and Niklaus made no effort to keep up. Unsure whether to walk — or eat — with either one of them, Adam angled off toward a table of young men and gladly helped to organize the walk. The same outing was far more pleasant in late spring or early fall than in August heat, but keeping to the shade along the route made the trek more bearable. A dozen and a half friends traipsed along a path, some pairing off for a few minutes at a time.

Susanna, who was rarely without her collection basket, had stopped to inspect loose bark when Adam caught up with her.

"I have a feeling I know just the shade you have in mind," he said.

Susanna gave a half smile. "You know me well."

Adam liked to think so. "May I walk with you?"

"If you do not mind the occasional pause to consider the possibilities of God's bounty," Susanna said.

"Never." Adam let her set the casual pace and adjusted his longer legs to her shorter stride. Susanna paused to touch the vibrant blue of a lone wildflower but did not pluck the petals. Her eyes would be looking for the place where the flowers were plentiful so that the few she carried home would leave no bare spot.

"How did you find church this morning?" he asked.

Her gait faltered for a split second but found steadiness again. "I always pray that God is present in our worship," she said.

Her answer told Adam nothing of her opinion. He tried again. "My *onkel* and the bishop seem to have had different responses."

"Your *onkel* gave a wonderful sermon," she said.

"Do you really think so?"

"Did you not?" Susanna turned her head to glance at Adam but did not meet his eyes.

"May I be honest?" he said.

218

"Of course."

"I am not sure what to think. Niklaus's sermon was very different today."

"Especially heartfelt."

"Too heartfelt, perhaps."

"Is that even possible?"

Adam shrugged. "The bishop seems to think so."

"The bishop is a good man," Susanna said, "but he is overly cautious about new ways."

"Is that not the manner of our people?" Adam said.

"I do not suggest that we should give up living apart," Susanna said, "but neither should we close ourselves off to the ways God may choose to speak."

Adam walked a few yards in silence. They were exchanging information, informed perspectives, but they were not linking hearts the way he craved.

"I came upon my *onkel* and Shem," he said, "and felt great discomfort between them."

"About the sermon?"

"Perhaps about the events that led Niklaus to take this new approach," Adam said.

"You mean the preaching trip."

"I cannot be certain what they were speaking of, but I suspect so."

"I wish you had come, Adam," Susanna said. "It was not what I expected, but I felt God move in my heart."

"And you think my *onkel* did as well?"

"If only you had been there to see for yourself," she said. Her countenance grew intense. "When people come to hear Noah at his house, they do so only out of curiosity or because they hope to find some judgment against him. But in the revival meeting, Charles made nothing of the way Noah falls under in his introduction. He simply gave those who came the opportunity to hear a fine sermon that moved many hearts."

"But if the bishop disapproves," Adam said, "was it right to go?"

"If you had been there," she said again, "you would have seen only how right it was — how the beauty of faith can truly gladden the heart."

"Your heart has been gladdened?" Adam played with the phrase in his mouth.

"It has. I wish you could know what I mean."

"What is right and true is not simply what we feel in the moment."

"Did I suggest that it was?"

Her brusque tone rang unfamiliar. Adam only wanted to talk with the person who knew him best about his own uncertainties. But whatever hesitancy she might have had about Noah's preaching in public had dissipated during the four days she was away. A chasm had opened between them. A gladdened heart was no match to what he felt.

Behind them a heavy breath caused them both to turn.

"Finally, I caught up with you." Barbara Glick smoothed her apron. "I want to see what you have in your basket, Susanna. I want to learn what you know about making colors."

"I am happy to show you." Susanna lifted her basket.

Two bonneted heads leaned toward each other as Adam withdrew. Susanna did not even catch his eye.

Galahad would run himself to exhaustion if Patsy allowed it, and as much as it thrilled her to be astride as he galloped, gradually she reined him in to cool him down. To think that her father had wanted to geld him and make a calm work animal of such a magnificent stallion! Only Patsy's protests spared Galahad the fate — and the reprieve had required Patsy's promise that she would make sure her favored horse earned his keep on the farm. He was far too expensive to raise and feed merely for her amusement. Having raced up Jacks Mountain and along the ridge before descending, they were still miles from home, and Patsy would soak up every ray of sunshine and every breath of the wind on her face. The heat bothered her not at all.

A bobbing black bonnet caught her eye. Patsy did not have to spur the horse in order to catch up with the pedestrian.

"Susanna, what are you doing way out here?"

Susanna tilted her head up to gaze at Patsy. Her bonnet, quilted and black, was years out of style, but that seemed to be true of most of the clothing the Amish women wore. Unspoken rules of dress kept them in clothing that might have been in style twenty years earlier. Patsy was hardly one to remark, though. While she owned gowns that would have been presentable in a downtown Philadelphia church, she much preferred comfortable cotton work dresses with a minimum of petticoats. The color or print of a dress mattered far less than how easily she could move, especially when she wanted to ride.

"Church was at the Planks'," Susanna said, "and we had an outing."

Patsy glanced down the road in the direction from which Susanna must have come.

"You are a long way from home on your own," Patsy said.

"So are you," Susanna said.

Patsy patted her horse's neck. "But I have my trusty steed to whisk me home."

"I have two equally trustworthy feet."

Patsy laughed. "Climb on and let me take you home." She would feel like a neglectful friend if she cantered off and left Susanna to traverse the miles home.

Susanna hesitated. "I wonder if taking the horse out and then asking it to carry two riders does not constitute work on the Sabbath."

"I prefer to think of it as the joy of the Sabbath," Patsy said. "Exodus tells us we are to delight in the Sabbath."

"But even animals are to have a Sabbath rest."

"Will it be a sin for you to ride home on a horse which God has so clearly created to find delight in running as fast as he can?" Even the Amish used their buggy horses to get to church. What could be so different in riding Galahad?

Susanna moved her basket from one arm to the other. "I suppose not."

Patsy held on to the saddle horn with one hand and reached down to offer the other to Susanna's grasp. Once her friend was settled behind her with her basket secure, Patsy put Galahad into motion again.

"Doesn't Adam usually see you home from your outings?" Patsy asked. "Especially one so far from home?"

"It does not always work out," Susanna said.

"I hope he is not unwell."

"No, he is not."

"Did his uncle need him today?"

"I do not believe so."

Without slowing the horse, Patsy twisted to look at her friend's face.

"Susanna Hooley, you tell me what is going on right this instant."

Susanna hesitated.

"Susanna." Patsy infused stern warning into her tone.

"Matters between us are strained," Susanna said softly.

"Between you and Adam? That's ridiculous."

" 'Tis true."

"Did he not offer to see you home?"

" 'Tis I who declined. Someone else had a wagon and could bring me most of the way home, and I was happy to walk the remaining distance."

"Happy?"

"Willing, at least," Susanna said.

"You must work it out," Patsy said.

Susanna was silent.

"Does this have to do with my father's preaching journey?"

Susanna remained silent.

"Niklaus seemed content enough while we were gone."

The horse *clip-clopped* another thirty yards.

"It's the bishop, isn't it?" Patsy said. "He's causing trouble."

"The bishop does what he believes is best for the congregation," Susanna said.

"And if he is wrong?"

Susanna shifted in the back of the saddle but did not speak.

Since the short preaching trip, Noah had not failed a single day to fall under. What Susanna found most remarkable was not that Noah preached daily now but that the time at which he would fall under was likely to occur within a specific thirty-minute period of time. News of this consistency only served to increase the size of the crowd that came to hear him. With the certainty that he would preach and an accurate estimate of the time this would occur, residents of the valley could plan the day's excursion in the same manner they would plan a visit to a neighboring farm or a trip into a town with sufficient shops to make the outing worthwhile. Every day or so another bench turned up, and others simply circled their carts and wagons to be able to see from the driving benches while children napped or played in the beds.

Susanna did not blame them for coming. She learned something new from God's Word every time she listened to Noah. At the same time, she suspected that many who gathered were there for the spectacle more than for the edification. Snippets of conversation she overheard still revolved around whether Noah could truly be unconscious as he preached or whether he was a charlatan and everyone who assisted him was complicit.

Susanna was not complicit in anything. She was there to make sure Noah was safe. Increasingly the task went beyond keeping him away from a hot stove, a glass lamp, or loose rugs he might trip on and also included keeping people out of the house and at a reasonable distance. Thursday's crowd was the largest Susanna had yet seen, and some moved to stand in front of the benches, even in the flower bed beneath the window. There was no point in asking them to leave, but as the time approached, she stood on the front step and called out polite requests for respectful observance of Noah and Phoebe's property and privacy. She or Patsy gave the same brief speech every day.

When Adam turned into the Kauffman farm on his horse, his interest lay not in listening to Noah's words but in the likelihood that Susanna was somewhere on the premises.

He had fumbled badly on Sunday. He and Susanna looked past each other, never meeting eyes, and surely not hearts. Trying again was imperative. Spying Galahad heartened him. Patsy's presence would give Susanna less reason to refuse to step out behind the house with him. He knew the rules, however. Once Noah fell under, no one must approach the house. He waited in plain view in the front until Susanna peeked out the front window beside Noah and caught his silent, pleading eyes. Only when she nodded did he lead his mount around to the back.

"I feel terrible," he said once they were face-to-face. It had been a miserable four days since Sunday, in the middle of a miserable few weeks.

"Me too," she said. "Thank you for coming."

"I miss you," he said. They had not had an impromptu forested walk for weeks, and none seemed likely soon.

"I miss you," she said.

"When can we be alone to talk?"

She glanced back toward the house. "I am here nearly every afternoon. It is difficult to get away from home more than I do."

"Can you come early one day and stop at my *onkel*'s farm?"

"That will be difficult. To please my *mamm,* I must keep up with my chores and work, but I have much less time to do so."

A shout from the front yard startled them both, and Susanna shot off to discover the reason. Adam was on her heels.

Susanna groaned. " 'Tis that *English* man again. He likes to toss pebbles at Noah to see if he will react, and others find it amusing."

As if to testify to the accuracy of Susanna's account, the man reached into a pocket and arranged something between his fingers.

"Can you help?" Susanna spun to face Adam.

"I am not sure I can do anything."

"He does not listen to me. You are a man.

He would listen to you," Susanna said. "Surely you can see that things are getting out of hand. I do not come to encourage this, but I am limited to prevent it."

The bishop's face floated through Adam's mind. He wanted Adam to speak up among his friends, not involve himself in the spectacle.

Susanna's dark eyes gripped him.

CHAPTER 19

Adam took a step back. Susanna could make no sense of the gesture. She moved toward him, and he stepped back again.

"Adam," she said. "We need help. Noah needs help."

Adam drew breath slowly. "He is an *English.* He has nothing to do with me."

"He means harm to Noah. Will you tell me that Noah is nothing to you?"

Susanna had no patience for the hesitation that followed. Moments ago they voiced that they missed each other, and she had spoken truth. But in this moment, she did not recognize the man who held her affections. Susanna pivoted away and marched toward the stone thrower.

"Once again, Mr. Grauman," Susanna said loudly, "I must ask you to refrain, and if you do not, I must ask you to leave."

He grunted but for now released the pebble in his hand. It skittered against his boot on its way to the ground. No doubt Mr. Grauman would try again. Even Susanna's youngest brother had more sense than this grown man. Every time he came, there was another incident. Through the window, Susanna saw Patsy inch into view. Spectators must never think that Noah was unattended. Perhaps it was a useful strategy for one of them to be inside but visible in the window, while the other maintained a presence among those who gathered outside. Would it have been so difficult for Adam to play this small role?

As much as Susanna would have liked to soak up Noah's words, the task of surveying the farmyard occupied her thoughts. Forty was becoming a usual number of people. It was not always the same forty people. Farms and shops and homes demanded attention. Even Mrs. Zimmerman did not come as frequently as she had in the beginning with her judgment and protests. Susanna did not try to convince herself that it was Noah's preaching that drew the crowds. Rather it was the trances. Charles Baxton called it falling under the Holy Ghost, but most of the *English* who came called it trance preaching. Was Noah truly unconscious? Did he truly have no recollection of his actions? Were the sermons one big scam?

Those were the questions that spread across the Kish Valley demanding individuals satisfy their own suspicions, with the indisputable evidence of personal visits.

"Susanna."

She turned toward Phoebe, unaware that her friend and relative had come to stand beside her at the back of the crowd.

"I saw Adam earlier," Phoebe said. "Do you think he has a bit of time to spare this afternoon?"

"I am not sure." At the moment, Susanna was unsure of anything except the pressure of the unknown rising in her chest.

"Our stalls are in need of mucking," Phoebe said. "The preaching takes so much out of Noah that in the mornings he often lacks his usual strength."

Susanna nodded. "I can muck."

"Two are better than one," Phoebe said. "Why not ask him to help you?"

Susanna glanced around, unsure whether Adam was still on the Kauffman farm.

"We will find him together," Phoebe announced.

Susanna said nothing when they found him lurking at the side of the barn, well away from the gathered onlookers but near enough to monitor the scene. As Phoebe explained her request, Susanna examined the ground at their feet.

"I would be happy to muck for you," Adam said.

Susanna's eyes snapped up. Adam would not stop a man from harassing Noah, lest it be interpreted as endorsing the preaching — the only explanation she had come up with for his hesitant silence at her request — yet he would willingly do Noah's work and muck stalls. Adam had some sort of invisible line in his conscience. Susanna's request was on one side and Phoebe's on the other.

"We will get to it, then," Susanna said. She would let Adam choose the stall he would muck first, and she would choose the one farthest from it.

Niklaus lugged the bucket of limestone ground into powder and mixed with water. He might not be a competent carpenter by Shem's standards — or his own — but he knew how to whitewash. The walls were up; the roof was on; the chinking and daubing were finished; and the siding was on one end wall that had no windows or doorways. Adam had said just yesterday that the wall was ready for whitewashing on the exterior. Niklaus situated the bucket, grasped the brush, and began applying whitewash. The upper areas would require a ladder, and Deborah would advise that he leave the task to Jonas and Adam. Even in his youth, Niklaus had never liked heights. But he was a tall man with long arms, so whitewashing did not intimidate him. Moving from end to end of the wall and working his way upward, he could not help but admire the construction. Niklaus had never seen such clean and consistent notches, and Adam had cut most of them himself.

An approaching horse drew Niklaus's eye away from the task. Shem had arrived. Niklaus dipped his brush in the whitewash and began another length. If Shem planned to stay, he knew what to do with his horse.

Niklaus dragged the brush as far as he could before returning to dip it once again in the whitewash. It looked like nothing more than a thin layer of liquid going on the wooden siding, but Niklaus had white-washed enough walls to know that within a few hours a bright white would emerge.

Shem stood at the bucket, a brush in his hand. Niklaus nodded at him but did not speak. Perhaps Shem's mood had shifted in the last few days. If so, it would be up to Shem to reveal himself. They white-washed side by side for a few minutes. Soon Niklaus would have to mix up more lime and water.

"I have but one simple request," Shem finally said.

Niklaus waited.

"I do not question the sincerity of your lively experience of the Spirit," Shem said, "but when you preach, I ask you to use the traditional style of sermon to which our people are accustomed."

Swish. Niklaus moved his brush.

"And if I do not feel that I can in good conscience promise to do so?" Niklaus said.

Swish.

"Can you in good conscience choose not to submit to the church?" Shem said.

Swish.

"Can you in good conscience ask me to do so if it might mean quenching the Spirit?" Niklaus said.

Plop. Shem lowered the bristles of his brush into the remaining mixture with a force Niklaus did not find necessary.

"Then," Shem said, "you must step aside."

Step aside. The congregation's members had voted to make Niklaus one of their ministers, and he had accepted the role for the rest of his life or until his health made it inadvisable to continue. In what manner was it Shem's role to suggest Niklaus step aside?

Niklaus said nothing. The bucket had little

left in it now, but he went through the motion of swirling his brush against the container.

"There is no need for you to rush your decision," Shem said. "There is still more than a week before the next church service — right here at your own home. And if you need more time, it is simple enough to arrange that Yohan and I will take the two sermons. That will give you more time to come to terms with submitting to the teaching of the church, just as you always have."

Niklaus picked up the empty bucket and walked toward the barn.

"Will you not agree to this sensible arrangement?" Shem said.

Niklaus did not turn around.

Another horse trotted toward him. Adam was returning, as he said he would, in plenty of time to resume his work.

"I hope you will approve of my whitewashing efforts." Niklaus put a grin on his face.

" 'Tis hard to go wrong with whitewashing," Adam said.

Niklaus laughed. It felt good.

"Hello, Bishop," Adam said, swinging off his mount.

"I am glad to see you," Shem said. "You have done well in the tasks I assigned. I am confident now that you will be able to complete the work on your own."

"I did not realize you were coming," Adam said, "or I would have been sure to be here to receive you."

If Adam had done as well as Shem said he had, then why was the bishop scowling?

"No need," Shem said. "You are more than capable to finish up on your own — or with your cousin's assistance. If you would like, I will have a word with Jonas about taking a greater role in helping you."

Adam gripped the reins still in his hand. "I am not sure I understand."

" 'Tis simple," Shem said. "I will gather the tools I have left here for you to use. Your *onkel* has sufficient implements for the work that remains."

Shem was speaking as if Niklaus were not standing just five feet away. Adam looked from one to the other.

"I appreciate your confidence," Adam said, "but I do not feel ready to be on my own."

"You will not be on your own. I will be here," Niklaus said. "Shem, thank you for all you have done to bring us this far. I am sure Jonas would also wish to express his gratitude."

Sealing the chimney. White oak interior

trim around the doors and windows to match the rest of the house. The bed frame. The shelves that Jonas's betrothed had asked for on one wall. In Adam's mind, many details remained.

Niklaus began to mix up a fresh batch of whitewash. Shem gathered tools, wrapped them in leather, and secured them in his saddlebags. The two men did not speak to each other again before Shem rode off the farm.

"Onkel," Adam said.

Niklaus positioned his bucket along the wall and began brushing.

"Onkel," Adam repeated.

Niklaus looked up.

"Is there to be no reconciliation?" Adam said. Though he had not — so far — found reconciliation with the father who had sent him to Kish Valley, nor with Susanna who might have made plain God's will for coming, surely the two spiritual leaders would find a way to move toward one another.

"We will wait on the Lord," Niklaus said.

Adam found less comfort in the words than he might have wished.

"Someone must make the first step toward forgiveness," Adam said. This is what every preacher Adam had ever heard said. Two hardened hearts would only cause more division. One must soften.

"The path is not yet plain," Niklaus said, "but I pray the Lord will make it so. Go put your horse away. As Shem suggested, we will work together on the labor that awaits us."

CHAPTER 20

Susanna might just as well have gotten off a train in an unknown town in Indiana for all the strength of the ties she felt with her own church right now. She ate with her parents, listened to her father's devotions, and kept up on chores. But her mother's smile was gone, and the boys only looked at Susanna with confusion. She rarely saw Adam, and when she did, they might not even speak. Not really speak. Noah and Phoebe came to expect her every day, and she was glad to go, but when she looked out at the crowds that gathered, even if there were Amish among them, her role with Noah set her apart from them. When she slid into the back row of the worship service on the Zug farm, she was not sure she wanted to meet anyone's eye.

Susanna found no expression to interpret in Niklaus's face or posture. Perhaps it was a simple prayerful discernment between the three ministers that he would not preach on this Sunday. If so, he was content with the choice. He sat with his Bible open in his lap, listening to the second sermon of the morning. Through the hymns and prayers, Niklaus's mouth moved, and Susanna heard his rich, unwavering baritone anchoring the congregation's progress through the stanzas. His brow held no furrow, his mouth no frown, his posture no slump.

As they always did, the ministers withdrew during an early hymn to discern who would bring the two sermons. The trio had left that morning and returned only a few minutes later to take their places for the rest of the service.

Yohan brought the first sermon. No doubt he was secretly relieved not to be responsible for the longer main sermon. Yohan never seemed at ease in his role as preacher. He was a devout man, a kind man, a studious man. For all these reasons, he had been nominated to serve as a minister, and in God's wisdom he had chosen the hymnal with a slip of paper between its pages that confirmed he was God's choice. Susanna once heard a rumor that Yohan studied his Bible by lamplight late into the night, making notes and committing them to memory lest he be called on to preach and have no insight to offer the congregation. Even still, his phrasing was often stilted, and beads of perspiration shone along his hairline. When he was assigned the long sermon, it was sure to be briefer than either Niklaus or Shem's. Today he had spoken on rejoicing in all things, quoting from Paul's letter to the Philippians without need to read from his Bible.

And then came Shem, always the preacher with the lengthiest sermon. Two weeks ago he had preached on the theme of submission, and today he returned to the topic. Yohan's brevity meant that Shem could speak for an hour and a half and the service would conclude at its usual time. It was as if he had a clock ticking in the pocket of his worn black frock coat reminding him, without need of a glance, of the time remaining so that he might fill every minute.

Submission in the family always led to submission in the church when Shem addressed the theme. Today's twist was submission to those whom God has placed in authority over us. Even Christ, Shem reminded the congregation, submitted to the will of His Father, even though it brought Him great suffering. It was no surprise when, at the conclusion of the service, Shem began to sing a hymn not of Yohan's glad rejoicing but remaining steadfast in suffering even unto death.

The Methodists do not sing seventeen stanzas of a hymn.

Susanna ousted the thought as quickly as it came into her mind. It mattered not what the Methodists did.

At last came the final *Aemen.*

Susanna eyed her little brothers sitting across the aisle. Her mother nodded to dispatch Susanna to round them up and assure they did not wander alone toward the creek that ran through this farm, especially Stephen, the youngest and most daring. Finding a group of children already eyeing the creek, Susanna redirected them to the safety of the horse pasture and paused at the edge of a group of women.

"I was glad to see that the bishop did not allow Niklaus to give a sermon. And the bishop's word of authority is quite timely."

The voice behind her was hushed and not directed to Susanna, but Susanna turned toward it nevertheless. Martha Zimmerman met her gaze but said nothing more.

Susanna hummed the bars of the hymn they had just sung. Suffering even unto death seemed an apt exhortation when it came to Martha Zimmerman. She once again expelled the thought before it could

243

distort into something she would have to confess.

At the top of the Hertzbergers' lane, Niklaus halted his horse. For more than twenty years, he had trotted around this corner, barely slowing down. No matter the reason for his call, his friend would be glad to see him. By the time Niklaus was ordained as a minister, Shem was seasoned in the role and the one who patiently guided Niklaus's adjustment to being a minister and learning to preach.

Today Shem would not likely welcome their conversation. For two weeks Niklaus had prayed and reflected and considered the nature of the last sermon he had preached. Shem's response mattered. His suggestion that Niklaus simply not preach for the time being was not unreasonable.

Neither was it sufficient. The church service two days earlier had confirmed the movement in Niklaus's heart.

He pressed his knees into the horse and rode all the way down to the Hertzberger house. Its spacious front porch was more than most of the homes in the valley featured. Meticulous craftsmanship, with the rocking chairs Shem had also fashioned, made it a beautiful and welcoming place.

Today, to Niklaus, standing on the porch felt like defacing its hospitality. He knocked on the front door and then backed down the steps.

Shem's wife opened the door and soon directed him to the stables, where Shem was examining horses' hooves and deciding which ones must be shoed first.

At the stable door, Niklaus paused once again. Shem spoke softly to one of his Belgian workhorses while he had a look at a shoe, murmuring a promise to visit the blacksmith soon. Niklaus inhaled and exhaled without sound, a habit he found himself cultivating more frequently in these weeks of befuddlement. He had no wish to harm his friend.

"Shem," he finally said.

Shem gently let the horse's leg down before looking up at Niklaus.

"I have thought a great deal about our conversations," Niklaus said, "and I have come to a decision."

"God is faithful and just to forgive us our sins," Shem said.

Inhale. Exhale.

"I have not come to confess or repent," Niklaus said.

Shem straightened to his full height.

"You are right that my sermon had the

possibility to cause some confusion for the congregation," Niklaus said. "They have trusted me to be their minister. I have no wish to confuse them."

Shem waited.

"You challenged me to consider whether my actions were in the interest of the congregation." Niklaus shifted his feet. "While I do not believe that a livelier style of preaching or an exhortation to know God in personal ways disrespects our tradition, I can see your point that our disagreement on the matter might be perceived as conflict. We should not pit minister against minister."

"Then perhaps we are not as far apart as I thought," Shem said. "You are thinking wisely. I am certain we will be of one mind again soon."

Niklaus shook his head. "Shem, my decision is that I will best serve the congregation by withdrawing. Then there can be no confusion in leadership."

"Withdraw?" Shem eyed another hoof. "I do not understand. Yohan and I will simply handle the preaching until you are ready to resume."

"I must withdraw," Niklaus said. "I do not regret the sermon that disturbed you, and I do not believe I ever will. I will step aside so that there should be no animosity between us in the midst of the congregation."

"Surely this is temporary," Shem said.

Niklaus shook his head. "You are awaiting repentance. At the risk that you will think my heart hardened, I must honestly say the wait will be futile. I have chosen another way forward."

At the sound of the galloping horse, Susanna looked up from her dye vat. Her brother Timothy did not slow the animal as he passed her shed and continued toward the house.

"Timothy!" Susanna called as she reached for the poker and gave the wood one last separating shove. The yardage she had simmered that morning was already spread on the lines. But her brother could not have heard her cry beneath his horse's hooves. On foot, Susanna chased him toward the house. By the time she reached him, breathless, Timothy was off his horse and broadcasting his news to their mother.

Veronica's face paled.

"What?" Susanna said. "What is it?"

"Your Adam will have something to say," Timothy said.

"He is not my Adam." Susanna fished for the memory of the errand her father had sent Timothy on after breakfast. "Is everyone all right?"

"This is just the kind of influence I try to protect my children from," Veronica said.

Only one topic would make Veronica make that statement. Noah.

"What is it, Timothy?" Susanna asked, striving for a tone calmer than her nerves.

"Niklaus plans to withdraw from the church."

"Oh no. Who would tell you such a thing?"

"Jonas."

"It is speculation," Susanna said.

Timothy shook his head. "Niklaus told the family himself as soon as he spoke to the bishop."

"But why?"

" 'Tis the preaching," Timothy said. "They cannot agree."

Veronica sobbed. "Your *daed* should never have agreed to any of this. Susanna, you must spend more time at home for the sake of your family."

"But Noah is our family as well," Susanna said. "Noah and Phoebe are our family."

Susanna had been a timid child, and Noah always made room for her. When she hid, he found her. When she laughed, he laughed with her. The thought that she might be removed from him against her will made her chest burn.

"You will be safer if you remain on the farm," her mother said.

"And Phoebe?" Susanna challenged. "And Noah? Are we to turn our backs on them?"

"We will discuss this later, once your *daed* is here," Veronica said.

Susanna contained her sigh. She could not refuse her mother's wishes, but her father's return would not be for hours.

"Phoebe is expecting me soon." Susanna avoided her mother's eyes as she whistled for the old mare in the pasture. The horse was the slowest creature on four legs, but Susanna managed to busy herself in preparations long enough for the mare to come to the pasture gate. She would take her back down to the shed and hitch her up.

Her head pounded with the rising conundrum, and she was unsure how long she had overlooked the sound of a second set of hooves before twisting to look.

"Timothy, what are you doing?"

"I am going with you." He pulled his horse up beside the cart.

"You know *Mamm* will be displeased." Susanna did not slow down.

"More and more people are talking about Noah, and I have not even heard him for myself except for a few minutes the first time it happened."

"What will you say to *Mamm*?" Susanna said. "Go home before you make things worse."

"Will you go home?"

"No. That is a different matter."

"How?"

"Phoebe is expecting me, and Daed has given his blessing." At least he had until this point. He might change his mind.

"I can do a man's work, if need be. I looked after their animals while you were gone. If it is all right for you to hear Cousin Noah and help on their farm, why should it not be so for me?"

Susanna blew out her breath. "He might not preach."

"I hear tell that it happens every day."

Susanna nudged the mare faster. "You may stay for a few minutes. Then you must go home before *Mamm* misses you."

With Susanna's help, Patsy settled the slouched and sleeping Noah on the davenport. Phoebe finally had rearranged the room so the davenport where Noah recovered from falling under was near the window. If he wandered while preaching, he nearly always returned to the window before speaking the Lord's Prayer.

"Another fine sermon." Patsy did not have

to lower her voice. A trail of children could march through the house beating pots and leading bleating goats and Noah would not stir.

Susanna rubbed her eyes. "Which of us shall go outside and encourage folks to go home?"

"I'll go this time." Patsy straightened her skirt and checked to be sure the blouse was well tucked at the waist.

"Thank you," Susanna said. "I am glad Phoebe is napping herself. I fear she hardly sleeps at night. I will tidy the kitchen and put something in the oven for a late supper when they wake."

Patsy nodded, spread a nine-patch quilt over Noah, and padded to the front door.

"Noah is resting now," she announced. "He will not preach again today."

Not many people could spare the time to remain on the Kauffman farm for the entire three hours that Noah was likely to preach. They had their own suppers to go home to, so the crowd had thinned already. Patsy would like to think that those who stayed until the end were the most devout, but more likely they were the most suspicious. Seven people remained, all of them Amish.

"I suppose your kind are very pleased."

Patsy did not know the woman's name,

but her tone held no mystery.

"My kind?" Patsy said.

"Your father is the Methodist minister, is he not?"

"He is."

"He might do well to reconsider what he is doing."

"I'm afraid I don't understand," Patsy said. No one coerced anyone to hear Noah preach. If this woman was displeased by Noah's actions, why had she come — more than once?

"We have no hard feelings about what your father chooses to preach to his own flock, but I would think he would understand the harm he causes by his evangelistic spirit."

Evangelistic spirit? "If you read the New Testament," Patsy said, "you will find that Jesus Himself had an evangelistic spirit and that the apostles Paul and Peter did not hesitate to preach the good news."

The woman gasped. "Young woman, I will pray for your soul."

"And I yours." Patsy glared.

Behind her the front door opened.

"May God go with you all," Susanna said. She yanked on Patsy's elbow and pulled her closer to the house.

"I am not certain you are much different," the woman said. "You encourage Noah when you know how the bishop feels about this. 'Tis no secret that you journeyed with them on the Methodist preaching tour."

"I did not intend it should be," Susanna said.

Patsy turned, surprised at Susanna's stance.

"If Noah had not gone with Mr. Baxton, perhaps this would have died out by now." An Amish man spoke.

"Why should it die out?" Patsy said. "If you come to hear him, you must find some merit in the experience."

"Then perhaps we shan't return."

Patsy raised an eyebrow. With Susanna's hand still on her elbow, she waited until the yard was cleared.

"Do you think that was wise?" Susanna said.

Patsy faced her friend. "Do you think it was avoidable?"

CHAPTER 21

For Adam, Friday morning was consumed with work inside Jonas's addition. Jonas had brought Anke to admire and anticipate, and her visit had turned into an inspection as well, as she ran her fingers over freshly installed woodwork.

Shem was earnest when he said he would leave the rest of the project to Adam, as evidenced by his absence from the Zug farm except to attend church. Niklaus tried to spend more time on the room, deferring to Adam's instructions in the details, and made sure Jonas was available for any remaining task that demanded the vigor of youth. Adam felt he had been thrown into an icy lake. Nevertheless, every day brought the project closer to completion, well before Jonas's wedding day.

After informing his household that he would not be attending church but they should feel free to do so, Niklaus did not speak of his conversation with the bishop. Jonas had. Adam had interrupted a conversation between Jonas and Timothy Hooley. Susanna would surely know by now. The entire congregation would surely know, and Niklaus's absence from worship on Sunday would be final confirmation of his intent.

Adam dropped his hammer into the toolbox and moved it to the corner of the room. He had built a room for his cousin's bride. Someday he would build a house for his own bride.

Susanna.

He avoided going to the Kauffmans' during the hours when he knew that Noah might be having one of his spells, especially after his last visit, when Mr. Grauman pestered Noah with pebbles. But Susanna spent as much time there as she could. Regardless of his personal opinions, if Adam wanted to see her, he would have to go to the Kauffman farm. It was much closer than the Hooley farm, but he missed the way Susanna used to wander through the Zug land on her collections and how easily he slipped into joining her.

Adam stepped into daylight, lifting his eyes to judge the time. It was late enough that Noah would have finished but early enough that Susanna might still be there helping Phoebe while Noah rested. Adam glanced at his horse and decided to walk. If he took the back paths that cut through the pastures, the distance was barely a mile and a half, and a brisk walk would settle his nerves.

When Adam emerged from the Kauffmans' fields — which looked as if they could do with some tending — he spied Susanna's cart. He was barely in time. In another few minutes, she would be finished hitching it to the old mare and on her way home.

"Susanna!" Adam called to her.

Susanna's head lifted, the bonnet rising first and then tilting back far enough for him to see her dark eyes. He knew the expression well — her impulse to be glad to see him. But it shifted, like a once vibrant color washed out and now only harboring memories.

"Hello, Adam," she finally said.

"Is your cousin well?" Now that he was close, he slowed his steps.

"Resting." Her eyes dropped to the shafts of the cart she gripped with both hands.

"Let me help you." Adam placed his hands next to hers on the shafts and breathed in her fragrance, a mixture of bark and berries and flowers that no *English* perfume maker could ever hope to duplicate.

Susanna released her grasp and allowed Adam to run the shafts to the waiting leather loops.

"Before you go," he said, "I want to invite you on an outing."

Her shoulders rose and fell with a breath. Had they become thinner?

"Jonas and Anke and some of the others will take a walk and a picnic supper tomorrow afternoon. I would love to have you with us."

She sucked her lips in slightly.

"Will Patsy be here?" Adam asked.

Susanna nodded.

"Then perhaps you can leave a little early and join us."

"Perhaps."

"We can hunt for what you need in your dyes."

"I do need a few things." Hesitation faded.

"Shall I come for you here?" Adam said. It almost felt like their old ways. The words were right for the most part, at least, and did not seem to be leading to a quarrel.

"I will walk over here tomorrow," she said, "so we will not have to worry about my horse and cart."

Adam nodded. She would want him to

take her home. And he would want to.

"And if my *mamm* does not object," she said.

Adam smiled. Veronica Hooley objected to many things, but he was certain he was not one of them.

Susanna and Adam straggled behind the others. Although on the surface it was simply a group outing of friends from the same church, everyone was well paired. These young men took these young women home from church and singings and picnics so predictably that parents looked out windows with slight smiles at their arrival — most of them. Trina's father was not fond of LeRoy, but Susanna doubted he would forbid their union when the time came. Once they got over their initial suspicion of Adam's reasons for moving away from his home district, the Hooleys never once suggested that he was unsuitable for their daughter. Susanna never spoke of it with her mother, but more than once she had seen Veronica's eyes in the candlelight of the upstairs window when Adam drove her home in his buggy, holding a mother's natural observance but no disapproval. He had even had supper with the Hooleys three times.

"Over there." Adam pointed.

Immediately Susanna saw what had caught his eye. "Wintergreen berries," he said. "Am I right?"

She smiled. His eagerness warmed her.

"You are exactly right," she said.

"Can you use them?"

Susanna nodded. The basket dangling from her fingers contained drawstring bags made of muslin for just this purpose.

They crossed the road to the prolific patch of lower shrubs growing with newly-ripened red berries against leaves of green. Adam squatted to pick berries and Susanna held open a bag.

"The leaves make good tea," she said. "Do not hesitate to take some."

He broke off some leaves and stacked them in one hand while continuing to drop berries into the tiny open sack.

"How many do you need?" he asked.

"A few will go a long way in altering a hue." She had little demand for fabric dyed the bright red of a wintergreen berry. Few of the Amish women would wear a color that drew such attention to themselves. Though they might use it in a quilt, they would first use scraps from their clothing. Susanna thought of the stacks of folded yardage in the *English* mercantile. What if she were to dye short lengths in brighter colors? The women of her church might purchase them for small piecework.

Susanna sighed as Adam placed the leaves in her basket and gently laid the berries against the cushioning he had created. She handed him another bag.

"More?" He raised his eyebrows.

She nodded. If no one else wanted the color, she would use it herself in her next quilt. And she would always remember this day that Adam found the berries. Not many men would walk the edge of the forest or go up the mountain with an eye for color. But Adam would. In the beginning, it was a guise for being able to walk and talk privately. In those days, Susanna had done all the spotting of bark and berries and roots. But Adam had learned well.

His devotedness was very sweet.

They could have decades together spotting color in God's creation and imagining how they might bring its beauty into their home. Certainly they both felt the possibility of this happiness.

But when Noah had begun preaching, everything changed.

Susanna's basket overflowed by the time the group reached their intended picnic spot.

Adam, who had taken it from her as it filled with berries and dandelion roots and acorns and leaves, set it safely in the shade of a tree before joining the men in spreading a couple of blankets and salivating at the food the women had packed. Cold sliced ham. Potato salad. Black bread. Juicy tomatoes. Peach and apple pies.

It was right that Adam and Susanna felt at ease among these friends. If any of them were not married by this time next year, Adam would be stunned. Certainly he wanted to be. He wanted more days like this, more days of just the two of them wandering the forest or one day guiding their toddling *boppli* to know the difference between safe and poisonous berries.

"Jonas," Seth said, "I heard about your *daed.*"

Everyone knew. Adam controlled his exhale, wishing that the perfection of the day were not sullied by such a discussion.

Jonas shrugged. "He is acting on his conscience. Is that not the way of our people?"

"Have you been to hear Noah?" LeRoy asked.

"I have not," Jonas said. "If you want to know about that, Susanna is the one to ask."

"So I understand," LeRoy said.

261

Adam scanned the group. Of the dozen gathered, at least three others had been to hear Noah. Why must they single out Susanna?

"I think I will go," Anke said. "I understand it happens every afternoon. Surely I can find the time one day."

"What of how the bishop feels?" Jonas said. Adam saw the surprise in his cousin's face that his betrothed would make this suggestion.

"If your *daed* is willing to make the decision he has, can there not be some merit?" Seth commented.

"I want to go," Anke said. "I just want to see for myself. We should all go. It would be a fun outing."

Beside Adam, Susanna bristled. Adam sat a little straighter, abandoning the bite of pie on its way to his mouth.

"Noah is not a spectacle for entertainment," Susanna said. "If you do not come seeking spiritual edification, it is best to seek other amusement."

"Of course I did not mean that," Anke said quickly.

Adam rearranged his legs, foundering to change the topic of conversation. What could they talk about that did not have to do with the church?

"We should come out here more often," Adam said, "especially before the harvest takes all our time and then the weather turns cold."

His effort went unheard.

"I agree with Anke," Trina said. "We should go listen to Noah — for the right reasons, as Susanna suggests."

"I have been several times," Barbara said. " 'Tis a sight, but he does speak the Word of God."

Seth chuckled. "But you also went to the Methodist tent meeting."

"I was not alone," Barbara said, eyeing Seth.

Adam ticked off in his mind the owners of rigs he had seen parked outside Charles Baxton's tent. Shem's words echoed. *You must speak up when you are with the young people.*

"I do not think what Noah does is right." Johannes offered his opinion while stretching out his form to lean on one elbow with a good view of Ruth. "The bishop is right to want it to stop. If you do something enough times, it becomes your habit, but that does not mean it is also genuine."

"Why can it not be real?" LeRoy challenged. "You must come and see for yourself before you can judge."

263

"Only God can judge a man's heart."

"But God looks at the heart before judging."

"Do not go." The words burst out of Adam's mouth before he could reconsider. He did not want to reconsider. The bishop was right. "We have all been baptized and made promises. Now is the time to keep them, for the good of the church."

"So you think my *daed* is wrong?" Jonas said.

Jonas's eyes burned into Adam's face, but he did not meet his cousin's eyes. He had no words to respond.

"Do you think Noah is doing something wrong?" Susanna said. "That he is being willful in disobedience to the church?"

Adam cleared his throat. "The bishop is concerned for the welfare of the congregation. I only mean to point out that we also have promised to be concerned for the welfare of the congregation and choose the path of submission. If the bishop believes we may come to harm, should we not heed the warning?"

Susanna began packing up leftover food. "I should get home."

When a few minutes later Adam bent to pick up her basket, Susanna snatched it from him and set a pace that she did not mean for him to keep up with.

CHAPTER 22

"I want to learn to do that." Patsy hinged at the waist to peer into the vat.

"I doubt it," Susanna said. "If you could see the way you scrunch up your nose when you look in my pots, you would know you do not want to learn to dye."

"I concede," Patsy said. There was no point in debating. She admired Susanna's skill and determination, but in the middle of the nineteenth century, with a mercantile in every town and factories in the cities, why would she don long gloves and stand over a simmering pot stirring with a wooden paddle?

"Thank you for keeping me company anyway," Susanna said.

Susanna had been quiet since Patsy's arrival nearly an hour ago. Patsy chalked it up to concentration on her task. Now it seemed something more. Fifteen years of friendship told her to wait. Susanna would speak when she was ready.

"It soothes me to do something normal," Susanna said, stirring. "So many things feel out of control."

"Noah?" Patsy asked.

Susanna chuckled. "Noah's preaching is starting to feel like the most unremarkable part of my day. 'Tis what everyone has to say about Noah — and Niklaus Zug and the bishop and your *daed,* and I suppose, even me. At church yesterday the bishop preached on submission for the third time in a row."

"Surely submission to God is what matters most," Patsy said. "True spiritual submission, not only obeying a man."

Susanna stirred, silent.

"I'm sorry," Patsy said. "I do not mean to criticize your faith."

"Our calling is to reside quietly in Christ," Susanna said.

Turn the other cheek. Go with him a second mile. Patsy could quote the same Bible verses Susanna knew about maintaining a mild spirit even when persecuted. But surely there were circumstances that cried out for righteousness.

"My father does not belong to your church," Patsy said. "They cannot ask him to submit to your bishop."

"They would not do such a thing," Susanna said.

"He is not even here to defend himself, because he is off preaching the gospel and ministering."

"That is what God calls him to do."

"Then why are they angry with him?"

"We live apart," Susanna said.

"You have been saying that for years." Patsy picked up a poker and stabbed at flames beneath Susanna's pot. "Yet you and I are friends. The Amish buy goods from others when they need to."

Susanna stirred. "Where the outside world influences us, danger lies."

Patsy circled around the pot. "Are you afraid the friend of your childhood will influence you to the point of sin?"

"You? No. You and I understand each other."

Patsy was not sure on that point in the moment.

" 'Tis not that way for everyone," Susanna said.

"You confuse me, Susanna Hooley." Patsy stood still and crossed her arms. "You hear Noah preach. You are moved by his sermons. I see it in your face. You saw for yourself how people responded when Noah preached with my father."

Susanna nodded.

"Then how can you defend Shem Hertzberger?"

"He is my bishop."

"I will have a word with your bishop. I will defend my father — and Niklaus and Noah and you and any other Amish who have found encouragement in Noah's ministry."

"Please do not do that."

"What about Adam?" Patsy said. "What are his opinions?"

Susanna's answer came a beat late. "He is mindful of the bishop's role as our spiritual leader."

"Does he not have an opinion of his own?"

Susanna lifted her paddle from the vat, took the poker from Patsy, and pushed apart the coals under the pot. Patsy's announced strategy would only make things worse. Susanna turned to look her friend in the eye but instead looked past her.

"Your mother is here," Susanna announced.

Patsy pivoted as the door closed behind her mother. "Mama, is everything all right?"

Mercy Baxton's visits to the Hooley farm were not unheard of, but they were infrequent. More often, Susanna saw Mercy when she visited the Baxton farm. She had always thought Patsy's mother was well named. Mercy. Had her character formed under the spiritual mantle of the name, or had her parents seen something in the disposition of their infant daughter that prompted the moniker?

"What wondrous hue are you concocting today?" Mercy asked. She looked into the pot without the least suggestion of scrunching her nose, but with eyes wide in curiosity.

"I am experimenting," Susanna said. If she had done well, the result would be a deep violet cloth, enough for at least three dresses. With the paddle, she found a loose edge of fabric and briefly lifted it from the bath of color.

"Lovely!" Mercy said. "Such beautiful colors you have in your imagination."

"Only those I see in God's world around me," Susanna said.

"Have you come for me, Mama?" Patsy said.

"I simply felt like a stroll and thought I might find the two of you here," Mercy said. "Susanna, may I be one of your customers? I would love to have a dress made from your cloth."

"Of course," Susanna said.

"Yellow, I think," Mercy said. "The color of a field of sunflowers on a golden summer day."

Yellow? Susanna had sometimes added a yellow hue to a brown bath, or even to tinge blue, but yellow cloth had not crossed her mind. The women in her congregation favored muted tones.

"I am not sure," Susanna said.

"You can do it," Patsy said.

Perhaps yellow would do for a quilt, just as red might. Even among the Amish she might find those who dared the occasional yellow triangle or square. But catering to the fashions of the *English* in a way she could not also serve her own people was a conundrum Susanna had not yet faced.

"Look, here comes your mother," Mercy said, at least temporarily distracted from her request.

Susanna once again removed the paddle from the vat to let the cloth rest in the liquid and absorb its tint. A conversation with one mother or the other was uneventful. But both mothers together was an event so infrequent — only a few times a year — as to be unpredictable in its outcome. Mercy would live up to her name. It was her own mother who made Susanna nervous.

"Hello, Mercy," Veronica said. "I pray God

271

is blessing you."

Mercy nodded. "He is faithful."

"And your husband is well?"

"By God's grace. He is ministering even now."

Veronica turned her attention to Patsy. "You look well also."

"I am very well," Patsy said, friendly caution falling on Susanna's ears in her tone.

"And how is your cloth?" Veronica said to Susanna.

"It seems to be taking the color well," Susanna said.

" 'Tis lovely you could both drop by for a visit." Veronica even smiled.

By nature, Susanna's mother was a person who got to the point. This string of polite inquiries unsettled Susanna. Her *mamm* could not have expected to find guests in the area where Susanna worked. She had come for a reason but held herself back in their presence.

Patsy shifted her weight from foot to foot. She would endure her own mother's chastisement for being rude if necessary, but a body could listen to innocuous inquiries about well-being for only so long.

"It's time I was off to the Kauffman place," Patsy said. "Susanna, will you be able to come today?"

The glance between Susanna and Veronica did not escape Patsy, and she wished she had not caused it. Perhaps she hadn't. Perhaps they looked at each other this way every day before Susanna left for Noah's.

"The fabric must stay in the bath another half hour," Susanna said. "Then I will have to spread it to dry."

Patsy nodded. "So you will come when you are able." *And if you are not able, I will understand.*

"Did neither of you bring a wagon?" Veronica asked.

"It's hardly any walk at all," Mercy said. "And the afternoon is fine."

"We can walk home together," Patsy said. She would saddle Galahad and ride swiftly to the Kauffmans'.

Mother and daughter said polite farewells and left their neighbors.

"I have never quite understood Veronica Hooley," Mercy said, once they were beyond earshot. "She can be quite a cordial woman until she gets a bee in her bonnet about something. Then her pleasantries begin to grate."

Patsy laughed. "I thought it was just me."

"The dilemma is that I rarely know what has put the bee in her bonnet."

"I'm pretty sure I know this time," Patsy said.

"You do?"

"Not specifically. But it has to do with Noah Kauffman. Apparently the Amish congregation is all in a dither with his preaching."

"I see," Mercy said. "Is there anything to be in a dither about? Your father says he does very well."

"He does. But he is not a minister, and the way he falls under the influence of the Holy Ghost is troublesome."

"You mean because he is in a trance or asleep?"

Patsy nodded.

"But we have heard of many other trance preachers," Mercy said. "Your father brings news of them when he meets with other ministers. God works in mysterious ways."

"It seems that the Amish prefer spiritual matters to be less mysterious." Patsy sighed. "Why don't you come with me today? It's about time you heard Noah for yourself."

"*Mamm,* I do not understand." Susanna kicked at a smoldering log in equal parts necessity and frustration.

" 'Tis clear enough," her mother said. " 'Tis not against *Ordnung* to move from

274

one district to another if God leads the way with opportunity or merely simple faith."

"But you have lived in the valley all your life. You and Daed have built this farm together." Using her largest paddle, Susanna lifted the soaking fabric out of the dye bath, impatient for the end of both her task and this conversation.

"And I pray we will live many more years together in a new land building a new farm."

A new land? Indiana was hardly the promised land of the Bible.

"So we will go through our belongings," Veronica said. "There is no need to keep every little thing we have ever owned."

Susanna could not think of what to say. Indiana! She squeezed excess liquid out of the fabric with less care than usual. As soon as she hung it from the line or spread it over the bushes, she could leave the farm.

"Do not look so shocked," Veronica said. "Belongings are material possessions of this world. They have no eternal value."

" 'Tis not the things I am surprised about," Susanna managed to say.

"Indiana, then?"

"Our church is here," Susanna said. "The people who know us. Your family is just in the next county, and Daed's also."

"Between your *daed* and me, we have

275

dozens of cousins — and so do you. We are likely to have relatives in any district we settle in."

Susanna could not dispute her mother's logic on that point. Both of her parents came from families with eight children, and her grandparents from families even larger. It would be hard for any Amish church member not to find a family thread tracing to a shared relative among nearly any congregation.

Veronica looked around. "You have mostly pots and jars out here. Indiana will have pots and jars and all the roots and bark you need."

"*Mamm,* I have spent years learning to dye."

"And you have done well, my daughter. No matter where we go, you will contribute to the congregation."

"What about the farm? The animals?" Susanna said. Surely her parents had not already made a firm decision. Daed would have told her. Or Timothy's nosiness would have come in handy and he would have reported what he overheard.

Veronica waved away Susanna's concerns. " 'Twill be only a matter of time. 'Tis a good farm, and the animals are sturdy and serviceable. Your old mare will be the only one difficult to sell. Your *daed* can just put her down."

"Mamm!"

"You must be realistic, Susanna. We may as well be ready. When the time comes, we can go without a fuss." Veronica pivoted and walked toward the house.

Susanna waited until her mother was out of sight before whistling for the mare and setting out for the Kauffmans' farm. Just shy of the Zugs' property, she slowed and then stopped.

"Noah?" she called. He was walking the other direction — away from home.

"Oh, Susanna. Lovely to run into you." Noah tipped his straw hat.

"Can I give you a ride somewhere?" Susanna dropped the reins and stepped out of the cart to meet Noah.

"I thought it was a nice day for a walk. That is all."

Susanna squinted into the sunlight. " 'Tis a very nice day. Have you been out walking very long?"

"Half an hour or so. Phoebe fusses too much, but surely a brief constitutional can do me no harm."

As long as you do not lose consciousness.

"Do you mind if I walk with you?" Susanna asked.

"You look like you were on your way somewhere," Noah said.

"Only to your house," she said, "to see how I might be of help to Phoebe."

"You are a sweet child. You always have been."

"*Danki,* Cousin Noah."

He was perspiring, and Susanna regretted not filling a jug at the well before she left home.

"Phoebe probably has some cold tea waiting for you." Susanna looked again at the sun, judging that Noah would fall under inside half an hour. "Did you tell her how long you expected to be gone?"

"She was busy," Noah said. "There was no need to bother her."

Susanna's stomach lurched. "I would be happy to take you home."

"I thought I might walk a bit farther."

"Then I would be happy to walk with you."

"What about your horse and cart?"

Susanna laughed. "You know this mare. She is not one for speed. I will just lead her."

"I suppose if I turned around now, I would still have a good walk."

Susanna nodded. "Two miles this way and two miles back."

Noah reached out for the reins. "Come

on, girl, let's go home."

Susanna wished she could spare Noah what awaited him on his own land, but the safest place for him was home.

"If you are looking for adventure," Susanna said, "we could go exploring on the way back." They could cut through the Zug property, go along the edge of the forest, and approach Noah's farm from the back. She might even get him into the house without being seen by the crowd.

"I think I might just be up for a bit of adventure," Noah said.

Susanna let out a breath of relief. Phoebe would be frantic if she discovered Noah had left the farm, but at least now he would not be alone if he collapsed before they reached home.

"You always were a child who wanted adventure," Noah said. "I have not forgotten the time you frightened the daylights out of all of us when you climbed down the old rope in an empty well."

"And then I could not get up," Susanna said. "But you were the one to find me just as I realized I ought to be afraid. I have never forgotten."

"Our little secret. I got you out, returned you to your parents, and that was the end of it."

"You never told them?"

"Never." Noah stopped walking. "I have changed my mind. It might be better if we rode in the cart."

"Of course," Susanna said, "but we shall still take the back way."

CHAPTER 23

Adam slid off his horse at the Kauffman
farm. The picnic had been a disaster, and
Susanna had barely looked in his direction
at church the following day. At the meal,
Adam found himself trapped at a table with
Mr. Zimmerman, who shared his wife's
public and suspicious views about Noah
Kauffman's trickery. Of course Susanna
would not catch his eye under those circumstances, and she had gone home with her
family rather than stay for the activities. On
Monday as he worked, Adam tried also to
pray. He had always imagined that doing
the right thing would be more straight-
forward than this. Before dawn on Tuesday,
Adam woke with the words of Isaiah in his
mind. *"For the Lord God will help me; therefore shall I not be confounded: therefore have
I set my face like a flint, and I know that I shall
not be ashamed."*

He set his face like a flint to make things

right with Susanna.

Somehow.

The benches outside Noah's window were full by the time Adam arrived that afternoon. He had not expected to sit, nor had he wanted to. Susanna, not Noah, drew him to the farm. Nevertheless, the number of the assembly alarmed him. This was the largest number he had witnessed. Would it continue to rise? Some of the Amish in the front benches had not even been in church two days earlier. The squirming and chattering were worse than you would find in a flock of jaybirds.

Adam's stomach hardened and soured. It was one thing for Shem to decide not to come to Niklaus's land any longer, but it was another to absent himself from this scene. Shem's incessant stern sermons about submission were not diminishing the interest in Noah, but one sight of the bishop might send the congregation's members back to their farms. What the *English* did would be up to them.

As he led his horse to a fence post where he could tie the animal, Adam's eyes swept the scene. Noah was in the window turning pages in his Bible. Even Adam knew he sometimes did this for several minutes before breaking forth in speech. Patsy was at his side. Phoebe would be in the kitchen or the barn or away at her sister's. If this was one of the rare days when Susanna did not come, Adam would ride over to the Hooley place. He circled to the side of the house, where his unexpected presence startled a young *English* girl and sent her scampering to the front yard where she belonged.

Except she did not belong there either. No one did.

The back door cracked open, and Susanna's dark eyes peeked out. "Adam."

If only they were walking in the forest. He would take the basket from her hands and lean in to kiss her. As it was, she might never let him do that again.

Adam swallowed. "The crowd today."

"Worse than ever," she said, stepping outside. "I want to believe the best of their hearts, but some of them make it difficult."

Adam nodded. "Where is the edification?"

"I asked the very same question just a few minutes ago. I fear it is drowned out."

At last they found something to agree on.

"If they cannot come with seeking hearts, they should not come."

Adam's heart sought only Susanna.

"I wanted to explain what happened on the picnic," he said.

Susanna covered her face with both hands and exhaled before moving them aside. "Adam, I know this is difficult for you to understand. But I must be here, and I do not believe Noah is willful."

"Neither do I," he said. " 'Tis the crowd in front that I find willful."

"Some of them," she said, guarded. "Some do come with pure motives."

"God sees the heart." If Adam knew the right words to say that would align his heart and Susanna's, he would say them with gladness. Instead, in the last few weeks, every thought that found spoken form had pushed him away from her. He heard them in his head as he lay in the dark and wondered whether he believed them.

Phoebe pushed open the back door and stepped out onto the stoop. "I pray every night for *Gottes wille,* and to know the patience of Christ, but I do not know how much more of this I can stand."

"The crowds?" Adam said.

"I try to ignore them, to reside quietly in Christ as we are taught, but they cackle like an overcrowded henhouse." Abruptly her face brightened.

"What is it?" Susanna said.

"I have an overcrowded henhouse," Phoebe said.

Adam did not understand.

"Come with me," Phoebe said.

"What about Noah?" Susanna glanced back into the house."

"Patsy will be all right on her own for a few minutes."

Adam looked at Susanna, who shrugged, and they followed Phoebe off the stoop, across the yard, and into the chicken coop. Phoebe unlatched the door, ducked in, and pulled a handful of flour sacks off a shelf.

Tossing them at Adam and Susanna, she said, "Grab some chickens."

"In the bags?" Adam said.

"Have you not ever picked up live chickens?" Phoebe asked.

A chuckle escaped Susanna.

Adam was glad to see her smile but was less enthused that her mirth came at his expense.

"I am not laughing at you," Susanna said. "I see what Phoebe means."

Susanna scooped up a chicken, deftly holding its wings to keep them from flapping.

"I will put this in your sack," she said. "Your job is to close it immediately until I get another."

"Do not forget Cranky Amos," Phoebe said, pointing at a rooster.

That a rooster should be so named made Adam take him seriously.

Within minutes they had four sacks filled with squawking, wriggling chickens. Adam and Susanna each grasped two bags in rigid fists. Phoebe picked up a pail of chicken feed and began dribbling it behind her as she left the coop and crossed the yard. Loose chickens followed and pecked.

"What are we doing?" Adam whispered to Susanna.

"Just watch."

Susanna tightened the grip of her left hand, holding both bags well away from her body. She and Adam followed Phoebe and her trail of fowl around the house to the front.

"God's call to repentance is a call of love," Noah bellowed from the window. "To repent is to receive His love."

Phoebe led the parade right up to the side of benches and then swung the pail with enough force to scatter chicken feed on the occupants. Undeterred chickens followed the food.

"Now!" Phoebe called, grabbing a bag from Adam.

They opened the bags and loosed the chickens.

The clacking and shrieking startled even

Adam. But if the outrageous scheme would sunder the crowd — and perhaps deter some from returning — there might yet be hope of bringing to an end the contentiousness around Noah's preaching.

Patsy laughed. She couldn't help it. Startled chickens flapping in the laps of doubters was as delicious as raspberry peach pie. Of course the devout were also under siege, and Patsy hoped Phoebe had the sense to use hens who were not long for the stew pot anyway, because the poor, frightened things might not lay for days after this. Cranky Amos crowed, standing tense at the base of the front bench. Patsy had fed Phoebe's chickens enough times to know what Amos might do if provoked — and it wouldn't take much to provoke him.

Noah preached on. "Hear the voice of the Lord calling you to repentance. Do not turn Him away when He knocks on the door of your heart desiring to sup with you."

Yet above the fray laughter rose. It was not the startled giggling decamping from Patsy's mouth against her best intentions, but mockery.

Mr. Grauman.

He pointed at Noah, who continued his sermon despite the disturbance outside the window at which he stood, and guffawed in an unseemly manner that defied Patsy's patience. Noah's oblivious persistence only spurred more laughter from Mr. Grauman. Patsy's clamped jaw thrust forward.

Phoebe and Susanna and Adam continued to lure and shoo chickens toward the benches, and not everyone laughed. A good number of people shoved chickens off their laps and stood up, some abandoning the bench arrangement altogether while raising elbows to shield faces from short bursts of feathered flight. Not everyone was a farmer, but chickens were common enough even for people who lived in the small town nearby. It was the distress Phoebe had stirred up in her own flock that made people reconsider their presence below the window.

"If God chastises you, it is because He loves you," Noah said. "Yield your heart to His in all things. This is what the Scripture teaches."

How could anyone see and hear Noah and not perceive God at work? The question befuddled Patsy.

Mr. Grauman was unperturbed, maintaining his position and beckoning others to come back with one hand while pointing at Noah with the other.

"Keep going, Mr. Kauffman," Mr. Grauman said, his belly rising in laughter. "That's right. Let nothing distract you. Show us what you are made of."

When Mr. Grauman bent for a pebble, Patsy reached her limit. The stove was not hot, the lamps were out of Noah's path if he should pace, and the furniture was permanently rearranged. Noah would be safe for the two minutes it would take for Patsy to execute her plan.

She scrambled out the front door, down two steps, and into the yard. Cranky Amos didn't frighten her. He would scratch her in protest, but the result would be worth the wound. Patsy marched straight for the crowing rooster with a layer of her skirt raised to wrap him. He squalled, but she triumphed. With the rooster tight in her arms, she stomped toward Mr. Grauman.

"Would you like to make fun of an angry rooster?" Patsy glared at the man. "Perhaps face-to-face?"

Mr. Grauman chortled. "That you would consider such a feat tells me you have not heard a word this man has been saying even as you stood right next to him."

Patsy lifted the rooster toward his face.

"You can be certain I will speak to your father when next I see him."

"As will I." If Patsy's father witnessed Mr.

Grauman's antics, he might well take charge of Cranky Amos himself.

"Noah!" Phoebe called her husband's name and barreled through the front door to go to his side.

Patsy heard Noah's voice but not his words. Most of the crowd, stunned, increased their distance from the altercation.

"Patsy," Adam said, coming from behind. "Let me have the rooster before he hurts you."

"I'm not afraid."

"I know."

With a slight grimace, Adam took the rooster from her. But he did not retreat with it as Patsy expected. Instead, he braced both of his feet, extended his arms forward, the cantankerous rooster in his grasp, and stood right in front of Mr. Grauman. The rooster stretched his neck toward the man's belly.

" 'Tis time for you to go," Adam said. "All of you. 'Tis time to go home."

Susanna's breath burst forth in relief. This was the Adam she craved. The man who had done what was needful to keep Noah safe during his first falling under all those weeks ago had found his footing again. They stood — Patsy, Adam, and Susanna — watching the crowd disperse.

"I am sorry that those who truly were listening could not stay," Susanna said, "but the matter is out of hand. Thank you, Adam, for your help."

Adam grinned. "Patsy, would you really have thrown the rooster in Mr. Grauman's face?"

Cranky Amos, released, continued to crow and flap his wings as if he might attack, and the three of them kept their distance.

"In the moment, it seemed right to at least give him pause," Patsy said.

"I love Noah's preaching," Susanna said, "but it is taking a toll on Phoebe."

"Perhaps she should keep the rooster in the front yard from now on," Adam said.

"Noah can preach again with my father," Patsy said. "He can still have a ministry. We could even arrange a tent meeting nearby."

Susanna appeared to consider the idea, but it was Adam who gave words.

"The bishop would never allow it," he said.

"The bishop, the bishop," Patsy said.

"Patsy!" The sharp edge in Susanna's voice surprised even her. "The bishop is not perfect, but he is still our bishop."

Patsy clamped her mouth closed.

"I apologize for my tone," Susanna said.

"We are all feeling the toll," Adam said.

We. Adam had held himself at a distance for weeks, and now he spoke of *we.* Susanna's spine tingled.

Noah's voice still carried across the yard.

"I'm going inside," Patsy said.

Standing beside Adam, Susanna let her fingers stray toward his. They faced Noah. Behind him in the front room, Patsy put an arm around Phoebe's shoulder.

"I miss Noah," Susanna said.

"But you see him every day," Adam said.

"I see this."

"I thought you like to hear him."

"I do, but by the time I come in the afternoons, he has fallen under, or will soon, and for hours afterward he sleeps deeply. I miss the talks we used to have."

"Can you not come in the mornings?"

In the mornings, Noah would be sweet and fine and himself. In the mornings, they could talk as they used to.

"I have my work," Susanna said. "Chores. My *mamm.*"

"She still disapproves?"

Susanna nodded. It was hard to find the balance between Noah's needs and her mother's shifting temperament.

"I have something you can take to your *aunti,*" she said.

They walked together to her cart, and Susanna handed Noah a bundle wrapped in brown paper and tied with string.

"I suspect you may have a new blue shirt soon," she said.

"Perhaps in time for Jonas's wedding."

Susanna nodded.

"Because you have colored the cloth," Adam said, " 'tis sure to be my favorite shirt."

Susanna flushed under his gaze, a sensation she had missed all this time.

CHAPTER 24

A few mornings later, the sizzle of sausage greeted Niklaus. Now that most of their children were married and settled in their own homes, Niklaus frequently told Deborah he could manage coffee and leftover coffee cake if he needed to eat something midmorning. Breakfast and devotions were hours ago, and as usual Deborah sent off Niklaus, Adam, and Jonas with a hearty morning meal. This offering, coming after Niklaus's morning barn chores were completed, would be just husband and wife sitting together. The effort Deborah still put into it after all these years, when her day was filled with mending, preparations for the midday dinner in another three hours, and the weeding of the vegetable garden, as well as the gathering of its ongoing summer harvest, cut straight through Niklaus. What tenderness God had given them when they married a lifetime ago, both of them barely eighteen. And what blessing it was that they should still share it now.

This is what the sizzling sausage meant.

Niklaus sat at the table, catching Deborah's free hand as she poured coffee with the other. He had nearly lost her when Jonas was born, and after that the babies came too soon. Three tiny mounds under the apple tree nearest the house marked their grief. Yet life was rich, their hearts full of abundance.

Deborah set a plate of steaming sausage and warm bread in front of Niklaus.

"I am thinking to visit Noah and Phoebe this afternoon," he said.

"They will be glad for it," Deborah said, lifting her own fork.

"Come with me."

She shook her head. "I have promised to help Mrs. Glick bind a quilt. 'Tis a gift, and she is running out of time for the occasion."

"Another time, then," Niklaus said.

"Will you go again?"

"Perhaps. I have only been in the early morning when Noah knows only the task at hand, but Adam has been going quite often when he has fallen under."

Fall under. Niklaus was still getting used to the term Charles Baxton used so easily.

Deborah smiled. "Obviously Adam goes

to see Susanna."

"Obviously," Niklaus said. "She does not happen by here as she used to. If she did, I am not sure Adam would go to the Kauffmans'."

"He seems fraught of late."

Niklaus nodded. "Change does not come easy for Adam." His nephew did not approve when Niklaus traveled with Noah and Charles, and whatever Shem said to Adam before dismissing himself from the building project had twisted the boy in knots. But his heart beat for God as surely as Niklaus's did.

"Will you go before Noah falls under?" Deborah asked.

"I will try," Niklaus said. "But even if he has begun preaching, I am sure his words will edify my spirit. And I can still speak to Phoebe to be sure she lacks for nothing until this passes."

"Will it pass? Is it that simple?"

"If it does not, I will still inquire from time to time."

"In your heart you are still a minister."

Niklaus swallowed the last of his sausage. He felt no different than he had before telling Shem he would withdraw from the congregation. No title was required for him to carry compassion to the farm next door.

■ ■ ■ ■

Adam arrived early enough to talk with Noah for a few minutes before he fell under. It was not hard to see why Susanna liked her cousin Noah as much as she did. His bright, eager eyes and wide smile put anyone at ease. But when he flushed and slumped and then stood up straight, Adam left it to Patsy and Susanna to help Noah to his place at the window. He and Noah were members of the same church. Turning his back when Noah was in danger was not something Adam would do again. But helping him to the window? Was that not condoning his preaching?

Three days had passed since Phoebe connived for Adam's complicity with the chickens. Adam had no regret. No doubt rumor left the Kauffman farm that day along with the listeners. Everyone in the Kish Valley soon would have heard that Phoebe Kauffman had turned as batty as her husband. The words would vary, but the sentiment would hold. Already three members of the Amish congregation had spoken to Adam about his own participation in the scheme. Nevertheless, the effort seemed to bring a good outcome. The benches were still there, and some people still came to sit on them, but the size of the crowd had been cut at least in half. And Mr. Grauman had not been back.

Yet.

No one could say what might happen. Noah could stop preaching tomorrow or return to the occasional nighttime rhythm.

Adam had taken to perching on the pasture fence, well away from the house, where he could survey the whole of the front portion of the Kauffman property. If there was more trouble, he would step in. If the crowd composed themselves, there would be no need to chase them off.

Niklaus strode into the Kauffman yard about twenty minutes into the sermon. Adam dropped from the fence to greet his uncle.

"I should have told you at dinner that I was thinking about coming," Niklaus said. "I did not decide for certain until after you were gone."

"So you have come to hear Noah preach?"

Niklaus lifted his bearded chin toward the house. "And to see how my friends are doing."

"As you can see, Noah has fallen under already, and Phoebe has gone to her sister's with half a wagon of food for the family."

"Then I shall try again another day," Niklaus said.

But Niklaus made no move to leave. Instead, he sauntered forward, following the sound of Noah's voice. Adam trailed.

"Onkel," Adam said, "people at church miss you. They want to hear your sermons again."

"You are kind to say so," Niklaus said, "but I am afraid that is unlikely."

"Even Noah preaches about repentance," Adam said. "He speaks of it as a way that we know God's kindness."

Niklaus nodded. "I would say the same."

Adam swallowed hard. "Then why do you not repent and return to church? Everything could go back to normal."

"Normal?" Niklaus halted his steps and turned to look at Adam. "And what is the true normal our hearts should desire? What we have always known or the glory that might lie ahead?"

"Mr. Zug!"

Niklaus turned his head to see both Susanna and Patsy crossing the yard to meet him. His conversation with Adam, whose shoulders slumped slightly at the intrusion, would have to wait. Niklaus had little more to say anyway. He had not, and would not, suggest that Adam or anyone follow his decision to withdraw from the Amish congregation. If he returned, it would be because the Spirit of God stirred him to do so, not because he feared Shem's opinion that he had become an unrepentant apostate.

"You've come to hear Noah?" Patsy's inquiry lilted with hope.

"I have," Niklaus said. "I visited Noah early one morning last week, but I can see it is quite different in the afternoon."

Noah was in the window, his voice projecting across the farm in a way Niklaus would not have thought possible for his mild-mannered neighbor if he had not heard it for himself on earlier occasions.

"God's mercies are new every morning." Susanna spoke for the first time. "That is the sermon today. A good word for everyone."

The four of them — Niklaus, Adam, Susanna, and Patsy — angled toward the house.

"This is the first time we've been together since the preaching trip," Patsy said. "Such a marvelous journey."

Niklaus had agreed to the four-day excursion for the safekeeping of his friend. But the trip had lit his spirit with the light of a thousand candles. No doubt remained in his mind that Noah was compelled to preach Christ — and that he recalled nothing of it. When Niklaus and Noah spoke, Noah could not recall what he had preached the day before or say what passage of Scripture might be the basis for the next falling under.

The benches below the window allowed Niklaus his choice of seating. He had heard about the chickens. A story like that did not stay hidden under a bushel for long. When it reached Shem's ears, it might result in consequences for Adam, Phoebe, and Susanna. Niklaus would defend them. Adam's account was persuasive. An element of the crowd had been out of hand.

They stood now behind the last row of benches.

"One of us should go back inside," Susanna said. "I will go."

"I will keep an eye on the back door," Patsy said. "Adam can watch the front — and now we have Mr. Zug to help if something happens."

Adam's eyes trailed Susanna's movements, and Niklaus's gaze traveled from his befuddled nephew to the young woman who was the best match God could bring to Adam's heart. She approached the front stoop, took two steps up, went inside, and took her place a few feet to one side of Noah. Phoebe leaned toward her for a brief word and then crossed the room out of sight.

They had a system for surrounding Noah with care — Phoebe, Susanna, Patsy, and it seemed, Adam, reluctant as he was.

"Patsy," Niklaus said, "when does your father return home?"

"He only just left again. I would not expect him home again for a couple of weeks."

Niklaus scratched under his chin. "Would you favor me by telling him that his old friend would like to see him?"

"Of course. Shall I tell him the matter you would like to discuss?"

"Preaching."

"Noah's?"

"No, mine."

"So you will go back to church?"

Niklaus shook his head. "Perhaps on a circuit."

Patsy squealed. "Papa would be delighted to have you with him."

"I am still praying on the matter." Niklaus ignored the stiffening of his nephew's posture. "Your father knows me well, and

302

he knows preaching. He will be a wise counselor."

"A circuit!" Patsy's eyes glowed. "Perhaps you and Papa and Noah will all go together someday."

"Perhaps."

Adam gripped his uncle's open elbow and gave a slight pull.

"Onkel."

"Yes, nephew."

"May we speak privately?"

Patsy's hand swept in a wave. "I must get back to my post in the back. Papa will be so excited."

Adam let her gain some distance before speaking again. He had always looked up to his uncle as a wise man, but the last few weeks were befuddling.

"Do you think the time is right for this?" Adam said. "Your status with the congregation is not settled."

Niklaus raised his eyebrows. "Is it not?"

"If you do this, Shem may ban you."

"First would come an official warning."

"Surely you do not want to provoke such a warning." Adam stared into his uncle's eyes.

Niklaus paused for a deep breath. "I do nothing on a whim, Adam."

"I know," Adam said, his voice soft. His uncle was reasonable, thoughtful. If he were not, his recent statements would not dumbfound Adam as they did.

Niklaus gestured toward Noah. "Do his words not touch you?"

"Of course they do."

"Do you hear truth in them?"

"I suppose so."

"When you have experienced the Holy Ghost as I have, you would see that it is difficult to turn back."

"But our unity, Onkel. Our vows."

"My nephew, you know all the hymns of our tradition."

Adam nodded.

"They are two hundred years old, yet we sing them."

"The truth of God does not change," Adam said.

"The hymns tell us our own history," Niklaus said. "Our faith came from the bravery of men who believed the church must change — that God called them to bring change. Shall I miss God's call because Shem does not hear it?"

CHAPTER 25

Susanna stood, took the thick German Bible from her father's hands, and hefted it onto the handcrafted stand where he liked to keep it. The Hooley family Bible was larger and heavier than the one Noah used. Still, Susanna was impressed Noah could hold his in one hand at times. Her little brothers dared to squirm now, having sat still while Elias read from the tome and offered his reflection on what the apostle Paul said about a man's duty for headship in his home. With four sons, and one of them old enough to have his head turned by the young women in the congregation, Elias had begun leading family devotions on this topic a couple of times a month, glancing at Timothy more than anyone else. Susanna's mother, on the other hand, steered her glances in Susanna's direction, as if she thought Susanna needed this lesson. They did not speak much of Susanna's afternoon excursions to the Kauffmans'. And Veronica had stopped staying away completely herself. She had visited her relatives twice immediately after breakfast, when Susanna could assure her that not only would Noah not be preaching but she was unlikely to encounter anyone else from the Amish congregation. Both times she returned home to report how well Noah looked and oozed optimism for a full recovery, for which she would earnestly pray. But every time Susanna left in the afternoon, she felt her mother's eyes on her, even from halfway across the farm.

Veronica cleared her throat. "As you all know, Daed and I have been praying about a move to Indiana."

Susanna's stomach clenched.

"I have told your *daed* that I feel in my spirit that the time may be drawing near," Veronica said. "We will need the house and farm to be in readiness, and each one of us must do our part."

Timothy leaned forward from his end of the davenport, which did not surprise Susanna. He was always eager for adventure and was not attached to a young woman yet. Pennsylvania or Indiana, it would matter little to him. Timothy had even wondered aloud what the countryside was like farther west than Indiana.

The other boys shuffled their feet and held the arms of the three identical wooden chairs in which they sat. Their eyes were wide with imagination and unspoken questions. Susanna recognized the expression because she felt the way their faces looked — and perhaps she would appear as wide-eyed as they if she could see her own face. But the boys could not be feeling the consternation that accompanied her confusion.

"You all know what you are supposed to be doing," Veronica said. "The corner just inside the barn is where we will gather the items to share with others who can use them. When the time comes, your *daed* will let the other men know."

Stephen, the youngest, scooted off his chair. "May I go with Susanna to see Cousin Noah today?"

Susanna froze.

"I like Cousin Noah," Stephen said. "If he is sick, I want to visit him."

"When he is recovered," Veronica said. "Then you may visit."

"Jeremiah Zimmerman said Cousin Noah is not really sick. His *mamm* has been to visit many times."

"Stephen," Elias said, "do not contradict

307

your *mamm.*"

Stephen slunk back in his chair. Elias's tone was not harsh. It never was. But the Hooley children knew when their father meant what he said.

"Go on, boys," Veronica said. "There is much to do. Get started with the mucking, and your *daed* will be out soon."

All four boys stood, and Susanna with them.

"You may stay, Susanna," Veronica said.

Susanna choked back her questions and sat again. Even her father's eyebrows lifted as he looked at his wife.

"Veronica," Elias said, "is something else on your mind?"

"Did you know Timothy has been to hear Noah preach?" Veronica said. "Mrs. Satzler told me she saw him there. I cannot control if Susanna chooses to attend these . . . I do not even know what to call them, but I do not want the boys there."

"Timothy is more man than boy," Elias said, "and he is of an age for his *rumspringa.* We must allow him his curiosity."

"He only came once," Susanna said, "and I sent him home after less than thirty minutes."

"You both heard Stephen," Veronica said. "Will he be next?"

308

"No," Elias said. "He is a child."

"A child who hears things," Veronica said. " 'Tis a difficult task to help him understand why he may not do what other children do when his own brother and sister partake."

"Stephen is a mild child," Elias said, "and you are a wise mother. You will do right by him."

"It is my opinion that Susanna's visits to Noah are taking a toll on the family," Veronica said. "It would be best if she no longer went in the afternoons."

"Mamm!" Susanna shot out of her chair.

"I am serious, Elias," Veronica said, not even looking at Susanna.

"I have no doubt of that," Elias said.

"I have seen for myself that a brief visit with Noah and Phoebe in the morning can be accomplished without putting the family at risk, but the afternoons are another matter."

So this was her mother's agenda with her visits to Noah. Susanna had no defense against the flush that burned down her neck and through her chest. Her mother had never heard Noah preach, apart from the day he fell under at the end of the church meal. If she would just come one time, she would see that Susanna's presence was needful, not frivolous, and that no harm

309

would come even if Stephen saw what his friends saw. Most of the children were soon bored and congregated in a wagon bed to amuse themselves while paying little attention to Noah.

"Of course you will make this important decision," Veronica said to her husband. "I felt it wise to include Susanna in the discussion because it will affect her directly. But this business with Noah has gone on long enough. It is hurting our family, and it is hurting the church. Look what has happened to Niklaus Zug, one of our ministers. If he can be led astray, what might happen to our children?"

"I have not spoken to Niklaus about his decision," Elias said, "so I will refrain from conclusions on that point."

Susanna held her breath.

"And I will not assume that whatever moved Niklaus to make his choice would likewise move Susanna or Timothy." Elias leaned forward, hands on knees. "I will speak to Timothy and caution him. And the other boys will do as you see fit."

"And Susanna?" Veronica said.

Elias looked at his daughter. "I suggest that she remain on the farm today with time to think."

Veronica nodded vigorously.

310

"But if her own searching leads her to return to Noah and Phoebe, I will not stand in her way."

"Husband!" Veronica said.

Elias's eyes remained on Susanna.

Slowly, she nodded.

Susanna kept her word. She did not leave the farm. With plenty of orders to attend to, both for dyes and finished cloth, the hours were well occupied, and she remained occupied in and near her shed. Her mother would look around and see clutter that could be left behind when the family moved to Indiana, but Susanna saw value in every jar, every muslin sack, every pot and implement. She would leave none of it behind.

The thought of moving was a hideous monster, and she chased it away repeatedly that day.

She had made no promise not to think of Cousin Noah as she worked, and surely no one would prescribe that she abandon praying for him. When she went to the house in time to help her mother with the midday meal, she thought of Noah and hoped he was eating heartily before falling under. She hoped Phoebe allowed herself respite from the heat of the day. And when the Hooley meal was finished and the washing up complete, Susanna resisted the urge to hitch up her cart and instead visited the garden where she grew some of her own root vegetables to use in dyes.

When the afternoon sun beat down as she carried a basket of vegetables back to the shed, she slipped her old mare a carrot at the pasture fence but did not let her eyes rest on the cart beside the shed.

When her mind filled with images of what might be happening at the Kauffmans', Susanna found the stub of a pencil and a scrap of rough paper and planned the next route she would take to deliver her goods. She would see her customers at church the next day, but only those who lived at significant distance along the edges of the church district would agree to discreetly receive her goods and deftly slip her something in return. The contact was brief and wordless, more like an exchange of gifts than conducting business on the Sabbath.

When her ears heard the timbre of Noah's preaching voice, she shook out a length of fabric to banish the sound that she could not possibly be hearing. Surely Patsy was there — and perhaps even Adam keeping his distance along the pasture fence but with a mind to step in if necessary. With a long paddle, Susanna pressed the cloth into the simmering pot, a task that would tie her to the farm for the afternoon. She would let it steep for a deep color, and then she would hang it from the line between the shed and a tree or spread it over bushes to dry, trying all the while not to think about the errands with which her father had charged Timothy. One of them would take him out to the Zugs'. Her father was a man of his word. No doubt already he had cautioned Timothy against stopping even for a few minutes.

The crops were growing well and the harvest would be upon them soon enough. Surely even if her father decided the family should move, it would not be until after the harvest. They might sell more of it than usual to supply cash for a move and because they would not need to lay in hay and straw for the animals to last through the winter. But after the harvest? Would her father want to be in Indiana, settled on new land, in time for spring planting?

He might not leave at all. Moving to Indiana was her mother's notion, and as her father liked to remind them all, a man's duty was to lead his household.

Susanna stirred the kettle, spreading the fabric with her paddle to make sure color seeped evenly into every crevice and wrinkle. When she had begun making and selling dyes, she had arranged the spot for her fire where she had the best view of the Hooley orchards. The trees were domesticated and purposely planted for the family's needs, but still they reminded her of the lovely wildness of the forest beyond the farm that cradled the Kishacoquillas Valley and that had cradled her life and every affection.

Indiana. Tears stung her eyes.

Horse hooves forced her to wipe her face with the backs of her hands and look up. Timothy reined in his horse.

"All is well?" Susanna said.

"More than well," Timothy said. "I met a man, and I think Daed should meet him."

"Oh?"

"He is new to the valley and looking for a farm."

Susanna lurched. "Surely you did not tell him ours was for sale."

"It might be," Timothy said. "If God sends us a buyer we did not seek, would that not be a sign of His will?"

Susanna pressed her lips together, unwilling to dispute her brother's faith. It was one thing for a sixteen-year-old boy to be enamored of the adventure a move west might bring, and another to seek a buyer on behalf of a father who had not yet said they would move.

"Where did you meet this man?" she said.

"In the mercantile in Lewistown. I happened to overhear him."

"So you intruded on a private conversation?"

"I assure you, the gentleman considered it no intrusion."

"You cannot force *Gottes wille,*" Susanna said, stirring more vigorously.

"Susanna, you fret too much."

And you are too nosy, she wanted to say.

"I told him he was welcome to come by at his earliest convenience," Timothy said. "Even today, if he can spare the time."

"Today?" Susanna's paddle stilled. "You had better tell Daed then. And *Mamm.*"

"She will go into a frenzy," Timothy said.

No doubt. Timothy should have thought of that before inviting a stranger to their land this very day.

"Go," Susanna said, stirring again. She could not undo his invitation to a stranger, but it was in everyone's interest that their mother be prepared.

Timothy cantered his horse toward the house. Susanna stirred and judged saturation and considered which of the Amish women she knew might find this violet-blue cloth appealing without considering it vain.

315

She had just finished hanging the cloth on the line when she again heard the *clip-clop* of a horse.

An *English* man sat astride.

Although the Hooleys sometimes saw *English* when they were off the farm, other than Patsy and her mother, no *English* had been on their land in years. Surely this was not the man to whom Timothy had spoken. An Amish family would appreciate the cleared and cultivated acreage. It was not unheard of for a family from a nearby church district to seek a farm in the valley. If her father did want to sell, surely it was not necessary to sell to an *English*.

"You must be the industrious Susanna," the man said.

She blanched and shielded her eyes from the waning afternoon glare. What had Timothy told this man?

"Your brother's instructions to find the farm were pleasingly exact. I had no trouble finding my way around its dimensions. I have only yet to see the buildings, for which of course I would want your father's permission."

Susanna stared up at him.

"I'm sorry. I have forgotten my manners."

He slid off the horse, and Susanna could better judge his age, probably not yet thirty.

If this were to be his first farm, he must already be a prosperous man.

"I promise a fair offer," he said. "Perhaps you would do me the kindness of taking me up to the house and helping to locate your father."

CHAPTER 26

Sitting in church alone was something Adam was not sure he would ever adjust to. Of course he was not alone. On one side of him was Seth and on the other LeRoy, but neither of them was his cousin Jonas, who had sat with him during every worship service for the last two years except one time when Jonas was too ill to attend. Side by side, they both listened to Jonas's father pray or preach and could readily glance across the aisle to see Deborah watching her husband with an expression bordering on pride. But today Jonas was not here, and neither was Deborah. Both had opted to worship at home privately with Niklaus, as they all did on Sundays that were not church Sundays. Surely this was not a permanent break. Both had been to church without Niklaus two weeks ago, and in a few weeks Jonas would marry Anke, who was sitting beside her own mother across the aisle. No one could hold Jonas account-able for his father's decisions. Jonas would do more to please his bride-to-be than any other young man Adam knew. He would not imperil his betrothal by a break from the church.

Would he?

Yohan Maist gave the short sermon. Shem Hertzberger led prayers longer than Yohan's sermon. Virtually any hymn in the *Ausbund* would take longer to sing than Yohan's typi-cal sermons. But the service would be no shorter than usual because Shem, as always, was more than eager to use the extra time. A child squalled in the back and was quickly quieted. A hymnal dropped, banging against a bench on its way to the bare wood floor of the host's home. The breeze that blew through the open windows an hour ago when Shem began had dissipated, leaving grit in the weave of Adam's new blue Sunday shirt.

"Some would have us believe," Shem said, shaking an index finger, "that salvation comes through words that we speak in a moment of emotional frenzy. Some would have us believe that weeping and clapping are signs of the regenerate heart. Some would have us believe that lofty rhetoric is what leads us to God and assures us we are saved. Some would have us believe that if we learn to describe God in certain ways, this is how the world will know our faith."

Shem paused to shake his head and move his glance back and forth among the eyes of his flock before settling on Adam as if daring him to look away.

"My children," Shem said, "I do not want you to be led astray. Young men and old men, stand firm in the truth. Our regeneration comes through our obedience, and our obedience from a heart of submission. The great apostle Paul wrote to the young Titus that we are heirs of the hope of salvation, not the certain knowledge of salvation. To claim such assurance is to manifestly declare to the world the pride of your heart. And when one is prideful, the entire congregation suffers.

" 'Are you saved?' some will ask you. I exhort you that your answer should be, 'Ask my family' or 'Ask my neighbor.' Let your deeds speak for the condition of your heart. For how can true salvation come from the words or prayer of a moment if they be not manifest in the actions of a lifetime? Only at the end of our lives, when the time of the Great Judgment comes, can we hope to hear, 'Well done, thou good and faithful servant.' "

Susanna could think of little but Noah during Shem's sermon, and even Adam's patient attempts to calm her after the church meal were futile. He took her home directly after she helped clean up, lest her mother have some other reason to doubt her piety. Susanna had clamped her mouth though. She would give neither her mother nor the bishop reason to gloat that they had been proven right about the dark condition of her heart, and she would not squeeze Adam into the middle of anyone's accusations if her tongue got the best of her. Neither did she tell Adam of the *English* visitor to whom her father had been more encouragingly cordial than Susanna expected. Timothy had followed the men around as her *daed* led the tour of the house, barn, stable, equipment shed, chicken coop, and odds and ends of outbuildings.

And Patsy. If she heard any word of Shem's sermon and the pointed way he had looked at both Susanna and Adam and others who had been to hear Noah preach, she would gallop Galahad directly to the Hertzberger farm and loose her tongue.

Susanna wore her oldest dress on Monday

for a long morning of mashing ingredients into batches of dye. Some of it she would barter with women who preferred to dye their own cloth, and some of it she eventually would use to color the newly woven cloth customers brought to her. Someday she would devote time to her weaving skills. If she could create cloth worthy to sell as well as color it, she would have a useful skill whether she married or not and whether she moved to Indiana or not.

Indiana. She could not move to Indiana.

She sealed a wide-necked jar that would provide a household with enough black dye for a family of garments — trousers, dresses, aprons, hats, bonnets — and plunged her hands into a pail of water to wash up with lye soap and a brush. Despite the income and bartered goods her skills brought to the family, her mother did not tolerate lines of color beneath Susanna's fingernails at the midday dinner.

"Susanna."

She looked up. "Phoebe! Is Noah all right?"

"For the moment," Phoebe said. "But he was up and down all night complaining that his head hurt. I did not dare leave him on his own. But this morning he has no recollection of any of it."

"Did he fall under?"

Phoebe shook her head. "He insists he is fine."

"But you do not believe him."

"And my sister was so unwell the last time I saw her," Phoebe said. "I never know when I might get word that I must go to her. I thought if I came to ask before you arrived this afternoon, you might come prepared to spend the night and I could go today if need be and stay as late as needed."

Susanna gulped. "My *mamm.*"

"We will tell her, of course," Phoebe said. "I do not mean to cause her alarm. But I need help."

Susanna blew out slow breath. "Then I will talk to her."

"We will go together," Phoebe said. "I have my wagon."

"Yes." Susanna quickly agreed with the strategy. Her mother's face might announce disapproval, but her tongue would not directly deny Noah or Phoebe the comfort of Susanna's presence, and if Susanna took neither the mare nor the cart, her mother could make no claim their absence was an inconvenience. Susanna would need her father's blessing, but he was sure to give it. It was just for a night — two at most.

■ ■ ■ ■

Patsy galloped toward the Hooley farm. At the speed with which Galahad moved, the time spent riding in the wrong direction would soon be recovered. Susanna was so pent-up lately. She needed a strong, swift ride on the back of Patsy's horse, and Patsy would be glad for the excuse to gallop the animal twice in one day in order to have Susanna home in time for supper. Undeterred by the orchard that lay between the main road and Susanna's shed, Patsy wove between the trees and emerged in the clearing. The shed's door was propped open by an arrangement of small crates.

"Susanna?" Patsy called, reining in Galahad.

Veronica's head poked out of the shed.

"Hello," Patsy said, sliding off her mount. The coals beneath the empty kettle were cold. Susanna had not been dyeing today. "Is Susanna in there?"

"You have missed her." Veronica dropped a tin into a crate. "She has gone early today."

Veronica disappeared into the shed. Patsy could have called out her thanks and hoisted herself back onto Galahad, but intuition tugged her into the shed. Susanna rarely

324

walked the miles to the Kauffmans' anymore. It was too risky when no one could be sure when Noah would stop preaching and Susanna had promised her mother she would always be home for supper. Susanna didn't ride, but even the old mare Susanna used to pull the cart was faster than walking. But the cart was there beside the shed. If Susanna had left already for the Kauffmans', what mode of transportation had she used?

Patsy was wasting time speculating. Susanna always said that her mother rarely stepped inside the ramshackle structure. This niggled at Patsy as she followed Veronica. Inside, Veronica clearly had two categories on the workbench, those items she was taking care to arrange and those she piled as if they held no value.

But it all held value to Susanna. Every small bit of crushed bark or reduced berry juice bore the potential to add nuance to a hue, to reveal a shade of nature that ninety-nine people out of a hundred would never notice but that Susanna's eye would memorize.

Veronica's haphazard pile was many times larger than her careful pile.

Patsy's gaze went to the crates propping open the door. Empty tins separated from

their lids. Jars with no stoppers. Flat —
emptied — muslin bags.

"What have you done?" Patsy marched to
the crates and picked up the top one. She
had sat for hours with Susanna stitching
these tiny muslin bags, and some of the tins
had come from her own mother's kitchen.

" 'Tis not practical to take everything,"
Veronica said. "I have asked Susanna half a
dozen times to sort through her things."

"Take them where?"

"Indiana, of course. I am hopeful we will
have a good faith offer on the farm any day
now."

Patsy's hands went to her face but only
for three seconds. Then she gripped the
crate in one hand, stepped into the shed,
and began sweeping Susanna's belongings
into it.

"Miss Baxton," Veronica said. "Need I
remind you this is none of your affair?"

"It is my affair until I hear with my own
ears Susanna say she is moving to Indiana
and does not intend to take these things."
Patsy picked up another crate, set it on the
workbench, and grabbed fistfuls of jars and
bags. Whatever sorting system Susanna had
used clearly was compromised. Veronica had
already seen to that. The important thing
now was to prevent destruction of anything

Susanna could reassemble. At least Veronica hadn't started burning anything.

"Is this how your mother raised you?" Veronica said. "To barge into other people's homes and wreak havoc?"

"To be a loyal friend!" Patsy started in on a third crate. "And I will thank you to leave my mother out of this."

Until recently, Patsy would not have imagined Veronica capable of what she had begun doing. She wanted to live apart in the Amish manner. All the Baxtons respected the boundaries Veronica guarded around their interactions. But this? Was she so frightened of her cousin's gift?

Crate after crate, flour sack after flour sack, Patsy loaded the remains of her friend's curated collection wherever the items would fit in the cart. She didn't often hitch Galahad to anything, but she would manage. She'd seen Susanna fasten the bridle and shafts to the mare enough times to know how to do it, and Galahad was loyal enough to cooperate. Several times Veronica protested and attempted to thwart Patsy's movements, but youth — and anger — gave Patsy the advantage. She didn't get everything, but she got as much as she could swiftly manage and left Veronica, without

remorse, red-faced and indignant at the
shed.

CHAPTER 27

Susanna knew the creak and rattle of her own wagon, and she knew the thundering gallop. Never before had the two been in combination. She and Phoebe had come at a more reasonable pace in the Kauffman wagon and had barely arrived. Phoebe had just let her horse into the pasture, and Susanna was waiting to see whether Phoebe wanted her help in the house or she might keep Noah company in the barn. Both of the Kauffmans now appeared in the yard, drifting toward Susanna as the horse and cart rolled down the lane.

Galahad!

"What in the world?" Susanna ran toward the rig, which came to a rough halt.

Patsy jumped down from the cart. "I've brought your things."

Susanna narrowed puzzled eyes. The small bag she'd filled with everything she would need to spend a night at the Kauffmans' sat on the stoop. When she came alongside the cart she gasped.

"What have you done with my dyes?"

"I saved them, that's what." Patsy un-hitched the cart. "Your mother decided to sort through them. Some ridiculous thing about an offer on the farm and Indiana."

"Susanna?"

Noah's voice was distant, as if he were half a mile away rather than standing right next to her. Susanna picked up a small jar that had lost its cork. What had become of the powder she had ground just after breakfast?

"Susanna," Noah said again, his voice breaking in more firmly now. "You must tell us what is going on."

Susanna fumbled for a starting point and arranged events as coherently as she could manage amid the shock of seeing the contents of her shed scattered in the cart.

Her mother's growing anxiousness over Susanna's daily visits to the Kauffmans'.

Veronica's correspondence with an old friend who had moved to Indiana and sent glowing accounts of God's blessing and the wonderful faithfulness of the believers there.

The conversation with other families who feared the church was becoming too pro-gressive.

Elias's permission for Susanna's choices

but not his agreement with the events.

The *English* man Timothy had turned up who looked eager to buy a farm in Kish Valley.

"You must stay with us indefinitely." Noah lifted Susanna's kettle out of the cart. "You can use the back corner of the barn for your things, and I will prepare a place just outside for your fires."

"One night," Susanna said. "That is all I asked my *daed* for."

"I doubt he knows what your *mamm* has done." Now Noah lifted out a crate of jumbled jars and tins. "It will not take much to persuade him this is the best place for you right now."

Susanna looked from Noah to Phoebe. "For how long?"

"As long as it takes," Phoebe said.

"It is too risky for me to go now, but I will speak to your parents first thing tomorrow morning," Noah said. "I will appeal to Veronica as her cousin, and Elias will not deny me. He is a good man."

Susanna looked down at her garments. She and Phoebe had left swiftly. Susanna had not even changed out of her old work dress or put on a suitable apron.

"Have no worry," Phoebe said. "I have dresses. If I have to, I will make you a new dress from your own cloth. Come. We will settle you in the small bedroom.

Voices woke Patsy the next morning. Her parents' murmurings spiraled up the back stairs, indistinct yet comforting. The sound was not unfamiliar, but it was rare. Her father's habit of slipping into the house in predawn hours to surprise his wife and daughter with his presence made Patsy smile every time. She threw off the light quilt she used during the warm months, sat on the side of the bed, and let her toes fish for her slippers.

"Papa, you were a rascal once again," Patsy said when she reached the bottom of the stairs in her nightdress and a cotton robe.

"I stand guilty." Charles pecked Patsy's cheek. "A man can only bear to be away from his family for so long before the Spirit moves him to go home."

"Eggs?" Mercy stood at the stove dropping butter into an iron skillet.

"Shall I make them?" Patsy said.

"Sit. It will only take a moment."

Bread and jam were already on the table. Patsy reached into a cupboard and took down three plates.

"Tell us the news, Papa," Patsy said as

soon as Charles had blessed the food.

Most of the people her father named, Patsy had never met and likely never would. Yet they were her father's scattered congregation, so she wanted to hear whose illness had improved, whose baby had come safely through a dangerous delivery, whose prodigal son might have sent his parents a letter, who had at last surrendered to God in a blissful conversion. Patsy bit into jam-laden bread and swallowed her mother's fluffy eggs while her father chattered about events on the circuit.

"Why can't they see how God works?" Patsy reached for her coffee mug.

"They do see," Charles said. "Have I told my stories so badly that you do not see God in them?"

"I mean the Amish," Patsy said. She told a few stories of her own, wishing that her father might stay home for a good long stretch and see for himself.

After breakfast, Patsy strolled the farm with her father while Harvey, the weathered farmhand, reported to Charles on the corn and wheat fields, when he thought the harvest might begin — Charles would try to be home to help with that — and how much cash they might expect the farm to yield.

After a while, Mercy's voice rode the

wind, faintly calling her husband's name. Then came the bell that could be heard across the acres. Patsy and Charles turned back toward the house and hastened their steps.

Shem Hertzberger stood at the base of the steps leading up to the front porch, his black frock coat announcing that he had come on official duty as a minister. Charles owned a similar coat, though he did not wear it when he was home on his own farm.

"Mr. Hertzberger," Charles said, "I do not believe we have ever had the privilege of hosting you in our home."

"I have offered refreshment," Mercy said. "Mr. Hertzberger tells me his visit will not be a long one."

"We can at least sit in the shade of the porch." Charles gestured up the steps.

Shem shook his head. "I have come only to ask that you take care with my flock."

Charles tilted his head. "I don't understand."

"Confusion courses through my congregation," Shem said. "Perhaps you do not understand the influence you have and that it is misplaced when directed toward our people."

"You are speaking of Noah," Charles said.

"And Niklaus," Shem said, "and all those

who are drawn to give or hear sermons that are not in the way of our people. The congregation finds itself in tension, and I ask that you mind your conversations carefully so as not to cause further rift than you have to this point."

Patsy boiled over in an instant. "You dare to come here and tell my father that he has caused a rift in your congregation!"

"Patsy," Charles said softly.

Mercy laid a hand on Patsy's elbow, but Patsy shook her off.

"If your people are confused," she said, "it is because their bishop scolds them for a true experience of the Spirit of God. You might open your heart first and then show them the way."

"Patricia!" There was nothing soft about Charles's voice this time.

"Come," Mercy said, "we'll go inside and let the ministers speak."

Patsy ought to feel sorry for her outburst. Her parents made that clear. But she didn't. It was about time someone stood up to the likes of Shem Hertzberger.

"You have a visitor."

Deborah stood in the open barn door, looking up at Niklaus in the hayloft. They would bale again soon. He wanted the loft ready to receive its fresh supply.

"Who is it?" Niklaus brought his hook down in a solid thrust into a bale so it would be safely stored until he could return to his task.

"That *English* girl Susanna is so friendly with."

"Patsy Baxton?" Niklaus looked down at his nodding wife before making his way to the ladder, down its rungs, out the barn door, and to the young woman sitting on his front stoop. Deborah went into the house through the back, leaving Niklaus to sit beside Patsy.

Her news of the bishop's visit to her family's farm surprised him. As long as he had known Shem, his old friend never ventured to tell the *English* how to behave.

"I lost my temper," Patsy muttered.

"I am sure you are sorry," Niklaus said.

"Not really."

Niklaus paused and then said, "You may want to reconsider."

"I believe what I believe," Patsy said.

"Of course you do. But it is not your beliefs that have brought you here to see me."

Silence expanded the inches between them.

"You're right," Patsy finally said. "I came

336

because I feel terrible about the things I said."

"Our old friend repentance arrives again."

"Will I have to apologize to your bishop?"

"First make your peace with God."

Patsy nodded.

Niklaus pressed the heels of his hands into his knees, his elbows swinging wide, and pushed himself upright.

"In the meantime," he said, "I will speak to Shem. You Methodists have your own bishops. Shem should not have approached your father that way."

"Then we agree!" Patsy said.

Niklaus gave a half smile. "Yes, we agree on that point. But we also agree that you have an opportunity to know God's mercy through repentance."

"That's what Noah always says."

"He is not wrong," Niklaus said. "I will get my horse and leave you to examine your own heart."

Bishop Hertzberger's arrival sent a shudder through the makeshift congregation gathered to hear Noah. Standing in the front room with a clear view out the window, Susanna saw Amish shoulders stiffen, as if they were children caught with a spoonful of sugar their mothers were carefully rationing. Patsy might be glad he had come — if she were there. Noah had fallen under at least half an hour ago, and Patsy had not come. Patsy advocated that if people would just hear Noah preach, they would see he was a true servant of God, and usually Susanna agreed. She was less certain of that result when it came to Bishop Hertzberger. His sermons the last two months made clear where he planted his feet.

Now the bishop trotted his horse alongside the benches. A handful of people immediately dashed for their wagons. But what was most remarkable about the bishop's arrival was that he was not alone. The *English* doctor was with him. Phoebe and Noah had been to doctors before. No one had a solution. If the bishop had bothered to speak to them, he would know this.

Shem eyed the side of the barn and steered his horse toward the hooks where he and the doctor could tie up their animals.

Noah preached with his usual kindly forcefulness, but Bishop Hertzberger did not halt a single step to take in Noah's words. Instead, he led the doctor in a straight path in full view past the benches and toward the front door.

Phoebe had gone to her sister's for the day. Patsy was unaccounted for. Susanna saw no sign of Adam, not even sitting on the pasture fence behind the gathered crowd. Gulping, she met the bishop at the door.

"Susanna," he said. "We must come in."

The one rule Phoebe was adamant be enforced was that no one be allowed in the house during Noah's sermons. Did such a rule apply to the bishop?

"I am sorry for your trouble, Doctor," Susanna said. "No one here requires your services."

"I asked him to come on this day," the bishop said. "It has been arranged for some time, so I ask you to permit entry."

She could have heard him perfectly well if he had spoken with a private tone. Instead, it was as if he wanted to best Noah's volume. Noah, of course, showed no awareness that his bishop had come calling.

"We are coming in." The bishop pushed past Susanna. The doctor followed tenuously.

"But we do not need a doctor," Susanna said.

"You are in great need of a bishop. I have chosen to bring the doctor to prove once and for all what this is."

This was Noah preaching the truth of God. Why was that so difficult to see?

"You have a kind spirit," the bishop said. "I do not doubt your intention is to help Noah in some way, but you have tangled yourself in his duplicity."

Duplicity!

"Doctor, are you ready?" Shem said.

The doctor unclasped his black bag and unfolded his leather surgical kit.

"What are you doing?" Susanna stepped between the doctor and Noah. Even if Noah was being duplicitous, how could the doctor possibly treat him with a surgical kit?

"This will just take a minute," Shem said. "A few seconds. A simple medical experiment."

The doctor removed a long needle from its place in the medical pouch.

"I cannot allow this," Susanna said. "There is no wound to close."

"You dare to speak to me that way? You are being far too emotional."

The bishop grabbed the needle from the doctor and jabbed it into Noah's thigh.

CHAPTER 28

Susanna gasped. "Bishop!" She tussled her way to Noah's side and stood with a hand on his shoulder.

But Noah made no response to the needle coming through the weave of his black trousers and into his thin thigh. Today's sermon was on forbearance, and the fluidity of his exhortation did not falter. God's divine forbearance toward us should most certainly inspire forbearance toward one another. Susanna, however, felt no inkling of the trait.

"Doctor," she hissed, "what results do you find from this medical experiment?"

The doctor shifted his feet as Shem slapped the syringe back into the surgical kit he held open in his hands.

Outside, listeners had left their seats and come closer to the window to peer up at Noah.

"Looks like he didn't even feel that,"

someone said.

"Or he is exercising great control because he wants us to think he didn't feel it."

"Hey, Doc, do you think he's sick?"

"Is this some kind of trick?"

Even the Amish who had guiltily abandoned their seats when Shem arrived inched their way back for a closer look.

Noah spoke of God's unending patience for the faithless Israelites and turned pages in his Bible.

Not so much as a wince.

No touch on his leg to acknowledge the intrusion.

No glance at Shem.

No quizzical look at the doctor.

Noah's hands did not move from his Bible, nor his eyes from the Word of God.

"There," Susanna said, stepping back from Noah. "You have your response."

"You verge on impudence, Susanna," Shem said, glancing at the onlookers on the other side of the window. He stepped deeper into the room. "Your parents have taught you better."

She held her tongue but could not constrain her thoughts.

"This proves nothing," Shem said. "I am not accustomed to handling such a delicate tool. Perhaps the doctor should show me how I ought to have done so."

So far the doctor had not spoken a word, as if he had come along simply because he was in possession of the longest, sharpest needle the bishop could find.

"Doctor," Susanna said, "in your medical opinion, is there any value to poking Noah again? Might not the action draw blood and create a needless wound?"

The doctor folded in the flaps of his kit. "I do not see advantage in repeating an experiment that has given clear results."

"Your opinion, Doctor?" Shem said.

"Clearly this man has no awareness of the events at which he is the center."

"Do you believe him to be sleeping or unconscious, as some have claimed?" Shem said.

"The mind is far more mysterious than our understanding of it." The doctor snapped closed the clasp on his black bag.

The warmth of a golden gloat infused Susanna's face as she met the bishop's eyes.

"I have other patients to see while I am out this way," the doctor said.

"I will show you both out through the kitchen," Susanna said. The least the bishop could do was leave quietly. Susanna was doing him a favor by not thrusting him out the front into a bevy of *English* onlookers asking questions.

Niklaus rode to the Hertzberger farm, miles across the valley, only to hear from Shem's wife that her husband had gone to visit Noah Kauffman on the farm next door to Niklaus's.

Still astride his horse, he saw through the window what Shem did while Noah innocently expounded the Scriptures. At the back door he dismounted, shaking his finger at a boy with his hand on the knob and shooing him off in time to hear the latch move on the inside. The boy would not have gotten in, but Niklaus's task would be easy. Shem stepped out of the house.

"Shem, my old friend, you have had a busy morning. First the Baxtons and now the Kauffmans."

"It is none of your concern."

Niklaus nodded his black hat at the doctor. "I hope you have not troubled yourself too much."

The doctor shrugged, thumbs fiddling with the handle to his bag.

"Shem," Niklaus said, "what were you hoping Charles Baxton would do? He is a Methodist minister who does what he believes God calls him to do."

"Then he can understand when I do the

same," Shem snapped.

"Our people have lived apart for two hundred years," Niklaus said. "It is not our habit to persuade others that their religious practices are in error."

"I only ask that he keep his ways to himself also," Shem said.

Two colorful hats leaned around the corner, two sets of shoulders following, with four eyes fixed on the three men.

Niklaus shook his head at the women. "If you would like to hear Noah preach, I suggest you remain in the front. This is a private conversation."

The women withdrew.

"Noah's behavior has become an occasion for too much interaction with the *English*," Shem said. "It is not good for the church."

"It causes no harm."

"Then why have you withdrawn?"

Niklaus looked away for a few seconds. "We have to be sensible in these matters."

Shem pointed a thumb over his shoulder toward the house. "Do you believe this is sensible?"

Niklaus exhaled. "If you go around to the front to leave, you will only cause a greater spectacle than what has already happened. I will fetch your horses. Ride through the fields to the road at the edge of the forest and depart that way."

He should have come earlier. Adam could see that now.

The bishop.

The *English* doctor Adam had seen only one other time in two years.

Niklaus leading two horses, neither his own.

No sign of Galahad — so Patsy was not there.

Empty dirt where Phoebe usually left her wagon.

Susanna was alone in her responsibility for Noah, and the afternoon had not been routine.

"Onkel." Adam left his horse and sprinted across the Kauffmans' backyard, sending pecking chickens fluttering.

Between the two mounts, reins in both hands, Niklaus's head turned.

"Please do not attract attention," Niklaus said, low and firm.

Adam glanced over his shoulder. At the moment, no one followed.

"What happened?" he asked.

"I cannot speak of it now," Niklaus said. "Shem and his needle must leave, and I will see that they do."

"Needle?"

"Go inside," Niklaus said. "Susanna needs someone."

Niklaus headed off toward Shem and the doctor. Adam targeted the back door, which was latched.

He knocked. "Susanna, 'tis me."

Hearing no footfalls, Adam leaned to one side to peer through a window. The door to the front room was propped open, giving him a clear view through the house. Susanna's eyes were fixed on Noah.

He knocked again. This time Susanna startled, and her head jerked toward the kitchen. He waved, catching her gaze. She glanced again at Noah and then lifted the hem of her skirt enough to allow quick steps. The expression on her face wrenched his heart as she lifted the latch and he slipped in. Susanna gripped his hand.

"What happened?"

"The bishop jabbed a needle into Noah's leg to prove his trickery."

"And Noah did not respond," Adam said.

"Of course not. Whatever you think of his preaching, Adam, you have seen for yourself that 'tis no malicious trickery."

Adam nodded. If Shem had been in the house while Noah preached, surely he had seen for himself that Noah's preaching was not an act of volition that could be constrained simply because the bishop had entered the room.

"I cannot go home now." Susanna released Adam's hand and pulled fingers across one eye. "*Mamm* will hear of this, and it will be the last straw. Besides, I want to stay here. Noah is right. This is where I belong right now. I am not even sure I can go back to church."

"Susanna!"

She heaved out her breath. "I am sorry, Adam. I am just telling you the truth."

"But leaving the church?"

"Your *onkel* did it."

"And I pray that he will return soon. God will not turn away from the one who repents."

"Can one repent of compassion?" Susanna turned and paced into the front room.

Adam followed. He was meant to be Susanna's husband, if not this year then next. But they must marry in the church.

Repentance was sluggish for Patsy. Even charging up Jacks Mountain when she left the Zug farm did not split her spirit open in exuberance as she had hoped. Instead, she felt undeserving of joy if it were true that she was displeasing God with her anger. Well into the afternoon, sincere repentance

348

was reluctant enough that she halted Galahad four times on the way to the Kauffmans' so that she might search her heart,
even though she knew she would miss the
falling under. Perhaps Noah was preaching
on repentance and his words would soften
her heart when her own self-examination
was insufficient.

The benches beneath Noah's window
were nearly empty — but the flower bed was
full. The summer's flowers were already
spent, but that was no reason to venture off
the benches and so near the house. Patsy
pressed her knees into her horse to speed
her arrival.

"Please step out of the garden," she said
in the officiating voice she had developed
over the last few weeks, imitating the authority she had grown up hearing in her father's
tone.

"Not on your life."

The man who retorted was a loyal listener
when Patsy's father preached, and she
would not have expected such disrespect in
the presence of anyone's sermon.

"I must insist," she said.

He shook his head. "You weren't here. You
didn't see what happened."

"Tell me." Patsy hastened out of her
saddle and approached the house.

"It's proof. No doubt about it."

"Proof of what?"

"Proof that he is unconscious."

"I was not aware you had any doubt." Patsy glanced up at Noah. Behind him, Susanna was unconcerned with the flower bed assembly. Or perhaps she had simply given up protesting.

A woman wearing an atrocious green hat shook her head. "It is no proof at all, not in the eyes of that bishop."

"Bishop?" Fresh irritation filled Patsy's chest.

"If it's trickery, it's of the highest level," the woman said.

"It's not trickery," Patsy said. "What about the bishop?"

"He went inside," the man said. Then he proceeded to tell her about the doctor, the tussle with Susanna, the needle.

Patsy fumed. "Is he still in the house?"

"I don't think so. My friend and I saw him in the back with Mr. Zug."

Patsy hadn't tied up Galahad, but she would trust him not to gallop off. She raced to the back to find only Niklaus.

"What have you done with the bishop?" she demanded.

"He is gone now. That is all that matters," Niklaus said.

"That is *not* all that matters. I heard what happened."

"I sent him away by the forest path, and I do not believe he will return."

Patsy scoffed. "You must have seen for yourself what his attitude is like."

"I did indeed."

"I am not afraid to speak to him. I have nothing to lose. He is not my bishop." The bishop could have gone far if the people out front did not yet know he had left Kauffman land. He was taking the sloped path at the base of the mountain, which would slow him. Galahad had more speed than any horse in the Kish Valley. She would catch the bishop within minutes.

"If you want to help Noah," Niklaus said, "you will not cause further disruption."

"I only want to settle the disruption Mr. Hertzberger seems intent to inflame."

"Have you so quickly forgotten our conversation a few hours ago?" Niklaus said. "Remember, we know God's mercy by repentance. Is that not what your own father preaches?"

Patsy balled her fists.

CHAPTER 29

Adam stood sentry beside Susanna. His ears heard the sounds coming from Noah's mouth, the punctuated consonants and elongated vowels. Surely the vibrations formed words and sentences and paragraphs, but Adam's mind could make no sense of them. He was stuck on Susanna's proclamation that she might not go back to church.

Would she change her mind if he suggested they become betrothed? Would she reconsider all that she was sacrificing, all she put at risk? Would he even want her to do that if it meant quenching the spirit he loved in her?

"Patsy is finally here," Susanna said. "I saw her getting people out of the flower bed. She just went around to the back. If anyone is there, she will make sure they disperse."

Adam nodded. He could still see Galahad where Patsy had left him.

"You can go if you want to," Susanna said. "The bishop is gone. The people who remain are back on the benches. Patsy will not let anyone else interfere with Noah."

Adam had no good answer. He hesitated to leave, but Susanna seemed not to want him to remain. Patsy's footfalls were fast and hard across the kitchen floor, and she came into the main room. Adam nodded at her, passing her on his way out.

Niklaus was still in the backyard, feet braced and arms crossed over his chest, looking in the direction of the forest path at the edge of the farm.

Adam stood beside him, silent for a few minutes.

"This is no trickery," Adam said.

Niklaus nodded. "I never suspected it was."

"It is befuddling," Adam said, "yet you moved so quickly to approval." Niklaus had even chased off the bishop.

Niklaus turned his head. "Approval? Is that what you think?"

"Is it not?"

"Noah means no harm," Niklaus said.

"The bishop believes he is harming the congregation."

"Any harm that comes is not Noah's doing. If folks would leave him be, the bishop would have no concern. If they did not trample Noah's farm every day, there would be nothing to upset Shem."

"But you have withdrawn from being a minister because of Noah," Adam said.

"No." Niklaus's rebuttal came swiftly. "Do not attach my choice to Noah when he remains separated from his own words. He is responsible for none of this."

"Then what?" Adam said. "What made you withdraw?"

"In all things I wish only to honor God."

Adam never doubted his uncle's motive, but this statement was no answer to his question. Surely Shem would say the same thing. No one in the congregation would suggest that in some matters they were free of duty to honor God.

"There are other sleeping preachers," Niklaus said, "many among the *English* but occasionally among our people as well. At our last gathering, fellow ministers mentioned this. Noah is not the only one. Do I understand what causes these curious events? No. Do I need to understand? No."

"But you are a minister — or were. Still are? What do you believe the Bible says about this?"

Niklaus rubbed the end of his beard between two fingers. "The Bible tells us to watch and pray. As far as I can recall, it says nothing about sleeping and praying."

"Onkel, you are confusing me."

Niklaus laughed softly. "I am sorry. You want me definitely to tell you the line is straight. But what if it bends and wiggles at times? Is not God present there as well?"

Adam resolved to stay away from the Kauffman farm the next day. Hearing Noah, being near Susanna, seeing Phoebe's weary distress — he could not think straight when he was there. At least he knew where the bishop stood, even if his actions had been shocking when he brought the doctor to see Noah. His uncle had offered little counsel. Adam needed time with his own thoughts to untangle the cryptic advice contained in his uncle's words.

Adam's morning was committed to a group of friends who recruited him to help build an equipment shed on the small farm Nathaniel Swigert had just acquired. They argued that he was the expert among them, having been taught by Bishop Hertzberger, the master carpenter himself, and having constructed the addition for Jonas and Anke. His afternoon was promised to Jonas for chores that would ready them for the harvest, which would begin any day. A few farmers had begun their harvests, depending on what they had planted. When the harvest season was under way in earnest, most people would be fully occupied with the task, and Noah would be preaching to an empty yard. Then the colder weather would begin, and few would want to bundle up to sit outside in a biting wind for long sermons. Perhaps it was simply a matter of time and all would settle down.

Except Niklaus would still not be in church.

Except Susanna might not be there either.

Except Phoebe and Noah would not feel welcome by their own bishop.

The others lined up logs, and Adam swung his ax over and over, notching with perfection as if he had been doing it all his life.

"I suppose they will be expecting you at the Kauffman place," Seth said, lifting one end of a log and dragging it out of Adam's way.

Adam simply swung his ax again, first from one angle and then from the opposite, to send a chunk of wood flying and leave a clean notch.

"We know you go," Johannes said. "You told us that day at the picnic we should submit to the church, yet you go to hear

Noah Kauffman."

He did not go to hear Noah but to help Noah. Even that was an excuse to see Susanna. Adam swung his ax again.

"You must have an opinion," Nathaniel said.

Adam let the weight of his ax fall to the ground and leaned on the handle. "The Bible says to watch and pray, not sleep and pray."

"Yet you go," Johannes said. "You think it is wrong, and I agree, yet you go. Is that not also wrong?"

The only reason any of these young men knew Adam sometimes went to the Kauffman farm was because their own family members or neighbors also went. Why did anyone go?

"Noah Kauffman is my nearest neighbor," Adam said. "Jesus told us to love our neighbors as ourselves."

"Do you believe what he does is right?" Seth said.

Adam did not believe it was wrong. Was that the same as saying it was right? This must be what his uncle was trying to say.

"Faith without works is dead," Johannes said. "If you say one thing but do another, are you any better than the hypocrites James warns us of?"

"If you do not believe it is a true calling that serves the church, then do not go," LeRoy said.

Adam swung his ax.

Noah preached only two hours that afternoon, for which Susanna was grateful. She welcomed a bit more time between making sure he was settled on the davenport to sleep for a few hours and helping to get supper under way. Supper was late on the Kauffman farm. Phoebe saw no reason to rush the meal if Noah would not yet be awake to partake, and Susanna found no reason to argue with the sensibility of the plan. They ate late and retired immediately. Phoebe arranged her household chores to be occupied in the house while Noah slept, freeing Susanna to leave the farm if she wished to work by lantern light in the barn and sort out the jars and bags her mother had jumbled. Each time she placed a tin on one of the shelves Noah had cleared off for her, she felt traitorous, as if she expected never to go home to her family again. Now perhaps she would have no home to return to, only a wagon loaded for the journey to Indiana.

Susanna's errand today was specific and close — and had nothing to do with her parents' impending decision. It seemed so long ago that she used to take her sagging mare and rickety cart and arrange to happen by the Zug farm in the afternoons at the same time that Adam would happen to be visible outdoors on his uncle's farm. She smiled when she recalled how Niklaus would wink at them as they eyed the forest path with her collecting basket dangling from her fingers. Whether they found anything to fill it was never important. Only a few weeks ago Susanna was certain Adam would propose and that she would accept with joy. Now she was certain of nothing.

But she did need Adam's help. She could have hitched her cart to Phoebe's most mild-mannered horse. She missed her old mare. The animal belonged to her parents, of course. Even the cart was not hers to take. Susanna was in possession of it simply because Patsy had not paused to ponder the technicalities of ownership the day she rescued Susanna's supplies. But her destination was not far — only to the Zugs' — and the day was not overly hot, so Susanna walked.

She saw Adam before he saw her and slowed her steps to watch his movements, a habit well rehearsed in the old days of happening by. The way he ran a finger under the brim of his hat to scratch where the straw made him itch. The way he never passed an animal without stopping to stroke a nose or offer an apple or carrot. The way he listened intently when his uncle spoke to him. The way he grinned at his aunt while feeding the chickens for her or elbowed his cousin to get to the well-pump first. She loved it all. It was not a difficult thing to imagine what life on a farm with Adam Yotter would be like.

He caught sight of her now as he lifted his head up from setting a fence rail properly in its slot. He lifted a hand in a wave.

She waved back and continued walking toward him.

"I pray you are well," she said as she approached.

He nodded. "And you?"

She nodded. She should have brought her collection basket, not because she expected a walk in the woods but because it would occupy her nervous hands.

"I come asking a favor," she said. "For Phoebe."

He stiffened — or perhaps she imagined he did.

" 'Tis the roof in the barn." Susanna plunged in. "One can see daylight in several places, and they seem to be enlarging. For obvious reasons, Phoebe is not eager that Noah should go up on a ladder to do the repairs."

"So you would like me to go up on the roof?"

Susanna nodded. "Noah keeps saying he is going to do it. It would ease Phoebe's mind if someone else would do it so he would stop talking about it."

"Would he not be safe if he went up in the morning, before he . . . falls under?"

"Likely, yes. But what if the pattern shifts once again? It would be one thing if he fell under while mucking a stall or plowing a row and quite another if it happened while he was on a pitched roof."

Adam nodded. "I see your point."

"So you will help?"

He hesitated.

"Adam?" Susanna said. Whatever was amiss between the two of them ought not to affect Noah and Phoebe. "It has nothing to do with the preaching. It has nothing even to do with the house where the preaching occurs. If you came in the morning, no one else would be there."

Still he hesitated, taking far too long to scratch the back of his neck.

"Adam."

"You were honest with me when you said

you might not go back to church," he said. "Now I will be honest with you. I am trying to discern if I ought to keep going to the Kauffmans'. People draw conclusions from what they observe."

"Conclusions? So what? You know the truth." Idle speculation should not keep him from neighborly helpfulness.

He drew a long, slow breath and swallowed hard. Whatever he was working up to saying would be hard for him, and it would stab Susanna. This much she knew.

"I must take leave of visiting the Kauffmans," he said. "There is too much at risk for the church."

She wanted to screech at him, *This cannot be your true mind!* But he was quite set on what he was saying. When she had prayed that they would once again speak truth to each other, this was not the truth she had hoped for.

"I see," she said. "Then perhaps I will have a word with your *onkel* about the roof."

CHAPTER 30

Susanna crept into Phoebe's kitchen by moonlight. A slice of Phoebe's egg bread might settle her stomach and allow her to sleep at last. If this effort did not succeed, she might as well dress, take a lantern, and go out to the barn to work while she awaited daylight. The grandfather clock Noah built as a wedding gift for Phoebe struck three just as Susanna swallowed the last bite of bread. She sat for a few more minutes in the kitchen, dreading the reality that she would not sleep if she returned to bed now even though in three short hours the household would liven. It might even be earlier, depending on what time Cranky Amos crowed.

Was Adam sleeping? She had never seen his bedroom, of course, so any image in her mind of its furnishings or the quilt Deborah had pieced for him or how he looked when he slept under it were fancies of her own

363

imagination, and she ought not to indulge them. Still Susanna wondered whether making up his mind to stay away from the Kauffmans', at least for a while, had let him embrace restful slumber or caused a disquiet similar to what prevented her from sleeping.

There was too much at risk, he said, and perhaps he was right. No doubt she had stirred the bishop's ire, though he was more likely to name it righteous indignation. Any who had not already heard of the incident soon would, and were she to attend church, all eyes would be on her. And if she did not attend, a dozen conclusions would circulate.

Her family would be drawn in. Elias would be stoic, Veronica agitated, Timothy nosy as usual, and the younger boys confused. Susanna could spare them all if she returned home and privately apologized to the bishop. And if Susanna ceased shouldering responsibility for Noah, perhaps her mother would cease planning for Indiana.

Early, even before Cranky Amos announced daybreak, Susanna donned a dress borrowed from Phoebe, tidied the sparse room where she slept, and whisked a half dozen eggs into a bowl of cheese and chopped bacon. She warmed the oven and placed the iron skillet inside to bake. Then

364

she left a note Phoebe would find in a few minutes along with the egg dish and set off to walk to the Hooley farm. If she had her old mare, she might have taken the cart, but she was fortunate to have her dyes, and though Phoebe would have been glad for her to hitch up one of her horses, Susanna needed the miles to pray.

Her heart pounded as she tried out one salutation after another and discarded them all as inadequate. How should she greet her mother, when Veronica was sure to feel ill-treated by her daughter's friend on top of Susanna's own insolence in the circumstances of her departure?

But someone must take the first step if there was to be reconciliation. It had only been a few days. Susanna still lived as a guest at the Kauffmans'. Surely there was hope.

In the end, Susanna said simply, *"Gut mariye, Mamm."*

Eyes of pain met hers when she stepped through the back door.

"Susanna," Veronica said, scanning Susanna's garb. "I suppose you have come for the rest of your things."

Susanna would welcome her own dresses and aprons but shook her head. "I hope we can talk."

"What is there to speak of?" Veronica's voice cracked. "I will always be your *mamm,* but you seem bent on no longer being my *dochter.*"

"Do not say such a thing, *Mamm.*"

"I have not changed my mind about Indiana. In time you will see that it was the right thing." Veronica sorted the household clothing into piles in the kitchen. Wednesday had been laundry day at the Hooleys' for as long as Susanna could remember.

"I will help you with the wash," Susanna said.

"No need."

Susanna prayed for the right words, but they did not come. Instead, her throat knotted until she gasped for air.

The resolute knock on the front door startled both mother and daughter.

"I will go." Susanna slipped past her mother and padded through the house to the front door, conflicted between relief that the conversation had been interrupted and dread that now she would have to muster the courage to begin again another time.

She opened the door. The *English* man stood on the stoop.

"Miss Hooley," he said. "I wonder if I might speak with your father."

Susanna could not remember the man's

name. In her mind she had only called him "Mr. Indiana," because his interest in the farm had stirred her mother into frantic action.

"I am not certain where he is," Susanna said.

"It would be worthwhile to find him," Mr. Indiana said. "I've brought papers, and the offer is more than fair. Quite generous, actually."

"I will do what I can to find him. Please come in."

She left him standing in the front room and scurried to the kitchen.

Veronica clapped her hands, careful not to let them make a sound as they met. "He came back! I hoped he would, but your *daed* said I should not be so eager."

"Where is Daed?" The man was here. Susanna could do nothing to prevent the conversation both her parents had agreed to have.

"The south field," Veronica said. "He took the boys out there to make sure they understand what they are to do once the harvest begins."

Susanna nodded.

"Go." Veronica put both hands on Susanna's shoulders and spun her toward the back door "Run quickly. We do not want to try Mr. Ingersolla's patience."

Ingersolla. That was it. Not so different from Indiana.

Susanna raced across the backyard. Was it wicked of her to hope her father might have finished in the south field and taken the boys to another corner of the farm? Perhaps they had finished to the south and rotated around to the north and she was now running in entirely the wrong direction. He could be anywhere, and Mr. Ingersolla's patience would have its limits. Surely he was a busy man.

She passed the fence where she used to meet Patsy when they were little girls and felt its tug to linger and remember easier days. Instead, she raced past and found her *daed* just where her *mamm* had said he would be. Breathless, she recounted the guest's arrival.

Elias handed the hoe in his hand to Timothy, who was grinning at the news, and set his face toward the house.

Susanna glared at Timothy. This was his doing. If he had ever learned to mind his own business, Mr. Ingersolla would not be in the Hooley front room encouraging their mother's fixation on Indiana.

Susanna paced after her father, two steps to each one of his strides.

"Daed, you would not really sell the farm, would you?"

"I promised your *mamm* I would hear him out," Elias said. "If he has come in good faith, I will keep my word to her."

"You have spent twenty-five years building this farm," Susanna said. "Your work is paying off now. There are enough acres for at least two of the boys to do well here."

"Susanna." His voice was calm, as always, but firm with caution. Susanna was overstepping.

By the time they reached the house, Veronica had poured Mr. Ingersolla a cup of coffee and set a thick slice of lemon coffee cake in front of him. He consumed both with visible enthusiasm.

"Here is my husband," Veronica said. "Thank you, Susanna. We will allow the men to conduct their business now."

Veronica took Susanna's hand, her grasp unrelenting as she led her daughter to the kitchen. Susanna raised a fist to her mouth to constrain herself as her mother discreetly set a tea tin in the threshold to keep the door from closing fully and then pulled a chair up to the opening she had created. She widened her eyes at Susanna and lifted a finger to her lips.

Susanna closed her eyes and took a deep

breath before inching closer to the door. She was here. She may as well know what was happening.

Mr. Ingersolla's voice was rich and full, and he seemed to have no reason not to speak robustly. Elias's voice was muffled, courteous, restrained — and difficult to hear. Susanna and her mother looked at each other and shrugged, neither of them able to hear both sides of the conversation.

They could hear Mr. Ingersolla saying, "You won't find a better value for your land. . . . Certainly we can discuss your terms. . . . You can be sure your land will be will cared for and will not go to ruin. . . . The new life you seek is within your reach with the price I am offering."

The inflection of her father's muffled voice made Susanna think his contribution was largely patient questions. Whether he was satisfied with Mr. Ingersolla's responses was less evident.

" 'Tis going well," Veronica whispered. "If your *daed* was not interested, the visit would not have lasted this long."

Panic rose through Susanna's core. Her mother was right. Her father was taking this offer seriously. His patience with the conversation went beyond his promise to hear out the *English* man merely to placate his wife.

Susanna's chest stung with every breath.

"I am sorry, *Mamm,*" Susanna said, whispering. "I cannot leave Noah. Please do not ask me to. I beg you. Please."

And I do not want to leave Adam. Not like this. Not ever. These weeks were a season that someday they would look back on and barely be able to recall the details. Never before had she wanted to believe anything as much as she wanted to believe this one thing.

Veronica met her daughter's eyes for the second time that morning. "This is a decision your *daed* and I will make, and we will not leave behind an unmarried daughter."

Finally, the two men stood, shook hands, and walked toward the front door, where they shook hands once again.

What did that mean? Were they shaking on an agreement? Had her father given his word in his reserved manner?

Susanna jumped back from the kitchen door, and her mother scraped her chair back to its place at the table and scooped up the tea tin just as Elias reached the door.

Elias looked from his wife to his daughter. "I hope you heard what you wanted to hear."

Veronica slapped his shoulder with the back of her fingers. "Would it hurt you to speak up for once in your life?"

"Daed," Susanna said, "do not tease us. What have you decided?"

"I have made a significant decision." His face sobered.

Susanna's stomach sank.

"You have accepted his offer?" Veronica said, her eyes bright.

Elias wagged a finger. "No, I have not."

Susanna's heart surged.

"But I have agreed to look at the papers very carefully," Elias said, "and take the matter under prayerful consideration. Mr. Ingersolla is of the Baptist faith and understands what it means to seek *Gottes wille* in a decision such as this one."

"What are the terms?" Veronica said.

"The land, the structures, the cows, the pig, as many chickens as we want to leave behind," Elias said.

"And the harvest?" Susanna asked.

"He offered to buy out the harvest," Elias said, "but I want the boys to see the harvest through, especially Timothy. It will not be long before he must be able to handle a farm from planting to harvest. He needs this season to learn."

Veronica nodded. "Yes, that is wise. And the horses?"

"We will take that under consideration,"

Elias said. "He will buy them if we wish to sell, but of course he understands we need to take at least four to see us to Indiana in the wagon.

Susanna could not bring herself to ask about the old mare, who would not be able to keep up on a lengthy journey but also had no value as a work animal.

Prayerful consideration was the least she would expect from her father, but it was not a decision.

"How long?" Susanna asked.

"We will meet again in one week, and I will give him my answer."

CHAPTER 31

After breakfast the following day, Adam made a list of tasks, all of which would keep him up close to the road or in the Zug farmyard where he had a clear view of passing traffic. It included checking the fence again for repairs — although he and Jonas had done this several times and the fence was more than ready for winter; trimming tree branches threatening to hang too low into the road; making sure the ditch alongside the road was unimpeded, in case a sudden fall rainstorm required rapid drainage; and exercising the horses in the pasture that had not been called on for service in recent days. None of it was essential. Adam settled for useful.

And none of it pleased him. His hope to catch sight of Susanna out making deliveries of cloth was not because he hoped to divert her for a walk with her collection basket. If only that were so. On this day, breathing did not come automatically. Every few minutes he caught himself short on breath and inhaled with sharp urgency. The sound of every approaching horse or buggy, few as they were, caused him to raise his head in a concoction of anticipation and dread.

But he must see her. Delay would bring no soothing balm.

Susanna's creaky cart gave her away. Adam had offered several times to oil every part of it, and Susanna shrugged, seeing no need. Flimsy as it was, the cart served her well enough. Seeing it hitched to one of the Kauffmans' tamest horses underscored the necessity of this conversation.

Adam flagged her down in the road. She halted the horse but said nothing.

"I thought we should talk again," Adam said, slipping fingers in the bridle lest Susanna decide to put the rig into motion prematurely.

She still said nothing, barely meeting his eyes.

"I am sorry that my decision to stay away from the Kauffmans' hurts you," Adam said. "You know I care for you."

Susanna looked up now. "Have you reconsidered?"

"I have further considered," he said.

"Prayerfully and daily."

She read his eyes. "And you have arrived at the same conclusion." Same, yes. And more.

"Susanna." He choked on her name.

"Do not say it, Adam. Please."

"So many days I have lingered in view of the road," he said, "imagining where we might walk and what we might find and what our words for each other would be."

He had not yet said the final words, and already her face wrenched. His own no doubt matched her contortions.

"I will not ask you to deny your conscience," he said. "I must only follow mine. And if that parts our paths . . ."

"Adam." Tears welled in her eyes. "I wish you could understand about Noah."

"Help me. Your loyalty is admirable, but if it should lead you from the church, I wonder if it can be right after all."

"I was a child," Susanna said. "I like to think I was no naughtier than any child, but I hated to be scolded. Noah was a young man, not even married to Phoebe yet, and he was the one person I knew who would listen before scolding. My own foolishness might have cost me my life, and it was Noah who found me and carried me home, just the way I imagine the Good Shepherd carries home the lost lamb."

"Why have I never heard this story before?" Adam asked.

"It was so long ago, and it was always just between Noah and me. I never imagined it would matter to anyone else."

"If it matters to you," Adam said, "then it matters to me."

"You know Noah. You know he is not malicious or self-seeking. You know he needs help. You know he speaks truth."

Adam kicked a rock. "I do not claim certainty about what to believe. But when I was baptized, I promised to submit to the church. When I transferred to this district, my promises came with me. If the bishop does not bless what Noah does, then how can assisting Noah be an act of submission?"

"So you will not see Noah, and you will not see me. Is this what you mean to say?"

Adam nodded. The only words that formed were ones he had promised himself not to speak.

Susanna picked up the reins, her face pale and shoulders slumped. Adam stood in the middle of the road and watched her disappear around the bend. Only then did he speak.

"Susanna Hooley, I love you."

■ ■ ■ ■

Susanna sobbed as she turned off the main road in favor of a less used route that would keep her tears from sight. The deliveries would have to wait. She wanted only to get back to the Kauffman farm, throw herself on the narrow cot where she spent her nights, and turn her face to the pillow. When the wind slammed the back door behind her, though, Phoebe appeared in the kitchen, and fresh engorging tears made it impossible for Susanna to hold her composure.

Phoebe took her by the shoulders and guided her to a chair.

The *English* man's offer on the farm.

Veronica's determination to take her children to spiritual safety in Indiana.

Adam's refusal to patch the roof.

Now his breaking off with Susanna.

She wept, and Phoebe held her until the shuddering stilled.

"Perhaps Noah and I were wrong to suggest you stay with us," Phoebe said softly into Susanna's ear.

Susanna drew back. "But you know what my *mamm* did to my things. You know she will keep trying to separate me from Noah."

Phoebe nodded. "I am not a mother, but I cannot be certain I would not do just as your *mamm* has. She is protecting you because she loves you, just as the other families that have moved to Indiana believe it is best for their children."

"But Noah is my *mamm*'s cousin. How can she have so little pity?"

Phoebe shook her head. "Noah and I do not need pity."

"I have chosen my words carelessly," Susanna said. "I am here out of love, not pity."

"We may not have counted the cost before we built this house."

"I would not change anything!"

"But I might," Phoebe said. "I have received your love without loving well in return."

"No!" Susanna gripped Phoebe's hand.

"No one need decide anything this moment," Phoebe said. "Think and pray, just as your *daed* has promised to do."

"But if I leave, what about you?"

"God will provide. *Gottes wille.*" Phoebe stood up. "I promised Mrs. Swigert three dozen eggs. She has a house full of relatives from Somerset County."

"I will stay with Noah." Susanna looked out the kitchen window. "Where is he?"

"In the barn building you more shelves."

Susanna sighed.

"I know what you are thinking," Phoebe said. "If you go home, he will have wasted his time."

Susanna nodded.

"Leave him be," Phoebe said. "We can always use more shelves in the barn. But you do not have to stay to watch him. 'Tis still before midday, and Noah has been remarking of late that he does not need to be hovered over quite so deliberately. He is himself in the morning without exception. Finish your deliveries."

"I will think about it." Susanna stood and smoothed her apron.

Splashing cold water on her face might erase the distress from her face and restore purpose to her day. Phoebe picked up her basket of eggs, and Susanna went outside to the well to raise a bucket of refreshing liquid. She wandered into the barn to reassure herself that Noah was making progress on an ordinary task for which he was more than capable and found him humming a hymn. He looked up and smiled.

"I did not realize you were back," he said.

"Just stopping in." Susanna choked back the urge to say more. The was no need to distress Noah. She needed time to think. Driving to make deliveries might be the right choice after all. "Phoebe has gone to see Mrs. Swigert. Do you need anything before I go?"

"Nothing at all." Noah picked up his hammer. "Go. I feel quite fit. We will see each other for our dinner in a little while."

Susanna calculated carefully. Despite Phoebe's best intentions to simply drop off the eggs and return home, Mrs. Swigert would foist coffee and pastries on her and make sure Phoebe met every visiting relative and chatted long enough to uncover where her family line might have crossed theirs sometime in the last hundred years. Mrs. Swigert, who had been to hear Noah preach on four occasions that Susanna could recall and whose husband had brought the benches Susanna detested, might even raise the subject as a point of fascinating conversation, making it even more difficult for Phoebe to make a swift departure. But it was barely midmorning. Susanna had time to make at least some of the deliveries she had planned for the day and still be back on the Kauffman farm before the earliest time she had ever seen Noah fall under and before spectators would begin to assemble.

First she went to the Maist farm with a pale gray length of fabric that would become dresses for three young daughters about the ages of her youngest brothers. Mrs. Maist paid her with newly woven cloth she thought Susanna might like to use to make herself a new dress.

"God will provide," Phoebe had said earlier. If Susanna decided not to return home, she would need a new dress. She could not share Phoebe's wardrobe indefinitely.

Next she took dye made from beet juice and dandelion roots to Mrs. Beiler, who gushed over the rich hue even though Susanna considered it quite ordinary. In exchange Susanna placed a meat pie and a fruit pie in the cart, a barter that would ease Phoebe's burden in the kitchen. Perhaps they would eat them for midday dinner.

Susanna judged she had time for one more stop. She owed Deborah Zug a tin of pale yellow dye meant for a tablecloth, but it would have to wait until Susanna could face the possibility of seeing Adam. If only she had thought to foist it on him while he stood there in the road. Instead of the Zugs', she went to the Hostetlers with the only color dye Mrs. Hostetler ever requested, black. The deeper and darker the black, the better, and it came as no surprise that Mrs. Hostetler's barter was a black apron.

"God will provide." Muslin for a dress, a complete meal, a perfectly stitched apron. Susanna whispered thanks for these provisions as she returned to the Kauffmans'. Phoebe's buggy was not yet back. Susanna slipped into the kitchen to leave the pies on the table, pleased that she could provide a meal for the household.

"Noah?" Susanna stuck her head into the front room. "Are you here?"

No answer came. Noah must still be in the barn. Susanna went out the back door and crossed the yard, supposing she would hear the sound of a hammer. The barn was empty.

Susanna stepped outside again. "Noah?"

A few chickens clucked and fluttered.

Susanna spun toward the shed where Noah kept his plow and other implements he needed only at planting or harvesting. Silent iron tools greeted her, with no sign Noah had been there recently. She scurried toward the pasture, where the cow lay in the dirt chewing cud and the horses nibbled at the grass. Noah was not in the pasture, nor walking along the fence. Susanna balled the fabric of her skirt in her hands to allow her feet speed, running toward the vegetable garden, where Noah sometimes weeded, and then toward the planted fields. She saw no one.

She must have missed him somewhere. Susanna retraced her steps — with urgency — fighting off the fright that he might have climbed to the barn roof.

"Cousin Noah!"

But he was not on the roof. He was not in the house. He was not in the chicken coop. He was not behind the shed. He was not in the fields or the pasture.

Noah was nowhere.

Noah was nowhere.

CHAPTER 32

Heat drenched Adam's shirt beyond what he would wish to sit in at his aunt's midday dinner table. At the well, he splashed himself clean, removed his shirt to rinse it in the bucket, and donned a fresh dry garment before anyone caught him shirtless. He ran his hands through his hair and settled his straw hat where it belonged, expecting that any moment now Deborah would call him to dinner.

The sight of Susanna racing her cart into the Zug yard startled him.

"Adam," she said as she reined the horse to an abrupt stop, "you must help. You must!"

He sucked in his breath. She was back about the barn roof, and in a fury.

"I am sure someone else will be glad to patch the roof." Adam would leave it to one of the men who went to hear Noah preach.

Susanna shook her head and jumped out

of the cart. "Not that. Noah is missing."

"Missing?"

"I have looked everywhere," Susanna said. "He is not on the farm."

"An errand," Adam suggested, though his pulse pushed faster.

Susanna shook her head with more vigor. "I do not think so. The horses are there."

"He might have walked."

"He left no note."

Noah was not the sort to jaunt off because of an impetuous thought. When he left the farm, he had a list long enough to make the excursion worthwhile.

"The fields, the outbuildings — I have looked everywhere," Susanna said.

"You think he has wandered off?"

"I do not know what to think, except that we must find him."

Adam glanced at the sun. "It is not yet time for his spell. He knows to be careful as the time approaches."

"Noah is not a Swiss watch," Susanna said. "We cannot be certain that the time will not vary. After all, it used to be in the middle of the night."

Adam's eyes darted around the Zug farm as if he might settle on something also present on the Kauffman land to suggest where Noah could have gone.

"We are wasting time," Susanna said. "You cannot say no. What if someone took Noah?"

Adam lurched. "Why would anyone take Noah?"

"To stop his preaching, of course."

"You do not mean Shem."

"I do not mean anyone in particular. I only mean that we must think of every possibility."

"How long has he been missing?"

"I only just discovered him gone," Susanna said, her voice cracking. "But he might have left soon after Phoebe and I did, and that was hours ago."

"But without a horse —"

Susanna interrupted him with a wide gesture toward the mountain. "With danger in his backyard, why should he need a horse to come to harm?"

Adam nodded. Susanna's breath came fast and shallow. Fright transformed her countenance.

"I am mindful of our previous conversation," she said, "but Adam, Noah is missing. He is vulnerable. You must help me find him."

Niklaus strode toward Susanna's familiar cart hitched to a Kauffman horse. Normally

387

Susanna constrained her manners in a becoming way, but now she stood in his yard in an unabashed plea for help, mindless of volume or tenor.

"Of course we will help," Niklaus said.

"And Jonas?" Susanna said.

Niklaus swung his head back and forth. "He is off the farm all day today."

Susanna trembled. "I would not make such a fuss if I did not believe Noah might be in danger."

"Of course." Niklaus ran a hand along the edge of her cart. "This will only slow you down. We will need to be on horseback, especially if we have to go up the mountain."

"I do not ride." Susanna's eyes puddled.

"Then we will find a horse sturdy enough for the two of you." Niklaus marched toward the stable with Adam and Susanna in his wake. Susanna was slight enough to settle comfortably behind Adam in one of the longer saddles.

In tandem, Niklaus and Adam bridled Adam's gray stallion and led it outside.

"I want the two of you to go back to Noah's farm," Niklaus said. "Ride the entire perimeter and then work your way toward the house and barn. Make sure he did not come home on his own or has not fallen somewhere."

"We are wasting time," Susanna said. "I told Adam I looked already."

"The most likely scenario is that he is still on the farm but out of sight," Niklaus said. "We will begin there. Get on the horse."

Adam slung himself into the saddle and offered a hand to Susanna. Niklaus stood behind her, ready if she should misjudge the mount.

"I will be right behind you," Niklaus said, "as soon as I can get another horse ready."

Susanna held Adam's waist more tentatively than Niklaus would have imagined. Once they found Noah, Niklaus would sort out what had gone wrong between the two of them.

"Go!" He slapped the stallion's rump and watched the animal gallop up the lane.

Niklaus turned to find his wife approaching.

"What is going on?" Deborah asked.

Niklaus explained.

"You will need food and water," she said. "When you find Noah, he will need refreshment. I will pack something while you get yourself ready."

Niklaus nodded.

"Take two horses," Deborah said. "And some ropes. You may have to tie him to the saddle. And the good lantern."

Niklaus met his wife's eyes, both of them mindful of the image her words created. If Noah had come to harm and could not sit upright, they would need the ropes.

And if he had come to ultimate harm — Niklaus banished the possibility and pushed back into the stable for two sure-footed animals and his best saddlebags. His charcoal-gray stallion was the strongest in the stable, and a black mare was gentle enough to carry an unconscious rider.

"It is good we are coming early," Patsy said to her father, their side-by-side mounts gently trotting toward the Kauffman farm after a vigorous run in which both riders had given the animals their heads. "You will get to speak to Noah. I'm sure he will be glad to see you."

"And I him," Charles said. "I want to know how he is in his spirit."

Patsy chuckled. "And you want to see him fall under again."

"It is a curious sight," Charles conceded. "The more I observe it, the more I may understand it."

"Is it not enough to hear his words and know that God brings it to be?"

Charles nodded. "For me, yes. But I encounter questioning souls about this phenomenon, and I should be more prepared to offer answers."

They turned into the path cut through the trees, barely wide enough for a wagon, and entered Kauffman land.

"I can also see what Phoebe needs help with," Patsy said.

Sometimes when Patsy arrived, Phoebe had not yet had a chance to collect the day's eggs, or milk awaited churning into butter, or the vegetable garden was heavy with abundance in need of picking. Their early arrival today would also allow her father to judge what Noah might need help with, or at least offer a few moments of companionship.

As Patsy expected, they had arrived in advance of the usual gathering crowd. Phoebe's angry chicken episode made some people more cautious about finding seats on the benches, but nearly always there would still be wagons lining up around the perimeter of the yard. A moment of relief that they had in fact arrived before the audience and could enjoy a cheerful visit with Noah and Phoebe soon morphed into befuddlement.

The farm was too still.

The horses were in the pasture, where Patsy expected to find them, but no sound of work rose from the house or barn — though the doors were wide open on both structures.

Patsy slid off Galahad, yanked open the barn door, and walked through the building to emerge on the other side. A few chickens flustered, but most lost interest once they saw she dropped no feed. The makeshift work area Noah had rigged for Susanna's dye pots showed no sign of recent use. The back door of the house was unlatched, and Patsy went in and called for Noah, Phoebe, or Susanna before walking through the house and returning to her father in the front yard.

"No one is home," she said. "It's very odd."

"They must have gone off together somewhere," Charles said.

"Perhaps." It was possible, though in Patsy's experience, Phoebe preferred that Noah be at home when the time came that he might fall under.

"As long as they are together, all is well," Charles said, leading the horses to the hooks on the barn wall to tie them with generous leash. "Will they mind if I take a place on one of the benches?"

"I'm sure not," Patsy said. She sat down herself, something she rarely did, and imagined what it must be like to come to the Kauffman farm simply to hear Noah preach the Word of God and not to be vigilant about those who came with other intentions or because there was work to do and someone needed to be with Noah.

Patsy and Charles sat side by side on the front bench. He was relaxed and smiled in anticipation. Patsy, though, grew stiffer with each moment. Something was wrong.

CHAPTER 33

Susanna had never ridden behind Adam before. On Galahad with Patsy, it was not unseemly to hold on to her friend and lean together into the gathering speed of the horse. A few weeks ago, the thought of hanging on to Adam for the same purpose would have stirred giddiness. More than once, in the secret of imagination, she had hoped that when they were married she could duck her head into his back, urging him to dare a fiercer gallop. Grief over a moment was not to be mingled with anxiety about Noah, though, and Susanna could not help but say, "Faster!"

And Adam had gone faster, so now she had her head against the back of his shoulder just as she had imagined but without exhilaration. In only a few yards, she had seen the insensibility of trying to keep her quilted black bonnet on her head and let it hang from her neck by the ties while her cheek felt the muscles of Adam's back rippling beneath his movements with the reins.

They thundered onto the Kauffman farm.

"Patsy has brought her father," Susanna called above the wind and clatter of hooves.

Two figures popped up from the front bench and turned toward them.

"Have you seen Noah?" Susanna said as Adam halted the stallion.

Patsy shook her head.

"Phoebe?" Susanna said.

Once again Patsy shook her head. "Is something amiss? I was surprised to arrive and find none of you here."

That had never been the plan. Noah was to remain on the farm, and Phoebe had meant to have a short visit. Both should have been cleaning up for dinner by the time Susanna returned from her deliveries.

Susanna managed some words and hoped they formed sentences.

"We'll help look," Charles said. "We have two good horses."

Susanna nodded. "Niklaus will be right behind us. We must search the farm again, every irrigation ditch and furrowed row."

"We'll go," Patsy said, marching toward Galahad. "We will meet you back here one way or the other. Papa, come with me."

Susanna released her grip on Adam's

waist, something she should have done as soon as the horse stilled. She hesitated to dismount if she was going to get back on soon. Every second would matter if they had to go up the mountain.

"What should we do?" she said as Patsy and Charles raced toward the Kauffman fields.

"We wait."

Adam's surety surprised her.

"My *onkel* will be here soon, and with two people searching the fields, we will have a report soon."

"And Phoebe," Susanna murmured.

Adam twisted in the saddle for a glimpse of her face, and Susanna did not turn away.

The next sound was an early arriving wagon. Susanna moaned and leaned out of the saddle until she could free both legs to drop to the ground. A busybody spreading rumors about impropriety would help nothing.

"Stay calm." Adam dismounted in the other direction and handed Susanna the reins.

He sauntered a few yards and met the wagon driven by Mrs. Henderson, an *English* woman. "Noah will not be preaching today."

"Why not? What happened?" Mrs. Henderson said.

"He does not preach every day," Adam said. "This is one of those days."

"How can you be sure?"

"I am quite sure. Noah will not be coming to the window this afternoon."

Fretting, Susanna was holding her breath. If they had to search further for Noah, they would need all the help possible, but a mother in a wagon with three children was not likely to be a swift addition to the search party.

"I might wait and see for myself," Mrs. Henderson said. "The children will be content to play in the wagon bed."

Adam lifted his eyes beyond the wagon, cocking his head slightly to listen for his uncle's galloping horse. Instead, another wagon rolled in, followed by two men on horses separated by twenty yards and both in unhurried trots.

Adam glanced at Susanna, who shrugged more with her eyes than her shoulders. He walked back toward her.

"Maybe we should go in the house and close the shutters," he said.

Susanna shook her head. "That will only raise more questions about whether Noah is inside ill or what we might be hiding.

Besides, Phoebe could turn up any minute."

"Maybe one of us should walk up to the lane to meet her there," Adam said.

"I will," Susanna said. "She should hear it from me."

"Remember," Adam said, "Patsy and Charles could also return with news that all is well."

Susanna squeezed her eyes. "All is not well, Adam."

Adam nudged her elbow. "Go."

She hurried up the lane. Another Amish wagon passed her on its way down, and a couple of *English* men on horses.

Where was Niklaus? He should have been right behind Adam and her.

"What is the matter, Adam?" Mr. Krabill said.

Adam's attention snapped back from Susanna's disappearing form to the scene magnifying before him.

"Why must anything be the matter?" Adam said.

"You look fidgety."

"I have tried to explain there will be no sermon today," Adam said.

The next wagon rattling down the hill was Phoebe's, and Susanna was beside her on the bench. Phoebe drove far too fast for the slope and the presence of other rigs and horses. Adam waved some people out of the way and went to greet her.

"Where is he?" Phoebe spoke loudly enough to make heads turn.

"His own wife doesn't know where he is?" someone said.

"Adam," Phoebe said, "send these people away."

"I have been trying," he said.

"I cannot manage their presence right now," Phoebe said. She called toward the benches, "Please go home. You may come again another day."

"No!" Susanna said. "There are men and horses here. They might help."

Adam spun around to address the crowd, even as it grew by another half dozen people.

"May I have your attention, please?" Adam strode toward the benches. "As I have explained, Noah will not be preaching today. This is because we fear Noah is not on the farm. I expect that in a very few minutes an organized search will begin to make sure that our brother has not come to harm. I stand before you and call upon you either to be prepared to help or to clear away so that you do not impede the effort."

"I knew something peculiar was happening," Mrs. Henderson said. "You and the

Hooley girl have been acting oddly since I arrived."

"Again," Adam said, "if you can help, we welcome your assistance. If your responsibilities prevent this, then I ask you to be on your way."

Ropes. Water. Blankets. Adam tried to think what else he might gather.

Lanterns.

In the early afternoon, it was difficult to imagine they might still be looking for Noah after nightfall, but if they were going up on the mountain, Adam wanted to be prepared.

Niklaus heard the ruckus before it came into view. As he turned into the Kauffman lane, leading a second saddled horse, Patsy and Charles galloped out of a field of cornstalks and headed straight for the farmyard. Niklaus pressed his knees into his horse again and followed them.

Somber, Patsy and Charles shook their heads at Susanna. Phoebe slumped into Susanna's arms.

"Who has a saddled horse?" Niklaus called out.

"I have a good wagon and a sturdy team," Mrs. Wagler said.

"A rig will be too cumbersome up on the ridge," Niklaus said.

Adam emerged from the barn with two lanterns. Niklaus nodded approval. Adam might be tentative about responding to conflict of opinion, but he had a good head on his shoulders in a situation like this one. They now had three lanterns that Niklaus hoped they would have no use for.

"Are we certain Noah did not take a horse?" Niklaus said.

Phoebe straightened and looked toward the pasture. "They are all there but the one Susanna took. He is on foot."

"Do you have extra saddles?" Niklaus said.

"Just the one Noah uses," Phoebe said. "The other has a broken strap."

"How far could he have gotten?" Susanna asked.

"Depends which direction he went," Niklaus said. He lifted his eyes to Jacks Mountain.

"We'll find him."

Niklaus did not know the name of the *English* man who spoke, but he nodded gratitude.

"If you can help, move over toward the barn," Niklaus said. He would need to know how many men were available before formulating further instructions.

Relief rushed through Susanna. Niklaus and

Adam were taking charge. The muddle of spectators — the number was still growing — gradually sorted itself out so that there was a clearer indication of who might ride with the search party.

"I want to go," Susanna blurted out.

"Someone must stay with Phoebe," Niklaus said.

It was the sensible choice, but Susanna's impulse fought it.

"If Noah comes home on his own," Niklaus said, "someone must be here — someone who knows his needs."

Still the notion that she must stay behind stuck in Susanna's throat.

"I will stay," Mrs. Krabill said.

"As will I," Mrs. Lantz said. "The children will be glad for the break from their chores waiting for them at home. Surely the search will be accomplished quickly."

Susanna met Niklaus's gaze. He nodded slightly.

"I'm coming, too," Patsy said.

"I would expect nothing else," Niklaus said. "You have the finest horse in the valley and can teach us all a thing or two about riding."

Adam dragged Noah's saddle out of the stable and bridled the horse Phoebe specified as the best the Kauffmans had before handing the reins to one of the men who had arrived encumbered with a wagon.

Susanna turned to Phoebe. "Forgive me. I was thinking of myself. I will stay if you want me to."

Phoebe squeezed Susanna's hand. "You go. It will comfort me to know you are there if they find him on the mountain."

"I pray that he steps out of the woods and into your arms," Susanna said, "and that we have all worried for nothing."

Niklaus was giving instructions, a strategy for riders to canvass the area around the Kauffman farm before heading up the mountain. A ridge halfway up the mountain would be the meeting place if no one spotted Noah before reaching it.

Adam swung his own horse around to where Susanna stood and leaned down to clasp her arm. Susanna forced down the knot in her neck and let him hoist her up. The search party stirred up dust as it thundered off the farm.

"Faster!" Susanna said to Adam's back for the second time that afternoon.

Maybe she should have ridden with Patsy. Galahad charged ahead of them.

CHAPTER 34

Adam's stallion was no Galahad, but he could be coaxed to give more than he was accustomed to giving as the riders surveyed the acres Niklaus had assigned them to inspect. Susanna gripped Adam's waist but sat up straight in the saddle behind him to look in every direction.

"He is not here," Susanna said.

"We have been around twice," Adam said.

"We should head for the ridge. Is this horse up for the climb?"

"Of course."

Adam pressed his knees into the horse. Susanna leaned into him. They gathered speed steadily.

Suddenly the horse began to rear. Adam yanked the reins to one side before the rising front legs could dump Susanna off the back. The road's shoulder was uneven and sloped, but once all four hooves were on the ground again, Adam stared back at the road.

The bishop's reddish-brown horse had bolted in from a side trail and halted abruptly, under the bishop's command, across the trampled earthen road, impeding progression from either direction.

"Good afternoon, Bishop," Adam said, turning his horse back in the right direction.

Disapproval flared in Shem's eyes, which quickly settled on Susanna sitting astride behind Adam.

"Please, Bishop," Susanna said, "let us pass. Noah Kauffman has gone missing, and we are searching for him."

Shem gave a slight nod. "I have encountered others from the search party."

"Has anyone seen Noah?" Susanna asked.

The tremble in her voice was something Adam wished he would never hear again.

"No," Shem said.

Adam urged his horse back to the flat, narrow road, but Shem's horse remained unmoved.

"None of this should have happened," Shem said.

Adam swallowed his reply. Lectures about "should" would not change the fact that Noah was missing.

"If Noah had been exposed for what he

is," Shem said, "it would not have come to this."

"Bishop." Susanna's single word held a tome of pleas.

From down the road, horses' hooves beat toward them. Charles and Patsy had circled back.

"Ah," Shem said, as Charles reined in his horse. "Here we have the true cause of these circumstances."

Charles's response was swift. "In my own ministry, I find that human willfulness is often the cause of undesirable circumstances, such as those who would stand in the way of good works and well-being."

"Willfulness, indeed."

Shem's ability to keep his animal completely still was remarkable, and without the distraction of even a dipping head, Adam's eyes saw the ire in the bishop's posture.

"You willfully encouraged a sheep of my flock," Shem said. "You willfully lured one of my fellow ministers into your snare."

"Snare?" Charles's eyebrows rose. " 'The Lord is known by the judgment which he executeth: the wicked is snared in the work of his own hands.' "

Shem glared. " 'The wicked is snared by the transgression of his lips: but the just shall come out of trouble.' "

406

"Noah is the one in trouble now," Patsy said, "and no one can possibly think him wicked."

"Is he not snared by his own words?" Shem lifted his heavy eyebrows. "Who are we to interfere with the will of God who chastises?"

"Will of God?" Charles's pitch rose. "The Good Shepherd cares only for his sheep and calls him by name."

They were losing time — precious minutes. Adam turned his head and whispered to Susanna, "Hang on with all you have."

Her arms tightened around him, and Adam secured his grip on the reins before signaling his horse forward. The road was blocked, but if his horse could not manage the ruggedness of the shoulder with speed, then Adam would think twice about taking him up to the ridge. He rushed around Shem and his statuesque horse and past Patsy and Charles on their restless beasts. Within seconds he was galloping again, with pounding hooves trailing behind.

Only when they reached the ridge did Susanna allow her lungs to fill and empty with capacity. The two *English* men were already there.

"Nothing?" Susanna searched their faces.

"We circled our area three times," one of them said. "Even made some inquiries. No one saw Mr. Kauffman come through that sector."

Patsy and Charles arrived.

"You must forgive me," Charles said to Susanna and Adam. "Frustration got the best of me, and I spoke with disrespect to your bishop."

Susanna's eyes rolled. Could anyone have maintained self-control during that encounter? They might be there still, sparring with Bible verses, if Adam had not had enough of it.

Niklaus arrived next, still leading the empty horse they all hoped Noah would ride home in his own strength.

Then came two more Amish men on horses.

After a few more minutes, it seemed no more would come. The search party was already diminishing.

"What did you see and hear?" Niklaus asked.

The *English* recounted the conversations they had instigated. The Amish men described the back roads they had thought to examine, places the *English* had no reason to go but which the Amish often used to travel between farms.

There had been more volunteers when they organized on the Kauffman farm, but Susanna had expected that some would drop out of the search, constrained by their own circumstances. Still, her gut clenched at the reduced number.

"One of the others might have found him," Susanna said. "They would have made sure he got home instead of coming up here."

"One of us could ride down," Patsy said, "to be sure."

Niklaus shook his head. "They know we are on the ridge. If someone found him, they would send a rider to us."

"Wherever he is," Charles said, "he is well hidden."

A final rider crested. Susanna's stomach sank.

"I cannot speak to the lost among this group," Shem said, "but to my own church members, I say that I believe you should return to your families and not interfere with the workings of God in this matter."

"Shem." Niklaus turned his horse toward the bishop. "Whether you count me among the lost or your own church members, I do not know. But I am certain God's will is compassion, and if we may be instruments of compassion, we will have served Him well."

"I must insist," Shem said.

None of the Amish moved. Susanna braced her hands on the back of Adam's saddle.

"Shem," Niklaus said, "this is not your true heart. You are not a severe man. Events of late are confusing for many of us. We will find our way out together, but in this moment we must think only of Noah."

Niklaus refused to let go of Shem's eyes. He barely recognized the old Shem in the features carved into fury. Shem had always been more tightly wound than Niklaus, but he did not become bishop because he threatened church members into obedience. A heart of submission was gladly given.

"You cannot change *Gottes wille,*" Shem said. "What God has decreed shall be."

"I do not wish to change *Gottes wille,*" Niklaus said, "only to accomplish it in the life of my friend and neighbor."

"Only God can accomplish His divine will."

Niklaus ran fingers across his mouth to mask his exasperation. This was not the time or place for theological nuances.

"I will say to you," Niklaus said, "what we

said to those who gathered in Noah's yard.
If you are able to help, we are grateful to
have you. If you feel you cannot in good
conscience do so, then please do not hinder
our efforts."

Shem did not move.

"What will we do now?" Charles said. "We
have come nearly a third of the way up the
mountain, using several different paths, and
we have not seen anything."

"Galahad can handle the whole mountain," Patsy said. "I take him up all the
time."

" 'Tis true," Susanna said.

Niklaus nodded. "Galahad is a virtuous
servant, and we may call on him to exceed
his best."

A couple of horses adjusted their feet, as
if recognizing what would soon be asked of
them.

"We are reduced to five pair," Niklaus
said, his eyes fastened on Shem again. He
pointed up Jacks Mountain. "I suggest we
pair off and comb the distance between here
and that ledge. Moreover, we should remain
within shouting distance of each other. If
one of us sees Noah — or even a thread
that may have come from his trousers — we
will call for the others."

Around the ragged circle, heads nodded.

"Patsy and Charles," Niklaus said, "you take your horses to the bend and begin there."

Father and daughter were on their way before Niklaus made further assignments, sending the two *English* men next and then the two Amish men.

"Adam and Susanna, since you are already sharing a horse, I see no cause to separate you now." Niklaus held up a hand to stave off Shem's imminent objection. "Go on. Waste no moment."

That left Niklaus with Shem. He might have scrambled the pairs differently, but at the moment, he did not trust Shem out of his sight. No one else should be left to endure Shem's perplexing tirades.

With her bonnet once again hanging by the ties, Susanna lifted her chin to prop it on Adam's shoulder.

"I do not know what I am looking for," Susanna said. "Daed taught Timothy to track but never thought I needed to learn."

"Watch the trees," Adam said, his breath warm on her face. "He may have caught a piece of clothing or lost a shoe. Or if he stumbled, there might be a batch of broken branches."

Susanna nodded.

"What color shirt was he wearing today?" Adam said. "White?"

Susanna squeezed her eyes and pictured the corner of the barn where she had last seen Noah. "Brown."

"That may be a little harder to see than white."

"I should never have left him."

"No one blames you, Susanna."

"I blame me."

Adam shortened the reins. "Hang on. 'Tis getting steep."

The horse took the incline ably, and when they reached a space flat enough, Adam halted.

"We must not go so quickly that we do not search well and carefully," Adam said.

Pressure built in Susanna's lungs. "Adam, I am frightened."

" 'Fear thou not; for I am with thee: be not dismayed; for I am thy God: I will strengthen thee; yea, I will help thee; yea, I will uphold thee with the right hand of my righteousness.' "

"Isaiah," Susanna murmured into his shoulder. " 'Be strong and of a good courage, fear not, nor be afraid of them: for the Lord thy God, he it is that doth go with thee; he will not fail thee, nor forsake thee.' "

"My favorite. Deuteronomy," Adam said. "Here is another: 'Be strong and of a good courage; be not afraid, neither be thou dismayed: for the Lord thy God is with thee whithersoever thou goest.' "

"Joshua 1:9."

In silence they peered into the thickening forest around them. Susanna lifted her eyes to the vastness of the Kish Valley below them. Her throat thickened.

"In all of this that has come from the hand of God," she whispered, her voice small, "Noah will be tiny. How will we find him? What if we are not looking in the right place?"

"One more," Adam said. " 'Thou shalt not be afraid for the terror by night; nor for the arrow that flieth by day.' "

Psalm 91. Susanna knew it well. *"There shall no evil befall thee, neither shall any plague come nigh thy dwelling. For he shall give his angels charge over thee, to keep thee in all thy ways. They shall bear thee up in their hands, lest thou dash thy foot against a stone."*

"Adam," she said.

"Yes?"

"How have we lost our way?"

She listened to him breathe, three times in and three times out.

"We will find it once again," he said.

CHAPTER 35

"Noah could be on Stone Mountain," Charles said. "We assumed Jacks Mountain because it's closer to the farm, but who is to say he didn't cross the valley in the other direction?"

Patsy shook her head at the thought that they had wasted valuable time on an erroneous assumption. What her father suggested was possible but unlikely.

"With no horse," Patsy said, "it makes the most sense that he would have left the farm by the back way, sticking to the paths the Amish use to visit each other." Stone Mountain was on the other side of the valley, a long way to walk.

"Perhaps he only meant to borrow a tool from someone," Charles said.

"Papa, I can't explain it, but I do believe he would have come this way." The search team had raced to adjoining farms and found no one who had seen Noah that morning. But what would take him up the mountain? He had begun to comment on the way Phoebe hovered. A few minutes of independence might have appealed, or a time of prayer without others measuring his every breath.

They were on their way up to the highest ridge, where the mountaintop flattened. Patsy scanned for the other pairs. The mountain's echo would keep them within shouting distance, but the sound might bounce around so that the origination would be hard to discern. Adam and Susanna still shared his white horse, making them easy to spot against the vegetation. The others rode darker animals and blended in, but she found them.

"What's that?" Charles pulled his horse to the right and looked down and over several yards.

Patsy followed. "A piece of cloth."

"It might be nothing."

"Or it might have torn off Noah's shirt." He had a brown shirt he fancied, and a dark green one that Phoebe preferred he wear when he worked.

"Now that I am closer," Charles said, "I believe it is nothing. Just a patch of muddied weeds."

"I am going to look." Patsy dropped off

her horse to navigate into the clump of trees. Varied evergreens populated the mountain this high up, nothing that would be dropping autumn leaves. She would assume nothing at this point. Anything that looked the least unusual bore inspection. The terrain angled down a few feet, and she turned her feet to slide down sideways, reaching for stray branches to sustain her balance.

"Can you reach it?" Charles asked.

"Just about." She would have to release one last branch, let her weight surrender to gravity on the descending ground, and catch herself on the tree sporting the patch of unexpected color. There should have been footprints, or at least disturbed earth, if Noah had been this way recently, but Patsy would take no chances.

She spread her fingers on the broad evergreen tree, ignoring the rough bark that scraped her palm and reaching with the other hand for the cloth.

It crumbled immediately under her touch. If it had ever been a piece of whole cloth or a scrap of a garment, it was stuck on that branch long ago. Most likely it belonged to a trapper who passed this way years ago. Patsy moaned at the lost time.

■ ■ ■ ■

Niklaus's horse was sure-footed and reliable, and the second horse tethered to his saddle seemed unbothered by the trek up Jacks Mountain.

Jacks Mountain. The name arose when *Jack* Armstrong died on this mountain a hundred years earlier after confiscating a horse from a Delaware Indian who owed him money. The Indian tracked *Jack* Armstrong and with finality made sure there would be no further conflict about the debt. If Niklaus did not bring Noah safely home on this day, the Amish families might well take to calling it Noah's Mountain. Losing Noah would be more on their minds than an *English* fur trader they had never known.

Niklaus would not let that happen. Despite Deborah's caution that he should take ropes in case he had to tie Noah across a horse, Niklaus prayed constantly under his breath for a joyful outcome. Behind him, Shem rode without speaking. They were off any sort of path used for horses. Noah was on foot. He could have wandered in any direction once he began his ascent of Jacks Mountain. And the ground was rife with slopes and indentations that could endanger the sturdiest of horses. Niklaus and Shem zigzagged back and forth across the stretch of mountain Niklaus had chosen for them, peering at the earth for any sign of recent disturbance. Dirt that had been kicked. Splotches of color that might signal clothing. Had Noah even been wearing shoes when Susanna last saw him working in the barn? Niklaus had not thought to ask.

The silence between Niklaus and Shem had begun the moment they split from the other teams and persisted undisturbed during the search. Niklaus vacillated between being grateful for the silence and wishing they might use this time alone to clear the air between them. Shem was not an unkind man. The excitable state he entered beginning the day Noah first preached after the church meal befuddled Niklaus. Shem took seriously his responsibilities as a spiritual leader. Niklaus credited him generously for that. But was a minister not first of all a gentle shepherd? Niklaus turned over phrase after phrase in his mind, searching for something conciliatory to say to his old friend and fellow laborer in the gospel, but every thought was fraught with risk under the present circumstances. The wrong phrase, the wrong word, the wrong inflection — anything might provoke a tirade from Shem that would distract both of them from their task.

Find Noah.

Niklaus wanted to find Noah. He was less sure of having Shem at his side when the moment came, a sentiment for which Niklaus immediately asked God's forgiveness. He then asked for discernment to choose his words wisely.

From the height of the mountain, Susanna looked westward above the valley that ran from west to east. The sun that ought to have cheered her was instead ominous. The afternoon was waning far too quickly and would soon yield to dusk. She thought back through the afternoon, calculating the time spans of each stage of discovering Noah missing, gathering help, eliminating the obvious possibilities closer to home, organizing a strategy for covering the terrain of Jacks Mountain.

Even the search party they began with was not nearly enough for the densely forested acreage. From her vantage point now, she could behold the entire valley, red barns dotting green and yellow fields, white houses, horses and cows in the pastures that looked as small as she felt. Against the challenge of finding one man on a sylvan mountainside, even ten pair of eyes were wholly insufficient. Yet had they taken time to gather a larger search party, they might have only sent Noah closer to danger. Susanna did not see the *English* pair. Most likely, now they were eight — or possibly only six, if the Amish duo did not come into view soon.

The time was well past when Noah would have fallen under. If he had left the farm consciously with a specific intent, by now he would be unaware of his surroundings. What did he see when he looked out the window of his house while he preached? Sometimes he seemed to look right at people, even point at them to underscore his words. But did he *see* them? Patsy and Susanna had spent weeks keeping him safe inside his own house, anticipating where he might step that could lead to harm, what he might touch that could injure him. How could he possibly be safe on Jacks Mountain when he ought to be home recovering on the davenport, sleeping while Phoebe prepared his late supper?

"Adam," she said.

"I know."

She needed to say no more. He understood her.

Adam reined in his horse, halting even the

slow progress they had been making.

"What?" Susanna said. "Do you see something?"

Adam shook his head. "I want to light a lantern while we can still see what we are doing."

Susanna shivered at the thought but nodded. She dismounted to allow Adam to unhook the lantern from the saddlebag and find matches. A breeze gusted just as he adjusted the wick, extinguishing the flame. It took him three times to make sure the flame would hold. Had he also put extra oil in the saddlebag? Susanna prayed they would not need it.

He handed her the lantern. "You will have to hold it. I have nothing to hang it from."

She nodded, parting her lips to breathe past the bulk in her throat.

"It will be dangerous to try to go down the mountain after dark," Adam said as they settled themselves back on the stallion.

"I do not care about that," Susanna said, "only that we find Noah."

"Even with a lantern it will become difficult to search." Reality muted Adam's voice. "We cannot serve him well if we are foolish in the short term."

Lighting the lantern was a precaution. It was not yet dark. Someone might be closer to Noah than she and Adam were.

"Where are the others?" Susanna said.

Sitting on the horse, they picked out three other pairs of searchers.

"The *English* have gone home," Adam said.

"Surely not."

"I do not see them."

Neither did Susanna. Eight. Half the number of people who left the Kauffman farm remained. She prayed the two Amish men were yet among the now eight pairs of eyes searching a darkening forest.

Adam guided the horse as gently as he could. Susanna had only one arm at his waist now, the other extended to light their way. They traversed the yards in slow, hushed deliberation, both of them tensing at every sound of an animal scurrying across the forest floor or the shifting light. The stallion dipped to one side, and the lantern flickered, trapping a shadow in uncertainty.

Adam pulled on the reins. "Hold still. Right there."

Susanna's outstretched arm froze in place.

"Higher," Adam said. A few minutes ago, the lantern had seemed precautionary. Now he could not be sure of what he saw twenty yards away, much less up the mountain.

Susanna raised the light. "What did you see?"

Adam pointed. "There." It might just be a play of light, the sun settling behind a tree trunk with outstretched branches. Adam inched the horse forward, his gaze not releasing what he thought he might have seen.

" 'Tis Noah!" Susanna said. "Faster."

"I do not want to lame the horse."

"Faster!" Susanna insisted. "You watch the ground. I will watch Noah."

Noah's voice echoed off the mountain.

"Is he preaching?" Adam nudged the horse to change direction. "Niklaus said we are to call out if we see him, yet I do not want to startle Noah."

"If he has fallen under, Noah will not hear us." Susanna lifted the lantern and swung it side to side, hoping it would catch someone's attention. "Patsy! Reverend Baxton! Niklaus! Bishop! Mr. Glick! Mr. Wagler!"

Returning shouts soon met their ears. Everyone came to the front of the mountain, out of the thickness of trees they had been weaving in and out of all afternoon. Susanna swung the lantern in the direction of Noah, but it was unnecessary. Noah's voice dominated the mountainside now, his words rising and bouncing.

"On this holy mountain," Noah said, his arms outstretched, "the Lord shall make his presence known. On this holy mountain, we shall behold his coming. His foundation is in the holy mountains. The Lord saith, 'They shall not hurt nor destroy in all my holy mountain: for the earth shall be full of the knowledge of the Lord.' He shall make his appearing and we will see the light of a new dawn break forth."

The booming echo made Noah sound closer than he was.

Stay right where you are. Adam scanned the way forward for the most direct route to reach Noah. *Preach all you want. Just do not move.*

CHAPTER 36

"Noah is moving." Susanna gripped Adam's waist more tightly with one arm while leaning forward to look over his shoulder. "He is starting to pace."

"He will stop," Adam said.

"You do not understand," Susanna twisted her spine to look beyond Adam. "We do not know what he sees."

"He will see a cliff."

"If he does not know to stay away from the hot stove," Susanna said, "why would he step back from a cliff?" Adam had witnessed Noah's falling under enough times to know he could not assume a reasonable response to the circumstances.

"He did not stay on a trail," Adam said. "I will do my best, but Patsy and her father may be closer."

Who might reach Noah first was difficult to ascertain. Distance, which was complex to judge and could not be measured as the crow flies, was only one factor. The steepness of the incline was another, and whether there might be a gully or chasm to navigate, or whether a horse might resist a needful jump. At least all four pair were aimed toward Noah.

The Amish men called Noah's name. Susanna sighed. Why could they not understand that he would not respond? Had they not observed this truth enough times on the Kauffman farm? Their intransigence vexed her. Did even they who had remained loyal to the search still believe falling under was a sort of trickery they could snap Noah out of simply by calling his name?

Susanna squinted into the burgeoning shadows. At least they still had eight searchers.

Noah took a step forward.

"Adam!"

Noah took another step forward. Then he dropped.

"Adam!"

Adam's gaze snapped up from the amorphous ground. "Where did he go?"

Susanna's heart was hurtling out of her chest. "We must get to him."

"I am doing my best."

"Cut to the west," Susanna said. "There must be a shorter way."

"I do not know this part of the mountain well," Adam said.

The blanketing darkness worked against them. Susanna panicked. "I am not sure I can see where he fell."

"He might just be kneeling," Adam said. "Praying."

"Something happened," Susanna said. Even when Noah knelt to pray, sometimes for nearly an hour at a time before beginning the Lord's Prayer that would signal the end of his preaching, his voice never faltered. She heard nothing now.

"Please, Adam, find a shortcut."

Adam swung his horse to the left. The animal's hoof sank into soft ground, taking the horse to his knees and jolting both riders loose in the saddle. Susanna jumped off, holding the lantern aloft. She was not at the reins, and she had no intention of getting caught beneath a falling horse. Adam righted himself without leaving the saddle, and the stallion found his footing.

"I will have to get off and have a look," Adam said.

"A look at what?" Her eyes once again searched for Noah. The horse was on four legs. What was there to inspect?

"It will only take a minute," Adam said, sliding off the horse. "Hold the lantern so

I can see."

Niklaus reached the ridge where he believed he had last seen Noah, though he was as much as a quarter mile away from where Noah dropped from view, and leading a second horse impeded speed.

"Shem," Niklaus said, "you know this mountain better than anyone else I can think of. You saw where he was. Would he have fallen, or could he have climbed down?"

Shem shook his head. "He was quite near the edge. My guess is he fell."

"What distance?" Perhaps a bed of bushes or a line of trees had cushioned the fall.

"That depends on whether he tumbled or fell straight down. To the north of that ridge is a rocky path that eventually leads to a stream."

"And to the south?" Niklaus asked.

"Quite a thick swath of forest," Shem said. "It can be difficult to sort out which branches belong to which tree."

"So he might have tumbled down the rocks, or he might be in the trees."

Shem nodded.

"You must lead the way," Niklaus said, pulling his horse to the side. If there was a direct path to Noah, Shem would know it.

The two men exchanged a silent stare before Shem pushed ahead, cutting at an angle Niklaus would not have supposed, and stopped abruptly on a narrow ridge.

"Down there," Shem said. "If he landed in the trees and not the rocks, we should be able to see him from here."

Niklaus saw nothing. Light failed by the moment, and he did not have the eyesight of a younger man.

Shem was dismounting, so Niklaus did the same. Together they fell to their knees, and then to their bellies, and crawled forward.

Below them about thirty feet, straight down off the ridge, Noah was sprawled on his back in a nest of towering evergreens. From above the trees, Niklaus could not count the trunks, and the number did not matter. Branches crisscrossed and intersected to form a delicate man-sized basket. If they did not support the weight of a man, they might at least have broken the fall and slowed Noah's descent.

"Shem," Niklaus said, "is Noah safe there? Might he fall through?"

"There are many branches," Shem said. "But he must be careful where he puts his feet."

"Noah," Niklaus called. "Do you hear me?"

Noah did not respond. Although Niklaus heard a smattering of words, they sounded more like the waning phrases of a robust sermon than a response to the question. At least he was speaking.

Susanna scrambled up behind them, lifting her lamp. "Is he all right?"

Niklaus looked past Susanna's shoulders. "Where is Adam?"

"Being careful with his horse. I could not wait another minute."

If Susanna came so quickly on her own through the dark, Adam could not be far.

"We are going to need Adam," Niklaus said.

Patsy and Charles converged.

"Be careful," Shem said. "This part of the mountain can be soft, and this ledge is not very wide."

Niklaus shifted from his belly to his haunches. "Patsy, watch for Mr. Glick and Mr. Wagler. Head them off. We do not need the weight of their horses near us right now, but find out what supplies they have with them."

Patsy expertly turned her horse around in the narrow space and trotted off.

"Adam has another lantern," Susanna

said. "And rope."

"Someone may have to find him. He can leave his horse tied up if he needs to, but he is the young man among us, and we need both him and his supplies."

"I do not want to leave Noah," Susanna said.

"It may be the best thing for him that you do," Niklaus said.

"On this holy mountain." Noah's faint voice wafted upward, and he began to shift in the treetop, pulling in limbs from where they draped the branches and shuffling his feet in search of support.

"Will he stand?" Niklaus asked.

Susanna's voice was small. "If he wants to."

Niklaus peered through the dark, hoping for a glimpse of Adam.

" 'In that day shalt thou not be ashamed of all thy doings,' " Noah said, " 'wherein thou hast transgressed against me: for then I will take away out of the midst of thee them that rejoice in thy pride, and thou shalt no more be haughty because of my holy mountain.' "

"We must get to him before he stands!" Susanna said. "He will not know that he should not take even a single step."

"This is a dangerous situation for all of

us," Niklaus said. "No one must do or say anything rash. We must all do what is best for our brother Noah."

Niklaus went to his saddlebags and began extracting supplies. They would need enough rope to lower at least one man down to Noah. Two would be better. Noah would have to be tied securely. They could tie the ropes to horses who could pull them up, but the horses must also be tied to trees to keep them from running too fast. Patsy or Shem would have to be in charge of the animals. Niklaus selected trees to knot ropes to. Another fall could endanger several of the men in the blink of an eye. He unhooked his lantern, taking time at last to light it, and hung it from a branch.

Patsy returned with Galahad.

Niklaus asked, "Did Mr. Glick and Mr. Wagler have any gear we can use?"

Patsy shrugged. "I called to them, but they were heading down the mountain and did not hear."

Niklaus expelled breath. A search party that had begun with fifteen volunteers was down to four men and two women.

Adam was behind Patsy, rope coiled over one shoulder and his second lantern in the other hand.

"Do we have enough rope?" Patsy stepped

aside for Adam to deliver his supplies.

Niklaus welcomed the lit lantern that arrived with Adam. That gave them three. "Is your horse all right?"

Adam nodded. "He's tied over there."

At the ledge, Charles squatted to look down at Noah. Patsy crept toward the edge and balanced herself with one hand on her father's shoulder to look down as well. Susanna extended her arm, holding a light as they all examined Noah from above.

"On this holy mountain," Noah said, still lying on his back, shuffling his feet occasionally and staring blankly up at them, "we will see that God acts for His people. On this holy mountain we will meet God in our spirits, just as Moses did when he carried the law down to the idolaters, just as Jesus did when He was transfigured before the eyes of Peter, James, and John. We do not come to this holy mountain lightly. We come expecting to find God here."

"He is amazing," Patsy said. "That he could keep preaching after what has happened, that he could still speak such timely words — I will never forget this day."

"None of us will," Shem said, still on his belly. "It is a day that should never have come to be."

"Does not God ordain our days?" Charles

said. "Who are we to say that this day should not have come to be? Do you not teach your own people that God's will is sovereign?"

"Sin is all around us," Shem snapped. "God is sovereign in the midst of sin, but that does not excuse us of our sin."

"Noah has not sinned," Charles said. "He has only obeyed."

Shem scowled.

Patsy squeezed her father's shoulder. "Perhaps this theological debate can wait until Noah is safely home."

"Shem," Niklaus said, "please help tie ropes to the trees. Adam and I will shinny down to Noah."

Patsy flicked a glance of thanks toward Niklaus. Shem and Charles side by side looking down on Noah was not an effective arrangement. Both of them would be in better service if their hands were fully occupied.

Shem exhaled and pushed himself up off the ground. "If Noah comes to greater harm, you will all be responsible."

Charles grunted and stood as well. "Is that how you propose to please God?"

"I propose to please God," Shem said, "by holding fast to the faith that was handed down to me and not to cater to softening toward the ways of the world."

Patsy was on her feet in an instant. "What a ridiculous thing to say."

Susanna tugged Patsy's arm, but Patsy shirked her off.

"I'm sick and tired of all this bickering," Patsy said. "We have in our midst three ministers and one poor preacher who did not ask for this calling or gift. The only one who seems to be speaking the Word of God is lying on his back in the trees. Do you feel no shame at the way you speak of him?"

"Patricia," Charles said. "Mind your tongue."

"And you yours."

Niklaus stepped between father and daughter. "We must all remain calm. We are here for Noah. No good will come from inflaming a quarrel."

Patsy nodded and turned away.

Charles followed Niklaus and Adam to secure ropes to the trees and to themselves.

"Noah is bleeding," Susanna said.

Both Patsy and her father turned their attention back to Noah.

"Are you sure?" Patsy said.

Susanna pointed.

"It is too dark and too far to see," Patsy said.

"I have been watching carefully," Susanna said. This was not the time for her best friend to doubt her.

"I agree with Patsy," Charles said. "We cannot be certain."

Must everything be an argument? Susanna leaned with her lantern as far out over the drop as she dared. She was the one who had been watching Noah all this time rather than bickering. Gradually she moved the lantern to the left and then swept it back toward the right. If only Noah would focus his eyes on the light, she might know that he was all right. His preaching voice was fading, though he still muttered and had not yet begun the Lord's Prayer. Even in his weakened state — Susanna was certain he was bleeding from the back of his head or shoulder — he remained fallen under. In that condition, he would not know to help himself.

"Please hurry," she said, turning toward Niklaus and Adam.

One wrong move would send Noah tumbling farther down the mountainside, and they would have to find another position from which to rescue him.

And it might be too late.

"On this holy mountain," was the only phrase Susanna could understand now.

His legs now straddling one of the thick-est branches and his hands fumbling to find where they belonged, Noah tried to sit up.

Susanna stomped a foot. "Someone must go down right now."

CHAPTER 37

Dragging a length of rope behind him, Niklaus ran back to the edge of the ridge and squatted to once again assess Noah's safety.

"Hold the lantern out," he said, "as far as you can."

Susanna complied, leaning farther forward than Niklaus would have allowed under other circumstances. He gripped her upper arm, ready to maintain his hold if she slipped any closer to the edge. Certainty was difficult to grasp as shadows lengthened and hues darkened from one moment to the next, but the peculiar spread of the color under Noah's back was convincing of Susanna's suspicion.

"Take care for yourselves," Niklaus said, and both Susanna and Patsy inched back.

Niklaus glanced at the trail of rope waving through the dirt. His was the longest. The two Adam had retrieved from Noah's barn were newer and more tightly braided but shorter. He may have underestimated the distance to Noah. If either of the other two pair of men, *English* and Amish, had turned up, they might have had more to work with. But they had not arrived, and Niklaus did not now expect them.

Beside Niklaus, Shem grabbed the end of the rope and began to tie it to his waist.

"Tie me to a tree," Shem said. "I will go down and talk some sense into Noah."

"He does not need talking to," Niklaus said. "He needs rescuing."

"I will impress upon him that he must participate in his own rescue." Shem finished his knot.

In one swift motion, Niklaus tugged a loop in the knot and undid it. Shem would be no help in the treetop where Noah sat muttering. Stabbing Noah with a needle should have made that clear. Shem resisted now, slapping away Niklaus's hand and grasping for the rope — and knocking against Susanna and disturbing her careful balance.

She shrieked as the lantern in her hand slipped off her fingers and banged against rock as it tumbled beyond reach and shattered.

Niklaus pulled her to her feet. "Are you all right?"

She nodded, breathing hard.

Niklaus turned to Shem. "You might have caused Susanna to fall and set the mountain on fire as well."

"Since I did not," Shem said, "clearly it was not *Gottes wille.*"

Niklaus exhaled heavily. "Shem, I must ask you to step away for the moment."

"*You* want to tell *me* what to do?" Shem's feet did not move. "Adam, bring me the spare rope."

Adam moved toward them, rope still coiled over a shoulder, his lantern on the ground.

"Adam," Niklaus said, "stay where you are." There was no spare rope. They needed every inch. Adam's eyes darted between uncle and bishop, caught between them as he had been too often of late. Niklaus put his hand out for the rope. Adam avoided meeting Shem's eyes as he slipped it off his shoulder and into his uncle's hands.

"We are wasting time." Susanna returned to her crouch at the ledge, this time without benefit of light. "Somebody do something."

"We are four men here," Niklaus said. "We will tie two of us to horses to pull us up once we have Noah. If the horses are tied to trees, we can be sure they will not bolt before we are ready. Is that understood?"

Every head but Shem's nodded.

Patsy shook her head in the dark. The moon was new, offering no light to the ledge, and the trees below remained in the thickest gloom. Whether the bleeding was worsening was impossible to say, but even a small wound seeping steadily would become severe soon enough. As long as Noah kept talking, even just to moan, they could be sure he had not expired in the silent shadows.

"We'll get to him," Patsy said to Susanna. "We must believe that."

Susanna did not turn her head toward Patsy's assurance, but a shimmer of starlight glistened through the tears on her cheek. Noah's volume had been steadily dissipating, but suddenly his voice once again burst out of the trees.

" 'Blow ye the trumpet in Zion, and sound an alarm in my holy mountain: let all the inhabitants of the land tremble: for the day of the LORD cometh, for it is nigh at hand.' "

"Cousin Noah has always liked the book of Joel," Susanna murmured.

"We can hear every word," Patsy said. "That's a good sign. He yet has strength in him even if he cannot stand."

If only there were a sense of holiness on this mountain ridge at this moment. Without looking — what point was there in watching the men squabble? — Patsy heard her father's voice rise in remarks aimed at the Amish bishop. His caustic inflection would help no one.

"I want to call to Noah," Susanna said, "just to let him know he is not alone, but he will not hear me."

"He knows," Patsy said. "He is wrapped in God's care."

"And if he moves?" Susanna said.

"Then he remains in God's care."

"Or if his wound is severe and the men cannot reach him?"

"He remains in God's care."

Patsy turned to watch the men. When they all left the Kauffman yard in the afternoon, Patsy had thought that the more searchers who volunteered, the better it would be for Noah. Now she was not so sure. They would have been better off without the bishop, who seemed to shout out every thought that entered his mind, and her own father was using his outdoor preaching voice to spew his irritation.

Susanna put a hand to her forehead and squeezed her skull. "When will they stop?"

"They are securing ropes," Patsy said.

"Soon they will descend. It looks like Adam will lead the way."

"Good."

Adam was the logical choice — young, strong, tall enough to repel down the side of the mountain without getting his feet caught in scrabble undergrowth. And Adam was the only one of the four men not accustomed to being in charge and seeking only to do what was needful.

"Too many ministers are stirring the pot," Patsy said. "They are all used to people turning to them for guidance, which they freely offer."

"Ministers," Susanna muttered. "Why can they not see that what is needed is submission to Christ alone?"

Adam flinched.

Shouts from the mouth of the bishop was not something he was accustomed to. Even if he disagreed with Charles Baxton or Niklaus, surely the circumstances called for more self-restraint rather than less.

"Mr. Baxton," Shem said, "I have determined that this is no concern of yours."

"Why is that up to you to determine?" Charles countered. "I am acquainted with Mr. Kauffman. My own daughter has been a faithful caretaker when he has needed it most, while I am given to understand that the only day you deigned to observe him at all was not to hear him speak the Word of the Lord but rather to further your own agenda of disproving his gifts."

"None of this would have happened had you not interfered." Shem poked a finger at Charles's chest.

"I will kindly ask you to keep your hands to yourself." Charles's tone was now more constrained than Shem's but no less fierce.

"Both of you!" The words left Adam's mouth before he could think better of them. "Noah. Noah is what matters."

Both ministers turned and stared at him.

"You will retract your impudence," Shem said.

Adam shook his head. It was not impudence, but rather truth.

"Niklaus has a plan," Adam said. "A good plan under far-less-than-ideal circumstances, and we would do well to assist him. Does our Lord not call us to unity and compassion?"

"Of course," Charles said, "yet it behooves us to act responsibly with the limited resources at our disposal."

"The resource of grace does not fail," Adam said. "Right doctrine may be a worthy conversation, but this is not the moment to undertake it."

"And who dares to preach now?" Shem said.

"I make no claim to preach," Adam said, "only to serve with every gift I have to offer."

Noah's voice grew faint once again, even the wall of the mountain insufficient to supply its echo. Only scattered words reached Adam's ears.

" 'In that day . . . wherein thou hast transgressed . . . thou shalt no more be haughty . . .' "

"What is he muttering now?" Shem spun toward the ledge.

"Zephaniah," Charles said. " 'In that day shalt thou not be ashamed for all thy doings, wherein thou hast transgressed against me: for then I will take away out of the midst of thee them that rejoice in my pride, and thou shalt no more be haughty because of my holy mountain.' "

Adam had not recognized the verse, and he was certain Noah had no awareness of what was happening ten yards above him, but the quotation was apt, and he left it in silence. Shem and Charles both shuffled their feet.

"I will harness myself now," Adam said.

Niklaus stood by with the longest rope,

tying one end to Galahad's bridle and double-knotting it. Adam began winding the other end around himself.

The only sounds coming up the mountainside were the skittering of an unseen animal and the caw of a crow.

"Stay right here," Susanna said, pushing off her haunches.

"Where are you going?" Patsy twisted to look at Susanna.

"We need another lantern." Susanna could barely make out Noah's supine form on its bed of branches, and for the moment he had ceased speaking. She ached to hear him begin the Lord's Prayer.

Susanna marched past Charles and Shem and even Adam to where he had left his lantern idle. When she snatched it up, it dimmed, but she neither sought nor required assistance in lighting it again. The men might think they had time to debate their strategy, but Susanna did not. She marched back to the edge, extended the lantern, fixed her eyes on Noah, and handed the light to Patsy.

"Right there," Susanna said. "Whatever happens, you must not lose sight of Noah."

"Of course not," Patsy said, "but what are you going to do?"

Susanna stood once again.

"Susanna?" Patsy swung the light toward Susanna and looked up at her.

"Patsy!" Susanna could not conceal the urge to scold. "I said whatever happens, you must not lose sight of Noah."

Patsy returned the lantern to the position Susanna had established. "What are you doing, Susanna?"

"Somebody must do something." Susanna brushed her hands against her apron, though they would be dusty again as soon as she began her descent. "As long as I can see your light, I will have my bearings."

She was not foolish enough to attempt an untethered direct descent. Her feet would remain on the ground, but she could find a less steep route and bank toward Noah from an oblique angle. Her mother had made her give up climbing trees years ago, but she could still do it if necessary. She glanced toward the men fumbling with their ropes and tempers.

"Go," Patsy whispered. "Quickly."

Susanna murmured thanksgiving for the stars spattering the sky. Even without the moon, she might find herself by the patterns of the stars if she paid close attention. Aggravation burned through her. Shem's carelessness had cost them the lantern she might have carried with her, but she could not leave them with nothing on the ledge. Niklaus's lantern still hung from a tree so the men could make their knots, and Patsy must keep her eyes focused on Noah.

How long had Noah preached? The hour was much later than his usual time to offer his final words of God's grace, but nothing about the afternoon reflected the pattern she had come to regard as usual. Noah had wandered from the farm when he knew he ought to remain close at hand. He could have fallen under later than expected and remained so for longer. He might even now be preparing to pray.

Or he might be unconscious from his injuries.

Susanna stepped off the only path available and into darkness shrouded by the forest. Only a few steps from Patsy and already she had lost the light.

CHAPTER 38

Adam tested the knots, both the ones that formed the harness around him and the ones connecting him to Galahad and the horse to a tree. He raised his eyes to meet his uncle's.

"Ready?" Niklaus said, his hands on Adam's shoulders.

Adam nodded.

"The *maedel* will hold the light, and Charles will help guide the rope," Niklaus said. "I will be right behind you. We will bring Noah up together."

Adam paced toward the overlook, stopping every few steps to once again tug the rope and reassure himself the knots showed no slippage. At the spot where he had left Susanna, he found only Patsy.

"Where is Susanna?" Adam said.

Patsy gave no answer but simply braced her arm on one knee as she squatted and held out the lantern.

Panic coursed through Adam's chest. "Patsy, where did Susanna go?"

"She was tired of waiting for someone to do something practical." Patsy's eyes did not leave the shaft of light the lantern cast into darkness over Noah.

"We were preparing as quickly as we could." Adam gripped the rope around his waist. "Could she not see that?"

"Noah is bleeding," Patsy said, "and he's hardly talking beyond infrequent bursts of speech. He stopped preaching but did not begin to pray. He never does that. And all the ministers could think to do was bicker."

"Do you mean Susanna is down there somewhere? Why did you not stop her?"

Patsy scoffed. "Stop Susanna once she has made up her mind?"

Adam peered into the darkness below, trying to find Noah's form. "But she took no equipment. She cannot possibly succeed."

"She will be with Noah. He will not be alone, no matter what is happening. That will be success. That is what she promised Phoebe she would do."

"Onkel!" Adam reversed his direction, stomping back toward the horses. "Susanna has taken matters into her own hands."

Niklaus released his grip on Galahad's bridle. "Where?"

Patsy pointed in the direction Susanna had departed.

Niklaus turned to Shem. "Will she find a path that way?"

Shem pressed his lips together, thinking. "Not a path, but enough opening between the trees that she will progress."

"But will she progress toward Noah?"

Shem shrugged. "This I do not know. 'Twill be difficult to maintain direction. She may find herself below Noah and have to climb up."

Adam fumbled with the knots he had been so careful to secure just moments ago. He wanted the whole mess off.

"I will find her," Adam said.

"What about Noah?" Charles said.

Adam looked to the ministers. "There are still three of you, and Patsy at the light. Susanna has naught, not even a lamp."

Niklaus watched Adam's face, saying nothing.

"I will go before harm multiplies," Adam said.

Niklaus nodded now and reached for the light on the tree. "Take the last lantern and the shortest length of rope."

"We need a sensible plan," Charles said.

If it were Patsy swallowed by the darkness, Charles would be halfway down the mountain by now. Adam shirked out of his harness, tossing the rope toward his uncle.

"We do have a sensible plan," Niklaus said to Charles. "I will go down to Noah on my own and assess his injuries. If necessary, you can follow me down. That still leaves Shem and Patsy to manage the horses when the time comes to pull us up."

Patsy's steadfast grip would have to do for light shed on the men's descent, and whoever was left with the horses would have to stand in darkness. Adam would not leave Susanna on the mountain in blackness.

"We will call to one another frequently," Niklaus said to Adam. "When you hear me, you must call in return."

Adam nodded. He would do as his uncle asked, but the voice he most wanted to hear when he called was Susanna's.

Adam may not always have gotten along with his father, but he had learned the essentials of tracking. Anytime they left the house together, his *daed* insisted on Adam's careful reporting of what he observed. What was different? What was missing? What did not belong? What was out of place?

Neglectful of any necessity for stealth, Susanna left plenty of clues. Crashing through bushes might have attracted animals and heightened danger to herself, but Susanna

453

would have only Noah on her mind. And in fact, her aggressive progress seemed to have silenced the animals that ought to have been scurrying across the mossy forest floor, scampering up tree trunks, or disturbing branches. Adam detected not so much as a gray squirrel.

Instead, the trail of branches someone had brushed against was obvious, a handful of needles missing here and there. It could be no one but Susanna, and perhaps she did not realize that six or nine or twelve inches at a time, her route through the forest was taking her downward at an angle sure to miss the mark. Adam dangled his lantern near the ground so that he might look upward and judge whether Patsy's was visible. From his immediate position, it was. From a few feet deeper into the forest, it would not be.

Whether Susanna lost her balance and slid downward or chose to turn her feet sideways and scrape through the dirt to maintain balance, Adam could not know. By God's grace her path was not difficult to track. No man's boot prints confused the smaller markings her shoes had rendered. No hunter or wood gatherer had been on this portion of the mountain in recent weeks. Adam witnessed a fresh canvas of movement through the

454

woods. Periodically, when he discerned a branch had been brushed or broken, he paused for closer inspection under the light of the lantern. This was how he found the patch of violet threads that must have come from the worn apron borrowed from Phoebe that Susanna had donned every day since leaving the Hooley farm and spending her nights with the Kauffmans. The evidence was slight. Most likely Susanna had not even noticed the snag. Adam picked the threads off the pine needles and closed his fist around them.

He was on the right path.

"Susanna!"

Silence.

He pressed on, holding the lantern in front of him lest he overlook another snag or even a compressed bed of pine needles that indicated she might have stopped to rest, catch her bearings, or shift direction. Above him, Patsy's light flickered. If he could see it, Susanna would have seen when she stood in this spot — though Adam did not know how long ago that was. She would have adjusted her path to take her as directly below the light as possible.

"Susanna!"

Silence. Then, "Adam!"

But it was not Susanna's voice. Niklaus

was calling from somewhere in the trees above him.

"Here!" Adam responded, turning his lantern upward and sweeping from side to side to make his presence known.

"What do you see?" Niklaus boomed.

"Nothing. No one."

Adam pushed forward, turning his own feet sideways against the slope of the mountain while trying to maintain level progress into a faltering shaft of light.

He slipped and caught himself on a tree trunk. Something slick was beneath his right foot, causing the slide. Adam reached for it.

Susanna's black quilted bonnet. Had she even noticed that it had fallen? He was on the right path. Up on the ridge, the stars provided little reassurance of direction. Under the canopy of trees on a near moonless night, discerning east from west and north from south was difficult.

"Susanna!"

He waited, then called her name again.

"Adam?" The response was faint, tentative.

"I am here," he bellowed. "Talk to me." *Say something. Say anything.*

"Here!" came her voice.

She was above and beyond him, not so far off the path he might have chosen himself

456

while aiming for Patsy's light. Adam lifted his own lantern high, catching her shadow.

"I am coming," he called out. "Stay there."

"I must get to Noah."

"Wait for me." *Please. Just wait for me.* Adam focused his eyes as best he could with limited light against a blanket of black.

There. She was there. He would have to clamber up toward her. "I am coming."

Susanna slipped from Adam's view. He stilled his movement to listen for hers, certain she had stumbled and was slow to rise.

"Susanna!"

Silence.

"Susanna, answer me! Please!"

Adam made his best guess and pushed through a thicket of new forest growth beneath the age-old trees.

"Here," she said finally. "I am here. I am waiting."

Niklaus rotated his stance and inched his boots back until just his toes remained on the ledge, both gloved hands gripping the rope lined up straight down the center of his body.

"You all understand?" he said.

In the light of Patsy's lantern, they nodded. Charles had hold of the rope as well and would feed it down a foot or two at a time, steadily enough that Niklaus would make continuous progress but controlled enough that the line remained taut enough to keep Niklaus from swinging. Shem was on horse duty, making sure Galahad remained as unperturbed as Patsy promised he would be. A second length of rope was tied to Charles's horse, and both animals were secured to trees with short leads that would prevent their departure if something spooked them in the dark.

Three heads nodded as Niklaus bounced on his toes three times before letting both feet slide off the ridge. Noah was straight below him, but he would have to zigzag past trees Noah must have tumbled through on his way down. Niklaus's boots scraped against the mountainside as he found footing and controlled his movement with more certainty. He must depend on Charles to give him as much rope as he needed but not enough to bring him harm by allowing him to swing wildly. And Charles would have to trust Shem not to suddenly decide he had a better plan than the one they all agreed to.

Niklaus wanted to look for Adam, but he did not dare take his eyes off his own task. *Let no man despise thy youth,* he reminded himself. He was past his own youth, but he spoke these words to Adam from time to time when the young man's confidence faltered. Niklaus could find his next mountain foothold while also praying that Adam would find his mountain wisdom and together — with Susanna — they would converge on Noah before it was too late.

CHAPTER 39

Lambent light licked its way through the leaves as Adam made his way toward her. Susanna dug the worn toes of her shoes into soft earth to suppress her impulse to keep her feet in motion even if she was uncertain of the direction in which she should aim. Adam was not so far behind her. He could not have wasted any time in noticing her departure amid the commotion on the ledge, nor in hastening his own. Every step she took away from the ridge and under the tree-covered path she had chosen — largely by guesswork — toward Noah had taken her deeper into darkness. She saw Patsy's light only intermittently, and she did not know how far off her bearings were. The lantern Adam carried now, flickering though it was, burst with comfort that she might have more to rely on than the glint of Patsy's light that seemed yards above and yards to one side.

Adam reached her, and Susanna let herself fall into his arms.

"You should not have done that," he said. But his voice held no scolding.

"It was the only thing to do, and you know it." Susanna gripped his hand. Together they looked upward toward Patsy's light.

Adam cupped one hand at the side of his mouth. "Onkel!"

"Here!" came a quick response. "On my way down."

"I have Susanna."

"Hold on to her!"

Adam turned to Susanna. "Charles will not be far behind."

"Then my impetuousness caused no harm at all," Susanna said. "Rather, we have doubled our possibilities that someone will reach Noah before further harm comes to him."

"But harm might have come to you," Adam said. He brushed dirt off her bonnet before putting it on her head, and then he straightened it and tied it loosely beneath her chin using only two fingers of each hand.

Susanna half-smiled in the darkness. His voice still was void of scolding.

"I found threads," he said, opening a fist.

461

She peered in the light of the lantern. "My apron."

"What has become of it?"

"It caught on a branch." She raised the remains in her free hand. "Then I thought I might as well rip it into strips as I walked. We will need bandages when we reach Noah."

"I cannot see him," Adam said softly.

"Nor I." Susanna led the way as they began to walk again. "But Patsy is steadfast at her post, and now you are here with another light. We will find him."

She pulled a length of cloth from her shoulder, fingered a width, and tore swiftly as she walked.

"Let me help," Adam said.

" 'Tis enough that you are here and hold the light." Susanna ripped another length. " 'Tis no different than tearing remnants for a quilt."

"At least let me carry the strips."

She nodded and laid a careful pile over his shoulder before pointing upward. They had gained enough yards to see that Patsy's light was clear, and Niklaus was well on his way down.

"We are too far over," Adam murmured.

"Then we will correct our course." Susanna ripped another strip and hastened the pace.

Niklaus's parting words to Patsy had been the same as Susanna's. Her job was to keep the lantern in view at all times so he would have a reference point in the dark. As long as he could see the light, he could give his best effort to dropping straight down the side of the mountain toward the last place he had seen Noah nestled in the tree limbs. Patsy's second task was to keep her eyes on Noah in her shaft of light. If he moved, she was to cry out the news. No one should reach his spot and discover that he had turned over or tried to stand or fallen four branches down or hung by one shoulder.

Beside Patsy, watching Niklaus repel carefully and successfully without getting caught in branches, her father was antsy for his turn. He squatted and shuffled toward the edge.

"Papa, don't." Patsy did not take her eyes off Noah and Niklaus. Her peripheral vision was enough to know her father was squirmy and might compromise the careful instructions he had received.

"I just want to be ready," Charles said.

"You are ready," Patsy said. "When Niklaus calls to you, that's when you go.

Not before."

"My goodness, you have become quite particular about these things."

"This is serious, Papa." If he moved as much as his little toe prematurely and it caused a complication that put Noah at greater risk — or Niklaus or Susanna — her father would never hear the end of it from Patsy. He was used to being a free spirit out on the circuit, with an occasional report to his bishop, but this was an entirely different sort of circumstance. She would not hesitate to impress the reality on him.

"If you want to help," Patsy said, "tell me if you see Susanna or Adam. You might at least spot Adam's light."

Charles shifted in the dirt but said nothing.

"Papa?"

"Sorry, sweetheart. He's with her now. We heard him call, and she answered. But the forest is just too thick to see."

"If we can't see their light, then they can't see mine."

"We don't know that."

Patsy dropped down onto her belly and stretched her arm its full length out over the nothingness before her.

"Patsy, take care," Charles said.

Patsy's only response was to dig her toes

into the dirt, forming twin depressions.

"Charles!"

Niklaus's voice startled them both.

"Ready?" Charles called down.

"Slow and steady," Niklaus advised. "Let Shem feed the rope."

Patsy pressed her lips together, resisting the urge to look at her father. She would not take her eyes off the shadow she believed to be Noah's shape even to wish her father Godspeed as he began his descent. But when he kissed the top of her head, she blinked, and for half a second she feared she had lost Noah. She did not watch her father's movements but only listened. Beside her, Shem gripped her father's rope.

Fifteen had left the Kauffman farm.

Ten had promised to meet on the ridge.

Six had arrived on the ridge.

And now Patsy was alone on the ridge with the Amish bishop — the person she trusted least.

Or perhaps she herself was the one she least trusted. Shem was doing what had been asked of him, bracing his feet against Charles's weight just as he was supposed to do and gripping her father's rope with both hands. As long as he did what was asked of him, maybe she would be able to keep her mouth closed.

■ ■ ■ ■

"Wait." Adam lowered a shoulder and let the loops of rope slide off onto the wrist that held the lantern while reaching for Susanna with the other hand. "I want you tied to me before we go any farther."

"There's no time," Susanna said.

But Adam would not let go. "Hold the light while I untangle the rope."

" 'Tis not necessary." Susanna did not take the lantern. "We can see Patsy's light. We are not far off."

"I will not have you slip and fall faster than I can catch you."

"I will not."

"You might." Adam thrust the lantern at her again, and this time she took it.

He let the rope hit the ground and fumbled for a loose end, dropping it twice before making his fingers stop trembling long enough to circle her middle and cinch a knot at her waist. In the process, the rope tangled itself and he had to pull the entire length of it through two loops while Susanna tapped her foot with undisguised impatience before he tied the other end to himself.

Susanna's eyes answered the lantern's

flicker, and in them he saw gratitude that he had caught up with her despite her annoyance for the time it was taking. He only wished to mitigate the possibility that they might complicate the circumstances by bringing harm to themselves in pursuit of safety for Noah. Her breath came fast, shallow, anxious. Adam tugged the last knot.

"Now?" she said, her head turning toward where they had last seen Noah.

"Now."

Susanna took off with the lantern, leaving Adam to scoop up the excess yards of rope and lope after her. When he pulled on his boots hours ago, the day had been ordinary and his reasons to trust their tread ordinary. Now he was glad he had not put off last month's trip to the cobbler any longer. His boots would serve him well scrabbling along an untrodden, ill-lit trail. As she gained distance, the rope went taut, and he pulled himself along it hand over hand toward the light she held high. With each step, Adam dug his heels in, making sure that if he must pull against her falling weight, he would be well prepared to do so.

Finally, the rope slackened and the distance closed. Susanna's shadow took form in the lantern's illumination.

Susanna's posture told Adam she had her

eyes on Noah once again. And that they were yet again in the wrong place.

"Adam!" Susanna shouted over her shoulder and then turned, relieved, to find that he was right behind her. She would not have to untether herself from him after all, an action she was fully prepared to accomplish if necessary in order to reach Noah. She had miscalculated long before Adam reached her, and rather than correcting her course, by stubbornly racing ahead of him, she had taken them farther from Noah. She had crashed through branch after branch, trying to keep her bearings by Patsy's light, only to find herself steeply below Noah.

She would not cry. She simply would not. Tears would not help Noah.

Adam caught her by the elbows from behind, his head coming alongside her to see what she saw.

"We will climb," he said. "We have the rope. We will get to him."

"He is not moving." She could barely push out the words.

"That may be the safest thing right now."

She nodded but felt no less foolish for having miscalculated to such an extreme.

"Susanna." Adam turned her to face him, but she could not meet his eyes.

"Susanna," he said again.

She pushed out her breath.

"We are all trying to reach Noah. You are not solely responsible for him. He is in God's care."

She raised her eyes toward Noah once again. Adam meant to be tender, but there was no time for such indulgence. She lifted the lantern to sort out whether it would be fastest to take the steepest route up toward Noah or to zigzag a path that was less direct but also less steep and so in the end might take less time.

"Do you still have the bandages?" she asked.

"Yes, of course," Adam said.

"Good." She would tear up her entire dress if that is what it would take to care for Noah properly when she reached him.

CHAPTER 40

If Niklaus had known Patsy Baxton was capable of such steadfastness in a crisis, he might have welcomed her into one years ago. She had muscles of steel and the determination of ten men. Each time Niklaus raised his eyes from where his feet pushed off the mountain, Patsy's lantern was directly above, unwavering in its duty of casting illumination straight down toward Noah. Three quarters of the men in the Amish congregation would have been shifting burning muscles and trembling with one more moment of effort, hoping for someone to step in and relieve them. But not Patsy. Never once did she so much as look over her shoulder or glance at her own father. At any moment, Niklaus could have called to her with an inquiry about Noah's position and she would have responded in detail.

Niklaus could hear for himself that Noah was no longer preaching nor praying nor muttering nor responding to his name, and he himself prayed that his friend was simply in his usual unconscious state following the exertion of falling under. While the circumstances of his preaching on this day had been even more unlikely than most days, if he was now simply asleep and in stillness unaware of his danger, this would be the most gracious blessing the Lord could bestow on his servant Noah and all those who loved him.

Above Niklaus, Charles descended steadily and with due caution. Not since their youthful days working in a lumber camp, when both of them had quicker reflexes, had Niklaus witnessed Charles in a situation that might have brought him danger, but he knew him to be steady of spirit. Patsy's light seemed to grow farther and farther away. The one they needed now was the one Adam carried — since Shem's recklessness had deprived them of the one that Niklaus had intended to carry down the mountainside. No one could fault Adam for taking the smallest lantern to look for Susanna, and perhaps the young pair would be the first to reach Noah. Who could say?

But no matter who reached Noah first, with which light and with which length of rope, all supplies would be needful.

"Charles?" Niklaus called up. His voice echoed.

"Yes, my friend."

The response warmed the loneliness of the dark task.

"I hope you are praying for our Lord's assistance." Niklaus spoke up for his voice to carry.

"And for the assurance of your heart," came Charles's answer.

Niklaus peered into the darkness for his next foothold and pushed off one more time, once again aligning himself to Patsy's lantern, which felt smaller with each push.

Where was Adam's light?

Patsy was accustomed to standing in the farmyard watching her father press his heels into his horse while lifting his hat in one hand to bid his wife and daughter farewell in rising morning sunlight. Watching him grip a rope in gloved hands, brace his boots against a mountainside, and gradually disappear into shadow was an experience for which she was not prepared.

Papa.

She wanted to call to him, but she didn't. He must not know how nervous she felt for him. No one must. Niklaus. Susanna. Adam. Her father. Noah. Even the bishop. She was

472

nervous for them all.

Two white circles with dark centers cast upward, and Patsy recognized them as her father's eyes. She allowed herself only a fleeting glance, first because her primary duty was to keep Noah within view as best she could with only one feeble lantern to assist the lights thrown across the night sky, and second because if she met her father's gaze, she might not be willing to look at anything else. Charles had a rope around his waist that was tied to a horse that was in turn tied to a tree. He might smash an ankle or find himself hanging upside down through his own carelessness, but he would not fall. Noah was tethered to nothing and in an unknown state of consciousness.

Patsy was already on her belly with her arm outstretched, but she dared to creep forward another two inches, her shoulder aching as if it might leave its socket. If only she were tied to something. She would gladly hang upside down against the side of the ridge if doing so would shed more light for those climbing down below. But there were no more lengths of rope. Adam had the only loose one.

"You had better have a good grip on Susanna," Patsy muttered. "If you can't reach Noah, at least bring Susanna back."

Patsy crept another inch forward, feeling the edge of the ridge at her waist now. If she risked another inch, the laws of gravity would send her tumbling. She stared at Noah's unmoving form, a dark blotch against a murky background, before daring to glance over her shoulder. No loose length of rope was available, but she was only inches from the rope that tied her father to his horse. If she scooted to the right, she could twist her ankle into his rope. Then she could lean farther over the ledge. If she ended up dangling from the cliff, it would be her own fault, but believing the rope would hold, she was willing to take the risk.

The bishop eyed her movements. She was alone with him after all, she stretched out holding the lantern over the edge of the ridge and he with his hands through the bridles of the two horses whose movements governed the fates of the men below. Patsy was sure of the horses — they were her own Galahad and her father's horse, after all. She knew them well. They would follow instructions in a trustworthy manner.

It was the bishop she was unsure of.

He held his position, his hands ready to guide the horses the instant the signal came. Remorse stung her conscience for not trusting him.

Patsy wriggled her foot into the rope that connected her both to her Methodist minister father and to the Amish bishop, feeling like a schoolgirl assigned to write an essay about a circumstance most unlikely to happen.

"Look! There!" Susanna held the lantern high and turned her head to make sure Adam's gaze followed its light.

"Niklaus reached him." Relief gushed out of Adam.

"And we will be there soon." Susanna pushed past another branch. The direct climb had been too steep, and they had calculated that weaving back and forth at longer distances but more yielding inclines would be a more efficient use of energy and time. She suspected they had been right but was nevertheless mollified that when they reached Noah they would not be on their own to assess his care and determine the best way to return him to safety.

"The bandages," she said.

"I have them," Adam said.

They pushed through another rank of trees, uncaring of the needles that scraped against their skin, leaving marks where blood would well, and now Susanna saw that Charles was not far above Niklaus.

There would be four of them to sort out how to care for Noah. She was not sorry she had taken matters into her own hands when she left the ridge while the men were quarreling and wasting precious moments. She might have gotten to Noah first if they had left even three or four minutes later than they did, or if they had run into trouble on the way down, or if she and Adam had not misjudged and had come out just a few yards closer to Noah. None of that mattered now. They were there, four of them converging on Noah.

Niklaus straddled a thick branch and scooted toward Noah six inches at a time. "Adam! Your light!"

"We're coming!" Susanna's next step snapped a dry branch on the forest floor, and a raccoon scurried across her path, but she did not break stride. Adam was near enough that his breath warmed her neck. She reached for his hand, and he obliged as they scrambled up the final yards of the slope in tandem.

"Is he all right?" Adam called up as his uncle slowed his tedious progress even further to test the weight the branch might bear.

Susanna squeezed Adam's hand as they came to a stop directly beneath the tree that cradled Noah. "How do we get up there?"

"Just wait," he whispered.

"We can climb to a different branch," she said, loosening her grasp on his hand.

He tightened his fingers around her. "Just wait."

They looked up. Charles had reached the treetop, chosen a different branch, and begun working his way toward Noah.

"We have bandages," Susanna called up.

"We are going to need them," Niklaus said.

Susanna widened her eyes at Adam, stripped the stack of bandages off his shoulder, hiked up her skirt, and chose her first foothold. He could come or not. She was going up with the light and bandages. In only seconds, she felt Adam beneath her, ready to catch her if she fell. Shooting up a tree trunk hand over hand was a skill that remained in a girl's muscles, whether she was four or twenty-one. The condition of her stockings was a small price to pay for being within reach of Noah almost as soon as Charles was.

Noah remained unconscious.

"I do not think he is simply sleeping." Susanna fought the panic that cracked her own voice.

"Nor I." Nicklaus slipped a hand beneath

Noah's head and shoulder. It came out damp and sticky.

"Blood?" Susanna whispered.

Niklaus nodded. "We will need those bandages now."

Susanna gripped them and extended her arm to first pass up the lantern and then the strips of her apron.

" 'Tis his shoulder, Susanna," Niklaus said. "Not his head. We must stop the bleeding either way, but it is not his head."

She blew out her breath. "I want to help."

"You have. You are the only one who had the sense to make sure we had bandages. Now Charles and I will patch up Noah, and we will figure out how to get him back up to the ridge."

Adam reluctantly admitted he would have to untether Susanna and surrender the extra rope for the good of Noah. Susanna's fingers were already fumbling at her waistline, and Adam certainly had no credible reason to constrain her. He made sure to keep an end tied to one wrist, lest he and Susanna both loose themselves at the same moment and send their valuable cable tumbling into uncertainty. He need not have worried. Her haste was not so foolhardy. She carefully wound several yards of rope before handing it to him. Only when he had secured charge of it did she swing to another branch where she could get a better look at Noah.

"Susanna!" Adam said.

She did not meet his eye.

"Are you certain that branch will support you?" They were all high up in the trees among thinner branches, uncertain whether some might only be shadows.

She ignored him, her hand on Noah's forehead.

Charles glanced at Adam. "She is well positioned."

Adam nodded. What else was there to do?

"We'll need your rope now," Charles said.

Susanna held the light, and Adam aimed and threw one end up.

Charles caught it on the first try. "We'll tie him to me."

"You?" Niklaus said. "I had supposed me."

"I feel some responsibility," Charles said.

"You are not responsible," Niklaus said. "No one is."

"Affinity then," Charles said.

"What's going on down there?" The shout came from Patsy.

"We have him," Adam shouted back. "We are all here. Give us a few minutes to tie him to your father, and we will send him up."

Adam ventured closer to Noah and Charles. He wanted to satisfy himself that the knots were right. If Noah should wake partway up the mountain, he must not be able to thrash, not one foot nor one hand, nor disturb the other man's balance to any degree. Once he was satisfied, Adam called instructions to Patsy, who passed them on to Shem to lead the horse gently, a step at a time, to pull the men up, with Charles shielding Noah at every turn from banging against trees or rocks.

CHAPTER 41

"Slow!" Susanna could not help adding her voice to the bevy of instructions bouncing among the rocks of the mountainside.

"A step at a time," Niklaus said.

The words had become a motto. The horse pulling up Charles and the inert Noah could move no faster than Charles could feel around for a foothold that would keep them from slamming too harshly into rock or tree, or perhaps allowing him enough time to swing around and make sure he, rather than Noah, took the brunt of any collision.

Charles had refused the offer of the only light available to the group below the ridge. Once he and Noah were harnessed and the knots had been tightened three times, what need had he for a lantern — or with which hand would he hold it? Surely no one would suggest it hang lose to smash into the first hard object it encountered.

So they watched, Niklaus, Adam, and Susanna, as the tangle of limbs and ropes that
was Charles and Noah rose foot by foot.
Niklaus held the lantern as high as he could
for as long as it was useful to do so, but the
time came that they were in a void beyond
the reach of Adam's small lantern and not
yet within the yellow spread of Patsy's.

"They are fine," Adam whispered in her
ear.

She reached for his hand in the dark.

He pointed up. "Let the stars light their
way. With every step of the horse, they are
closer to the God who placed the lights of
the night."

" 'Who is God save the Lord? Or who is a
rock save our God?' " Susanna murmured.

" 'For thou art my rock and my fortress;
therefore for thy name's sake lead me, and
guide me.' " Adam jumped from Psalm 18
to Psalm 31.

Susanna's response took her to Psalm 78.
" 'And they remembered that God was their
rock, and the high God their redeemer.' "

"He is almost up," Niklaus said. His
lantern hung at his side, but now Patsy's
hand also went out of sight.

"What happened?" Susanna lurched
against Adam. "Why can we not see them?
Where is the light?"

Niklaus breathed the laughter of relief. "I imagine she had to put it down so she could grab the rope and guide them to safety."

"Of course." Susanna let her own breath out. Shem was at the horse. Patsy would have done nothing else than to reach for Noah, just as Susanna would have.

A moment later, Patsy's light reappeared and she waved her free arm. "They're here," she called down. "They're safe."

The trio cheered.

"I'll try to throw the rope down for you and Adam," Patsy said.

Noah was at the top. That was all that mattered. Susanna would scramble back up in the dark if she had to.

"The rope could snag on the way down." Adam cupped his hands at his mouth and called up to Patsy. No one had thought beyond getting Noah up the mountain.

"I have to try," Patsy said. "There are three of you, and only one rope down there."

"Is it too much for Galahad?" Adam asked.

Patsy scoffed. "Do you expect me to receive that inquiry seriously? Too much for Galahad? Don't be ridiculous. It's not helpful at a moment like this."

Behind Adam, Susanna snickered, and he

turned to glare at her.

"Sorry," she muttered.

"We will figure it out," Adam called up to Patsy.

"Not with one rope, you won't. You've got my best friend down there, the man she loves, and his uncle, who is one of my father's dear friends. I am not leaving all that to one spindly rope."

"Let her throw it down," Susanna said. "If it catches in a tree, I will climb to get it."

"The two of you should just take this rope," Niklaus said, pulling at the one around his waist, "and I will sort things out."

Adam and Susanna rejected the idea simultaneously.

"We are not leaving you here."

"We need a better plan than that."

"We can go back the way we came down."

Three heads tilted back and looked up at Patsy.

"Is Noah still unconscious?" Niklaus shouted up.

Patsy paused to look over her shoulder. "Yes."

"Then you must keep one rope to secure him to the spare horse. You must not risk losing both ropes in the trees."

"Swing wide and throw far," Adam said.

"And make sure it's tied to one of the horses."

Susanna cleared her throat. "She does not like people telling her what to do."

Above them, Patsy set the lantern on the ground, braced her feet, and swung the rope as if she had spent the last ten years lassoing bulls at a rodeo. Perhaps she had lassoed bulls, Adam realized. Her father was gone most of the time, and Harvey the farmhand seemed to accommodate Patsy's request when she demanded to learn peculiar skills.

The loop of the rope left the range of Patsy's lantern and entered the void. Susanna squinted, trying to catch sight of its movement. The rustle above told her Patsy's effort had very nearly found its mark. She turned and grinned at the dumbfounded Adam.

Niklaus leaned his head back and waved, while Susanna scrambled up the tree and pulled the rope clear of impediment.

"Susanna should go up next," Adam said when the three stood with the rope. He pulled on it, as if to test that it was in fact tied to a horse, hoping that it was his stallion.

"I agree," Niklaus said.

"Alone?" Susanna said.

485

"You are slight of weight with quick reflexes," Adam said. "The journey up will be far easier than the route you chose down."

She elbowed him. "You will be right behind?"

Uncle and nephew nodded.

"You can trust me to send Adam up next," Niklaus said. "As soon you're off the rope, make sure Patsy throws it down again."

"There could not be a better horse to entrust with our welfare than Galahad," Adam said. "I will not take my eyes off you."

Susanna fiddled with an end of the rope, considering the knots. Adam took it from her.

"I will harness you myself," he said. "Remember Psalm 31. 'Bow down thine ear to me; deliver me speedily: be thou my strong rock, for an house of defence to save me.' "

Susanna nodded.

Niklaus watched Susanna make swift progress, her skirts conformed closely to her legs, giving her clear sight of her feet and where she must put them. Charles had to calculate how Noah's limp weight might affect how they swung and how it would be up to Charles alone to compensate, but Susanna was free and clear to climb with her feet while also moving hand over hand up the rope. It took no time at all before she was above them. The spunk and determination she had shown in the last few hours, even in moments of anxiety, were remarkable.

"Nephew," Niklaus said.

"*Ja,* Onkel."

"If you do not tether yourself to that girl in marriage, I may have to take you to one of those *English* doctors to see what is wrong with your mind.

"Onkel!"

"Adam, my boy, I am as fond of you as I am of my own son, but she will not wait for you forever."

Adam kicked the dirt.

"I hear she may not have a choice," Niklaus continued. "Her family would not be the first to up and move west looking for a new start for their children."

"You need say no more," Adam said. "I do not know what I was thinking, telling her that I could not see her. The reasons seem so petty when life is full of moments like these last hours. Moments that matter. Moments when everything might change, and not for petty reasons."

"You know the bishop may still not agree

that the reasons are petty," Niklaus said.

"I suppose not," Adam said, his eyes fixed on the light above. "But I am not proposing to plight my troth to the bishop."

"That might be an unsubmissive position to hold."

"Said the kettle to the pot."

Niklaus laughed.

" 'And though I bestow all my goods to feed the poor,' " Adam said, " 'and though I give my body to be burned, and have not charity, it profiteth me nothing.' "

"That is a truth each man must find for himself."

"I am here!" Susanna's voice rang through the night.

The two men looked up. Susanna bounced close to the edge, but there she was, in the light of the lantern. There could not be much oil left in it after all this time, but they still had Adam's.

Adam caught the rope when it swung back down. "You should go next."

"We promised Susanna it would be you." Niklaus took the rope from Adam's hands and started to tie the light to it."

"I will not take the light." Adam poked his finger into Niklaus's knot and undid it. "If you remain here alone, the light must be yours."

Niklaus held the light while Adam secured himself and called up to Patsy. If Niklaus knew his nephew, Adam had packed extra oil to see them through the night.

Safe. Everyone was safe. Her father and Noah and Susanna and Adam and Niklaus. They were scratched up, disheveled, and smudged. Their clothes were beyond mending and could go to the rag piles once they got home. The cobbler would be glad for the leather repair work on their boots.

But they were safe.

Noah, limp, was still unconscious and tied into a saddle with his head resting against the horse's long neck and his hands secured underneath. While Adam refilled the canisters of the lanterns with enough fuel to get them down the mountain, Patsy rounded Noah's horse to stand beside Susanna.

"I think he should be awake by now," Patsy said softly.

Susanna nodded.

"Should we be worried?"

"Niklaus said the wound was on his shoulder, not his head," Susanna said.

"That doesn't mean he didn't hit his head on the way down," Patsy said. "I've been doing the arithmetic all afternoon and evening. It comes out the same every time.

We don't know when he began preaching, but we have a good idea when he stopped. Even allowing for one of the longer recovery naps we've seen him take on the davenport . . ."

"I know. He should be awake — and he might be at any moment. We must make sure that one of us rides beside him all the way down."

"It should be you," Patsy said. "Since Phoebe is not here, the first face he sees should be yours."

Niklaus approached. "Charles wonders if we should wait for daylight. The later it gets, the harder it is to argue with his point."

"No," Susanna said. "Absolutely not."

"We would go at first light," Niklaus said. "And we call this a mountain, but folks out in Colorado Territory would laugh at us for getting so worked up over a hill. At dawn we would all be safely home in no time."

"I'll deal with my father," Patsy said. "Mama is used to having him gone, and as long as she knows I am with him, she won't worry for me. But Phoebe will be out of her mind. Making her wait for dawn would be a great unkindness."

"She might already be alone," Susanna said. "The men who offered to help never made it all the way up here. How do we know the women did not go home when it was suppertime?"

"I do not suppose we do," Niklaus said.

"Phoebe will be frantic," Susanna said. "I will not have any part in multiplying her distress."

Nicklaus nodded. "Shem knows every inch of mountain even in the dark."

"And Patsy has been all over it with Galahad," Susanna said.

"Then the two of them shall lead," Niklaus said.

"Me? Lead with your bishop?" Patsy said. "He will have none of it."

"You handle your father," Niklaus said. "I will handle Shem."

Moments later the entourage began the descent, Patsy and Shem at the head, Susanna and Adam riding on either side of the horse bearing the sleeping Noah whenever the width of the path allowed it, and Niklaus in the rear. One light beamed in the front and one in the back. They would go as slowly as necessary, but Patsy would feel relief when at last the stars began to fade.

CHAPTER 42

Mrs. Krabill and Mrs. Lantz had indeed remained at Phoebe's side, though Susanna could well imagine there had been moments when Phoebe wished they felt less inclination to chatter as much as was their nature. Normally Phoebe enjoyed long stretches of peace and quiet, even in the middle of a quilting bee. But under the circumstances, with her vulnerable husband lost in a mountainous void, Susanna hoped Phoebe had appreciated companionship in a vigil of brooding hours.

Every candle in the house was burning when Susanna rode side by side with Noah onto the Kauffman farm, and within seconds the front door was thrown open and the three women charged out in welcome. Phoebe held a candle over her husband and then up in Susanna's face.

"He is alive," Susanna said, "and as far as we can tell breathing well."

"Just asleep?"

"We hope so."

"Help me get him down."

Adam was already on the other side of the horse, pulling just the right length of rope to swiftly undo one knot after another before receiving Noah into his arms.

"Straight to bed?" Adam asked.

Phoebe shook her head. "The davenport. If he is just sleeping after preaching, that is where he will expect to find himself when he wakes."

They carried him inside, where Phoebe warmed water and sponged him off and satisfied herself that the bleeding from his shoulder had been stemmed. The other men saw to the horses before coming in through the kitchen.

Charles was the first to emerge into the front room. "Your friends have the stove fired up and eggs and flour and sausage everywhere."

Susanna laughed. "Give them a few minutes. They will have enough to feed four times more people than are here."

"I should see what they need," Phoebe said "A pot or something."

"You stay put," Patsy said. "Noah will wake soon. He'll want to see your face."

"He will not remember any of this night."

Phoebe sighed.

"But none of us will forget," Patsy said. "I will check to see if the kitchen crew will allow me to join them."

In the chair pulled close to the davenport across from the fire, Susanna allowed her head to loll back, tracking the comings and goings from the kitchen through slits in her eyes.

Charles pulled a hardback chair from the table and sat with a view of Noah. Susanna could not discern what he might be thinking.

Shem was next to come out of the kitchen, pausing to speak to Patsy before following the tip of her finger. Patsy directed Shem to Charles. Shem went to the dining table and, with a glance toward the davenport and mindful of any noise that might disturb Noah, gently pulled out a chair.

With all the empty seats in the room, Shem sought the one beside Charles. Even after all that happened on Jacks Mountain that night, this one gesture was enough to make Susanna's eyes flip open wide. Surely Shem did not think this the time or place to confront Charles. Susanna edged forward in her chair. But Shem simply angled his head toward Charles and murmured peaceably.

This was as it should be. Friends gathered

in a time of need.

Mrs. Krabill stuck her head out the kitchen door. "All is ready. Come and eat."

Having been shooed out of the kitchen, Patsy gasped at what she saw at the table. It would have made more sense for her father to sit next to Niklaus. Or Adam. Or Susanna. Or Patsy herself. Sitting beside the bishop would only stir embers that had cooled during the night. With a glance across the table toward wide-eyed Susanna, Patsy took a place on the other side of her father. If he got out of hand with his erudite yet pointed comments toward the Amish bishop, Patsy would reach under the table and pinch his knee. This was an Amish home. Noah's home. They were there because of a harrowing night and being fed by the kindness of Amish women who had every reason to be home with own families at this hour — hours and hours ago.

The women came out of the kitchen with platters of food, arranged them on the table, and then stood back ready to serve as the ravenous rescuers, who had not eaten since breakfast, gathered around the table. Patsy took her cue from the Amish, awaiting the silent prayer with which they began every meal, waiting for Shem to raise his head and say, *"Aemen."*

Charles cut his fried ham into polite-sized bites and swallowed one. "Certainly we have seen God at work this night."

No one could argue with that simple statement.

Charles pulled open a steaming biscuit and slathered it with butter. "Might I inquire if you have a secret ingredient for such a delicious concoction?"

The women beamed.

So far so good. Patsy ate with a fork in one hand, leaving the other idle — yet available to pinch her father's knee if necessary — in her lap.

"I wonder if I might say something to Shem," Charles said, "something that might edify others of you as well."

Patsy crept to the edge of her chair. *Papa, this is not the time.*

"I want to say I'm sorry," Charles said. "With my sincerest, deepest apologies."

Forks clinked to plates and stilled.

Charles pushed food around on his plate, not taking any bites.

"I was raised by my grandmother," he said, "and she made sure I was in church every time the doors were open."

Grandma Pat. Patsy had never met her great-grandmother, who died before her parents married, but she bore her name, Patricia Louise Baxton.

"She read her Bible faithfully," Charles said, "and I learned my letters at her knees by sounding out her favorite verses." He paused to chuckle. "Of course, I had heard her recite them so many times that the process was to my benefit and she thought me an exceptionally bright child."

Laughter erupted. Patsy glanced around the table, uncertain.

Shem had turned in his chair to listen attentively, and others around the table found the story captivating as well.

"My grandmother believed," Charles said. "I had no doubt as to the state of her soul, though some in many groups believe we will only be sure on Judgment Day."

Even Patsy was hearing a chapter of the story her father had never told before.

"But you see," Charles said, "I had fallen in with some friends who were Methodist youth, and I had my heart strangely warmed. I knew I had been saved and that I would give my life to God's work, just as John Wesley had done after his heart was strangely warmed. My grandmother could never sort out what that meant, or what it said about the state of my own soul in all those years she was hiding God's Word in

497

my heart. And all I could talk about was how she needed to have her heart strangely warmed, too, because I knew the joy that awaited her once she did. She took it to mean I did not believe her to be saved, and she took offense."

More tears filled Patsy's eyes than they could contain.

"My new minister said that if you have good news, of course you want to share it, but to Grandma Pat my news was not good news. I tried to work it into conversation at least once a day, and that was my downfall. Eventually she calmly and firmly suggested I look for other accommodations."

Niklaus caught Charles's eye. "That is why you were in the lumber camp where I met you," Niklaus said.

Charles nodded. "I learned a few things about hard work and a tamed tongue. And here we are. At the table with your bishop, to whom I owe an apology."

Patsy held her breath.

"I have always wondered," Charles said, "if there might have been a third way I could have taken with my grandmother — something other than right or wrong, some middle ground of understanding each other. But she passed suddenly before I mustered the courage to try."

Patsy's sleeve was grimy from a night on the ridge and on horseback, but it was the nearest thing she had to dab at her eyes.

Charles held out his hand to Shem. "I would like to think that the lesson I learned too late so long ago will not be a complete waste. Will you forgive me?"

As famished as he was, Niklaus had set down his fork at the beginning of Charles's story, even if it was loaded with potatoes crisped to golden perfection and even if they were quickly losing their steam.

How could he have been ignorant of the circumstances that brought Charles to that lumber camp a quarter of a century ago? Men came for all sorts of reasons. Saving the family farm. Sending a younger brother to college. Running from trouble with the law by venturing into territory where few cared about real names or details of the past as long as a man gave an honest day's work. Even Niklaus, who had left behind his young bride, had hoped to make a modest but rapid fortune that would secure his own future on the very farm where he had raised his children. No one would have supposed that Charles's grandmother had thrown him out because of his religious conversion and he had nowhere else to go.

But if she had not thrown Charles out and he had not labored in that lumber camp, Niklaus would not have met him, and his own life in the Lord would not be what it was.

Charles's face was white with the truth he had told.

"Papa," Patsy said, "I never knew."

Charles cleared his throat. "I always thought that once I had a wife and child, Grandma Pat would want to know you both, and that would smooth things over. I guess I waited too long."

"Shem?" Niklaus said, his question laden with every plea their decades of friendship entitled him to ask, despite the crooked path they had taken lately. Making their own crooked places straight was yet to come. For now it was Charles whom Niklaus ached for. Niklaus had known Shem long enough to read his every expression. The bishop looked dubious but was beginning to bend.

The stirring behind Niklaus turned everyone's heads.

"Noah!" Phoebe cried.

Niklaus scraped back his chair.

Noah threw off his quilt. "Have I missed supper again?"

"Stay right there." Phoebe scurried to her

husband. "You are wounded."

"Wounded?" But Noah's wince testified that he had discovered the gash at the back of his shoulder. He was quiet for a moment. "This did not happen preaching in the window, did it?"

Phoebe shook her head.

"The bishop?" Noah said.

"Of course not." Niklaus was on the davenport now, looking to Phoebe for some clue as to what they should tell Noah. They would tell him the truth, of course. But how quickly?

"You truly remember nothing of this day?" Shem crossed the room slowly.

"I remember that Phoebe went to take some eggs to Mrs. Swigert, and Susanna had deliveries. I was quite insistent there was no need for them to watch my every move. Then I realized I lacked long nails for hooks in the barn and thought Niklaus might have some. Since it was a nice day, and his farm is so close, I decided to walk over and ask."

Niklaus and Adam exchanged glances.

"You never made it," Niklaus said.

"You must have fallen under," Charles said, standing at the table, "and wandered."

Noah peered again at the bishop. "Quite a ways, I gather."

"The bishop helped us find you," Niklaus said.

"I repent," Shem said.

Noah drew back. "Of finding me?"

"Of ever doubting you. Of shouting at you. Of the needle. Of speaking of you in a malicious manner. Of all of it. Please forgive me."

"Well," Noah said, "since I do not specifically have personal memory of these events and only secondhand knowledge, then I do not find it reasonable to hold a grudge. I surely know our Lord would not."

CHAPTER 43

The Amish wives were the first to go. Susanna had expected they would leave to care for their own households as soon as they were certain Phoebe would not be left on her own, but instead they had left the returning entourage to recount their feats and perils and disappeared into the kitchen to rustle up a middle-of-the-night meal. Afterward, though, Patsy and Susanna assured them they could look after the cleaning up, and the two women hitched up the wagon they had come in half a day ago and journeyed toward home and a few hours of sleep before their own *boppli* clamored for breakfast.

Shem was next. His wife knew that occasionally he was up late ministering to a family in their congregation in a turmoil, but her habit was to wait for him. It was two in the morning. It was time she heard the night's story — not only Noah's but his own.

Charles fretted that Mercy might be worried — more for Patsy than for Charles. She was used to his absence, but she was unaccustomed to their daughter gallivanting at night, and there had been no time to explain the circumstances.

One by one, Susanna watched them leave. In another three hours, Phoebe would have been up for twenty-four hours straight. Susanna would have to make sure Phoebe got some rest.

"No need to make Deborah worry longer than she has to." Niklaus made his usual effort to be sure his hat was on straight, but as usual it cocked to the left. That he still had possession of his hat after the night's ropes and knots and horses and lanterns and rocks astounded Susanna, but there it was.

Niklaus glanced at Adam. "Ready?"

"I will be right behind you," Adam said. "I will bring the extra horse, if you like."

Niklaus glanced from Adam to Susanna. She almost blushed, but Niklaus was on Adam's side, no matter what.

"I thought we might have one last look at the barn animals," Adam said.

We.

Why was that such a delicious word when it came from Adam's mouth?

"Do as you please," Phoebe said, straightening the quilt on the back of the davenport. "Noah and I are going to bed."

The animals were fine. Susanna knew that, and Adam knew that. As they stepped out the back door, Adam offered her his hand. This was his real reason for staying behind when his uncle left.

Under starlight they lit a lantern one more time before going in the front door of the barn. They went through the motions of checking on the cows bedded there, and the one mule Noah kept. The chickens were in their coop, and the horses in the stable that opened onto the same pastures where the cows spent their days.

Just before they emerged from the back end of the barn, the place where yesterday morning Noah was building shelves, Adam turned down the glow.

He was going to kiss her.

At least she wanted him to.

But as his face lowered toward hers, it looked far too stern for a kiss.

Susanna drew back, but Adam reached for her again.

Susanna swallowed hard, but still he saw

the flush in her face. She was not going to say one way or another, and he did not blame her. Right until the last moment, he was unsure himself whether he would lean in for her waiting lips and the sensation he had ached for since — he had lost count of the days. Just as easily he might pull back to speak needful words.

"I am sorry," he said. "I misled you. Forgive me." He once again offered his hand, and she took it. When he began to walk again, she followed.

" 'Tis your parents," Adam said. "Should we not speak to them?"

"I do not know what to say," Susanna whispered. "My *mamm* has her mind made up. Daed always sees both sides of an issue but in the end is unlikely to find a reason to make his wife unhappy on such a matter. Timothy is old enough to make his voice heard and his presence known even if it is not welcome."

"You are older than Timothy. Have you no voice?"

"You are a son. 'Tis difficult to explain what it is like to be a daughter."

"Then I hope that someday you will explain it to me. Perhaps when we have our own daughter."

Her head snapped up and her gaze into

focus at this suggestion. Adam turned, stood before her, and squeezed both hands. "If we are to have any future, we must have their consent, if not their blessing."

"I know you are right," Susanna said. "But 'tis a hard thing, like hauling ice on a winter's morn. 'Tis right and necessary, but no one wants to do it."

"I will be there," Adam said. "If we have learned any lesson from what happened today — yesterday — 'tis that no one can pretend that what they see right in front of their eyes is not happening."

Susanna nodded.

"No one can pretend Noah does not preach," Adam said, "or that Shem and Niklaus have not had a falling out, or that Charles Baxton wandered into waters whose depths he did not know. And I will not pretend that Shem did not try to separate me from my own *onkel* and you. I do not want to be part of anything that separates you from your parents — or an excuse to find an easy path out of our conundrum."

"You would never be just an excuse," Susanna said. "I would never . . . If I married you, it would be because I could not bear the thought of life without you, not just so I did not have to go to Indiana."

Adam rubbed his chin between two fingers. "Maybe Indiana is not such a bad place."

Susanna slapped his forearm, and he caught her hand once more.

And this time he did kiss her. With surety. With abandon. With relief. With delight.

"I should have thought as much," Phoebe said, unable to make her voice stern even with the broom in her hand for stability.

Susanna scrambled up from the back porch, looking away from Adam. They had been sitting there for hours, sleeping on each other's shoulders. "When did it get so light?"

Phoebe looked at her, befuddled. "The sun has been up nearly an hour."

"The cows," Susanna said. Milking was one of the chores she had offered to take on when she moved in with the Kauffmans, and if the last couple of days were any measure, they would find Crazy Amos reliable for the task of announcing the day. "I slept though the rooster?"

"I do concede that your day yesterday was long and tiresome," Phoebe said, laughing. "Since in the end you did bring my husband home in one piece, I bear you no grudge."

"I will milk," Adam said, jogging toward the barn before Susanna could object.

Susanna's shoulder, where his head had been piled against hers as they shared one buggy blanket, was still warm, and she was sorrowed by the knowledge that the heat would soon dissipate.

"He is going home with me this morning," Susanna said.

Phoebe nodded. "It must be done, and I can think of no better man to go with you."

Adam slipped inside the barn, and Susanna faced Phoebe. "Do you think so, truly?"

"Take one of our buggies," Phoebe said. "And a decent horse. Do not turn up looking as if Adam cannot do better for you than that mare you are so enamored of. I will heat water so you can have a proper bath and a clean dress. After hearing about your escapade, your *mamm* will be especially anxious to know that no great harm has come to you after all."

Susanna had a bath and Adam cleaned up at the well and put on a shirt borrowed from Noah. Despite the hearty midnight offering only a few hours earlier, Phoebe's breakfast was robust, as was Adam's appetite.

"Take your time," Phoebe said as she saw them off.

Regardless of Adam's confidence and Phoebe's reassurance — and a fine horse and buggy, even if her mother would recognize it as Noah's and not Adam's — Susanna trembled across the miles, few as they were. With every step of the horse, she wanted to turn around and go back to the shelter the Kauffmans offered. She could help Phoebe and be with Noah. And when the time came, they could wed there. Would that be so distressful? Her parents would be in Indiana, too far away to attend anyway.

Timothy was the first to spy them coming. Of course. How did he do that? It was as if he had some device that sat on top of a weathervane, itself atop the barn, with eyes that scanned for motion coming toward the Hooley farm from any direction.

There he was, once again the first to shake the hand of a visitor.

"Philip," Timothy said to one of his brothers, "go find *Mamm* and Daed. Tell them we have visitors."

Visitors. Susanna winced at Timothy's choice of words and her application of it to his own sister.

Veronica and Elias settled side by side on the settee, with Timothy comfortable in a side chair. Susanna and Adam had no choice but to sit across the room. The other boys draped themselves across the back of furniture. One pulled in a chair from the

510

dining room.

"Boys," Elias said, "you will leave us now. This is a conversation for the grown-ups."

Daniel, Philip, and Stephen, after a stunned moment during which their father's request sank in, complied. Timothy settled back in his chair.

Adam cleared his throat and leaned forward. "I thought we might do well to give you an account of last night. I am sure it will run the length of the valley before the sun sets today."

Elias held up one hand to interrupt Adam. "Timothy, you will go with the boys."

"But Daed —"

It took only a quarter inch shake of her father's head for Susanna to know that Timothy would protest again. But wherever the other boys had gone, Timothy was likely to go no farther than the kitchen.

"Please begin again," Elias said.

Susanna pushed air past the knot in her throat. "There is much to tell. I hope that in the telling we may find peace between us."

Veronica's dubious expression remained in place, but Elias leaned forward, hands on knees, in genuine interest.

Adam began again. This time he got through it all. The dangers. The rescue. The reconciliations no one dreamed possible. The forgiveness.

"I feel you must know," Susanna said, "that Adam and I hope that our differences will be likewise healed as we understand each other better. And if we should marry, it will be for all the right reasons, with no guile nor guise. I want to say aloud that I understand your decision to sell the farm and move."

"But we have not decided anything," Veronica said.

"You seemed quite set on the acceptability of the offer," Susanna said.

"It is a more generous offer than we had imagined possible," Veronica said, "but we can scarce expect your *daed* to make such a decision in a scant two days.

Two days? Is that all it had been since this all began?

Niklaus let himself sleep late — in theory. Slumbering past six was only for times of illness. Even that hour was an indulgence. After their late night, Deborah insisted on it, though she was aghast at his suggestion that she should do the same. Let Jonas do the early chores, she said on this morning. He was the only one who had a decent night's sleep. Breakfast could be fried

512

leftover *yamasetti* that would take only minutes to heat through.

But of course none of that was possible for either of them. It mattered not how long the night was. Their inner clocks woke them at the same time as always.

Adam had never come home. Niklaus would have a word with him about that, not because he harbored any distrust about how Adam spent those hours in the deepest darkness of the night but because he preferred not to have to dodge questions from his brother-in-law about whether Adam, who had been sent to his uncle's care, was in fact behaving appropriately. When he heard footsteps behind him, Niklaus assumed Adam had finally come home. Instead, it was Shem.

"Long night," Niklaus said.

"Very. For all of us," Shem said. "But now we are back at it. I never properly inspected Adam's work."

"Remarkable, as always." Niklaus gestured to the back of the house, now extended with enviable space. "But you knew that."

Shem nodded. "Niklaus."

Niklaus looked up. "Yes."

"Last night."

Niklaus waited. He knew what Shem wanted, but it would be best if Shem spoke it for himself.

"What Charles said," Shem said, "about a third way. There could be a third way for us."

"Could be." Niklaus ran fingers through his beard. "A third way that lets us understand each other even if we cannot explain everything."

"And Noah?"

Shem crossed his wrists behind his back. Niklaus waited.

"I am certain you can find your way with Noah as well," Niklaus said.

"I pray so," Shem said.

"And church?"

"Perhaps you may preach from time to time," Shem said.

"As I am moved." Niklaus's fingers stilled under his chin.

"Of course."

"And Noah? He will be welcome?"

Shem nodded once.

Niklaus matched the gesture. "We will find our way."

Timothy burst into the room. "This is not at all what I expected."

Veronica turned to her eldest son. "Timothy, what did you expect?"

Beside Susanna, Adam stiffened. She

wanted to reach for his hand but did not dare.

"Indiana, of course," Timothy said.

Elias stood. "This has never been your decision to make. Your *mamm* and I will decide."

Awkward, Adam was on his feet.

"But, Daed —" Timothy said.

"Timothy, you will wait outside. In the garden."

Timothy dragged his feet out of the room. Adam sat again and reached for Susanna's hand, gripping it as he never had before.

"I wonder how your garden is." Adam's voice cracked.

"Our garden?" Veronica said. "It has yielded well."

Adam's mouth turned up one corner. Veronica understood well.

"Beans?" Adam said.

Veronica nodded.

"Squash?"

Another nod.

"Carrots?"

One nod after another as Adam named vegetables.

"And celery," he said. "Perhaps more celery than usual?"

Finally, Susanna saw the path of this discourse. Celery was a common wedding decoration. All summer, uncertain whether Adam would propose, she had not let herself monitor the end of the garden where her mother grew celery.

"As a matter of fact," Veronica said, "a great deal of celery."

Elias slapped his knees. "Veronica, it looks like we have a wedding to plan."

AUTHOR'S NOTE

I'm a church history fan. This book began when I was reading about the revivalism of the late eighteenth and nineteenth century, and I learned that the Amish lost a larger percentage of their members to the open-air revival preachers than other established traditional denominations. Part of the reason for this was because the preaching and the message were distinctly different from that of their own tradition. I began to think that might be interesting to write about.

Like any curious historical novelist, I did a Google search to see what I might find to spark a story. And I found the "sleeping preachers" phenomenon. One author described it as "widespread" in the nineteenth century, but it didn't strike me as a very Amish experience. Yet several accounts are in circulation of Mennonite and Amish laymen falling unconscious, preaching for hours at a time, gaining audiences, and remembering nothing.

My character Noah Kauffman is a blend of the names of two historical Amish sleeping preachers, Noah Troyer and John Kauffman. They were born into two different church districts, both in Ohio. During their lifetimes they both moved to other states, where their preaching became widely known. Some of the events and symptoms I used to create Noah Kauffman's preaching are based on detailed descriptions of the real-life Noah Troyer and John Kauffman.

The other theme that caught my imagination is the question of what constitutes a genuine religious experience. None of us has a spiritual journey identical to anyone else's, and the church history tree has diverse branches. None of us gets everything right. Nevertheless, we don't always make room for each other. We don't always look for what we have in common before jumping into what separates us.

As I wrote *Gladden the Heart,* I pondered this question — not just on a church or societal level, but on a personal level. May I know God's grace in challenging relationships, even when I don't deserve it, and may I also be a vessel of God's grace to others.

Every new book is a reminder that I cannot do this alone. I'm grateful for Rachelle Gardner, my friend and agent, who has steadfast confidence in me. I'm grateful for Annie Tipton, the editor who helped brainstorm options for a next book and got intrigued with the sleeping preachers right along with me. I'm grateful for JoAnne Simmons, the editor who looks after the details when I can no longer see straight and inevitably straightens out a chronology glitch. They are a faithful, supportive team. And this time around, I'm also grateful for the help of Joanna Rendon, on duty at the research desk at the public library down the street, whose help filled my research binder.

And to everyone who has ever said, "I love your books," thank you! You keep me going.

ABOUT THE AUTHOR

Olivia Newport's novels twist through time to find where faith and passions meet. Her husband and twentysomething children provide welcome distraction from the people stomping through her head on their way into her books. She chases joy in stunning Colorado at the foot of the Rockies, where daylilies grow as tall as she is.

The employees of Thorndike Press hope you have enjoyed this Large Print book. All our Thorndike, Wheeler, and Kennebec Large Print titles are designed for easy reading, and all our books are made to last. Other Thorndike Press Large Print books are available at your library, through selected bookstores, or directly from us.

For information about titles, please call:
(800) 223-1244

or visit our website at:
gale.com/thorndike

To share your comments, please write:
Publisher
Thorndike Press
10 Water St., Suite 310
Waterville, ME 04901